TEN CENTS A DANCE

TEN CENTS A DANCE

CHRISTINE FLETCHER

BLOOMSBURY

This is a work of fiction. Any resemblance to actual people, places,
or events is purely coincidental and not the intention of the author.

Published by Bloomsbury U.S.A. Children's Books
175 Fifth Avenue, New York, New York 10010
Distributed to the trade by Macmillan

Library of Congress Cataloging-in-Publication Data
available upon request
ISBN-13: 978-1-59990-164-0 • ISBN-10: 1-59990-164-1

First U.S. Edition 2008
Typeset by Westchester Book Composition
Printed in the U.S.A. by Quebecor World Fairfield
1   3   5   7   9   10   8   6   4   2

All papers used by Bloomsbury U.S.A. are natural, recyclable products
made from wood grown in well-managed forests. The manufacturing processes
conform to the environmental regulations of the country of origin.

For Mitch

Ten Cents a Dance

ONE

We heard the music even before we got to Union Hall. Turned the corner and there it was, big double doors flung open, yellow light bright as butter spilling into the cold October air. Kids swarmed the front steps of the hall, the boys in ties and their good shoes, the girls' skirts shimmying below wool coats. More were coming. Hustling up the sidewalks from all directions. I didn't recognize a single person.

"Mother of God," Angie said, "the whole Back of the Yards must be here!"

"Go on, go!" I said, pushing her, and in two shakes we were in the thick of the crowd.

This wasn't any Saturday night at the corner drugstore, hoofing it to a dinged-up jukebox with the same kids we saw every day of our lives. This was the Young Men's Club annual dance, the biggest in the Yards. Some said the biggest in Chicago. I'd been trying to talk Ma into letting me go since I was eleven. This year, she said yes.

Not that it didn't take some work. But if fifteen and a half was old enough to drop out of school and get a job, then it was old enough for the Young Men's Club. Ma had to see that, and I'd kept after her until finally, she gave in.

At the front door of the hall, Angie grabbed my coat sleeve. "Ruby, wait! Damn, this girdle's tight . . . How do I look?"

"Gorgeous," I said. I meant it. Angie had a kitten's face, wide across the eyes and a little pointed chin. "How about me?" I asked.

"Hotsy-totsy," Angie said. "Togged to the bricks."

This was why I loved Angie. She'd give you the truth straight—but she knew when a lie would do you better. I was wearing the only good dress I owned, a lime green wool crepe handed down from my cousins in Wicker Park. Ma had sewn on lace cuffs, to hide the grape jelly stain on the left sleeve, but she'd refused to let me dye it a decent color. Lime green made my skin look three days dead. The dress showed off my figure, at least. Angie was prettier, but below the neck I won, no contest.

We plunked our quarters into the can at the door and shoved our way inside. A real five-piece band, drums crashing and saxophone wailing, maybe two hundred kids already jitterbugging and plenty of room for more. First thing, we dumped our coats and pocketbooks in the checkroom, then headed for the ladies' room to put on lipstick. Angie loaned me hers: Magnet Red. I loved the way it made my mouth feel heavy. Important. I'd have to remember to wash it off before I went home, though, or Ma would make me scrub my face until I was raw.

As soon as we left the ladies', someone hollered, "Hey, Ruby! How about a dance?"

"You bet, handsome!" I yelled back.

"Who is it?" Angie said.

"I don't know and I don't care," I said, just as Stan Dudek came side-shoulders through the crowd. Stan wasn't good-looking—his face had too many knobs and angles, somehow—but he was a sweet guy, he'd had a crush on me since third grade, and, most important, he was the best hoofer I knew. Smooth and snappy, plus he let a girl show her stuff. He'd make me look so good, the boys would line up for me the rest of the night.

And they did. Not just fellows I'd grown up with, either. Why should I care if someone was from my parish, or from St. Rose of Lima or Holy Cross, or if he lived north of Forty-seventh Street or west of Ashland? Other girls did, but not me. Me, all I cared was that he could stomp to the beat.

I'd always loved to dance. But now that I was working, I couldn't get enough. Maybe if I'd kept my big mouth shut and kept my place in sliced bacon, it wouldn't be so bad. Sliced bacon was the easiest job in the whole packinghouse, and the cleanest. But no, I had to tell the girl working with me to move her fat, lazy tush or I'd move it for her. It was only my second day on the job, how was I supposed to know she was the foreman's girlfriend?

Quicker than you could spit, they stuck me in pickled hog's feet. Hog's feet wasn't easy. It sure as hell wasn't clean. Grab glass quart jars—ten at a time, one on each finger—rush to your table, shove in the pig's feet, don't drop them, fill the jars with brine, everything slick—the feet, your hands, the glass. Shove the jars onto the belt, run back for more, start over. Slipping on floors sopping in greasy pig-water, the stench enough to make you puke, every knuckle scraped bloody from the rough jar edges. Tape the cuts but the vinegar seeps underneath the tape

· 3 ·

and boy howdy, then you see stars. But can't slow down or the foreman hollers. Got to hustle. Get them trotters packed. Half hour for lunch, then back at it. If you don't make your quota by the end of the day—every day—they'll can you sure. Lots of girls in line for your job, the foreman won't waste time on you. That's how Ma got sacked. Her hands got bad, she couldn't make the base rate. Ten years in the packinghouse, and they booted her out the door.

I'd been there only a month and already I felt a hundred years old. Just another packinghouse worker in a bloody, soaking apron; fingernails soft and cracking from the brine; and a smell I couldn't get out of my skin. Eight hours a day in a stinking gray room with a bunch of ladies older than Ma, listening to them complain about their bunions and hammertoes and changes of life. That's why I'd pestered Ma to let me come tonight. I needed to feel good, and nothing made me feel better than jitterbugging until I was ready to drop.

So I danced, with one boy after the next, until I had to rest my dogs. Then I searched through the crowd for Angie, finally spotting her with Helen Orszak and Viola Bauer and all our bunch from school. Their heads together, throwing narrow-eyed looks at someone on the dance floor. I made a beeline. I didn't miss memorizing battle dates and writing essays—I was no egghead, like my little sister, Betty—but I hadn't heard a down-and-dirty gossip session since I'd dropped out. My palms itched to get in on it.

". . . caught them kissing," Helen was saying, "in the alley behind the Olympia, and . . ."

"Who?" I shoved between her and Angie. "Who?"

"Bea and Eddie," Angie said.

"Who cares about that?" I said, disappointed. "They've been sweethearts for years."

"Not since she jilted him for Jack Cipinski."

"What? When?" But nobody paid attention. Even Angie batted her hand at me: *Hush, I'm trying to listen!* And then they went on to somebody else, while I stood there with nothing to say.

Well, I'd come here to dance, not listen to tittle-tattle nobody cared about anyway. A little ways off stood a dark-haired boy; I didn't know him, but I'd seen him Lindy. Not half-bad, and no girl on his arm. One smile later, we were out on the floor. When the dance ended, the boy shouted over the hubbub, "Buy you a soda?"

"Sure!" I yelled. We threaded hand in hand through the crowd to the refreshment stand. I was glad he knew where he was going; short as I was, I couldn't see a thing.

A girl bobbed in front of us. Skinny, like she was built out of rectangles, sharp corners everywhere. My partner—what did he say his name was? Robert? Roger?—stopped so suddenly I practically ran up on his heels.

The girl looked past him at me, tucking one of her bony shoulders back, like she was thinking about round-housing me. "What parish are you from?"

It was the first question you asked anybody, in the Back of the Yards, and you could ask it two ways. Friendly, like nice-to-meet-you talk. Or like the way she said it. *Get home before you get hurt.*

"Excuse us," I said. "You're in our way." The boy wasn't going to be any help, I could tell. He still had hold of my hand, but his had gone limp, as though he'd died.

The bony girl grabbed his other hand and pulled. "Come on, Ronald!" To me, she said, "Word of advice. Leave the St. Augustine boys alone. You'll live longer."

I smiled at her, sweet as pie. "You can have him," I said, "*after* he buys me my soda."

She shoved me. Reached out with both hands, smacked them on my chest. Right away, the boys started hollering for a catfight. If I'd walked away, they'd be calling me yellow to this day.

So I shoved her back. She started flailing her arms, the way some girls do who don't know better, and landed a lucky shot. A good one, right across my eye. That's when I got mad. She was goggling at her fist—I think she was more surprised than me—and I saw my opening, under her elbow, a nice spot of belly. I hauled back my own fist and let fly.

But instead of a good solid *thwack,* my hand whooshed through empty air. Somebody had grabbed the back of my collar, and it wasn't the bony girl, number one because she was in front of me, and number two, because at the same time I was yelling, "Let me go! Let me GO!" I heard her shrieking, "Ow! That's my EAR, sweet Jesus, OW!" I was getting dragged. I stumbled, trying to keep my feet, yelling for Angie, yelling at the gorilla who had hold of me to let go. All around us, roars of laughter. Then the gorilla said, "You wanna fight, take it into the alley!" and he shoved me out the Union Hall door. I tripped and stubbed my big toe hard—somewhere, I'd lost a shoe—and grabbed a lamppost to keep from falling.

"That oughta cool 'em off," someone said. More laughter.

Cool? I was cold. More than cold. Mother Mary on a shingle, it was raining.

Over by the wall, the bony girl was crying. Well, she could stand out here and get soaked if she wanted to. I was going back for my coat and my pocketbook. And my other shoe. And if any of those boys had swiped it, they'd regret it. I was little, but I was mad. Mad counts for a lot.

I limped to the Union Hall door—walking tippy-toe on my shoeless foot, trying to keep my ankle sock dry—and jerked it open. Two big Irish galoots from the Young Men's Club blocked my way.

"No fighting," one of them said.

"I'm not fighting, I'm getting my coat." They didn't budge. I tried shoving between them, but they each took hold of an arm and pushed me back. My sock foot landed smack in a puddle of water. "ANGIE!" I bawled. "Angie, get me my coat! My *shoe*! *ANGIE!*" The galoots slammed the door in my face.

If it wasn't for the shoe, I might have left and gotten my stuff from Angie later. Maybe not, though. I was steamed but good. After all, I hadn't started the fight, and what do they expect a girl to do when she gets provoked like that?

I pounded on the door hard. No answer. "Open up, I need my COAT!" I hollered.

"What's it look like?" a man's voice said behind me.

"None of your business," I snapped. And then I turned around.

He was wearing a blue shirt, the sleeves rolled

halfway up. No tie, brown trousers. "I can make it my business," he said. He stepped close, put out a hand. "Paulie Suelze."

For a second, the name didn't mean anything. Then I remembered. Clothesline gossip, whispers in the grocery store or the butcher shop that hushed whenever his mother came in.

The whispers said he was handsome. He wasn't. Not like the movie stars in Angie's magazines—but they were so handsome they were boring, and Paulie Suelze wasn't boring. His eyes shone pale under the streetlamps. I couldn't tell their color. Blue, maybe.

He looked at his hand, hanging out in the air. Just as he started to pull it back, I grabbed it. Too hard. But he gripped harder, so that my cut-up knuckles hollered and stung. I blinked back tears.

"Come on," he said. "Let's get this coat of yours." He glanced down. His face crumpled when he grinned, messy as an unmade bed. On another man, it might have been ugly. On him, it looked perfect. "Your shoe, too."

I'd tucked my shoeless foot behind my other leg, hoping he wouldn't notice. But of course he had. Eyes like that must notice everything.

"They won't let me in," I said.

He stepped close and put his arm around my shoulders. "They will now," he said.

When he opened the door, the galoots faded back like smoke. "Hey, Paulie! It's Paulie Suelze!" they said. "How long you been back, Paulie?"

Paulie dropped two quarters into the can on the table. Paulie paying admission to the dance struck me as strange as a grown-up running after the ice wagon in summer or playing crack-the-whip in the street. He must have been the same age as the boys of the Young Men's Club, nineteen or twenty, but next to him they seemed like a bunch of snot-nosed kids.

"Those blowers up there know any Benny Goodman?" Paulie asked.

"Sure, Paulie!" "You bet, Paulie!" Boys scrambling to tell the band what Paulie wanted. The kids who weren't dancing poked each other and pointed, *sss*'s and *zzz*'s like bees humming, *suelzesuelzesuelze.*

Paulie looked down at me. He wasn't tall, or big around. But he was solid. Tough. Like the harder you pushed him, the harder he'd push back. He'd been a boxer in the army, people said. Won all his fights. Then—this was when voices lowered—he'd half killed a private in a bar fight over a girl. Did time in military prison. The ladies on their stoops *tsk*'d and shook their heads. A disgrace to the neighborhood, they said. His poor mother, God bless her.

His arm was warm and heavy across my shoulders. Thick with muscle. He smelled different from all the boys I knew. Better. Across the hall, Stan Dudek stared at us openmouthed. So did all the other boys. Most of the girls, too. But some of the girls stared at me, the looks on their faces saying, *If only I'd been the one thrown out in the rain when Paulie Suelze came walking up.*

"You want your coat, I can get it," Paulie said. "Or you can stay and dance with me."

The band struck up "In the Mood." I tipped my head back against Paulie's arm. His eyes were gray. Not cold, though. Like rain with sun behind it. Flecks of blue, green, yellow mixed deep. Dark blond hair, not as streaky as mine, more gold on top. Pale blond eyebrows and ears that stuck out the tiniest bit too much.

Not boring at all.

"You don't know it yet," I said, "but I'm the best dancer you ever saw."

He grinned his rumpled grin again. "Yeah? Prove it."

I kicked off my other shoe. And then I was doing the boogie-woogie in Union Hall with Paulie Suelze, and didn't nobody laugh at me then.

He walked us home. Me and Angie. It had stopped raining, but the wind had kicked up. My wet sock clung inside my shoe, and the wind on it made it feel like an anklet of ice. I jammed my hands deep in my coat pockets. Freezing weather and only going to get worse. Ma's gloves were too old and too thin, she'd have to have new ones. But first the back rent had to be paid. New gloves wouldn't help if we were out on the street.

Only ten minutes gone since the last dance, and here came all my worries, skittering back like rats.

Paulie walked between us, Angie on the other side firing questions at him like a Tommy gun. Paulie didn't seem to mind. Yeah, he'd missed the Back of the Yards. No, he didn't think it smelled worse than when he'd left. He was staying in a rooming house over on Forty-ninth and Marshfield. Yeah, right by the railroad tracks. What was he doing? Still looking around, getting the lay of the land. Seeing which way the wind blew. When Angie asked if it was true he'd killed two sergeants with his bare hands, he laughed.

"If I did, they asked for it," he said.

When we got to Angie's building—her folks' tavern

on the first floor, their flat on the second—she offered to keep walking with us. "We'll both see you home, Ruby," she said.

"You're here, you better go in," Paulie said. "I ain't coming back this way."

It wasn't every day a boy told Angie Wachowski she wasn't worth his time. But Paulie wasn't any boy, and besides, he'd seen me first. He must have liked what he saw.

Sure enough, as soon as the door closed on Angie, he put his arm around me. I smiled, ducking my head a little so he wouldn't see. He'd try something for sure now. Kiss me, run a hand up under my coat. Ever since I was thirteen, boys always tried something. Kissing I liked, but mostly I put the kibosh on hands. You let a hand get someplace it wants to be, good luck getting it out again anytime soon. And then word goes around you're easy, and that's it for you.

It wasn't very late, but the streets were almost empty. Windows closed, drapes pulled down against the cold. I prayed nobody would recognize me. Otherwise, by the end of first Mass tomorrow, the whole Back of the Yards would know Paulie Suelze had walked me home, and Ma would have a fit. Just last month I'd stayed out past ten o'clock with Hank Majewski, and she'd grounded me for a week. And Hank hadn't almost killed anyone.

Maybe Paulie hadn't really hurt that private. Maybe none of it was true at all. Just rumors people made up to make themselves feel important.

We kept walking, our heels hitting, *tunk, tunk,* on the sidewalk, keeping perfect time. Away behind us, a train whistle shrieked; on Forty-seventh Street, streetcar bells clanged. Just a couple more blocks to home. I wished I lived across the city so it would take us all night to get there.

"Let's go to Davis Square," Paulie said.

He must have been thinking the same thing. I smiled up at him. "You bet," I said.

Only a few boys rambled across the park, kicking a can between them as they went. The hottest nights this summer, when it was too stifling to sleep inside, we'd come here along with half our neighbors to spread blankets and sleep on the grass. That had been only two months ago. Now it was almost Halloween, and the weather had turned sharp.

"What school you go to? Sacred Heart?" Paulie asked.

I shook my head. "I work," I said, and then wavered over telling him everything. About Ma losing her job, and the back rent, and the grocery stores not extending us any more credit. About the two days last week the three of us—me, Ma, my little sister, Betty—lived off canned milk and a sack of stale, broken cookies Ma had bought for a quarter from Loose-Wiles.

I didn't say anything.

We came to the benches in front of the fieldhouse and sat down. Damp leaves whirled high on the wind. In the light of the lampposts, they looked like shining, crazy wings. Wings with no birds attached.

"Cold?" Paulie asked. I nodded so that he'd put his arm around me again. He did. It felt more than nice. It felt like it belonged there.

"So you work in one of the packinghouses, or what?"

"Yeah. But just in the offices. Not . . . not on the floor."

He grunted. "I've lived in the Back of the Yards all my life. All that time, I never met a girl from the packing-houses who actually packed meat."

"Really?" I'd known dozens.

"Nope. They all worked in the offices." He dug in his pocket, pulled out a cigarette pack. "Every single one."

Another girl might have gotten mad. But I busted out laughing. "Let me guess," Paulie said. "They put you in bacon. Right?"

"How'd you know?"

"My ma used to work for Scully's. She said the pretti-est girls always got put on bacon, 'cause that's where they bring the visitors through."

I felt myself blush. *He thinks I'm pretty.* For sure I wasn't going to tell him about the pickled hog's feet.

He lifted his arm off my shoulders. Cold air drifted across the back of my neck, and I shivered. "Any girl can hoof it good as you," he said, "don't need to work in no packinghouse."

"There aren't any other jobs." Not for me, anyway. If I'd been smart, and taken classes in typing and short-hand, maybe I could've landed something in an office. But the typing instructor insisted all the girls cut their nails. And I'd had no patience for shorthand's squiggles and lines.

Paulie offered me a cigarette. I took it. He lit a match and I leaned into the tiny flame, puffed until the cig caught.

"What are they paying you?" he asked. "Twelve a week? Thirteen? I know it ain't more than that."

"Twelve and a quarter." All of which went straight to Ma. I walked to work, to save the streetcar fare. I'd had to borrow a quarter from Angie to get into the dance tonight.

"Girl like you could pull down forty, fifty a week," Paulie said. "Easy."

I laughed. "Pull the other one." I'd never heard of any girl making that much, not even in an office.

"No joke. A guy I know runs a dance academy. He's always on the lookout for girls to teach fellows the newest steps. You"—he turned on the bench, eyed me up and down—"the way you dance, the way you look . . . yeah, you'd do good."

He seemed serious. Fifty bucks a week . . . we'd have the back rent and the grocery bill paid off in no time. We could buy meat for dinner again. I could get Ma's wedding ring back for her . . . I'd pull it out of my pocket and there it would be, shining in my palm. I imagined her mouth falling open in surprise.

"I never heard of anything like that," I said. "What kind of girls work there? I mean, are they respectable?"

"Sure they are. You think this guy wants the cops raiding his joint? But hey, if you're not interested, it's no skin off my nose. Stay in sliced bacon." He stood up, dropped his cigarette, and ground it out underfoot. He reached down a hand. I took it. His palm was so warm, I thought my fingers must feel like icicles to him. I was embarrassed, but he didn't seem to notice.

Fifty dollars a week. Warm gloves. Pork roast. Ma's ring.

But Ma wouldn't even let me wear lipstick. I could only imagine what she'd say about dancing with strange men for money.

We crossed South Wood Street. Home only a block away. Tomorrow was Sunday. Mass at Sacred Heart, then sit around the flat, listening to the radio, helping Ma make the bean soup we'd eat all week for dinner. Then Monday, seven in the morning, slopping hog's feet in brine. Bone tired, wondering if this was the day I'd see the first sign of pickle hands, like all the old ladies had. Great red blotches, and sores that took months to heal.

At the corner of Honore Street, I stopped. I could just see my building from here, gray like most of the other two-flats and four-flats on the block, with a wrought-iron rail on the front stoop.

"If . . . *if* I was interested in this dancing thing," I said, "where would I go?"

"It's called the Starlight," Paulie said. "Madison and Western, on the Near West Side. Ask for Del. He's the manager." He looked up the street, squinting a little. Already thinking where he was headed next, probably.

I wanted him to ask if he could see me again. I wanted him to say, *Boy, Ruby, am I glad I came to the dance tonight. I sure am glad I met you.* I wanted him to try something.

"I should go," I said. Ma would be sitting up, waiting for me.

"Yeah, okay." Neither of us moved. Paulie's eyes like rain clouds in the dark. I wondered if I'd imagined the little flecks of color.

"Thanks for getting my coat for me," I said.

He kissed me. Not like Hank Majewski, who'd fidgeted and fussed until I'd felt like telling him to get on with it. Or like Robbie O'Brien, who'd grabbed me like I was a piece of ice on a hot day, and he'd better slurp me up before I melted. Paulie cupped his hand under my ear—how did his fingers stay so warm?—and he leaned down and laid his mouth on mine, easy, everything he did was easy, and his lips were gentle and warm and then he opened them and he was warmer yet. He tasted of cigarettes and beer and earth. I slid my hands under his coat. He felt solid. Tough.

The kiss ended. Paulie tilted my face toward the streetlight. His fingertip brushed the bone over my left eye. It hurt. I jerked away in surprise.

"You're gonna have a shiner," he said. "You better cover that up. Del thinks you're a scrapper, he won't take you on."

"I'm only thinking about it. I didn't say I was going to do it."

"I bet you will." Paulie's gaze wandered down my face to my mouth. "Just like I bet," he said, "you'll go out with me."

It was cold enough now to make our breaths puff like smoke. Mine and Paulie's, clouds mixing between us. The look on his face smug and sure, like he knew exactly which way I'd jump. And he was right, and more than anything that rubbed me the wrong way.

I stepped back. "I don't know," I said. "Maybe I have to think about that, too."

He laughed, short and hard. Surprised. And angry. *Ruby, you and your big mouth! Take it back, tell him, Sure, anytime, Paulie . . .*

"Think you're a pretty tough cookie, don't you?" Paulie said. He reached up and mussed my hair, like I was some kind of baby. I ducked and swatted at his arm, and he laughed again, still angry, a little mean.

"So long, squirt," he said, and walked away. I tried to

think up something bad enough to yell after him, to show him I didn't care. But the rain started coming down again, and I couldn't think of anything, and then he was gone. I turned to run home, and that's when I saw Mr. Maczarek, our front-flat neighbor, standing on the stoop of our building watching me.

TWO

The next morning, Sunday, I woke up shivering. Betty had stolen the blanket again. I tried to pull it off her, but she muttered in her sleep and turned away from me toward the wall.

Paulie Suelze. Last night, that kiss. I drew a sharp, cold breath, suddenly and completely awake.

That kiss. Then right after, Paulie treating me like I was barely out of diapers. *So long, squirt.* I flopped onto my side, my face flushing hot.

Was it because I'd turned him down? Or maybe . . . could I be . . . a bad kisser?

All the other boys I'd kissed seemed to like it. Then again, they'd been kids from school, boys I'd grown up with. Paulie was different. He'd left and come back. He'd done things. Kissed a hundred girls, maybe. Girls in high heels and snappy dresses, not crummy saddle shoes and ankle socks.

A man's voice bellowed from the flat next door. I groaned. The Schenkers' window was only three feet from ours, and once old man Schenker started belting his

German operas, nothing could stop him. Except Mrs. Schenker, and she was deaf.

He never woke up Betty; she could snore through anything. I got up and pulled on my flannel housecoat, then shut the door behind me on my way out of the room. We left the door open at night, to get heat from the coal stove in the kitchen. Now Betty would wake up freezing, in spite of the blanket she stole, and I wouldn't have to listen to Mr. Schenker.

Two birds with one stone.

I slipped through the parlor and out our front door, then up the hallway to the bathroom. Good, it was empty. Since there was only one bathroom for all four flats—us in the downstairs back, Mr. Maczarek in the downstairs front, plus the Artyms and the Gurskis, upstairs—if you waited too long, you could be out of luck for hours.

We hadn't always lived in the Back of the Yards. We'd had a house, once, near my grandparents, Pop's parents, in Wicker Park. I barely remembered it: the long carpet with blue flowers that ran down the stairs, the white voile curtains Ma made for the front windows. Me coaxing Betty into the cellar, then jumping out like the bogeyman to make her scream. A sunny yellow bathroom with a tile floor instead of chipped-up wood. A bathtub. Hot water that ran out of the tap.

Then Pop passed away. Ma went to work in the packing-houses, and we moved here.

Back in our flat, the kitchen felt like a cave of warmth. Ma sat at the green-painted table, in a pool of light from the bulb overhead, darning one of Betty's socks. A few pin-curl pins glinted beneath the edge of her head scarf. I'd set her hair last night, before the dance. She couldn't manage it herself anymore.

"Morning, Ma." I bent to kiss her. She smelled like herself, like cold cream and raisins. Whenever she went out, she dabbed on lavender water; but I liked her better without it.

Ma didn't look up. "Coffee's on the stove," she said. Her voice flat and tight.

"Do you need some aspirin?" I asked.

"No." Not, *No thank you, dear.* Not even her usual glance and smile. A twinge of unease pulled tight in my chest, like a snagged thread.

Heat shimmered off the stovetop. The air smelled of hot metal and coffee and coal smoke. Cold weather smells. I poured two cups of coffee from the percolator. Last night, Ma had been cheerful enough—at least, until she'd noticed my shiner. But by the time I got done telling the story, she was madder at that stuck-up St. Augustine crowd than she was at me.

I brought the coffee to the table and sat down. Under the glare of the lightbulb, Ma's face looked set and grim. While I worried about gloves for her, she'd probably been fretting about the almost-empty coal bin, and where we'd get the money to buy the ton we needed to last through the winter.

Fifty dollars a week, Paulie had said. Just for teaching fellows the Lindy Hop.

Would she let me try? I'd had to argue for days just to go to the dance last night. But Paulie said the place was respectable. If I could convince her . . .

I warmed my hands on my cup. Pretended to look out the frosty window into the back lot, but really watching her instead. Trying to figure her mood. She stabbed her needle into the sock. Frowned, took it back out, aimed again. She used to be able to whip up an entire dress in a day. Now it could take her half an hour to sew on a button.

"I heard the most interesting thing last night," I said. My voice wavered upward, like I was asking a question. I sipped my coffee, swallowed hard. "This girl was saying she works at a, well, a kind of a da—"

"Ow!" Ma's hand jerked, and the needle fell to the table. Blood rose in a red bead on her fingertip. She made her aggravated noise, a sort of deep growling sigh, and put the hurt place to her mouth.

I reached for the darning ball. "Here, Ma, let me."

"Leave it alone!"

I pulled my hand back, surprised. "I was only—"

"Only what? Trying to help? Oh, yes, you're the good daughter, when you're not kissing thugs and hooligans on the street corner in plain view of everyone!"

My stomach knotted. That spying old coot of a neighbor must've pounced on Ma at the crack of dawn. "Ma, wait, you don't understand . . ."

"Bad enough if it was one of the neighborhood boys." Her blue eyes brittle. "But Paulie Suelze!"

"You kissed Paulie Suelze?" Ma and I both swiveled to see Betty standing in the kitchen doorway, in her nightgown and bare feet, her chocolate-dark hair tangled and wild from sleep. She pointed to my eye. "Wow! What happened to you?"

"None of your business," I said, at the same time Ma ordered, "Go back to bed!"

"It's freezing in there. And Mr. Schenker is singing,"

Betty said. Sure enough, with the bedroom door open I could hear him thundering away. She padded to the stove and poured herself a cup of coffee. Ma threw her hands in the air.

"You see the kind of example you set for your sister?" she said. As if Betty were eleven years younger than me, instead of only eleven months.

"It's not how Mr. Maczarek said, Ma. Paulie was just walking us home. Me and Angie. She was with us practically the whole way." Ma's lips thinned. Maybe I shouldn't have mentioned Angie. Ma thought she was wild, because her parents let her wear makeup. "Anyway, it's not like I *asked* him to kiss me. He just did, that's all."

"Then you let him believe he could get away with it. How many times do I have to tell you? You have no father to protect you and these boys know it. Thugs like Paulie Suelze are going to take advantage."

I shoved my chair back. "He's not a thug and he didn't take advantage, he—"

Her voice rose up sharp. "Remember Elena Radowski? Her parents still can't hold their heads up for shame. Is that what you want? To ruin our good name?"

You're not my daughter anymore. That's what Elena's mother had said when she threw Elena out. Elena had gone to stay with "relatives," which everyone knew was just a polite way of saying a maternity home. "Of course not, Ma, but will you listen? Paulie—"

"I knew that dance last night was a mistake. From now on, if you want to dance with your friends, you can go to Pulaski's drugstore. He doesn't let any funny stuff go on."

The *drugstore?* Ten couples crammed between the counter stools and the window booths, barely room to turn around, and old goat-faced Pulaski glaring at us? "But I didn't *do* anything!"

Ma shook her head and stood up, bracing her palms flat on the table. Part of me noticed and knew her knees must be hurting. A bigger part was too mad to care.

"And anyway," I went on, "what's so terrible about Paulie? He was nice to me—"

I heard Betty suck in her breath. Ma froze. "*Nice* to you?" she said. "Jesus, Mary, and Joseph, the boy was in an army prison!"

"—nicer than any of those stupid YMC galoots, and just because a bunch of old cats with nothing better to do tell stories about him that probably aren't even true—"

Ma leaned across the table. Close enough to see the broken threads in her pink quilted housecoat, close enough to catch the coffee scent of her breath. Her eyes icy as the window. "You are not to have anything to do with Paulie Suelze," she said. "If he speaks to you, you will ignore him. If he follows you, you tell me and I'll tell Father Redisz and he'll set him straight. Do you understand me?"

Speak to me? Follow me? As if a boy rumpled a girl's hair, said, *So long, squirt,* then started hanging around like a lovesick puppy. Paulie gave me a chance, probably the only one I'd ever get. I'd played the tough cookie, and I blew it. But if—*if*—he ever gave me another one . . .

"I said, do you understa—"

"Yes! I heard you."

Ma eased back into her chair. "Start the water heating for your baths," she said. "I won't have us late to Mass."

We didn't talk much the rest of the morning. Betty bathed first, in the big galvanized washtub in front of the stove. Then me. Before I got dressed, I combed out Ma's pincurls. Usually I loved arranging Ma's hair: smoothing the pale gold into a sleek crown, coaxing her bangs into fluffy curls. I had the same gold in my hair, but Ma's was pure, while mine was as mixed up as me. Polish and Irish. Streaks of honey and ash, and underneath, a dark blond that was almost brown.

Sometimes it seemed Ma's hair was the only part of her that hadn't changed. The pain had started a year ago, in her ankles first. She'd slept with her feet on a pillow, and that helped for a little while. Then her fingers started hurting. Then her knees, her hips, her shoulders, the pain worse all the time. Until she was taking so much aspirin she couldn't eat because of the new pain in her stomach. That was when she finally went to the doctor. A "real" doctor, as she put it, not the one at the packinghouse, even though the packinghouse doctor was free. I figured out later she must have known already what it was. The minute the packinghouse found out, her days would be numbered.

I'd gone with her to her appointment, to help her undo her buttons. The doctor glanced at her hands. Asked where she worked. Then he said, "Rheumatoid arthritis. Classic case."

"Can you do anything?" Ma asked.

The doctor shrugged. "Take aspirin," he'd said, and left the room.

Most Sundays, I fussed over Ma's hair. Today I tugged out the pins, ran the comb through to lift the curls, and that was that. When I started cleaning up, she blinked as though she was surprised, then patted the sides of her hair, the back. Checking my work, her fingers stiff and crooked as sticks. But all she said was, in that same flat, tight voice, "I suppose you'll have to powder that eye. If Father Redisz sees it, there's no telling what he'll think."

I dug her compact out of her purse and brought it into the bedroom. Mr. Schenker had finally finished his opera, thank God. Betty sat on the bed, still in her slip and bra, her hair half-combed. As soon as I walked in, she got up and closed the door.

"One of the boys in my class saw Paulie last week," she said. Her big eyes shiny as brand-new pennies. "Hanging around a tavern on Fiftieth Street. Said he looked like a real tough guy. Said you could tell just looking at him that he'd killed someone."

I ignored her and went to the little mirror hanging on the wall over our dresser. A deep red mark curved like a comma above my left eye, shaded to purple under my eyebrow. The lid wasn't swollen, at least. That was something.

Betty reached past me and snagged the hairbrush off the dresser. "Let me have that powder when you're done," she said.

"Are you crazy? Ma'll have a stroke if she catches you wearing face powder."

Betty stopped brushing. She leaned back against the wall, facing me. "So is Paulie a good kisser?"

His mouth pressed against mine had been soft and hard all at once. Like a question and answer both. Warm breath of cigarettes and earth. Better than good. Wonderful. And probably he'd never kiss me again.

"Get dressed," I said. "Ma's mad enough without you making us late."

I'd laid the powder on thick, but at Mass, Father

Redisz did a double take before he laid the Host on my tongue. At least there weren't too many neighbors there to stare at me. The noon service was the only one where the sermon was in English, not Polish, so it was the least crowded. I didn't care, I hardly listened anyway. But Ma said she got enough Polish just walking down the street; she didn't need it in church, too.

Walking the two blocks home, Ma took Betty's arm instead of mine. I pretended not to notice. Wind whistled down the street, sending tin cans and trash skittering and our skirts fluttering out ahead of us. When we got to our corner, I said, "I'm going to Angie's."

"No, you're not," Ma said. "I told Mr. Maczarek you'd clean his flat this afternoon."

I'd already started toward the Wachowskis' tavern. At that, I turned and gaped at her. "You *what*?"

Betty shot me a look, half-triumphant, half-pitying. Cleaning for Mr. Maczarek was Ma's worst punishment. I gritted my teeth. Was one kiss worth this? Father Redisz's sermon had been all about God's plan for us. What kind of plan was it, to dangle Paulie Suelze in front of me, then snatch him away? "It's not *fair*," I said.

"So what is?" Ma took up Betty's arm again and started walking. "Hurry up," she called over her shoulder. "I want you finished with Mr. Maczarek's by dinner. There's still the chores at home to do, and tomorrow's a workday."

.   .   .

I dropped out of school the day we pawned Ma's wedding ring.

A few weeks after she saw the doctor, Ma lost her job. She couldn't get another. Factories, hotels, laundries, it didn't matter. One look at her hands, and that was that. She had to apply for government relief. Instead of money, we got a box of goods every month: oatmeal, prunes, coffee, soap, flour, sugar, canned tomatoes, canned milk, beans. The landlord didn't want beans. He'd been patient, but after three months of no rent, he'd had enough.

The day after the landlord came, the three of us sat down at the kitchen table. Ma laid her hands in front of her. Her terrible twisted hands, the knuckles big as knots in a rope.

"Get it over with," she said.

The ring was beautiful; no diamonds, but a broad band of three-color gold worked in the shapes of leaves, with three tiny garnets tucked in a row. It took me and Betty half an hour to get it off. We started with ice, but the swelling in the joint wouldn't go down. Then we smeared on oleo, and I pulled and twisted until I thought I'd break Ma's finger sure. But every time I stopped, she said, "Go on, hurry up!" By the time we were done, her knuckle was scraped bloody and all of us were in tears.

Ma took the ring from me and held it to her lips. Not kissing it, but just pressing it there.

That beautiful Irish Jacinski. That's what our Polish neighborhood always used to call her. They didn't much, anymore. Her hands looked a hundred years old. She still had her pretty, high-bridged nose—the nose I wish I had, and Betty had gotten, instead—but her cheeks had started sliding down into jowls, as if invisible hands pulled at her. For the first time in my life, she looked like other people's mothers. Like Stan's, like Angie's. Fading and old.

She said, "You'll have to go to work, Ruby."

I watched her press a piece of ice to her knuckle. "I know," I said.

The next day, I'd gone to the packinghouse.

. . .

I carried two pails and an armful of rags over to Mr. Maczarek's. Pulled a pile of dirty undershirts out from under his bed. Heated a kettle of water on the stove and washed the dishes piled in his sink. Heated another kettle and scrubbed his floors. Meanwhile he sat at his window, listening to the radio and watching the neighbors pass by, telling me everything they wore or did. If it had been warm enough to open the window, he would have told me what they said, too. Old busybody, he was worse than any babushka biddie in the entire Yards. I nodded and said, "Uh-huh" and "Oh really," but I hardly heard a word.

The money Ma got from pawning her ring had gone straight to the landlord to keep him from throwing us out. I spent eight hours a day stuffing hog's feet in jars, and we still ate beans. We had nothing, and we were going to have nothing. Once, right after Ma lost her job, I'd suggested borrowing money from my grandparents. She'd lost her temper then.

"Those Poles already think I'm no-good shanty Irish," she shouted. "I'll be damned if I'll give them another reason to call me names behind my back."

I'd argued with her, until finally she said, "Nothing comes for free, Ruby. Everything has its price. There's some things I'm not willing to pay, so just leave it alone already."

On my hands and knees, I worked my way backward over Mr. Maczarek's kitchen floor. The rough, dented boards stretched in front of me like the years. In no time,

I'd be just like the old ladies I worked with. Just like Ma. Respectable and broken down. Proud, and hurting everywhere. Every chance in my life gone.

I wrung out the rags and dumped them in the empty pails. "I'm done, Mr. Maczarek, good-bye!" I shouted from his front door. He raised a hand but didn't answer; he was too busy trying to see into the flat across the street. In the hallway, I set down the pails and stretched. Feeling the ache of every muscle in my back, my shoulders, my arms. Seven o'clock tomorrow morning, I'd be hustling across a wet, greasy floor with ten quart jars hooked on my fingers, brine seeping under the tape on my knuckles.

From the hall, I could smell the bean soup. Relief beans. I hated them.

When I came into the kitchen, Ma smiled at me, the first time that day. "You're a good girl, Ruby," she said. "There's hot water on the stove to wash up with. As soon as you're ready, we'll eat."

I didn't feel like a good girl. I felt used up. I felt old. At the sink Betty nudged me aside, pretending to wash her hands too. "I got a Baby Ruth at the matinee today," she whispered. "I saved you half, if you want it later." I smiled and bumped her shoulder with my own to say thanks. She must have borrowed the nickel from one of her friends. Ma didn't like us borrowing; if she knew Angie had spotted me the quarter for the dance last night, she'd have a fit.

If I had fifty dollars a week, what could I do?

A ton of coal. Pork roast. Ma's ring.

"Oh, Ma, I almost forgot to tell you," I said. She was at the stove, ladling the soup into bowls. "Angie invited me for dinner tomorrow. If it's all right, I'll go straight from work."

"Dinner? On a Monday?" Ma asked. I didn't answer; I concentrated on working a lather out of the soap. "Well, all right," she said finally. "I want you home by eight, though."

"Sure," I said.

Our good name, Ma kept saying. How good was our name, if we couldn't pay the grocers, if Ma had to keep her ratty old gloves on in church so people wouldn't notice her wedding ring was gone?

I wouldn't ask Ma about the dance academy. She'd never let me go and I knew it. If she thought bean soup was more respectable than teaching a few fellows how to dance . . . then maybe Ma didn't know what was best for us anymore.

Maybe I did.

THREE

By day, the dance academy was a dump. I walked past it twice before a shoeshine boy finally put me right. I'd been looking for something more glamorous than a plain-Jane second-story walk-up over a butcher shop.

By night, though, I could spot the neon signs all the way from the streetcar stop. STARLIGHT DANCE ACADEMY in yellow, then in pink, underneath, FIFTY BEAUTIFUL FEMALE INSTRUCTRESSES. The street even more bustling than in the daytime. Honking cars, taxicabs swooping up to the curbs, crowds of folks going to movie theaters and restaurants and clubs and taverns. Everything lit up like Christmas. I clacked up the sidewalk in the three-inch heels I'd borrowed from Angie, my dress box tucked under my arm. I grinned at everyone I saw. All this electricity, and I was part of it. Me, a Beautiful Female Instructress!

I could still hardly believe I got the job. All day Monday, at the packinghouse, I'd been so nervous I could barely do my work. In my head, I practiced the Lindy Hop. The fox-trot. The rumba. All the dances I'd learned from Ma, back when Ma could still hoof it, when she used to teach us to music on the radio. All the dances I'd learned from Angie and Stan and the kids at school.

Whatsa matter, Jacinski, you got the jimmy legs over there? the foreman yelled. *You break them jars, there'll be hell to pay.* I didn't care. The quitting whistle hadn't finished blowing before I was running for the ladies' room. I scoured my hands until the scabs on my knuckles bled. Patted the face powder I'd snitched from Ma over my banged-up eye. Rolled on the Magnet Red lipstick I'd borrowed from Angie.

Then I caught the streetcar uptown. In the dump above the butcher shop, I met Del.

Del Giannopoulos was a squatty little man in a squatty little office that smelled like Italian meatballs. He sat behind a beat-up wooden desk, a racing form open in front of him and a plate smeared with red sauce at his elbow. He glanced up from his paper when I walked in. Hound-dog eyes, pouches underneath gray as old meat. He sucked his teeth, like he had a scrap of meatball wedged in there. He looked bored.

Wow 'em first thing. Show 'em what you got. I walked up to Del's desk, stuck one hip out to the side and my tits to the front. Me and Angie picked that up from the movies. If you practice—the twist in the middle is tricky—it looks swell. But only if you've got the goods. One of those stick girls tries it, she looks like a scarecrow in a high wind.

Me, I've got the goods. Sure enough, Del leaned forward. There, I thought. Got you.

"What's with the eye?" he said. "You been in a fight?"

My hand dropped off my hip, I was so surprised. I

started putting it back, then crossed my arms, but that felt wrong, so I ended up with my hands folded in front of me as if Del was Father Redisz at church. "Fight? No I, um, I banged it on a door."

"You married?"

I shook my head. "No."

"Boyfriend?"

"No."

"No boyfriend?" He sounded like I'd just told him I didn't have feet.

"My mother doesn't let me date," I mumbled.

"Good for your mother." Del scraped one thumbnail under the other, then pulled out a handkerchief and wiped it clean. "Door, huh." He balled the handkerchief up in his fist. "You eighteen?"

"Sure I am." Del narrowed his hound-dog eyes. I matched him, look for look. He sat back in his chair, and I let my breath out.

"You fight, you're out," he said. "I don't care which dame says what to you, raise a hand and I'll can you that same minute. That's a rule. Got that?"

I nodded. Del's gaze flicked to my tits, stuck there a few seconds, then slid down to my hips.

Ever since I was thirteen, men had stared. Most talked straight to my chest. A few—old men at church, my foreman at the packinghouse—gave me the once-over with their eyes slitted and their lips tight. Disapproving. As if where their eyes went was my fault.

Del, though—he sized me up the way Ma taught me and Betty to size up a hat. Did it go with the outfits we had? Did it make us look good, or would it be a waste of a dollar-fifty?

"You start tomorrow," Del said. "I don't care what time you get here, so long as you're in your gown, gussied up and ready to hustle by eight sharp." He raised his voice on the *sharp,* like it was spelled in letters of fire. "Streetcar breaks down, you better take a cab. There ain't no cabs, you better run. You're late twice, you're fired. That's another rule. Got that?"

I had the job. Fifty dollars a week. No more pickle juice wrinkling my fingers, no more scraping myself raw on jars. I felt like I'd jumped off a cliff, the wind carrying me safe away from every worry I'd ever had.

"Mondays will be your night off," Del was saying. "You got a gown?"

I blinked back a vision of steaks and mashed potatoes. "A gown?" I said.

"A gown! An evening gown, whatsa matter, don't you speak English?" Del waved a hand at my blue plaid skirt. "Think you're gonna dance in *that?*"

"Of course not," I said, although I hadn't thought about it at all. I had my bridesmaid dress, from my cousin's wedding last year. It wasn't an evening gown, exactly. But it was pretty as could be, and floor length. "Yeah," I said. "I got a gown."

"Good. Some girls hardly got clothes on their backs when they show up here." He flicked over a page of his racing form. When he picked up a pen and circled something, I turned to go. Just as I got to the door, he said, "Hey, I ain't finished with you. What's your name, anyway?"

I turned back around. "Ruby Jacinski," I said.

"Another Polack." His tone like he had Polish girls

coming out of his woodwork. "All right, Jaworski. Park it in that chair and listen up. I'm gonna explain to you the rest of the rules."

. . .

I told Ma I got a job as a telephone operator.

I'd seen a newsreel once about telephone operators. Dozens of women in a room, wearing headsets. They had to be polite and cheerful and efficient, and they had to dress nice, even though the customers never saw them. Most important, though: they had to work all hours.

"The phone lines don't sleep," I told Ma. I remembered that line particularly, from the newsreel. "Only girls with seniority get the day shift. I'm new, so they put me on swing. Eight at night until two in the morning."

"I don't understand," Ma said, flustered. The napkin she was folding scrunched in her hands. "You never mentioned a word about it."

"I tried to tell you yesterday. I overheard a girl talking at the Union Hall dance. I didn't say anything because I didn't think I'd get the job."

"How much?"

"Eighteen a week," I said.

I had no idea how much telephone operators made. I only knew it couldn't be fifty dollars a week. Not even foremen at the packinghouse made that kind of money. I picked eighteen dollars out of the air and held my breath, ready, if she didn't believe me, to take it back, to start over, to explain.

Ma's eyes opened wide. She raised a hand with the napkin still crumpled in it to her chest.

"So what do you think?" I asked. "Is it all right?"

"Ruby," she said, "it's wonderful."

. . .

Under the yellow and pink neon of the Starlight, I hesitated. It was only seven thirty, but already a dozen men milled in front of the building. They hunched their shoulders against the wind, collars turned up, hands in their pockets. I'd have to push through them to get to the stairs. I shifted the dress box in front of me, hugging it with both arms. All my life I'd always had someone, Betty or Angie or any of the couple dozen kids on our street, tagging after or leading the way, arguing or egging me on or threatening to tell Ma. I imagined Angie watching me now. *What are you, chicken?* she'd say.

Just as I'd almost made up my mind to go in, a taxi pulled up to the curb. Three girls spilled out of it, one after the other, clutching their coats around them. The men stepped aside, opening a path.

"You boys better make sure you don't freeze out here," one of the girls said. "I'm cold enough already, I ain't dancing with any Popsicles!" Some of the men laughed. I darted up behind the girls, as if I belonged with them, as if I was just running to catch up.

Inside, we trotted up narrow wooden stairs. At the top we passed the ticket booth with its sign, $1 ADMISSION, in bold red letters. Down that dim hallway to the left was Del's office. But the girls sailed straight ahead through a set of double doors, and before I knew it I was walking across the dance floor. Except for the four of us, the room was empty. The girls aimed kitty-corner across the hall, walking fast and chatting loud. I hustled after them. At first, the hall seemed like nothing more than an enormous bare, cold box. Then I noticed the row of high windows along one wall. The dozens of lights strung from the low ceiling. That raised platform at the far end, that must be the bandstand . . . over in the near corner, opposite, two dozen small round tables and oodles of bent-back chairs. Next to them, a middle-aged woman in a white waitress's cap wiped down a long counter. The lounge. Del had told me some rule about the lounge, what was it?

The clicking of our heels echoed back at us. I swept a glance over the pockmarked shine of the floor. In no time at all, Angie's borrowed heels would be making their own dings and dents . . . I felt my arms break out in goose-flesh.

The girls vanished through a swinging door at the far end of the dance hall. Through it, another dim hallway, and straight ahead, a door marked LADIES. I shifted the dress box higher under my arm and pushed the door open.

The room was bright and loud, humid as July, thirty girls at least crowded inside and all of them, it seemed, talking at once. "Hey, Marie!" someone called. "Lipstick express, catch!" A small glinting something whizzed past my face. I jerked backward, and I heard the slap of it landing in a palm.

"This ain't no slumber party, chickie," said someone behind me. "Move it." Her voice raspy and deep, what Angie's movie magazines called *smoky*. She pushed past me, a tall, dark-haired woman, and I might have shoved her back except for the honest-to-God red fox jacket draped across her shoulders. I'd seen fur only in the movies, in magazines. I had no idea it shimmered like this. Tawny and red and cream, fire-bright. I followed it like it was a magnet.

Paulie was right. This *was* the real deal. I could work at the packinghouse all my life and never have a crack at owning something like that.

The woman headed toward a row of lockers, barreling through knots of girls in dressing gowns and slips and girdles. Another set of lockers stood against the opposite wall. Between them ran a double row of dressing tables, back to back, each one with its own mirror and lightbulbs. I drifted behind the chairs, glancing at the faces in the mirrors, eyeshadow and hair curlers and rouge, breathing in clouds of perfume and hair spray and cigarette smoke. One of the girls caught me staring and frowned. I didn't care. I felt like I was in a movie. It was the most glamorous thing I'd ever seen. From the first moment I stepped into the Ladies', I knew.

I belonged here.

I looked around for a locker, but they all seemed taken: crammed with clothes, underthings tossed over open doors, the doors hung with pictures cut out of magazines—Clark Gable, Cary Grant—or smaller, white-bordered photos of regular boys.

"Hey, you! With the box," a girl called. "There's a spot over here, if you want it."

"Thanks," I said. I hurried over and set my box on the bench next to her. She looked about twenty, with the most perfect waves in her reddish brown hair: rolling and soft, as if she'd bottled them right off Lake Michigan on a spring day. I wondered what brand of setting lotion she used.

"Looks like Del robbed the cradle, hiring you," the girl said. "What are you, sixteen?"

"Eighteen."

The girl laughed.

"Look, you don't believe me, go ask Mr. Giannopoulos! He'll tell you."

"All right, all right. Touchy, aren't you?" She took a flat narrow hosiery box out of her locker. "But don't imagine you pulled the wool over Del's eyes. He ain't that dumb. He knows plenty of customers go for the babies." She stuck out a hand. "Peggy deGroot. From Wisconsin."

She had a crooked tooth in front, pushing a little ahead of the others. Freckles and clear hazel eyes.

"Ruby Jacinski." I shook her hand. "I love your nails." They were long and rounded, painted carmine red with the moons left bare. I busied my hands with my pocketbook, so she couldn't see the scrapes across my knuckles.

"Thanks." Peggy unrolled a nylon stocking up to her thigh and clipped it front and back to her garter. I kicked off my shoes and shimmied out of my lime green dress, then rummaged in my pocketbook for the makeup I'd brought.

"Don't bother looking for a dressing table," Peggy said. "This late, you won't get one. There's only twenty tables, and thirty-five of us."

"The sign outside said fifty girls. And there's a table open right there."

"The Starlight has fifty girls the same way you're eighteen. As far as that table, that's Yvonne's. Sit there and she'll bust your lip for you. If you go crying to Del, she'll say you started it and get you canned."

"Who is she? The Queen of Sheba?"

"And Queen of the May and Queen Bee, too." Peggy pulled a slip over her head, tugged it down past her hips. "Yvonne's the top earner in the place, and nobody forgets it. Least of all Del. There's a mirror by the sinks, you can use that." She nodded toward a dozen girls crammed shoulder to shoulder, standing on tiptoe and craning their necks, trying to see past each other in a mirror hung over four sinks.

Shove into that mob, when there was a perfectly good table not ten feet away? I didn't think so. I walked over and sat down. The girl at the next table didn't move her head, but she rolled enormous eyes sideways at me, an orange red lipstick suspended in her hand. "You can't sit there," she said.

I ignored her. She shrugged and turned away.

The tabletop was littered with makeup. I put my own down—the Magnet Red lipstick, rouge, and powder I'd filched from Ma—careful not to bother anything. See, I argued to an imaginary Yvonne, I'm not touching your precious stuff.

The bruise above my eye had faded, thank God. A little powder, and nobody could tell. Rouge . . . *Just enough for a healthy glow*, said the makeup articles in Angie's magazines. *No boy wants to be seen with a clown.* Somebody really ought to give that Peggy a hint—she was pretty, but she'd plastered on so much mascara it was a wonder she could hold her eyes open. And the girl at the next table, with her orange red lipstick—it was far too bright, hardly becoming at all.

I'd just finished my rouge when the most gorgeous robe I'd ever seen appeared in my mirror. I actually leaned forward a little, to get a better look. Could that be *silk*? Brilliant blue and peach, dashes of red. Wide sleeves. I barely noticed the strong tan arms below them, or the hands set on the hips. My eyes followed a line of scarlet piping upward, to see the same dark-haired woman who'd come in wearing the fox. She glared at me in the mirror.

"What in hell," she said, "are you doing in my chair?"

"I told her, Yvonne," the girl next to me said. She stood up, all graceful arms and legs, and padded away, barefoot.

"I'm not bothering anything," I said.

"Oh." She said it *ohhhh*, rounding her full red mouth into a circle, eyebrows hitched high. She seemed older than most of the others, maybe twenty-five or so, and she had a hard-edged look to her. Not rough, like some of the girls in the Yards. Polished. But hard all the same.

"Well, chickie"—she grabbed the back of the chair and, with a grunt, tilted it up—"you're bothering *me*." She wasn't any weakling; she threw me halfway off the chair. I scrambled to my feet, rubbing my elbow where I'd knocked it against the edge of the table. Before I could say anything, Yvonne's arm shot forward and she grabbed my wrist. "What on earth?" she said. She peered at my scabbed knuckles. At my fingernails, cut short and stained yellow from brine. Her nostrils flared. Delicate, like she was sniffing a flower. I balled my hand into a fist and wrenched it free.

"What a smell!" Yvonne wrinkled her nose. "What've you been doing, digging graves? Del must be desperate. It's getting so he'll let in anything with two legs and tits."

That raised a laugh. My cheeks burning, I snatched my makeup and strode to my locker.

"I tried to tell you," Peggy said.

"Leave me alone," I snapped. From outside the dressing room came a *rat-tatt*ing of drums, the single bleats of a trumpet. "It can't be eight o'clock already!" I said.

"Band's frisking the whiskers," Peggy said coolly. She glanced at my face and rolled her eyes. "Warming up. You've got five minutes."

I lifted the dress out of its box, letting the skirt fall to the floor in a cascade of pink dotted swiss. As soon as I saw it, I felt better. It didn't matter how many fox coats that girl Yvonne owned—nobody could outshine me on the dance floor. And I looked gorgeous in this dress, everyone at my cousin's wedding had said so. I gathered up the skirt and popped it over my head, then fit my arms through the short puffed sleeves. How wonderful to be able to wear it again . . . Of course, I'd had to smuggle it out of our flat without Ma seeing. Telephone operators didn't wear party gowns.

I lifted my hair and turned sideways, my back to Peggy. "Zip me up?" I asked.

No answer. Maybe I'd made her mad. I was about to turn around and apologize—she had tried to warn me, after all—when a raspy, smoky voice said, "Here. I'll get it." I felt a rough tug on the zipper, then a pat on my shoulder blade. "There now. Let's see."

I pivoted high on my toes, making the skirt swirl out, and came down on my heels smack in front of Yvonne. As soon as I saw her, I knew my mistake.

"Oh . . . my . . . God," Yvonne said, between gasps of laughter. "It's Little Bo Peep!"

She'd changed out of the silk robe into an emerald green gown, halter cut, with a plunging neckline and a rhinestone buckle at her waist. Her hair was caught back neatly in a sequined snood. Alarmed, I glanced past her at the other girls. Royal blue, apple red, gold, silver, mauve, every gown either glittering with rhinestones or rich with embroidery. Not a pale pink in sight. Not a single puffed sleeve or high Peter Pan collar with a pink grosgrain ribbon tied in a bow. Not one tiny white polka dot.

"Hey Bo Peep, where's your sheep?" another girl called.

I didn't blush. I went cold. My fingers, my face.

Yvonne laughed. She had a rich, lilting laugh, like something you might hear on a radio program. "This one won't last a week," she said, to no one in particular. She sashayed out of the Ladies' on high Cuban heels, the enormous-eyed girl following her, snorting giggles.

From the hall outside, a sudden swell of music. "Time to hoof it," somebody said. Compacts were snapped shut and shoved into lockers, bosoms adjusted, hair flipped back. Peggy—lovely, a numb part of me noticed, in a canary yellow number with a wide sequined belt—hustled over from the long mirror.

"I'd change, if I were you," she said, tossing a hairbrush into her locker. "Fast."

I made my lips move. They felt like frozen wood. "It's all I have," I said.

She slammed her locker shut. "What I wouldn't give to see the look on Del's face," she said, and walked away.

I closed my eyes. In for a penny, in for a pound, Ma would say. Ma's wedding ring stuck in a pawnshop, its three colors of gold, its smooth, fat leaves. I'd wrestled it off her finger. I'd stuffed hog's feet into jars.

A week, huh? You just wait and see how long I last, sister.

I opened my eyes and joined the surge of skirts for the door.

fOUR

Someone had turned down the lights, so that the bare corners of the hall vanished into a velvet dark. A warm glow lit the dance floor, making it shine like clear water. Dozens of tiny colored lights glided over the walls, and the floor, and the girls crossing to the opposite side of the room. Even they looked different. In the dim light, their sequins and rhinestones and gold lamé flashed and sparked, jazzy as the trumpet notes soaring from the bandstand.

Yvonne and the enormous-eyed girl—the others called her Gabby—led the way across the floor. A couple of wolf whistles split the air. Yvonne smiled and waved. Already twenty or thirty men were drifting toward us from the entrance, folding long strips of paper tickets, shoving them in their trouser pockets. Behind them, more men came streaming in.

"Gentlemen, here they are . . ." a voice boomed. Del stood on the bandstand, the microphone tilted down to his face. He was shorter than I'd guessed, but aside from that, he cleaned up pretty good. Brown suit, cream silk handkerchief in the coat pocket, gleaming wingtip shoes.

He spread his arms, swelled his chest: ". . . the ladies of the Starlight Dance Academy!"

Ragged clapping from the men, a few more whistles. The girls strolled in a loose bunch, heading for the far wall. A few of them waved, like Yvonne. One or two snapped their fingers to the music. Most of the rest walked like they were on their way to the grocery store. I brought up the rear in pink dotted swiss.

Illusion, Del had told me yesterday. *Don't ever forget. In the taxi-dance business, if you ain't got illusion, you ain't got nothing.*

I passed in front of the bandstand. My breath skated high and fast in my throat. The beat of the music was like stones tripping my feet. I couldn't find the rhythm. I glanced up at Del. He stared, blinking hard, like he hoped he was imagining me. Ahead of me, the sequins in Peggy's belt threw yellow sparks into the shadows, left, then right, with the sway of her hips.

Glamorous. While I was Little Bo Peep.

If you ain't got illusion, you ain't got nothing.

I stopped. I let Peggy and the others get ahead a little, so I stood in the middle of the floor by myself. Then I turned, twist in the middle, hand on my hip thrust sideways, bosom to the front. A whistle shrilled from near the entrance. Then another one, closer. I kissed my fingertips and waved, and as I strode off the floor *there* was the rhythm, my heels striking *two-three-four—*

"*Fif*-ty beautiful female partners!" Del boomed as I joined the other girls. "Your choice, for the price of a ticket!"

"Nice move, kid," Peggy said as I came up next to her. "Almost makes up for that pink sack you're wearing."

The girls started taking seats in rows of folding chairs, ten across and four deep, set across the dance floor from the men. The front row was taken immediately. I was heading for a chair at the end of the second row when Del's voice snapped behind me.

"You!" he said.

The other girls scattered as if I had a catching rash. Del took my elbow and hustled me over to a shadowed corner, next to the bandstand, out of sight of the customers. Raising his voice above the music, he jerked his chin at my dress and said, "What in hell's name is *that*?"

"A gown," I said.

"That," Del said, "is not a gown. *Those*"—he jabbed a finger at the other girls—"are gowns. *That's* the kind of thing the men who come here expect. Sophistication. Beauty. Not—" He raised both hands in a gesture of disgust. Apparently, no words contained the awfulness of me. "Go home," he said.

"No!" I grabbed his sleeve. "You haven't even seen me dance. I'm good, I'm . . . Please, Mr. Giannopoulos. You've at least got to let me try."

"I don't have to let you do a damn thing." He stared again, his nose wrinkling, as though I smelled. "A gown," he said. "By tomorrow. Or don't come back."

He walked away. I listened to him spread *Good evenings* right and left among the customers. I pressed my hands together to stop them shaking. While he'd hollered, all I could think about were piles of hog's feet. Bottles of brine.

And then he'd said *tomorrow*.

I had one night to make good.

As I turned back to the folding chairs, my eye caught

one of the musicians. At the Union Hall dance, the band had been white. This band was Negro, and it was bigger, ten pieces instead of five. All of them old, I saw, except for this boy maybe a year or two older than me. Tall, his wrists sticking out from his tuxedo jacket. Wide-set eyes, a smooth, quick face. But it was his look—amused, like I'd gotten lost from the kiddie parade—that started a slow burn up my cheeks. As if he had any call to be high and mighty, with his pant hems floating above his ankles. He saw I'd noticed, but he didn't hide his legs under his chair, like another boy might have. He stood up, and he raised a trumpet, and he blasted a fast scat riff that made my feet feel like leaping right up to my heart. The look on his face then: Yeah, I know. And I'm so good, I don't care.

I went back to the other girls and worked my way to an empty chair in the fourth row. So far only three couples were dancing. Across the floor, sitting in chairs or leaning against the wall, a hundred men watched us. In the dimness, their cigarettes glowed like the eyes of wild animals. More fellows still coming in.

Ten cents a dance, that's what Del had told me. Customers bought tickets and gave them to us. At the end of the night, we turned the tickets in. For every ticket a girl got, a nickel went to the Starlight. The girl kept a nickel, plus whatever tip her customer gave her.

I eyed the gown of the girl in front of me, a sweet floral in chocolate and blue. I bet it cost fifteen dollars, at least. How many nickels was that?

The music paused, couples broke apart. A fellow wandered by, a ticket in his hand. I sat up straight and smiled right at him, but I was in the thick of the herd and he didn't even see me. A girl in front jumped up and strutted out with him, just as the band struck up "Sing, Sing, Sing." My favorite. The trumpet screaming and wailing, the beat like it could pick me up by my ankles and spin me right across Lake Michigan, my feet flying too fast to get wet.

Well, these bumps on a log might be able to sit through the hottest jazz God ever made, but I couldn't. I got up and strolled along the edge of the dance floor, snapping my fingers. That trumpet blowing so good, I forgot I was Little Bo Peep. I forgot I was a Beautiful Female Instructress. All I knew was, the music rippled across my skin, tiny colored lights dappled the air, and I wanted to dance.

"Well, aren't you a live wire!" A man stepped up, grinning. He waved a ticket in the air. "Hey, I remember you. You did that little strut there, when you gals came on the floor." He was old, as old as Ma at least, with a pot belly bigger than Mr. Maczarek's. He could've been Frankenstein, for all I cared. I took the ticket like I was in a dream, like I was watching someone else do it, and then I was on the dance floor with my very first student.

Only he didn't wait for me to show him anything. He wrapped a big arm around my waist and shuffled us into a box step. He smelled like cheap bay rum: musty wood, sprinkled with cinnamon and talcum powder.

"Excuse me, mister, this isn't a waltz," I told him. "Jitterbug's best for this tune. Here, I'll show you." I tried to wiggle free but the man only grinned wider.

"I haven't seen you here before tonight," he said. "Am I right?"

"That's right, but I . . ."

"I'm your first, aren't I? Come on, you can tell me. I don't mind." He stepped back suddenly and twirled me so hard, my feet twisted and I would have fallen, except he caught me.

"Ho-ho!" he said. "There, I've got you. What's your name, sister?"

"Ruby," I said, a little breathless. I knew the jitterbug, the fox-trot, the rumba, the quickstep, the Peabody, and the boogie-woogie. I even knew the Charleston, though with luck I'd never have to do that fuddy-duddy in public. At the parish festivals, the old folks still thought it was the latest thing, probably because it was the only dance they knew that wasn't a polka.

But what kind of dancing was this?

Before I could figure it out, the man stepped back again. This time, though, I was ready. I twirled but I stayed on my feet and that was when I felt, clear as ice on a hot day, the squeeze of his fingers around my keister. The next moment, the music ended. Quick as that, he let me go, and quick as that, I drew back my fist to whop the living daylights out of him.

He held out his hand. Between his finger and thumb was a silver dollar. "A pleasure, little Ruby," he said.

Slug him, Ruby! I heard Angie say it, loud as if she was standing next to me. He deserved it. I knew it and he knew it.

I snatched the dollar out of his hand.

The man winked. "See you around." He darted at another girl, a ticket held high. I stood in the middle of the dance floor, babble and commotion all around as men snagged partners. Music swelled from the bandstand. I looked up to see the young trumpeter staring straight at me, his eyebrows raised. Like he was waiting to see what I'd do next.

Nothing here was what I'd expected. I wanted to go home and I wanted to dance. I wanted the trumpet player to have seen me deck that rotten jerk, instead of take his money. I made a fist around the dollar, pressing it hard into my palm. In my other hand was the ticket. A nickel for the Starlight. A nickel for me. A dollar and five cents, for two minutes of dancing.

At the packinghouse, it would take me almost half a day to earn that much.

In front of me, a man handed a ticket to a girl. I watched her, then did what she did. Stuck my leg a little out to the side, lifted my hem—more than a few fellows stopped to watch—and tucked the ticket and the silver dollar under my front garter. The weight of the coin against my thigh felt like good luck. And maybe it was, because when I looked up there was another fellow, this one thin with a wrinkled neck and a bitty scrap of a mustache, a fellow who, if I saw him on the street, I wouldn't look at twice.

I gave him a smile that made him blink. Then I took his ticket, stuffed it into my stocking, and trotted out onto the floor with him.

The hall, so big and cold at first, had gotten crowded and stuffy. There must be two hundred men in here by now. I got a third customer, and to my surprise, he actually wanted a lesson. He was a young chubby fellow and I swear he was a menace, I never saw anyone so clumsy. I made him stop what he was doing and look at my feet and practice. Nothing fancy, just a plain box step. He took that dance and the next one, too, and by the end he was at least putting his feet in the right places, even if he couldn't keep the beat. He seemed grateful to learn. He'd been coming to the dance academy a week, he said, and none of the girls had showed him a thing. I said I thought that was a shame. He tipped me fifteen cents.

The real shame was that people like him didn't have the brains God gave a goose. Coming here a week, and he still believed this was a dancing school. I'd only been working an hour, and already I knew better. I still wasn't sure what the real game was, but for sure it wasn't teaching these fellows the quickstep.

I looked around, eager for my next customer. And there, right next to me, stood a Chinaman holding out a ticket.

In the Ladies', earlier, I'd overheard a broad-faced blonde say, "I know some girls don't mind the chinks and flips, but it's getting so you can't turn around without bumping into one. If I had my way, Del would keep 'em outta here, same as the Negroes."

"Well, you don't have to dance with them," another girl said.

"I'll say I don't. They come here and dance with us, and the next thing you know, they think they can marry us. Don't laugh. Believe it or not, there's plenty of nickel hoppers who've married flips, and I say it's a damn shame."

I whirled and ran for the Ladies'. At the door, I snuck a peek to see if he was following. No, he was dancing with a pretty little brunette in a red dress. She didn't seem to care she had a Chinaman's arms around her. She was chatting him up like anything. Well, she could have him.

Half a dozen girls lounged at the dressing tables,

smoking or fixing their faces. "Hey, Bo Peep," a plump redhead called. "Found your sheep?" Shrieks of laughter. I ignored them and went to my locker. The coins had fallen down to my ankle and were chafing something fierce. I'd just gotten my stocking unhooked from the garter and was rolling it down when Peggy came in and plopped next to me. She hauled her yellow gown up over her knee.

"So, how you like it so far?" she said.

I fished the coins out of my stocking.

"Huh!" Peggy said. "You may be a slow starter, but you sure catch on quick enough."

Yesterday, Del had told me, *I run a clean place. Respectable. You don't dance decent, you're out. I canned a girl just last week for rubbing up a guy in a corner. You know what I'm talking about?*

My face had blazed so hot, it could've lit up his office.

Same time, Del had gone on, *you gotta be a sport. A customer steps over the line, sure, that's different. Tell the bouncer, O'Malley, and he'll take care of them. But don't come squawking just because a fellow's hand slips a little. Savvy?*

Yeah, I savvied. I dropped the dollar into my pocketbook along with the rest of my tips. I noticed Peggy kept hers in a little satin purse attached to her garter. I'd have to ask her where she got it.

Peggy stood up. "Come on," she said. "Band's about to take a break, we better hit the toilets. Unless you want to spend the whole ten minutes in line. Me, I'd rather get an orangeade."

"I'm with you," I said.

After the ten-minute break, we hit the floor again. My feet were killing me. Angie's shoes were darling, but all the Wachowskis had tiny feet and hers were a size smaller than mine. I couldn't sit down to rest, though; the second I did, the dances dried up. The only way I could get tickets was to sashay around like I had all the pep in the world and couldn't wait for some nice fellow to take me for a spin. Even then, half the time the customer would sail right past me to a dame with some flash and sparkle to her.

By ten o'clock I was dragging. Except for "Sing, Sing, Sing," the band had played hardly any hot numbers all night. It was all corny stuff from before I was born, groaners like "Tiptoe Through the Tulips" and "Cheerful Little Earful." Hardly a jitterbug in the bunch. Even so, if some of these clodhoppers could only dance, it might not have been so bad. But between the sappy tunes, and trying to keep up with all their galloping and bouncing and plodding, I was wearing thin.

I was in the middle of a strange kind of waltz with an old Italian man when, over by the bandstand, I spotted the man in a charcoal gray suit.

The man was dancing—I mean, *really* dancing—with the girl in the chocolate and blue gown. Her smile was plastered on, the way it gets when you're not sure of your feet but you don't want your partner to know. Only he will, every time. The man swiveled, *one-two!* He looked up and I caught his eye, and I smiled like blazes.

When the dance ended, I grabbed my tip from the Italian and dashed toward the bandstand. I had a hunch.

I was right.

His name was Art Dobbins. From Philadelphia. The band swung into "The Glory of Love," Art swung us into a snappy quickstep, and for the first time that night, I wasn't afraid for my toes.

Art was a salesman, traveling all over. He came to the Starlight whenever he was in Chicago. "Although I'll tell you, sister, I was about to give up this dump and move over to the New American. So many of these girls, dancing's their livelihood but darned if they have the first idea how! That last hobbledy-horse, I swear I sprained my wrist hauling her around."

The band ended—so soon! But Art didn't let go my hand. "Just let me get another ticket . . . there you are . . . what'd you say your name was? Ruby? Say, that's a fine little name. How long you been here? No kidding, your first night? Say, how lucky does that make *me*?"

Art was old, but he wasn't some doddery granddad, like some of the men here. The only wrinkles he had were laugh lines around his eyes, and on a man, that just meant he was grown up, not a young pup who didn't know what was what. And could he dance!

"You're too good for this place," I told him. "You should be at the Aragon, hoofing it with all the swells." The Aragon was the biggest dance palace in Chicago; everybody who was anybody went there. Angie and me dreamed of going there ourselves someday. Burn up the floor, the swing kings falling at our feet.

"The Aragon, huh?" Art said. "And if I saw you there, would you dance with me?"

I tossed my hair back. "Sure I would," I said.

"Little liar. You know perfectly well I'd stand around all night, watching the young bucks get the dances. When I come here, see, I can take my pick." His arm tightened around my waist. "I think I'll stick with you, doll. Once I've found a good thing, I hate to let go."

After four dances, Art bought me an orangeade, and a

coffee for himself, and we sat at one of the little tables in the lounge. He told a bunch of traveling-salesman stories he thought were funny, and I laughed and drank my pop and eased my heels out of my shoes. My toes ached and throbbed. Behind Art, I saw Peggy sit down with two Filipino men. She was laughing and joking around like they were regular fellows. And here I'd thought she was so savvy.

Art pushed his empty coffee cup to the middle of the table. "Shake a leg, sister?" he asked. I smiled and shoved my feet back into Angie's shoes, trying not to wince.

The dance was halfway over before I remembered what Del had told me about the lounge. *If a customer wants to spend time with you, he has to pay*, he'd said. *Time in the lounge is a ticket a dance, same as if you're on the floor. Keep track and make sure he antes up.*

How many songs had we sat through? Four? Five? Art must not know about the rule. I thought about asking him for the money, but somehow it seemed rude. After all, he'd bought me a pop. And he was being awfully nice, sticking with me. Saved me a lot of work and trouble.

The next dance, though, Art didn't reach into his pocket. He held my hand, chattering about nothing in particular, and when the band started up, he swung me into a fox-trot.

"The ticket, Art," I said.

He looked surprised. "Don't I get this one on the house? Oh, say, I forgot. You're new. Well look here, Ruby, you like me, right? I like you."

"Sure, but . . ."

"Well, that's what the girls do, you see. Give out some free dances. Kind of a tradition. Not to just anybody, not all the time. But when they like a fellow . . ."

"But I . . . The thing is, I'm in kind of a jam. See, my mother's sick and she lost her jo—"

Art let go. Just like that, in the middle of the dance floor, so suddenly that I teetered on my heels. "Look, sister, I didn't come here to be panhandled," he said. "Next thing, you'll be telling me your poor sick mother needs an operation. You skirts, I swear you ought to think up some new lines."

I gaped at him. Fun-loving Art was gone—this man eyed me like his shoes stunk and I was the dog turd he'd stepped in.

"I'm sorry," I said. "I didn't mean it that way, honest, it's just it's my first night and I'm—" Somebody bumped my shoulder. I jumped, startled, and turned to see Peggy quickstepping past with one of the Filipinos. She gave her head a tiny shake, then danced on by.

"Now you're cute enough," Art was saying, "and I thought we were square. I've got reservations at a fine steakhouse tonight—I'm a regular there, they treat me pretty much like royalty—and I was going to take you for a late supper, but . . ."

All around us, couples swirled and bobbed. Not ten feet away, Yvonne glided past, her arms around a heavy fellow who barely came up to her chin. She didn't seem to mind; she was smiling at him like he was the only man in the place worth looking at.

". . . plenty of girls would jump at the chance to step out with old Artie. I'd like it to be you, but . . . What do you say? Are we square?"

Supper at a club. Out on the town, just like one of the uptown swells. I'd never done anything like that in my life. "Sure, Art," I said. "Sure, we're square." The next dance, when Art tried to give me a ticket, I made him take it back. I wasn't any panhandler. I was a sport.

Ma would be mad, me getting in late. I'd tell her I missed the streetcar. Or that I'd been kept late for . . . for training. Yes, that was better.

After another couple of dances, Art said he needed to stop in the little boys' room. Fine by me. I needed to visit the Ladies' myself.

Peggy followed me in. "About time," she said. "I've been giving you the signal for ten minutes. You've been with that dried-up stick long enough, I figured you needed someone to throw you a lifesaver."

I glanced at myself in the full-length mirror by the door and made a face; my curls were flying every which way. I crossed to the sinks, wedged in between two other girls. "Art's no stick," I said over my shoulder. "He dances better than any other man here." I wet my fingers and smoothed down a corkscrew stray.

"*Art*, that's it," Peggy said. "I was trying to remember. 'Kiddo, you're the only reason Art comes here . . . Say, honey, be a pal . . . how about a free dance for old Artie?' "

"You talking about that skinflint in the good suit?" the girl next to me butted in. "He took me in once—had me on a string all night, one night."

"Don't feel bad," Peggy said to me. "Guys like him, they like to pick on the new babies. Listen, I've got two fish on the hook out there, but if I'm gonna reel 'em in, I need another girl. Dump that bag of bones and get some real action. What do you say?"

I had no idea what she was talking about—*fish? real action?*—but I was no dummy. Dance with Filipinos? Not on your life. "Thanks very much, I'm sure," I said. "But Art's taking me to a fancy steakhouse."

They hooted at that. *Ooh, a fancy steakhouse. Thanks very much, I'm sure!* Rolling their eyes at my dress, elbowing each other. Jealous cats. When I was digging into my steak, later, I'd be the one laughing. I shook the water off my fingers and turned for the door, past Peggy's grin and her outstretched hand. "Hey, kid, wait," she said. I didn't even slow down.

Art wasn't where I'd left him. If some tart in sequins had pinched him from me, I'd tell her a thing or two . . . I walked up one side of the dance floor and down the other. I searched the lounge. It was past one o'clock, and the crowd of men had thinned out; less than a hundred left, and none of them Art. I waited where I could see the door of the men's room. Two dances rolled by. Five. Art didn't come out.

He couldn't have left. Could he? Surely not. He hadn't even tipped me yet. I had a dollar coming, at least.

I made another round of the hall, a sick feeling growing in my stomach.

He was gone.

I pressed my hands against my girdle. The sick feeling only got stronger. When Peggy went dancing by, I edged back into the shadows so she wouldn't see me standing alone.

Art's taking me to a fancy steakhouse. No wonder they'd all laughed. Little Bo Peep. The baby. The stupid little fool.

I'd tell the other girls I'd gotten sick. That I'd had to give Art a rain check, that he'd been so disappointed he'd gone on home.

But hide until the night was done, and then what? If I slinked off, I might as well just walk out.

I'd wasted three hours with Art. I had one hour to make up for it.

I closed my eyes and took a breath. My stomach did a slow flop, front to back, but I ignored it. Started snapping my fingers. Walked into the swirling lights. Strolled down the sidelines as if the sweet, sappy tune the band was playing was the hottest swing in the jukebox. Angie's shoes chewing my toes like wild animals, and not a single fellow looking my way. The hall was emptying out. Only fifteen or twenty girls were still dancing. Yvonne—she'd had fellows lining up for her all night. Her big-eyed friend, Gabby, and the plump redhead who'd heckled me before. Stella. And Peggy. I didn't see her Filipino friends. Maybe she hadn't found another girl to reel them in, whatever that meant.

I picked up a ticket here and there, but it was hard slogging. The dance tunes had gotten downright skimpy. Everyone seemed tired. On the bandstand, the trumpeter looked bored enough to fall over dead.

The music scraped to a stop. The lights came up. Two o'clock, and I hadn't had a dance for the last twenty minutes. O'Malley, the bouncer, herded the men ahead of him toward the door. "That's it for tonight," he kept saying. "You want more company, come back tomorrow."

In the Ladies', I slipped off my dress and hung it up in my locker. Then scooped out the handful of tickets from the top of my stocking. Across the room, Yvonne propped her foot on a chair and flipped up the hem of her gown. The tickets crammed under her nylons looked like a blue tumor on the side of her leg. It took her both hands to get them all, and even then two or three fluttered to the floor.

Big deal. Give me time, and a swell dress, and I could do that, too.

We lined up in front of the ticket-seller's booth. Yvonne—no surprise—was first. I ended up last, behind the girl in the chocolate and blue gown who'd given Art a sprained wrist. Alice, she said her name was. She wore her hair in big fat sausage curls, like Shirley Temple. I wondered if she knew even Shirley Temple didn't wear sausage curls anymore.

When I finally got to the booth, I laid down my handful of tickets. Little Bo Peep or not, I hadn't done too bad. Tomorrow I'd go down to Maxwell Street. See if I could find a bargain. Probably I wouldn't be able to afford rhinestones and sequins, but that could come later. Right now, I needed just good enough for Del to let me back in the door.

The ticket man counted fast, shoving the tickets aside, two by two. His hand crawled in a drawer, coins clinking. He pushed the money across the counter to me. I drifted to the door, adding it all up.

Three dollars sixty-five cents, including tips.

That couldn't be right. I stopped and counted again. Fifty, seventy-five, one, one-fifty . . .

"You, Jablonsky!" Del yelled from across the hall. "Either show up with a gown tomorrow, or don't show up!"

The sick feeling bloomed in my belly, worse than before. I hadn't even earned enough to buy two pairs of stockings. How many free dances had I given Art? How many had I wasted, waiting for him to come back? I couldn't remember. I couldn't think. The other girls clattered down the stairs and I trailed behind in a daze. He might as well have stolen from me. Reached into my pocketbook, taken my gown away from me. I rubbed my knuckles. The scabs like whips on my skin.

Where could I possibly get more money? Ma used to keep a few dollars saved in a sugar tin, but that had been spent months ago. Betty didn't have a nickel to her name. Angie? She loaned me a quarter sometimes. Nothing like what I needed.

Freezing outside, an icy wind whipping up the street. The door to the Starlight latched shut behind me. It was over. Just like that.

I headed for the streetcar stop. Ahead, a group of people laughed and chattered. Under the streetlights, the cigarette smoke around their heads was a bright haze; between that, and the shadows of their hats, I couldn't see their faces. But I'd recognize that tawny shimmer of fox fur anywhere. Yvonne. The thin-shouldered slouch next to her must be Gabby. Three men with them. From around the corner, behind them, a fourth man came walking. A tall, lean man.

Surprise jolted through me. Then relief, like cool water on a burn. I raised my hand and waved. "Art!"

It's Bo Peep, I heard Gabby say. The men laughed. I didn't care. I started toward Art, but instead of walking to me, he stopped. A cab swerved up to the curb, and in the sweep of headlights, I saw my mistake.

It wasn't Art. It was the trumpet player from the band. He'd changed from his too-short tuxedo into regular clothes and a derby hat. A piece of paper gleamed white in his hands.

"What is she *doing*?" Gabby said, at the same time one

of the men said, "That the kind of thing you girls go for at this place?"

I spun on my heel and walked away, my heart hammering hard. The wind bashed my face, stung my eyes.

"What is this, a joke?" another of the men said. Angry. At me? *It's not my fault, I made a mistake.* The words ready to fly out of my mouth. But when I turned, I saw they were staring at the trumpeter, not me. He'd unfolded his paper and was holding it out. The men stepped in front of Yvonne and Gabby, as if the paper might bite.

The man raised his voice louder. "You think these fine ladies want to drink homebrew rotgut at some two-bit black and tan?"

"No sir, no rotgut. We—"

"Wait a minute," Yvonne said. "You're in the band, aren't you?"

"Yes, ma'am," the trumpeter said. "Just started last week."

"And *this* week'll be your last, if I catch you bothering our customers again. I'll go to Del, and he'll make sure you don't blow another note at any taxi-dance hall in Chicago. Now, go on, get out of here."

"Yes, ma'am. I didn't mean to bother you, I just—"

One of the men took a step toward him. The trumpeter folded the paper. Touched his hat, walked away.

"Let's go," Yvonne said. "I'm freezing."

They didn't spare me a glance. I watched the cabs' taillights until they turned the corner at Western Avenue. A gust of wind raised gooseflesh up the backs of my legs. A car passed by, its engine knocking hard. The air smelled like snow. I pulled my coat tight and started walking.

At the corner, a man stepped out of the shadows. I

almost screamed, then saw it was only the trumpet player. Again.

"Jesus, Mary, and Joseph!" I snapped.

"Excuse me?"

"Nothing. Never mind." I turned to go, but he held out the paper. I hesitated.

"New after-hours club," the trumpeter said. "Give it a try, when you get tired of the Hoot Owl or the Rhumboogie."

I'd never heard of those places. I took the paper but I didn't look at it. A bit of his face was lit up by the streetlamp: the long curved cheek, the corner of his mouth. The line between light and shadow so sharp, the edge of his lip looked cut from stone.

"Club just opened," he said, "so the cabbies, they don't know about it yet. I'm in the band. You got a customer wants to hear the hottest jazz in Chicago, you bring him down."

"Hot as 'Tiptoe Through the Tulips'?" I said.

That surprised a laugh out of him. He had a nice laugh, low and rolling. "That off-the-cob stuff," he said, his voice spiky with contempt. "Geezer music. If I'd known that was all they played here, I wouldn't have taken this gig."

Fast riffs, the screaming of his trumpet. Better than the Union Hall band. Better even than the scratchy jukebox at Pulaski's drugstore. "I liked 'Sing, Sing, Sing,'" I said.

"Yeah, that's solid. You want to hear even better, come to Lily's." He nodded at the paper. "It's my cousin's place. Tell her you know me. Name's Ozzie. She'll take care of you."

I won't be back. This is the last you'll see of me, right here.

"Okay," I said.

The wind tugged at his hat. He pushed it backward on his head, just a second, before snugging it low again. "I saw how you was gonna deck one of those geezers." His lip curved up in a grin. "Only interesting thing that almost happened all night." He touched his hat brim. "Evening," he said, and walked away.

On the streetcar home, I folded the paper into squares. When it was so small I couldn't fold it anymore, I slipped it into my pocket.

I knew I'd be angry tomorrow. I was too numb now. Numb from cold. From not wanting to believe that Art had made a fool out of me. From not wanting to think about a mountain of hog's feet in a stinking gray room.

The streetcar clanged. One bell, stopping. I leaned my head against the window and closed my eyes. Two bells, starting. My head shuddered along the glass and we were moving again.

FIVE

Ma had waited up for me. She'd splurged on hot chocolate, to celebrate my becoming a telephone operator, and when I got home she insisted on making me a cup, even though it was a quarter to three and I was dead on my feet.

"Your lips are practically blue," she said. "Eighteen dollars a week won't do us any good if you catch your death of cold."

My lips were blue because I'd scrubbed off my makeup before coming into the flat. Like all the plumbing in the building, the sink in the hall toilet had only cold water. When it got icy outside, so did the tap.

Well, I wouldn't have that problem anymore. I sipped my chocolate and thought about telling Ma that starting tomorrow, she wouldn't have to sit up for me.

In the end, I kept quiet. Maybe something would come to me by morning.

. . .

Nothing did. All I knew was, if I ever saw Art Dobbins again, I'd throw him a punch so hard that the trumpet player—what was his name, Ozzie?—would think he had ringside seats at a prize fight.

But that didn't help me any.

In the kitchen, Ma called good morning from behind two clotheslines sagging with clean, dry laundry. I ducked behind them and kissed her. She was dressed already; Betty must have helped her before going to school.

"There's oatmeal on the stove," Ma said. Cheerful, the way she always used to be in the mornings, the way she hadn't been in a long time. "Oh, and put the iron on while you're there, will you?" She unpinned one of Betty's blouses, folded it in half and dropped it in the laundry basket.

I spooned oatmeal into a bowl, chucked a little sugar over the top. Then lifted the iron out of the cupboard and set the heavy metal triangle on the stovetop to heat.

"I can't tell you, Ruby, how excited everyone is that you're a telephone operator. Mr. Maczarek said—"

The bowl slipped from my fingers and thudded to the counter. I grabbed it just before it spun off the edge. "You told Mr. Maczarek? Who else did you tell?"

"Well—not so many people. Mrs. Dudek, and Mrs. Artym upstairs, and Rose Terasek when the vegetable man came by . . . why, what's wrong? Why shouldn't I?"

"Nothing. It's just . . ." I carried the bowl to the table. A bedsheet hung between us and I was glad for it. "Ma, this telephone operator thing. It . . . it might not work out."

"Not work out?" The bedsheet twitched aside. I sat down quick, mashing at the oatmeal with my spoon, so that I didn't have to see the disappointment on her face. "Why? Did you . . ." Even without looking I knew she was peering at my eye, where the St. Augustine girl had socked me. "You didn't get into another fight, did you?"

"No! Of course not. It's just . . ." I laid my forehead in my hands. It wasn't only the gown, or even losing the job. It was that Ma's worries had somehow become my worries, and I was tired of it. I thought I'd found the solution but instead, we were in the same dumb mess as before. The back rent and owing money to the grocers. Bean soup. I didn't want to have to think about any of it anymore. But I had to.

"There's all these . . . I don't know, wires and . . . and things, and the other girls are so much better at it than me, and I just don't . . . I don't fit in, I guess." Which was the biggest lie of all, because I did fit in, I *could*, all I needed was a proper dress and I could show them, Peggy and Yvonne and all of them . . . and those beautiful dressing tables, each one with its own mirror, lightbulbs on either side, the most glamorous thing I'd ever seen, and now I'd never sit at one again. It was just like Paulie— something perfect dangled in front of me, then snatched away for no reason. At the thought, my throat closed up as if it was a rag in a pair of hands, wrung hard and squeezed . . . "And now Mr. Maczarek knows, and Mrs. Dudek and everyone, and they'll know I couldn't do it and it's all I'll hear everywhere I go for the rest of my life!" I picked up the spoon and stabbed it into the oatmeal.

"Ruby. Ruby! Look at me."

Ma's face wavered through my tears. She dragged a handkerchief off the line and handed it to me. I blew my nose.

"Did they fire you?" she asked.

I shook my head. I rubbed my knuckles, felt the scabs rough under my fingers. "Not yet. But I think . . ." *Either show up with a gown tomorrow, or don't show up.* I felt gray inside, heavy, as if a chunk of lead had appeared where my heart should be. "They will," I said. I pushed my chair back. "I'll go to the packinghouse. Maybe they'll give me my old job back."

"No." She said it with such firmness that I looked up at her, startled. Ma brushed a wisp of hair off her forehead. Then she sat down. Slowly, the way she had to do everything now. Little winces, the corner of her mouth twitching back. Watching her, I felt the grayness spreading through me. Dank, dark, dull. This was the way we were now. It would never be any different.

"I never had the gumption to leave the packinghouse and find another job," Ma said. "I wouldn't even join the union, when it came. I didn't want the bosses to think I was ungrateful." She gazed into her lap. I knew she was looking at her hands. The expression on her face the same as when we lost our gloves, or forgot our schoolbooks on the streetcar. Like she couldn't understand how anything that belonged to her could be so stupid.

"It'll be all right, Ma. I'll see the foreman and explain . . . something."

"Every mother wants better for her child than what she got. I never graduated school, and I'd hoped . . ."

What did school have to do with anything? I knew only one girl who'd ever made good: Angie's big sister, Clara. And that was because she married a mason with a good union job. She'd had a real satin wedding dress, which took Angie and her mother weeks to make, and then on their honeymoon what did her husband do but buy her *more* dresses, from Marshall Fields no less, one of them a gorgeous thing loaded with beads all down the neckli—

Inside me, suddenly, everything went quiet.

"Ruby! Are you listening to me?"

I blinked. Ma was frowning at me. "I *said*, you're as smart as any girl there. When they tell you something, you're to pay attention and do your best."

I nodded. I was almost afraid to breathe, afraid this bubble, this hope, might turn gray and sink. "Yes, Ma," I said.

"If they fire you, they fire you. But I won't have you quitting. Is that understood?"

"Yes, Ma."

She stood up and went back to the clotheslines. Creak of clothespins, the laundry falling like snow into the basket. The iron was heating up, the smell of hot metal cutting past the scents of clean cotton, oatmeal, coffee. I picked up my spoon again. Then dropped it clattering into the bowl and jumped to my feet.

Ma tugged on the bedsheet, trying to get it down. "Where are you going?"

I swooped around the table and kissed her cheek again, smacking loud. "Getting dressed. Then I'll run all your errands."

"This early? The shops aren't even open!"

"Then I'll be the first in line." I threw the sheet over the line and caught it on the other side. Ma laughed.

"I can't keep up. What's gotten into you this morning?"

I hugged her, until she batted at my arms, giggling. I couldn't remember the last time I heard Ma giggle. The gray lead inside vanished; my heart felt free and red again and warm, skipping like hopscotch.

When I let her go, she poked me in the ribs. "Sit back down and eat your breakfast. It's a sin to waste food."

"Yes, Ma," I said, and I went to get dressed.

. . .

When Angie and me played hooky, we always met up by the school's east gate. From there, we could hop the streetcar to the movie theaters on Ashland Avenue. Or to the lakeshore, if it was hot. Or ride the el to the Loop, if we felt like window shopping at Marshall Fields and Carson Pirie Scott, pretending we were swells who could buy whatever we wanted.

At noon, when school let out for lunch, I was waiting.

I hadn't seen Angie since the Union Hall dance, three nights ago. Since Paulie, since the Starlight. I didn't have to talk her into cutting class. She saw me, turned right instead of left, and we headed out the gate into the street. As soon as we were safe on the streetcar, I raised my right hand and stuck out the little finger. "Pinkie secret." Angie hooked her little finger around mine. Her kitten's eyes button-round.

"Pinkie secret," she repeated, serious as sin.

We'd started pinkie secrets in the fifth grade, when I had a crush on Barry Jenkins and Angie was in love with George Scepanovic. Whoever blabbed a pinkie secret would lose all her hair, never get married, and end up living with her mother for the rest of her life. We squeezed, let go, and kissed our pinkie knuckles. And then I told her about the Starlight.

"Dancing all night and getting paid for it?" Angie

said. "What a lucky break! And it's a real orchestra, not a jukebox?"

"Ten-piece band," I said. "The trumpet player, he's just as good as anything you'd hear on the radio."

"And little colored lights . . . it must be so *romantic*." She laid her head back against the seat and sighed. "Are the fellows swell? Do they have a good line, or are they a bunch of drips? I bet they're drips," she went on, before I could answer, "because any fellow with a good line would already know how to dance. Right?"

A good line? No customer at the Starlight needed to think up a line to get a girl to dance with him. All he needed was a ticket. In fact, the only fellow with any line at all had been Art, and all his sweet talk was just so he could cheat me.

It's taxi dancing, Del had told me. *The customers rent you. Like a taxi. Get it?*

"No, the fellows are swell," I said. "Hardly any drips at all."

She sighed again. "I bet they fall in love with the instructresses all the time. Don't you think they would?" She gasped so loudly, I jumped. She sat up, a hand pressed to her mouth. "If that happens, you know what you should do? Write in to *True Confessions* magazine. They pay fifty dollars a story—you'd be *rich*."

I barely heard her—I'd had a lightning strike of my own. I grabbed her arm. "Why don't you come with me?"

Angie blinked. "What do you mean? You mean work there?"

"Sure! Why not?" Should I tell her now about how the Starlight wasn't really a dance academy? How I'd gotten a dollar for letting a dirty-minded man pinch my ass?

No. She'd find out quick enough. I had.

So instead, I said, "You should see the gowns, Angie. And the *shoes*!" Angie was a nut for shoes; if she could, she'd own a hundred pairs. "Ma bought the telephone operator story hook, line, and sinker. You can tell your folks the same thing. Come on, say you will! We can go to the Starlight right now, I'll introduce you to Del."

Her eyes had gone dreamy at the shoes. But as soon as I mentioned telephone operators, her face changed. Like she'd woken up. "I can't," she said. "You know I have to watch the brats, now that Ma's working every night in the tavern."

Dammit. I'd forgotten Angie's little sisters and brothers. Five of them, the youngest only six years old. "But Reena's thirteen," I pointed out. "She's plenty old enough to watch them."

"Maybe . . ." Angie shook her head. "No. I couldn't lie to my parents like that."

I gestured out the window. "You lie to them all the time. Since when has that ever stopped you?"

"Cutting class, so what? If they find out, sure they'll get mad, but . . ." She shrugged. "Something like that, though, that's . . . I don't know. *Big.* It would be like . . ." She bit the inside of her cheek, frowning. "Like suddenly you're a whole different person behind their backs. Like if I found out my *mother* worked there. You know?"

I turned away from her and looked out the window. Ashland Avenue jolted past: People's Bank, Goldblatt's Department Store, Olympia Theater. Next to me, Angie sighed. Exasperated this time. "Look, I don't mean *you*," she said. "It's different for you. What choice do you have, really?"

I turned back toward her. She looked me dead in the eyes. Straight up, no fooling. That was my Angie.

"Pinkie secret," I said.

She looked a little surprised, but she nodded. Kissed her knuckle again.

"I need you to get something for me," I said.

· · ·

"Not bad," Peggy said that evening in the Ladies'. "Not bad at all. You didn't get this out of that old stick Artie, did you?"

"No." I ran my hands down both hips, savoring the silky rayon crepe. "You were right about him." I waited for her to ask what happened, to say *I told you so*. To make me eat crow. But all she said was, "Good riddance to bad rubbish," and took her makeup bag to a dressing table. I was glad. I needed to get on Peggy's good side, and if she was nice, that made things easier for me.

So did Clara's gown. Creamy ivory, a sweetheart neckline. Not low cut, which was too bad. But the sparkles made up for it: silver bugle beads, laid on thick in a kind of collar, and below that, round ones scattered like stars over the bosom and down to the waist.

Angie had nabbed it from her sister's flat that afternoon. Piece of cake, she said. Slipped it off the hanger, bundled it under her coat, then suddenly remembered she'd promised to be home early. Clara hadn't suspected a thing. "I have to have it back next Friday," Angie had told me, when she'd smuggled the dress to me outside the Wachowskis' tavern. "Clara's husband is taking her to some fancy shindig next Saturday night."

I'd counted in my head: eight days. I ought to have

plenty of dough to buy my own gown by then—but still, it would be nice to keep this one for a while. "Why can't she wear one of her other dresses?"

"What other dresses? She hasn't got any other ones like this."

"Sure she does. Her husband bought her a dozen on their honeymoon, you told me so."

"I never told you any such thing! She's got this one and she's wearing it next Saturday. If she finds out it's missing, she'll holler bloody murder from here to Pough-keepsie and I'm the first person she's gonna suspect. So just get it back to me, all right? And be careful with it! If she finds so much as a fingerprint, she'll scream like a banshee."

"Yeah, okay, but . . ."

"Promise!"

Of course I'd promised. Angie was my best friend, and she'd come through for me like a dream. I'd never worn a dress where Ma didn't have to sew lace or an appliqué over somebody else's coffee stain, where the hems weren't ratty from years of taking up and letting down. I'd never worn anything so gorgeous.

I snagged the dressing table next to Peggy. Snuck peeks, copied what she did. Last night, I'd thought the girls looked clownish. But that was in the Ladies'. In the low light of the dance floor, I'd seen how their eyes seemed smoky, their lips full. Next to them, my face must have been pale, as babyish as the dotted swiss. So tonight, on the way here, I'd stopped at a drugstore and bought eyeshadow—two shades, I couldn't decide which was better—plus mascara, and a redder rouge. It had cost me most of what I'd earned the night before.

Well, Ma always said you had to give a little to get a little. And I hoped I'd get a lot.

I had my gown. Now I had to get my "wages." Every place I'd ever heard of, Saturdays were paydays. Ma would be expecting an envelope with eighteen dollars cash, and I had four nights to earn it. If that meant dancing with—well, with anyone, then that's what I'd do.

I leaned my elbow on Peggy's table. "Those fish you mentioned. I thought about it, and I've made up my mind. I'm in."

She glanced at me in the mirror. Her expression as uninterested as if I'd said it was raining outside. Cool as an icebox, she said, "Fish don't keep. Better luck next time." She zipped her makeup bag closed, stood up, and walked away. Leaving me leaning on her table like a fool, my girdle pinching my waist.

I grabbed my comb, yanked it hard through my hair. My cheeks burned red in the mirror, and not from the rouge. Who did she think she was? Who needed her anyway, with her fancy makeup bag and her garter purse and perfectly waved hair?

If only I'd been able to talk Angie into working here . . . Between the two of us, we'd rule this roost. We'd show them, Peggy and Yvonne and Gabby and all these other cats.

But I was on my own. I gathered my makeup and got up from the dressing table.

"Well, take a gander at the new baby!" It was Nora, the snub-nosed blonde who didn't want any Chinese in the Starlight. "I guess we can't call you Bo Peep anymore," she said.

"Guess not," I said. Going back to my locker, I passed

behind the tables where Yvonne and Gabby were putting on their faces. Yvonne glanced at me in her mirror, then away again, fast as butter off a hot knife, like she hadn't seen a thing. Which told me she had, all right. I smiled, satisfied.

What a difference a dress made! The gown floated like a cloud against my legs, its beads flickering and flashing. I danced almost every dance, and I was happy enough about it to let it show. So many of these girls looked like they were taking a turn around their own kitchen. Where was their pep, their spark? Sure, Angie's shoes pinched like clothespins over my toes, and there were more sappy tunes than snappy ones. But then the band punched up "Sing, Sing, Sing," Ozzie's trumpet screaming, and I felt like I could dance up to the sky and kick a hole right through it with my heels. I grinned up at Ozzie on the bandstand, and he gave me the tiniest nod, just before the band slogged into "Cheerful Little Earful." Ozzie grimaced, then raised the trumpet to his lips.

"Now, *this* is real music," the geezer I was dancing with said. He dragged me from one end of the hall to the other, and at the end of the number he dropped a penny into my palm. I was staring at it—a *penny*? What did he think I was, a piece of candy?—when he tried to pinch my cheek. I'd learned a little about being a sport, and I wasn't playing for any measly cent. So I ducked out of his reach and almost fell over Peggy, right next to me.

"There you are! I couldn't imagine where you'd gotten to," Peggy said, as though she'd been looking for me all night. She turned to two men standing behind her. "Boys, this is Ruby. I told you she's a doll. Did I lie?"

"Hell, no," one of the fellows said.

"Name's Tom," the other man said. He held out a ticket. "Care to go for a spin?"

They were about twenty-five or so. Tom was the taller one. I would have rather had Jack; he was short but better dressed, in a chesty-front herringbone suit with a nipped-in waist, like a real swing king. Tom wasn't even wearing a tie, just slacks and a blue and gray zip-front sweater. But he wasn't bad-looking, he wasn't fat, and he didn't smell of sweat or cigars or garlic. I'd danced with worse.

He held me tighter than he should, for a fox-trot. When he said, "Slow down, honey, these dances are short enough as it is," and pressed me close, I figured he was trying to get the most he could for his dime. I could put up with that all right; those fellows almost always tipped. The next dance was a waltz, and Tom slowed down even more until we ended up barely shuffling side to side.

"Sure feels nice to dance with a nice girl," he said.

"Mmm," I answered. Up close, the wool of his sweater smelled doggy. What was Peggy up to? Was this another fish, or had she dumped Tom on me to get Jack for herself?

The waltz ended. A quarter tip, not bad. Then, even better: "Care for a coffee?"

You bet I did. I hadn't rested my dogs all night.

In the lounge, his friend Jack was already in line for drinks. Tom joined him. I found Peggy at a table near the back, where the light from the dance hall was even dimmer.

"What's the scoop?" I said.

"Dinner, if we play our cards right," Peggy said. "Don't say anything. Here they come."

They were steelworkers from south Chicago. "Tom's

never been to a taxi-dance joint, if you can believe it," Jack said. "I thought maybe it was about time he met some nice gals, you know?"

Tom smiled, but uneasy, like it didn't come naturally. He had a long, serious face, his cheeks smooth and straight as walls.

"I bet you've been around the block a time or two," Jack said to Peggy.

"Me? No sir, I stick close to home. You two boys been pals long?"

We chatted maybe ten minutes. Then Peggy drained her coffee cup and set it down.

"Come on, Ruby," she said. "Time to hit it."

"Hey, don't break up the party," Jack said. He'd unbuttoned his swing-king jacket and stretched his legs under the table, one arm flung across the back of Peggy's chair. "We'll buy you another cuppa, how about that?"

Peggy stood up. "We're glad to take a break with you boys, but the management hired us to dance. How many numbers did the band play while we were here, Ruby? Five?"

So much for dinner. "Five, that's right," I said. Honestly, I thought it'd been only three, but I wasn't about to argue. The men tore off five tickets apiece and handed them to us. When Peggy put her foot up on her chair rung and lifted her hem to slip hers into her garter, I did, too.

"Well, this is kind of rough," Jack said. Peggy smiled at him and shrugged—*what can we do?* "Maybe you'll see us for a dance later," she said.

"Forget dancing," Tom said. "You gals want to grab a bite?"

I started to grin—*bingo!*—but at the doubtful look on

Peggy's face, I stifled it. "We're working girls," she said. "If we stay out late, we'll be dead on our feet tomorrow."

Tom turned to me. "My mother waits up," I said truthfully. "I have to be home by two thirty."

"Then that settles it," Jack said. "Come on, girls, get your stuff. We're clocking you out right now."

SIX

While Peggy and I went to the Ladies' to get ready, Tom and Jack headed to the ticket booth. It was almost one in the morning. For two dollars and eighty cents each, Tom and Jack could clock us out of the Starlight an hour early. It was a good deal for us, Peggy explained: we still got half the dough, which was as much money as we'd make if we'd danced every dance straight until closing. Except that we got to save our feet and get a free meal, besides. She gave me the credit for pushing the fellows into it.

" 'My mother expects me home by two thirty! ' " she said in a fake-innocent voice, batting her eyes. She laughed. "Did you see the look on Tom's face when he thought you were going to throw him over for your *mother*? Like somebody'd pulled a steak right out of his hands. Here, unzip me, will you?"

A girl in a peacock blue gown and no shoes looked up from one of the wicker chairs by the door. "Clocking out, huh? Anyplace good?"

"Anyplace free is good enough for me," Peggy said.

"Lucky stiffs," the girl said, and went back to rubbing her feet.

I unzipped down the length of Peggy's back. "I wasn't making it up. My mother really does wait up for me."

Peggy laughed and shucked out of her gown, careful not to step on the hem with her heels. "Oh, yeah? And what does your mother think you do?"

"Telephone operator." I kicked off my shoes. My big toes felt like somebody'd been stabbing them with knives.

"Alice—you know her, the girl with the ringlets?—her parents think she works swing shift at the box factory," Peggy said. "Telephone operator's good, too, though."

"What about you?"

"The landlady doesn't give a rip what I do, so long as I don't do it in her rooms and I pay up the first of every month."

"No, I mean your mo—"

"I know what you meant. You're not wearing that to go out, are you?"

I'd pulled on my coat over the ivory gown. "You bet I am. I'm not going out on the town in this patched-up old thing." I rolled up the lime green dress and stuffed it into my bag. A quick change in the hall toilet as soon as I got home, and nobody'd be the wiser.

"A chop suey joint is hardly going out on the town," Peggy said.

Easy for her to say. If I had a cute outfit like hers—a herrringbone tweed skirt and matching jacket—it'd be different. But I'd never been out to a restaurant in my life, and I wasn't about to go in ashes and pumpkins. Although at least Cinderella had shoes that fit, I thought, easing my feet back into Angie's heels.

"Now listen," Peggy said as we walked out of the Ladies'. "Those two guys are out for more than a gabfest over chow mein, and they think they'll get it. But they won't. Not if you follow my lead. Get me?"

"I didn't figure Tom was looking down my dress to see where he'd dropped his keys," I said.

"Good. You're not as dumb as you look. Come on, let's cash in our tickets and blow this joint. I'm starving."

My haul for the night was seven dollars and sixteen cents. Clara's gown was the real deal, all right. My luck was finally changing. I was sure of it now.

"Shake a leg, kiddo," Peggy said. I stuffed the money into my pocketbook and followed her down the stairs. The men already had a cab waiting. They hustled us into the backseat: Tom first, then me, then Peggy, then Jack. I hadn't been in an automobile in years, not since Pop died, when I was five. I'd forgotten how smooth they were, how fast. I sat forward the whole way, so I could look out the window, see the buildings streaming past.

The restaurant was tiny, just half a dozen tables. But it had red paper lampshades and smelled wonderful, of meat and oil and spices I'd never smelled before.

"What'll you have, Ruby?" Tom asked.

I squinted at the menu, but it was hard to read, and anyway I didn't recognize any of the words. "I guess . . . chop suey?"

Peggy set down her menu. "Ruby, do you even know what chop suey is?"

"No," I admitted.

The men thought this was hilarious. Jack lifted his beer glass. "Here's to chop suey. And to the prettiest girls in Chicago."

"Hear, hear," Tom said.

I'd had a sip of gin once, from a boy who'd snuck a flask into school. I'd never had beer before, but now I had a whole glass of my own. I tried not to think what Ma would say if she knew.

Jack and Peggy were yakking a mile a minute about some Chinese dish that sounded like baby talk: *goo-goo* or *guy-guy*. I waited for Tom to strike up a conversation, but he concentrated on scraping at a black mark on his thumb.

Finally, I asked, "What did you think of the Starlight?"

"Tell the truth, I can't see why Jack's so gung-ho for that place," Tom said. "Before we met with you two, I wasn't having much of a good time."

"Really? How come?"

He dug a little harder at his thumb. "I'd heard the girls at those places are supposed to be pretty. Some of them are, I mean, you and Peggy sure are." He nodded in my direction. "But some of them . . . They're hard look-ing. Like they're"—he cut a sideways look at me—"well, never mind. And some are plain homely. How'd they even get the job, I wonder?"

"Good thing you met us then, I guess. Here, let me see," I said, reaching for his hand. I dipped the corner of my napkin in my water glass; three good swipes, and the spot on his thumb was gone.

"Seems like no matter how much I wash, I always miss something," Tom said.

"My pop was the same way. Ma wouldn't let him come to the table unless I looked his hands over good first. He worked for the railroads, before he passed away."

"Sounds like good honest people," Tom said. "That's

the other beef I had with that place tonight. All those foreigners in there dancing with American women. How come that is?"

"All I know is, the first time a Chinaman tried to give me a ticket, I about died."

Peggy butted in. "I haven't seen you dancing with any Chinese men, Ruby."

"That's because I ran to the Ladies'!" I said. Tom and Jack busted a gut at that; Tom almost choked on his beer, he was laughing so hard.

"That's showing spunk! Good for you!" he kept saying.

This was just how I imagined it would be, out on the town: me, witty and smart, the whole table laughing at what I said. I gulped another mouthful of beer—why didn't the dance hall serve beer, anyway? It beat back the thirst a million times better than that kiddie orangeade—and said, "It does make it hard, though, all those Chinamen. I always have to look before I take someone's ticket."

"Now, Ruby, there's not *that* many," Peggy said.

"Listen to her!" I turned to Jack, laughing. "Just last night, she was sitting in the lounge with two flips!"

Jack and Tom both stared at her. Jack laughed along with me, but Tom didn't. Something pointy and hard dug into my ankle. "Ow!" I looked up from my beer to see Peggy glaring at me.

"I wasn't *sitting* with them," she said. "They came over and started talking to me. I left as soon as I politely could."

Under her glare, the beer fizzled out of my blood like a drop of water under a match. "That's right," I said. "I remember now. You walked out on those boys just as . . . just as cool as a cucumber." The pain in my ankle eased. I reached down and rubbed the sore spot.

The food arrived. Tom loaded my plate with noodles, some kind of meat in a red sauce, vegetables in a brown sauce.

"Now look, you've got to promise me," Tom said. "I don't care what your boss says you have to do, I don't want you dancing with any flips or Chinese or any of that kind. Will you do that?"

Who did he think he was, telling me who to dance with? I opened my mouth to tell him so, but Peggy's shoe dug into my ankle again.

"You fellows forget," Peggy said. She reached for the ashtray. Her sleeve turned a dull red under the lamp. "This is our living. Sure, we try to stay white. But if the boss gets complaints, we lose our jobs. And then what?"

"That's a shame," Tom said. "That's a damn shame."

"Well, look, we're here now, aren't we?" Peggy raised her beer glass. "Here's to a couple of swell fellows!"

"Hear, hear!" I said. I grabbed for my glass and drained the last of my beer. But when I went to put down the glass, nothing seemed to be where I'd left it. The bottom of my glass cracked hard against china and I caught a glimpse of my plate flipping up toward me like a jack-in-the-box, and then Chinese food and plate and all were tumbling into my lap.

I shrieked and jumped to my feet. Red sauce, brown sauce, bits of food rolled down the front of my gown. Clara's gown. The one I'd promised not to get so much as a fingerprint on.

"Hold still, hold still," Tom said. He started swiping at me with his napkin, but even tipsy as I was, I knew I hadn't spilled food on my tits. I slapped his hand and stepped back. Then the floor seemed to upend itself, and I staggered. Tom grabbed my arm, and this time I didn't push him away.

"What am I going to do?" I said. "What am I going to do?"

"Cleaner's, looks like," Jack said around the two cigarettes he had stuck in his mouth. He lit both, gave one to Peggy. She drew a lungful, blew it out.

"Cleaner's, hell," she said. "They'll never get out that sweet-and-sour pork." She set the cigarette in the ashtray and pushed her chair back. "Come on, Ruby," she said. "Let's get some water on those stains before they set." I hardly heard her. She had to grab my hand and yank to get me moving.

Once we were in the ladies' room, though, she was no help at all. There were no clean towels left, so I dug a handkerchief out of my purse and blotted up every blottable gob of food. From the mirror, where she was freshening her lipstick, Peggy said, "I wouldn't work those stains too hard, if I were you."

"But I've got to get this out. It's got to come clean!"

"Yeah, well, what I meant was, don't make it look too much better. Not yet." She turned away from the mirror and looked me up and down. "Oh, much worse. Good."

"You don't understand. This isn't my dress!"

"So what? Like Jack said, take it to the cleaner's."

"You said the pork wouldn't come out!"

"You ninny, of course I said that in front of *them*. That Tom's a fish and no mistake, and baby, you've about got him hooked. And here you are bawling about some dress. You wouldn't have dropped noodles on it if Tom hadn't brought you here, right?"

I must have looked as stupid as I felt, because she

sighed and closed her eyes for a moment, exactly the way my math teacher used to in school, when she prayed for patience.

"Look," she said, "I know a cleaner who'll do that dress for a dollar and two bits, and get all the stains out, too. Well . . ."—she narrowed her eyes at the smear on my hip—". . . almost all. But you make Tom give you three. Men never know how much those things cost."

I looked back down at the ruin of the gown. . . . *If Tom hadn't brought you here, then . . .*

"Oh," I said. *"Oh."*

"Glory hallelujah, baby sees the light." Peggy snapped her pocketbook closed. "Word of advice, though? Don't wear a working gown out on dates. You ruin a four-fifty skirt, big deal. Ruin a gown, that's half a week's wages."

"You could have said something before!"

"Me? Not on your life. You're not the type to take advice, and I'm not the type to waste my breath. We're a perfect pair." She handed me her lipstick. "Come on, put on your pretty face. We've kept those boys waiting long enough."

We decided she should walk out first, me behind. The gown would make a better effect that way. The men stood up when they saw us coming. Tom blinked at the dress. "It'll come out okay, won't it?" he said.

"I was just telling her," Peggy said, "the cleaner's—"

"It's ruined, all right," I said. I dropped my gaze to the gray wool of Tom's sweater. I managed a little laugh, then looked back up at his face. "But really, I don't mind. I wouldn't have missed stepping out with you for the world. It's just a gown, right?"

Now, Peggy, I thought, you follow *my* lead.

"Oh, come on, now. What they can do these days, why, it's practically a miracle," Jack said. He held Peggy's coat for her; she slipped one tweed arm in, then the other. "I'll bet any amount of money a top-notch dry-cleaning man will have that dress good as new."

"I'll take that bet," Peggy said. "I never met a cleaner yet could get a nasty food stain out of silk." Playing along for all she was worth. Gotta hand it to her, she could roll with it.

"That's silk?" Jack said. Thank God, just then the waiter brought the check. He made a move for his wallet, but Tom beat him to it. I almost cried for real when he laid a five-spot on the table. What would it be like, to pay for something and not feel like you were handing over your own sweat and blood? Five dollars more or less must not make an ounce of difference to Tom. It wasn't a treasure, to him.

He lifted my coat off the back of my chair and held it for me. He wasn't even going to offer to pay for the cleaner's. Well, why should he? A baby, that's what he probably thought I was. Spilling food all over myself. A dumb squirt.

An hour ago, my biggest worry had been earning enough dough to buy my own dress and stuff a pay envelope for Ma. Now I had nothing. Again. Worse, if this gown didn't come clean . . . no. I couldn't even think about facing Angie.

At the front door of the restaurant, Jack said, "We'll flag a cab. You girls wait here."

Next to me, I felt Tom hesitate. Just a little, but—

I didn't stop to think what I was doing. I laid my hand on his arm. "Tom, wait." I glanced right and left. Saw a statue of a bald fat man on a shelf, pointed at it. "Look at that! Isn't it something?" Behind me, Peggy said, "Good Lord, there she goes . . . I never saw a girl so nutty about bric-a-brac. Come on, Jack, let's get that cab, or we'll be here half the night." The door tinkled open, then shut. Tom and I were alone.

Go on. Ask him for the dough.

Through the plate-glass window, out of the corner of my eye, I saw a cab already pulling up to the curb. How long would Peggy and Jack wait for us? A minute? Two?

Ask him!

"Tom," I blurted, at the same time he said, "Ruby . . ." He laid a hand on my shoulder. He had big hands. His fingers could wrap all the way around my arm.

"I feel awful," he said. "This was supposed to be a good time, and here you are, miserable."

"It's not your fault I'm so clumsy," I said. "Besides, it's just a . . ."

"Just a dress, yeah, I know." He edged closer. "And I'll bet it's the only one you have. It is, isn't it?"

My heart hit the gas. Suddenly I was aware of everything: the pressure of his fingers, the stirring of his breath in my hair, the anxiety in his voice. I wondered what he had to be anxious about, this man who could throw five dollars away on a single dinner. *I'd* scraped my mother's knuckle bloody so we could pawn her ring and not get thrown into the street.

The statue blurred and trembled. I groped for my handkerchief.

"Don't cry," Tom said. "Ruby, don't. If . . . if I . . ." He took his hand away. I thought he was getting his own handkerchief. But the hand came back, and it was holding a wallet.

It was as if Tom disappeared. All I saw was brown leather, scratched and scarred, held together at one corner by a bit of tape. Hands opened the leather. In that moment—I knew it was blasphemy, sorry, Ma—they seemed like the hands of God.

"If I loan it to you . . . ," I heard him say.

"I'll pay you back. I promise. I will." I slashed across my chest with my finger. *Cross my heart, hope to die.*

Fingers reached into the wallet. Pulled out a bill and folded it neatly into thirds, and then the fingers tucked the bill into my palm. It shouldn't have felt right to take money from a strange man. It should have felt wrong. Terrible.

I stared at the *10* in the corner of the bill. I'd never held ten dollars all at once in my life.

It felt wonderful.

"Is it enough?" Tom said. "I mean, to buy something as nice as . . ." He gestured at the dress.

Men never know how much those things cost. "This? Oh, well, *this* was twenty . . . But I have a little money of my own, and besides, I don't need anything nearly so pretty to dance in." I gave a little laugh. "You don't like the Starlight, anyway. I won't be dressing up for you."

Outside, the cabbie honked. The wallet still lay open in Tom's hands. He pulled out another bill. "Here."

"No, I . . ."

"Please, Ruby. It'll make me happy." He waggled the money. "Please?"

I took it. "Thank you." My voice cracked against a

sudden ache in my throat. "You have no idea what . . . I'll pay you back. I promise."

"I know you will," Tom said.

In the cab, Jack tried to get us to go with them to a party at his friend's house ("Be our dates for an hour, come on!") but Peggy was firm. Supper was fine, but we were working stiffs and we had to be up early. I let her do all the talking. I clutched my pocketbook to my side, as if the twenty dollars might escape. I hardly even noticed when Tom put his arm around me.

"You sure are nice," he murmured. "Such a sweet little thing." He nuzzled my ear, and I moved away. It tickled.

His arm tightened around my shoulders. "Well, that's a little hard, considering . . ."

He'd been nice to me. I supposed I ought to be nice to him. Besides, if I wasn't, maybe he'd demand his money back right now. That thought made me nervous enough that when he nuzzled my ear again, I let him, and when he turned my face toward his and kissed me, I let him do that, too. His kiss didn't make me thrill, not like Paulie's. Well, that only proved there was no harm in it.

My stomach had another opinion, though. Between my keyed-up nerves, and the chop suey, and the beer—inside me and on Tom's breath—I felt a little sick. When the kiss was over, I ducked my head and snuggled into his shoulder, hoping he wouldn't take it into his head to do it again. I wouldn't answer for my stomach, if he did. But he only kissed the top of my head.

"Remember what you promised about those flips," he said. "I'll watch you, I'll hold you to it."

"Sure." I hardly paid attention to what we were saying. With the four of us crammed close, the cab was too warm, and Tom's sweater smelled doggier than ever. I was relieved when we got back to the Starlight. Stepping out onto the sidewalk, I took a long, clean breath of cold air, to clear my head.

"That cheapskate Jack," Peggy said after the men dropped us off and pulled away in the cab again. "His friend pays for dinner, you'd think he could spring for cab fare to get us home. Well, how'd it go with you? Did you get the money?" I nodded. "I knew he was a sap," she said, and then, "Where are you going?"

"My streetcar's this way."

"Uh-uh. It's your big night out, remember?" Another cab was passing; Peggy flagged it down. I got in after her and kicked my shoes off and closed my eyes. She was right. I felt like I was flying on a magic carpet, winging my way home.

"So how much does a gown like yours cost?" I asked. "With sequins and things?"

"Sequins?" Peggy sounded puzzled. "You were just supposed to get a couple of bucks for dry cleaning. How much did you end up soaking him for?"

I smiled and snuggled deeper into the seat.

"You mean to tell me"—her voice disbelieving—"he gave you enough for a new *gown*? Just like that?"

"Well, not *gave*. Not exactly. More like a loan."

"More like? You mean exactly like, don't you?" At the sharpness in her tone, I opened my eyes. Light from the passing streetlamps flickered across her face: glimpses of finger-waved hair and one dark, serious eye.

"I don't know. He just said . . ." What *had* Tom said? "Well, what difference does it make? I got the money, didn't I?"

Peggy blew her breath out. "You little ninny . . . Look, this isn't borrowing a dime from your girlfriend for the movies. No man gives a girl money without expecting something back. If it's a gift, you can pretend there's no strings. If he says otherwise, then you act insulted, or like you don't know what he's talking about. But if it's a loan, God help you. Because then he'll make sure you pay. One way or another."

I straightened up in my seat just as the cab rounded a corner. Waves seemed to crash against the inside of my skull, and I fell back against the door. I was so tired . . . All I could remember was the wallet's cracked leather, the bill sliding free. I'd promised something. Hadn't I? And the money had slipped into my hand.

The cab pulled up to a curb in front of a narrow brick building. By the light over the front door, I read its sign: GREELEY ARMS HOTEL FOR WOMEN. "My stop," Peggy said. Getting out, she told the cabbie, "My friend'll pay the fare."

"Hey!" I yelled after her.

She stuck her head back in the door. "I got you that fish. You may have reeled him in, but I snagged him. And now you're rolling in dough. Aren't you?"

Back in the restaurant, my finger skimming across my chest. *Cross my heart, hope to die.* I'd promised, all right.

"Fine," I said. "We're even. And I'm no fool, you know. I'll pay Tom back."

Peggy straightened up. "If I were you," she said, her voice drifting down into the cab, "I wouldn't wait too long."

SEVEN

The next morning, I woke to a noise. Not wind. Not the trains delivering cattle and pigs to the stockyard, or the shift change whistles from the packinghouses, or the bells of Sacred Heart church. Not Betty snoring.

I blinked. My eyes stung, as if my lids were lined with sandpaper. Barely light outside. Must be before six. Not even three hours' sleep . . . the inside of my mouth tasted as doggy as Tom's sweater smelled. Maybe I'd dreamed it . . .

Then, from the window, a sharp double tap. I sat up and immediately sagged back on one elbow. Laid a hand over my eyes. It didn't help the throbbing.

Another tap, loud enough this time to rattle the glass. Next to me, Betty stirred and muttered. I reached for my housecoat and shrugged it on, then crossed the two steps to the window and parted the curtain.

Our flat was separated from the one next door by a narrow alley. No streetlight reached between the buildings—or much sun, either, during the day—and it was almost as dark as inside.

"Ruby!" Faint, through the glass.

I unsnapped the latch and raised the window. Freezing air gusted over my arms. Cigarette smoke and garbage reek came with it. The wood frame squeaked and caught, the glass shuddering so hard I thought it might break—it already had a crack halfway down its length, from a thrown rock years ago.

"Ruby!"

I pulled the curtain around behind me, then slid the window open just enough to let my head and shoulders through. We were on the first floor, but the windows were high off the ground. In the dim quarter-light, I could just make out Paulie's face, a few feet below mine. My heart skidded into a fast jazz beat.

"Morning," he said.

"What are you doing here?" I whispered.

"You still working in that packinghouse . . . office?" Grinning, the rat. Reminding me that I'd lied. Despite the pain in my head, I couldn't help grinning back.

"I'm at the Starlight now. Not that it's any of your business." I tucked my housecoat higher around my neck and glanced at the Schenkers' window across the way. Mrs. Schenker might be deaf, but her husband wasn't.

"Told you before," Paulie said. "I can make it my business." His cigarette end flared bright orange. Suck and puff of a draw, then a fresh waft of smoke drifting through the window. "You like it over there?"

Bedsprings squeaked behind me. "Ruby, are you nuts?" Betty said. "Shut the window!"

I settled my arms on the windowsill, not caring about the cold. "I like it fine, thank you. Why, just last night a *very* nice man took me out to dinner." I remembered sweet-and-sour pork tumbling over Clara's gown and shoved the image away. I didn't want to think about that. Not yet.

"A nice man, huh? What about me? Am I nice?"

"You know good and well you're not. You know how much trouble you got me in last time? If my mother catches me talking to you . . ."

The cigarette tumbled to the ground. Grinding of a shoe on dirt. "Gee, I'd hate for you to get in trouble," he said. "Guess I'll take back what I brought you, too." He turned away, a blur of ash in the dark.

Baby. Squirt. I shoved myself farther out the window. "No, wait!" I whispered. My voice sounded strangled. "Paulie!"

From farther up the alley, I heard him laugh. "Tell you what," he said. Loud, as if he was talking across a room. "It's in your back lot. You find it, you can keep it."

"Shhh!" I hissed. I shoved myself back inside just as Mr. Schenker's face appeared across the way. I grabbed the sash but before I could yank it closed, Betty ducked under my arms and stuck her head out the window.

"Who are you talking to?" she said. "Oh. Mr. Schenker."

"Ruby!" Paulie called. "You like it, go to Reinhard's. On Madison. Tell 'em I sent you."

Betty gasped and hoisted herself half out of the window. "Who is that?" she said. Paulie's laugh bounced between the walls. "Who's there? Is that—"

"Get back in here!" I grabbed the collar of her nightgown and hauled her inside, then slammed the window shut. I caught a glimpse of Mr. Schenker leaning out his own window, peering up the alley, his gray hair sticking up in back like a patch of weeds.

Betty tried to dodge past me. "Was that Paulie Suelze?" she said. "It was, wasn't it? What did he say?"

I spun her around and shoved her toward the bed. "No it wasn't. Go back to sleep!" I yanked my shawl on over my housecoat, kicked on my slippers, and hurried out of the room.

Ma was up already, stoking the stove. The kitchen light stabbed like a ten-penny nail to the back of my eyes. I closed them to slits and stumbled to the back door.

"Where are you going?" Ma asked.

"The privy," I called over my shoulder. "The toilet's clogged."

"But I was just there, it was fine," she said as I stepped onto the back porch. I shut the door behind me and hurried down the stoop, gripping the handrail so as not to slip on the ice. I ran through the back lot to the alley behind, and peered up the gangway between our building and the Schenkers'. Betty hung out the window, looking away from me toward the street. Nothing in the gangway but scraps of wood, bashed-up tin cans, bits of old newspapers scurrying in the wind. The Schenkers' window was closed. Paulie was gone.

He'd brought me something. *You find it, you can keep it.* Darned right I'd find it, and right now, too. Betty might've heard more than she let on. I dodged around our ash heap and began searching the back lot.

Nothing along the fence. Surely Paulie wouldn't hide something in the privy. Under the back stoop? Shivering, I started toward it. Then stopped opposite the coal bins.

Four in a row, one for each flat in our building. Three bins locked. Our lock hanging open.

I lifted the lid. Our bin was almost empty; Ma had been putting off calling the coal man for weeks. The morning light was brighter now, dull gray instead of dull almost-black. Enough to see a paper sack lying on the dregs of coal.

I almost upended myself, reaching in to grab it. Whatever was inside was soft. Light. I opened the sack and peeked inside, and for a stretch of heartbeats, I forgot about the cold.

Too dark to tell the color for sure. Too dark to tell if it was real silk. I didn't dare touch it, for the coal dust on my hands.

I rolled the sack and laid it back down. Closed the bin, locked it, and ran inside.

The two hours until Betty left for school seemed to stretch like days. "What did he *say?*" she whispered, the moment Ma left us alone in the kitchen.

"Nothing. Hello, that's all."

"Why would he wake everybody up just to say hello?"

"Will you *hush?*" I said, just as Ma came back into the room.

"You look worn out," Ma said to me. "No wonder, as little sleep as you got. You should take a nap this afternoon."

"Yes, Ma." I knew why I looked terrible. My head ached something fierce. I must have drunk more beer than I'd thought. I'd have to be careful. Buy a bottle of mouthwash, stash it someplace in the hall toilet. Ma hadn't noticed anything last night, thank God. But if she caught me coming home with alcohol on my breath, there'd be hell to pay.

As soon as Betty left, I nabbed Ma's biggest whale of a purse, whipped Clara's stained gown out of the bottom drawer of our dresser where I'd hidden it, and stuffed it inside. I slung the purse over my arm, yelled, "I'll go run your errands, Ma, bye!" then slipped out the back door and was running for the coal bin before she remembered she didn't have any errands today.

I opened up the bag as soon as I was out of sight of our flat. Dark, smoky blue. Silk for sure. I longed to pull it out, but across the street Mrs. Dudek was sweeping her front stoop, talking to Mrs. Pavlak. I waved to them and headed for school. I could find Angie easy enough. Signal her through a window, meet up at the east gate. Her mother would be home, but we could go to a movie theater, the ladies' room, where I could try it on, whatever it was, and Angie could tell me what Paulie meant by it. Just yesterday, I'd told Angie about Paulie kissing me. She'd gotten jealous—inspecting her nails, like she wasn't listening—but then I told her the rest, about him calling me *squirt*, and she got good and mad at him. Just like a best friend should. And now this! Angie read romance magazines by the truckload—if anyone could figure out a man, she could.

But she'd be sure to ask about her sister's gown, and what would I say? I slowed my steps. Worse, what if she caught sight of it in Ma's purse? I imagined her shrieking and crying, and my stomach clenched. I'd have to explain about the date with Tom and Jack. I'd have to tell her about the twenty dollars. I remembered how

I'd let Tom kiss me, in the cab, and I felt my face go hot. She would think I was a bad person. Maybe she already did. *I couldn't lie to my parents . . . it's different for you.*

But I didn't have a choice. She'd said so herself.

I turned away from the school. I'd take Clara's gown to the cleaner's first. Once it was fixed, and I'd given it back, then I'd tell Angie everything. It would just have to wait a little while, that was all.

Half a block away was Hirsch's candy store. Nobody on our block had their own phone; we all used the candy store's. If a call came in for you, the Hirsches either yelled for you—if you were in earshot—or sent a willing kid to your flat with the message, or told you about it the next time you came by.

I plunked the nickel into the coin slot and dialed zero. "Greeley Arms Hotel for Women," I told the operator. My voice low, so Mrs. Hirsch couldn't hear.

Ringing on the other end. "Greeley Arms Hotel," a woman answered.

"Peggy deGroot, please," I said.

. . .

Peggy's room at the hotel was tiny, just big enough for a bed, a chair, and a cramped narrow armoire. But the chair was upholstered in a red flower print, a thick blue rug cushioned the floor, and the tall window let in bright winter light. At first, I barely noticed any of these things. I was too busy staring at myself in the mirror.

The silk fell like water over my skin to the floor. The bodice was sleeveless, lower cut than Clara's gown. The shoulder straps were wide set, covered with sequins the exact same dark, smoky blue as the silk. The same color as my eyes.

"It's perfect," I breathed.

Peggy pinched the fabric over either side of my ribs. "Needs to be taken in a little. You're not *that* big in the bust." She let go and stepped back. Slipped a cigarette case off the top of the armoire, flipped it open, and offered me one. I shook my head. She lit one for herself, then walked around me, studying me up and down.

"So who gave it to you?" she asked. "Not that steelworker Tom, or I'll eat my radio."

I shook my head. Still staring at myself. Clara's gown was beautiful—but for the first time, I realized there was beautiful, and then there was beautiful on *me*. I looked like someone out of Angie's romance magazines. An heiress. A movie star. I looked like someone who'd never heard of the Back of the Yards. "He's just a fellow I know," I said.

Peggy laughed, a short dry *ha*, and leaned to tap her cigarette into an ashtray. "If I knew a fellow with that kind of taste in stolen dresses, I'd latch on to him so hard he'd think he picked up a leech. Does he have a brother?"

I blinked at her in the mirror. "What do you mean, *stolen*?"

"Didn't you notice?" She gestured at the back of the dress. "The label's cut out."

"You mean Pau . . . this fellow . . . he pinched this right out of a store?"

Peggy grinned so that her crooked tooth showed. She laughed a lot, but she didn't smile much, I'd noticed. "If he has the brains of a monkey, maybe. No, this got boosted from a warehouse somewhere. Or a delivery truck. They swipe a dozen or two, cut out the labels so nobody can tell where they came from. Then sell them to a fence. That's where your fellow got it, probably, from the fence."

"Reinhard's," I said. "On Madison."

"How'd you know—" Peggy laughed again, shaking her head. "I can't decide if you're the luckiest babe in woods I've ever met, or just savvy and putting on an act." She crushed her cigarette. "Here, get out of that thing. There's a girl on the third floor who'll take in the bust. Unless you do your own sewing."

"And try to explain to my mother where I got this from? No, thank you." She unzipped me. Reluctantly, I lifted the straps off my shoulders. A stolen dress. I should've been mad. Or afraid, or insulted. Instead, a thrill stirred, shivery-cold, under my ribs. I looked at the long, shimmering fall of silk. The way the color made my eyes seem deeper, darker blue. Just the way Paulie'd known it would. I was sure of it.

. . .

I brought the dress to the girl on the third floor. I gave her a dollar to do the alterations and another fifty cents to finish by six o'clock that night. Peggy'd promised to bring the gown to the Starlight with her.

At the dry cleaner's, the man behind the counter *tsk*'d when he unrolled Clara's gown. I tried to make him guarantee he could get the stains out, but he only shook his head and said he'd try. Well, I'd have to keep my fingers crossed, that was all.

The streetcar jolted and clanged. I sat with Ma's purse

on my lap, almost flat now that the gown was gone, and I chewed my lip, thinking.

If only Paulie had given me the dress yesterday, instead of today, things would be so much simpler. I'd never have borrowed Clara's gown. I wouldn't have spilled Chinese food on it, and I wouldn't have had to take money from Tom to buy a new dress.

But now . . . I had the money. *And* the dress.

Peggy would tell me to give Tom his money back. *If I were you, I wouldn't wait too long.* But how could I? He'd given it to me because the only dress I had was ruined. If I handed him his twenty dollars, while wearing Paulie's gown, he'd think I was a liar.

Of course, I could buy another dress. I was dancing six nights a week, after all, eventually I'd have to have more than one. The other girls each had four or five at least.

Then again . . . I reached inside Ma's purse and pulled out the pawn ticket for her wedding ring. The shop's address was all the way over in Canaryville, the Irish neighborhood east of the Yards. Ma hadn't wanted anybody to find out. That was why she hid her left hand anytime she went out of our flat, so no one would notice her bare finger.

What I must've looked like, lifting Paulie's gown out of the paper sack—that's what Ma would look like, if I pulled her ring out of my pocket. Gasping, covering her mouth with her hand. Touching it like maybe it wasn't real. Only it was. It would be.

At the next stop, I changed streetcars.

Last year, in English class, we'd read a story where a fellow was so happy he felt like he was walking on air. I'd thought that was the silliest thing I'd ever heard. Ground was ground, and how anyone could mistake it for air or clouds or what-have-you was beyond me.

But when I stepped out of the pawnshop with Ma's ring in my hand, I knew just how that fellow felt. Like I could walk taller than anyone, dance faster, shout louder. Like there wasn't anything I couldn't do.

Best of all, I had plenty of money left. And I knew exactly what to do with it.

In Ma's purse, too, were the store books that showed how much we owed at the shops in our neighborhood. I stopped at Graboski's first. When I asked Mr. Graboski for a box of Rice Krispies and one of Kix, his lips tightened. Fancy cereals were for people who paid their bills, not charity cases who owed six months' credit. I laid the tattered little book next to the boxes. Cash on top. "Ma asked if you could clear the book, too," I said.

"Well, now," he said. His face like I'd parted the clouds. "Telephone work must pay pretty good, huh, Ruby?"

"Pretty good," I said. I grinned, and he grinned back. He counted my money, wrote *0* in the balance column of the book, and handed it to me. Then he reached onto a shelf behind him. Took down a can of peaches, added it to the sack.

"Free of charge," he said. "Give my best to your mother."

At Burkot's, I bought coffee and canned milk and three Hershey's bars. Mrs. Burkot didn't give me a gift for clearing the book. But she did smile, the old sourpuss. *"Gratuluje,"* she said, when I told her about my new job. "Enjoy it in the best of health. My regards to your mother, how is she?"

Better, I thought with a sudden, fierce satisfaction, *now that you won't give her the evil eye every time she walks past.*

At Stawarz's, the butcher, I eyed the roasts but settled for a pound of ground chuck. I took the wrapped package, tied in string, and the butcher book, with its brand-new *0* in thick blue pencil. I stepped out onto the sidewalk, parcels in both arms, singing "Beat Me Daddy, Eight to the Bar." Not caring if people stared.

I was almost home when the noon whistles blew at the packinghouses. A few women chatting on their stoops stood up and went inside. Ma did that—timed her baking by the whistle. In the plants, everybody would be stopping work and heading for the lunch rooms. Hustle and wolf down your food, hustle back. My hands just starting to warm up, when it was time to plunge them into the brine again.

All that work and nastiness, and I'd never accomplished anything like what I'd done in the past two hours. Tomorrow I'd go to Goldblatt's, the department store on Ashland Avenue, and buy Ma some wool gloves. I'd have enough for that. Then a coal delivery for the winter, that was next. Although, if I had my way, I'd toss that old junkheap of a coal stove out the back door and buy us a modern gas one, like my cousins in Wicker Park had. Like everyone had, except us. We might as well wear long skirts and bustles and put our hair up in buns. In fact, if it was up to me, we wouldn't live in that dark cramped flat at all. How would it be, to live in a pretty little place with tall windows that let in the light?

Why not?

The thought was so startling, I stopped dead in the

middle of the sidewalk. "Watch out, Ruby, I almost ran the baby carriage right into you," said a woman behind me.

"Sorry, Mrs. Nowak," I said. I stepped aside and let her go by. Away beyond, smoke plumes from the packing-houses trailed up into the sky. Hardly any wind today. The plumes spread under the clouds like mold.

If I made fifty dollars a week, and gave eighteen to Ma as my "wages" . . . and then of course I'd have to buy at least one more dress, and a pair of heels that fit me, but it wasn't as if I'd be buying gowns every week and if I saved what was left . . .

I could do what Ma never could. I could get us out of the Yards.

I stared at the smokestacks. But I wasn't seeing them anymore. I was seeing a clean, pretty neighborhood. With trees. No more everlasting soot, from the packinghouse smokestacks outside and from the stove inside. Lamps with soft, pretty shades instead of bare bulbs. Our own bathroom, tile and chrome, and a porcelain tub. We'd be happy, the way we used to be before Ma lost her job. Happier, even, because we'd have enough money to buy whatever we wanted.

The pictures in my head were too big for walking. I ran the rest of the way home, the groceries jouncing in their sacks. Flew up the front stoop, up the hall, through our door.

"Surprise, Ma!" I yelled.

She came out of her bedroom, a dustrag in her hands. "Ruby, where have you . . ." She frowned at the parcels. "What did you buy?" she said, her voice sharp.

"Gifts," I said. I bustled into the kitchen, set down the sacks on the kitchen table, shrugged out of my coat. "Come see."

She did. And she threw a fit.

"Meat!" she cried. And then, in an even more scandalized voice, "Peaches!"

My victorious mood began to flatten. I hadn't expected this. Suddenly, it seemed I should have. "Ma, it's fine. Really. Don't worry." The ring lay tucked in my fist.

"Worry? Why on earth should I worry?" She stood with her back to me, poking in one of the sacks. She threw her hands in the air. "Fifteen cents for Hershey's bars! Jesus, Mary, and Joseph, Ruby, what possessed you? When we owe so much already I'm embarrassed to walk past their stores! What must they be thinking?"

"Mr. Graboski sends his regards." I held out my hand. The ring a dull gleam in my palm. "Mrs. Burkot asked after you, too. Ma, look."

She didn't turn around. "I bet she did. Rice Krispies? What in the world . . ."

"Betty hates oatmeal. Ma, please, will you just look?"

"God only knows how much we owe now. Where are the books? Ruby, get my pur—"

I walked around to the end of the table. Stuck my hand in front of her face.

She didn't gasp. Her mouth didn't fall open. The only part of her that moved was her eyes, blinking. Twice, three times. Then she swung her hips sideways and sat down, falling so heavily the chair scraped an inch or so across the floor. For a second I thought maybe I'd killed her.

"Get the grocery books," she said. Her voice as grim and tight as her face. She made no move to take the ring.

What's wrong with you? I wanted to shout. *You're supposed to be happy!* "Ma, what . . ."

"Get the books!"

I slammed the ring down on the table. Reached in her purse and grabbed the books. One by one she studied them and laid them aside.

"Where did you get the money for all this?" she said.

Of course she would wonder. Of course she would ask. Why hadn't I thought she would? Why would I suppose she'd just accept what I gave her, without having to know everything?

"Working," I said.

"Working." As if I'd said *flying*. She pointed to the books. "Do you think I can't add? You've only been at the telephone company three days. How much did it cost to redeem the ring?"

"Eight-fifty," I said.

"It was more than that, there would've been interest. Where's the receipt?"

The receipt was in my coat pocket, where I'd stuffed it, after the clerk had added, *Crystal butterfly hairpin . . . 75 cents.* The hairpin was blue. I'd thought it would look nice with the gown.

"I don't have it. I . . . I lost it." And then the answer came to me, and before I knew it, the lie was in the air. "I got an advance," I said.

That surprised her. "An advance? On your pay?" she said. "After only three days?"

I licked my lips. Thinking fast. Ma'd gotten an advance once, years ago. I cast back, trying to remember. "I guess I'm doing pretty good. Better than I thought. Anyway, I asked, and they said okay."

"You should've checked with me first," Ma said. She looked at the books, the ring. "This is a week's wages. What are we supposed to do next week? What are we supposed to give the landlord for the back rent? Did you think about that?"

The back rent. I'd forgotten. I sat down and tried to call back all the pretty pictures, the glory I'd felt right up until I'd walked through the door. Why couldn't things just be simple? What was so hard about saying, *Thank you, Ruby, you're a wonderful daughter?*

"I thought this was a good thing," I said. "I thought it would make you happy."

"Oh, Ruby, don't you see . . . ?" Ma sighed and rubbed the side of her face with her hand. "We can't think about happiness, the situation we're in. We have to be practical."

She was wrong. Maybe she'd forgotten. Maybe she never knew. There was more out there than just scraping by. I'd touched it.

"You're telling the truth. About where you got the money." She didn't ask it like a question. I lifted my eyes and met hers. Pale blue and afraid. What was she afraid of?

"I told you," I said. The lie smooth as a cab ride now. "They gave me an advance."

She nodded. Her mouth relaxed, the lines around her eyes eased. "After last week," she said, "with you and that Suelze thug, I thought maybe . . ."

"He doesn't have anything to do with it," I said. Too quickly, maybe. Ma gave me a sharp look.

"Have you seen him since then?" she asked.

I dropped my eyes. "No."

She didn't say anything and for a minute I thought she didn't believe me. If she took it into her head to ask Betty . . .

Ma leaned forward and picked up the ring. Brought it to her lips and kissed it. Then she smiled at me.

"Better get the oleo," she said.

EIGHT

"Customers always rush the new girls," Yvonne said. Loud, so the entire Ladies' could hear her. "They'd line up for a mule, so long as they hadn't seen it before. It doesn't mean a thing."

It was the first break of the evening, almost a week after Paulie had given me the blue gown. I sat in front of my locker, emptying tips out of my new satin garter purse. Yvonne perched on one of the dressing tables—not hers, of course—her back against the mirror and her ankles crossed on the back of a chair. She wore her hair down tonight, coiling loose and dark over her shoulders, a beaded barrette at each temple.

"I give her a month before the chumps catch on," Gabby said. She sprawled in the next chair, looking like a dropped egg in her gold and white gown. Next to her, the redhead, Stella, spritzed her pompadour with hairspray.

"A month, my eye." Yvonne took a last drag off her cigarette, hollowing out her cheeks. Grinding the stub into an ashtray, she said, "As soon as the men get a good whiff of her, she'll be cooling her heels in the meatpen with Fat Alice over there." The meatpen was what the girls called the folding chairs on the side of the dance floor. Alice always spent half the night sitting there.

"Hey, Alice!" Stella called. "Be sure and save Cinderella a seat. She's about to turn into a pumpkin, just like you." Chuckles from around the room. From my locker, I saw Alice duck her head, so that her sausage curls hid her face.

"And then it's back to the ash heaps for Cinderella," Yvonne said. "What *do* you do, darling, that gives you such a lovely stench?"

She asked me that at least once a night, always at the top of her voice, always when the Ladies' was packed. Yvonne was like my sister, Betty, that way—once she got an idea into her head, she was like a dog with a bone, gnawing and gnashing and refusing to let go. Of course I wasn't going to spill anything about the packinghouse. First—as I knew from living with Betty—it was the surest way to drive Yvonne crazy. Second, the last thing I wanted was for these cats to find out I'd been a meat-packer. Paulie told the truth when he said girls wouldn't admit it, not even when they lived in the Yards. Not even when everyone knew they worked in pork trim, or sausage casings, or canned ham, and the girls knew they knew. It wasn't about being a snob. It was because people looked at you differently. As if, because you worked there, you must not mind the smell, the grease, the filth. As if— almost—you were an animal yourself.

"Hey, Yvonne, I forgot to ask you. How'd it go with the suckers last night?" Stella said.

"Those chumps?" Yvonne said. "Me and Gabby took 'em to the El Palacio. Kept 'em there until they were plastered. Then we let on that we'd go back to their hotel to . . . you know."

"Twenty each, up front," Gabby put in.

"They kept saying"—Yvonne dropped her voice low, like a man's—"'You'll get the money after, not before.' No sir, we told 'em, you gotta pay to play. Then we made like we were gonna walk out. That greased the skids plenty."

"They forked it over?" someone asked.

"Cold, hard cash, chickie. On the way out, they turned left, we turned right, slipped a buck to the waiter to zip his lip which way we'd gone, and out the back door we went. Slick as a goddamn whistle."

"I bet they spent half the night looking for us!" Gabby crowed.

Most of the girls whooped with laughter—although I noticed a few pretending not to hear. Alice actually turned her back. I snapped my garter purse closed and stood up, letting the blue silk unfurl to the floor. I raised my voice over the commotion. "How do you know they won't show up tonight to get their money back?"

The laughter trailed off into giggles. Yvonne swung her legs to the floor. "Because, Bo Peep, the chumps had to catch a plane back to New York first thing this morning." Clapping, more laughter. She sauntered away to a chorus of snickers.

"Well, I think it's disgusting," I said to Peggy. "Cheating fellows out of their money."

"Spoken like a true Girl Scout," Peggy said. "I guess you think the girls should've gone through with it, then."

"Of course not!" At her sudden grin, I shook my head. "Stop trying to confuse me. What I mean is, those men were nice enough to take them out on the town. And then they got cheated. It's not right."

"Uh-huh," Peggy said. "You pay Tom back his money yet?"

I'd bent down to adjust a garter; at that, I snapped my head up to look at her. "I borrowed that, it's not the same thing at all! And yes, for your information, I did pay it back. Last night, when he took me out to eat."

The surprise on Peggy's face was satisfying enough—almost—to squash the twinge I felt at the lie.

Tom had showed up about ten thirty, without Jack this time. The blue silk gown made an impression—it was an hour, at least, before he raised his eyes enough to look at my face. At midnight, he clocked me out and took me to a steakhouse to eat. Just like that louse Artie had promised. But Tom was the real deal.

I meant to pay him back. I did try. I had a whole week's wages in my change purse. In the cab, I counted out three fives and five ones and gave it to him. It was one of the hardest things I'd ever done: taking that money out, handing it away. Money I'd danced myself into blisters for, money we needed.

Tom took it. Riffled through it. But he didn't put it in his wallet. "You're so pretty in that dress," he said. "Did you . . . did you think of me, when you bought it?"

It took me a second to remember; I was staring at the bills in his hand. "Mmm? Oh. Sure. Of course I did."

Tom tucked the money back into my palm, folded my fingers over it. I closed my hand tight, crumpling the thick paper against my skin. It felt just as wonderful as the first time. He put his arm across my shoulders. Drew me close. "Buy something else pretty," he whispered, and kissed me.

I didn't tell Peggy any of this. Ma believed I'd taken a whole week's advance on my pay. Tom wouldn't take his money back. That meant every penny in my change purse was mine. Entirely mine. Thirty-four dollars and seventeen cents. The sight of it made me dizzy.

The next day, I told Ma I was going to a matinee with a friend from work, and Peggy took me to Reinhard's on Madison.

Reinhard's was a tailor's shop, not five minutes from the Starlight. The front room looked like any other tailor's: shelves with boxes stacked high, a counter strewn with scissors and tape measures. The tailor, a thin man with small, watery eyes, nodded at Peggy.

"I ain't seen her before," he said, jerking his chin at me. "She okay?"

"Paulie Suelze sent me," I said. Right away, the tailor waved us to come back.

"Well, isn't that the magic word," Peggy murmured as we followed the tailor into a back room. I smiled but didn't answer.

The back room was tiny, stuffed with trunks and boxes and racks of clothes. Curtains hung against the far wall—changing rooms, I guessed. We wandered between the racks: every kind of smart outfit you could imagine, matching skirts and jackets, day dresses, and—dear Jesus—two whole racks just of gowns. Angie would die if she saw this. Betty, too. Not a plain housedress in the bunch, not a single one with a label. I pulled out a backless metallic gray sheath, held it up against myself. *Paulie stole this.* At the thought, the cold-shivery thrill bloomed again under my ribs. I hadn't seen him since he'd knocked on the bedroom window, a week ago. Betty made sure to whisper to me every scrap of gossip she heard at school: Paulie had been seen at this tavern or that poolroom; he was buddying up to a bunch of tough

Lithuanians from Forty-fifth Street; no, he was in with an Irish outfit from Canaryville. It seemed like he was everywhere but near me. Did he like me or didn't he?

I wished I could talk it over with Angie. But Angie and I weren't talking.

The cleaner had gotten most of the stains out of Clara's dress, but a ghost of pink still splotched one hip. You could barely see it, but of course Angie noticed. We'd had a screaming fight, and she hadn't spoken to me since.

Well, she'd come around. She always had before, when we'd fought. She'd say she was sorry, and then I'd say, "Me too"—I'd already apologized a dozen times, but still, this was what you did, for friendship's sake—and everything would go back to the way it was.

I held the gray sheath up to myself, turned to Peggy. "What do you think?" I asked.

She shook her head. "Not your color. Try that navy one, with the gold skirt."

I bought the navy gown and an adorable red wool jacket and skirt to wear out after hours. Peggy told me all the savvy girls bought their duds from places like Reinhard's. Not just Starlight girls, either—taxi-dance halls and after-hours joints were thick as a caterpillar's eyebrows in this part of town. That meant a lot of competition, with every girl trying to look more smashing than the next—at swag prices—because all of us were after the same pool of fish.

You could play taxi dancing two ways. Straight, like Alice and a few others. Wear your feet down to stubs at a nickel a dance, go right home afterward. But even if you had a string of regulars—fellows who were each good for ten or twenty tickets a night, every night—well, you'd work and work and work and still your best coat would be a black wool with a Persian lamb collar, and you'd have to take the streetcar everywhere. No, if you wanted to win at this game—*really* win—you needed men who would do more than dance.

You needed fish.

Fish were easy to catch for a single night. They'd buy you a meal at a chop suey joint or an all-night diner or, if you were lucky, a swell after-hours club, and that would be that. Sometimes a fish might stick around for a few weeks, or a few months. A girl never knew how long it might last, so she got what she could. Cash, if she could manage it. If not, then meals. Gowns. Jewelry.

There were different ways of getting fish, I learned. Peggy liked Filipinos—most of them had money, she said, and they didn't mind spending a little extra on a girl if she treated them nice. Nora, on the other hand, wouldn't have anything to do with Orientals. But anytime Del and O'Malley, the bouncer, had their backs turned, she was waltzing her customers into dark corners. Why not? she said. It's only a bump and tickle, it pays better than fox-trotting, and I don't wear out so many shoes.

A lot of the other girls played customers off each other, to make them jealous. Keeps 'em on their toes, Gabby said. Makes 'em think they gotta win. Or, a girl might play it the other way. Stella, the redhead, once threatened to cut a fellow's throat if she caught him dancing with anyone else. She got a new dress and a gold necklace out of that.

And Yvonne? Her fish weren't the handsomest; in fact, a few of them were downright ugly. I watched her, though. Saw how, when she was dancing with them, it was like no other fellow was in the room. Maybe that was why they'd wait all night, sometimes, for a chance to get in with her.

They ought to hear how she talks about them in the Ladies', I thought. Calling them chumps and suckers, laughing at their looks or how they talked. She didn't laugh at their money, though. Yvonne hadn't bought that fox fur. She didn't even pay her own rent. Her fish took care of that. Four of them, Peggy told me, whom she'd had on the string for years. Not only did they pay her way, but each thought he was the only one who had a "special arrangement" with her.

"I figure maybe she hires a social secretary, to keep 'em from bumping into each other in the hall outside her flat. So," Peggy said, "still want a fur coat of your own?"

"I never said I wanted one at all." When Peggy started laughing, I turned my back and walked away.

Somewhere between straight-arrow Alice and Yvonne's scams and schemes—and worse—there had to be a middle way. I still hadn't figured out what it was, though, when, the night after we'd gone to Reinhard's, Peggy set us up on an after-hours date with a couple of Filipino men.

So far I'd managed to avoid dancing with the Chinese and Filipinos. It wasn't hard, with practice—all a girl had to do was pretend not to see them. But this all happened so fast—Peggy introduced us, and then she was dancing away with the one named Alonso, while Manny stood in front of me, holding out his ticket. Obviously, I'd seen him. That and the fact that I knew his name made it seem unspeakably rude to turn my back and run.

Manny was shorter than Alonso, and if he wasn't as slim,

he wasn't heavy, either. He was dressed a lot better than my usual customer: snazzy pinstripe suit, spectator shoes. Flip or not, I had to admit that after all we did to put on the dog, it was nice to see a man make a little effort.

We danced a little bit without talking. Then Manny asked, "You dig music like this?"

"Oh, I don't know. It's a little sweet for me," I said. *Sweet* was the nice way of saying *cornball*. "I like swing best, but if the band plays too much of it, the geezers won't dance, and then they complain to Del. A lot of them can't hoof it to anything faster than this."

Actually, I'd already come to hate most of the music the Starlight's band played. I wasn't the only one, either.

One night last week, Yvonne hadn't let up on me all evening, plus my head was fit to split from all that tinkly stuff Del insisted the band play. At break time, I'd headed for the Ladies'. From behind the door came the usual babble and laughter, Yvonne loudest of all. To my right, the hall stretched down to a far window. It was dark. It looked quiet.

I just got to the window when I heard what sounded like a *taaaah* . . . I stopped. Nothing. I must have imagined it. I laid my hand on the glass, and the cold seemed to jump into the bones of my fingers. And then I heard it again, coming from a dark room off the hall. Humming—no, not humming, not exactly—more like notes being sung. *Do-re-mi,* only this wasn't any baby music, and it was no baby singing. I'd only heard his voice once. But I recognized it.

He paused in midnote, then started over, the same melody. Slowed at a tricky spot, then pushed past to end on a high *taaahh* . . . Then over again, faster. And faster. I could imagine the same notes flying out of his trumpet. Feel the music waking up my bones.

I glided to the doorway and peeked inside. Another window in here, and next to it, I could make out the pale glimmer of a shirt. A long gleam of brass and, on the windowsill, in a sliver of light from a streetlamp, papers covered with scratches and musical notes.

"Are you going to play that after the break?" I asked.

The brass gleam shifted. Scrape of a match. I glimpsed him in the tiny sudden flame, bending to it with his cigarette. Strong curved cheeks, blunt nose. Eyelashes curling up, almost as pretty as a girl's. I wondered if he'd ever gotten teased about them.

Ozzie shook out the match. Behind me, up the hallway, I heard girls' chatter loud, then faint. Girls coming out of the Ladies'. I eased inside the doorway so they wouldn't see me.

Ozzie said, "You ever hear anything like that in this dump?"

"No," I said.

"Then no. I'm not playing it after the break."

"Where, then?"

"Lily's. My cousin's joint."

The flyer he'd given me, my first night at the Starlight. Yvonne threatening to have him fired if he bothered the customers.

"Hottest jazz in Chicago," I said. "You're in the band."

"That's right," Ozzie said, surprised. By this time I could make him out pretty good in the dim light: he'd taken off his too-small tuxedo jacket, loosened his tie. He tilted his head back, looking at me more closely. "Okay, I know you. You almost slugged one of the customers."

The silver dollar. I decided to ignore that. "Can I have one of those?" I asked, pointing to his cigarette.

Rustle of a pack. He leaned forward, the cigarette in his hand. I took it and put it in my mouth and bent to the match and lit it. The flame snuffed out. Prickly scent of match smoke.

"You just flick your ashes on the floor?" Ozzie said.

"No," I said, even though I had.

"That pipsqueak Del sees ashes on the floor, he'll chase me outta here. Then I'll have to sit with those geezy old-timers in the band, listen to them jawing about the old days until I'm about to pull my own head off. Maybe you better get back where you belong."

"Maybe I'll invite all the girls back here. It gets awfully crowded in that Ladies' room."

Ozzie could've been a dragon, he blew his smoke that hard. His chair creaked, and an ashtray thumped onto the windowsill. I stepped over and tapped my cig against the rim. Before I could thank him, he started humming again, his fingers floating over the trumpet keys. Message plain as day: shut up. So I did. I laid my aching head back against the wall, and I listened. My fingers caught the beat and tapped in the air, silent.

The rap on the door almost made me gasp. I was standing behind it, and it swung inward, toward my face. "Man, what you always got to be sitting in the dark like this for?" The voice rusty-old. Not Del. "You want to write music, ought to do it in the light."

"I think better in the dark," Ozzie said. Scraping his papers together fast. He grabbed his trumpet and his jacket and then they both were gone.

I wondered what Del would do, if he caught a girl talking with a colored musician. It seemed like one of those things you wouldn't have to make a rule about, because nobody would dream of doing it.

So I hadn't gone back to the little room. Ozzie and I kept catching each other's eyes at least once a night, though, usually when Hamp, the bandleader, struck up groaners like "Sweet Sue, Just You" or "Champagne Charlie." Ozzie'd make a face, or I would. Once he let his eyes flutter upward, like he was dying. I'd busted up into giggles just as I was taking a fellow's ticket. He'd snatched it back and walked off, muttering he didn't see what was so danged funny.

Manny steered me smooth and easy across the floor. "I bet we can find you some real music," he said. "What do you say?"

He had a nice round face. Lively eyes, a sweet smile. A lot of snap in his moves, too. I bit my lip and glanced away. Saw Nora slip into the shadows with a customer, his hand already gripping her keister. Across the hall, Yvonne tipped her head and smiled at one of her fish. Not an hour ago, in the Ladies', I'd heard her call him a toad with the brains of a brick. The song ended, and from the bandstand came the first strains of "Tiptoe Through the Tulips."

I looked up at Manny and smiled. "Sounds swell," I said.

I didn't worry anymore about getting home late. Overtime, I'd told Ma. At first she made a fuss, but that didn't last long. I think she was secretly glad—not only because overtime meant extra wages, but now she had an excuse not to sit up for me. Night after night in the parlor chair was making her joints hurt so bad, she could barely walk.

By the time me and Peggy changed our clothes and cashed in our tickets, Manny and Alonso had a cab waiting. We ran for it through stinging sleet, jamming in together, us girls sandwiched between the men. Once we were in the cab, Manny pulled a hip flask out of his pocket. He offered it to me. I hesitated, then tipped it back.

It was all I could do not to cough. My eyes watered and I blinked back tears, afraid if they fell they'd take half my mascara with them. I passed the flask to Peggy.

"So where you boys taking us?" she asked, after she'd taken a slug, her voice gaspy and hoarse as if it'd been squashed by a car.

"If you want a black and tan," the cabbie called over his shoulder, "then you want the Hoot Owl." He shifted the cab into gear.

"Hold your horses, we haven't decided yet," Alonso said.

The cabbie threw his elbow over the seat and hoisted himself around. "Look, Pinoy," he said, "you know damn well you ain't headed nowhere with these girls but to a black and tan. Now, the meter's running, the Hoot Owl is the best in town, that's all there is to it." He shlumped around again and pulled into the street. I wondered what a black and tan was, but Peggy was talking to Alonso and I couldn't ask her.

"Hell with him," Alonso said. "I'm not going to the Hoot Owl just so he can get a kickback for steering us there."

The swallow of whiskey had turned into a small sun in my stomach. Warmth oozed into my muscles, and the

aches in my feet turned dull and distant, as though someone had swathed my feet in cotton. The buildings on the
street seemed to float past, blurry from sleet.

"I want someplace different," Alonso was saying.
"Someplace with real wild jazz."

Real wild jazz. Where had I heard that before? *Best jazz
in Chicago . . . you got a customer wants to hear* real *music, you
bring him down.*

"I know someplace," I said.

"You?" Peggy laughed. "Since when?" But I was
already digging through my coat pocket. Where was that
flyer Ozzie had given me? Had I thrown it out? I'd meant
to . . . a folded bit of paper tumbled past my fingertips. I
grabbed it, flattened it open on my knee. Manny took it
from me and tilted it toward the window, trying to catch
the light of streetlamps as we cruised down Western
Avenue. *"Lily's,"* he read. *"Jump and jive . . ."*

Alonso glanced across me at Manny. I felt Manny
shrug. He peered at the flyer and read the address to the
cabbie, who snorted and changed direction.

"You know that's in Bronzeville," Peggy whispered to
me. I didn't answer. Bronzeville was the Negro neighborhood, east of the Yards, between us and Lake Michigan.
I'd never been there. Ma once said she'd skin us alive if
she found us within a mile of it.

I didn't glimpse much of it that night. Outside, it was
black as the inside of a coal bin, sleeting and howling with
wind, that's all I saw, and you can bet we didn't stand
around gawking. Me and Peggy jumped out of the cab and
ran down the outside stairs to the basement entry, snatch-
ing at the iron rail to keep from slipping, our pocketbooks
held over our heads. We found ourselves in a tiny front

room with unpainted wood walls and a gray-haired Negro man sitting on a stool behind a cash register. To our right was an even tinier checkroom; to our left, a heavy velvet curtain. From behind the curtain came the stomp of drums, a hail of beats too fast to sort out, and over them, the scream and soar of a trumpet. Kicking my heart into high gear, thrumming down to my feet. I forgot the ache.

"Swell joint, kid." Peggy shook the sleet off her pocketbook. Glanced around at the bare walls. "Good thing I've had my tetanus shot."

I was already shimmying out of my coat and hat and handing them to the hatcheck girl. Alonso paid our admission, and then, Manny behind me, I stepped through the curtain into a blast of trombone. The entire club was maybe half the size of the Starlight's dance floor. Dimmer, and warm, stale with cigarettes, perfume, beer. A dozen or so little square tables, about half of them full. Mostly Negroes, a few whites, their foreheads and cheeks shining in the light of tiny yellow-shaded lamps, shining coffee-and-milk, shining pink, shining mahogany-wood brown.

Of course, I saw Negroes all the time, on the streetcar and the el, and when I was at the packinghouse I'd even worked with one, Evelyn, who cleaned the floors. But I'd never been in a place that was mostly Negro. I'd certainly never seen Negro and white sitting together. Dancing together. Holding hands. I stood frozen, unsure what to do.

Someone touched my elbow. I jumped, and looked up to see Manny grinning. He nodded at the band, crammed on a platform barely raised above the floor, at the tables, at the three couples dancing.

"Great!" he shouted over the music. "This is great!"

I grabbed Peggy's arm and put my mouth up to her ear. "What kind of place is this?"

"You're the one who brought us here, don't you know? This is a black and tan. You think a regular joint would let us in, with *them*?" She tipped her head toward the men. Alonso caught her eye, and she smiled at him. "Let go of my dress," she said to me. "You're wrinkling it."

A woman slipped past a knot of people toward us. "Welcome to Lily's," she said. She was tiny, and Ozzie was tall, but I could see the resemblance: wide-apart eyes, curved cheeks. Hers rounder than his but ending in the same strong chin. She was shorter than me but bigger hipped, her black hair rolled into an elegant updo.

"We're from the Starlight Dance Academy," I said. I had to raise my voice over the music. "Ozzie told us about this place!"

She nodded and waved us to follow her. She slipped between tables and I had to scoot to keep up, sure I was going to trip over someone's foot or my own. She put us at a table off to the side, just a few feet from the band and the couples jitterbugging on a bare patch of floor.

I felt like I had eyes all over my skin, taking in everything. The blue tablecloths and battered tin ashtrays. The rippling waves of the men's hair, combed straight back and gleaming. The men in zoot suits—I didn't know the name for them, I asked Manny, later—sharkskin gray, kelly green, royal blue, each with broad shoulders and nipped-in waists, coats and silver watch chains hanging almost to their baggy knees.

A trumpet blare caught my ear, a ratta-tat-tat solo so catchy my feet started jitterbugging under the table. It was Ozzie, all right, only an Ozzie so different from the trumpeter at the dance hall I hardly recognized him. Instead of a tuxedo, he wore a checked cotton shirt and a regular tie, and his jacket was unbuttoned. He wasn't bored now. He leaned back like a tree in a gale, his trumpet aimed someplace far gone from here, his cheeks puffed out and eyes squeezed shut and the sweat pouring down. Did he do this every night—play six hours at the Starlight, then come straight here?

Ozzie poured on the gas and so did the dancers. I thought I knew how to Lindy Hop—but I didn't, not like this. One girl threw her arm high in the air, her other hand gripping the man's hard, and they twisted low to the floor, knees wide, her body one long curve from fingers to hips, both of them light and lively on the balls of their feet. Kicking out to the side, the girl's Cuban heel flashing an inch from our table. Peggy jerked backward.

Ozzie lowered his trumpet, his solo done. People clapped and shouted. Alonso whistled.

"Dance?" Manny shouted in my ear. I grabbed his hand and leaped to my feet. I didn't care if he was Filipino or Chinese or Negro or Polish. I didn't care that I didn't know how to dance like this. I could hoof it well enough, the beat was fast and wild and I couldn't stay sitting.

Manny danced a hundred times better than Stan Dudek, a thousand times better than Art. He twirled and finger-popped, and we twisted and swung, my skirt flaring wide. After a while we staggered back to the table, and I found a drink at my seat. Coca-Cola and some kind of liquor, harsh under the sweetness. I didn't care; I was thirsty. I drank it down and we headed out to the floor again. A tall, thin Negro girl had stepped up onstage. She wore a pretty red dress that showed a scatter of freckles, big as raindrops, across her chest. She didn't look any older than Ozzie, no older than me. She carried herself like she wasn't sure where to put her hands or what to do with her shoulders, and for a second I thought she'd wandered up there by mistake. But the people at the tables whistled and called *Sing it, Ophelia,* and she did. There was no microphone, but she had the pipes to carry the whole room, a throaty scat and wail and, I tell you, my feet flew and Manny was right there, jump and turn and swing, his hand tight on mine. I glanced up at the bandstand and saw Ozzie watching her. He'd been so wrapped up in the music all night, I didn't think he'd noticed anything past the end of his trumpet. He sure hadn't noticed me. But he saw Ophelia, all right, the look on his face like the music itself had put on a dress and come up to him and said hello. But she didn't toss so much as a glance his way.

After a while, Ophelia took a break. Manny and Alonso lit up cigarettes at the table. I followed Peggy to the ladies' room. My legs shook, my dress stuck to my back, my hair felt five feet wide and a yard high. I didn't care. My feet hurt, but I didn't care about that, either. Let them be sore tomorrow, just please, keep them hopping tonight.

The ladies' room had only one stall and one mirror, although the mirror was a good size and had Hollywood lights over it. That'd be Lily's touch. A man wouldn't know about girls trying to fix their faces in shadows. Not that those lights did me any good. I tapped shoulders and said, "Excuse me," and these Negro girls said, "Yes, ma'am, hang on just a sec," and went right on dabbing their faces. Except that they were colored, it was just like the Starlight during a break: too many girls and not enough mirror, and every girl out for herself.

Peggy stood by the wall, holding her compact high, to catch the light. I did the same.

"I have to hand it to you," Peggy said. "Alonso said this is just what the doctor ordered. No big fancy floor show, just a band that can really cook."

I imagined coming here with Paulie. Imagined him saying, *What great music, what a great place. You're something else, Ruby*. I wondered if I'd ever have the chance.

We stayed over an hour. By the time we left, the weather had let up, a little. Alonso and Manny went out first to get a cab. When Peggy and I followed, a white girl was standing next to them, talking. She was blond—a dye job, even under the streetlamp you could tell, it was too all-over yellow—and so much rouge her face looked like a painted doll's. I didn't remember seeing her in the club. Manny looked embarrassed. Alonso turned his back to her.

Peggy bumped me hard with her shoulder. "For Pete's sake, Ruby, it's *freezing*." I ducked past the woman into the cab. Through the window, I glimpsed her turn on her heel and stride away. Then Manny slid onto the seat next to me, and we were moving. "Who was that?" I asked. Nobody answered. Alonso told the cabbie to drop them off at their flat, then take us home.

"What gentlemen," Peggy said as we waved to the boys through the cab window, after letting them off. "But then, Pinoys always are. Do you want the cab to drop you first, or me?"

"You're closer," I said. It didn't matter where we were; I always said Peggy was closer. I didn't want her to know I was from the Back of the Yards. I didn't want her to smell the packinghouses and the stockyards, that stench of carcass and manure and smoke. The smell of work, the

Yards called it. I was used to it, but I'd ridden the street-car with plenty of people who weren't. I didn't care to see their reaction on Peggy's face.

"I've never had so much fun in my life," I said. "Wasn't the music amazing?"

Peggy stretched, then collapsed into the corner of the seat. "We hear nothing but jazz all night, every night," she said, yawning. "What's amazing about more of it?"

"But this, it was . . ." *Different*, I was going to say. *Exciting*. They hadn't just played popular stuff from the radio; half the songs I'd never heard before. I tried to explain, but Peggy didn't care. I took off a shoe and pressed my fingertips deep along my instep, massaging the ache. How could anyone hear those glorious horns, the belting voice of the tall, freckled singer, and not tell the difference between that and the stuff they dished up at the Starlight?

Ozzie sure knew the difference. Somebody who could play like that, I wondered why he bothered with the Starlight at all.

"Are all the black and tans like Lily's?" I said.

I meant the music, but Peggy said, "No, thank God. The ones I've been to are all fancier than that dump. The Hoot Owl, for instance. You'll go there, if you keep going out with Pinoys. They won't let them in the regular clubs, you know, so you don't have much choice." She yawned again. "I think you've got yourself another fish, with that Manny. He likes you."

"Where do Filipinos come from?" I said sleepily. "I never thought to wonder before."

The cab pulled up in front of Peggy's hotel. She wrapped her hand around the door handle. Then she ducked her head down, close to her shoulder, as if she were talking to the floor.

"They're called the Philippine Islands," she said. "Tiny. Compared to here." Her eyes met mine then; they had an odd look, almost as if she was angry, but her voice was as light and casual as ever. She yanked open the cab door. "You remember those taxi dancers Nora talked about, who married flips?"

My very first night at the Starlight. "Yeah, I remember."

Peggy stepped out of the cab. "I'm one of them," she said, and slammed the door shut behind her.

NINE

I didn't even wait for Peggy to get her coat off, the next night at the Starlight. "You're *married*?" I said.

"Hush!" Peggy said. She glanced around at the hub-bub in the Ladies', then jerked open her locker. "I knew I should've kept my big mouth shut. Just do me a favor and keep it quiet, all right?"

"But who is he? When did—"

Peggy leaned down and clapped a cool hand over my mouth. Her skin smelled faintly of lemon. "Look, I was feeling nostalgic and I let it slip. Okay? Blame the rum and Cokes. That part of my life is over and done with, and it's a brand stinking new day. But if these witches find out, I'll never hear the end of it, and you know that's a fact." I nodded. She took her hand away.

It was a Sunday night. Slow, only half the usual num-ber of customers. I couldn't help but watch Peggy. She was only a few years older than me—not that that mat-tered, plenty of girls got hitched by eighteen. Ma had been only sixteen when she got married. But to a Filipino! How did that happen? And what on earth did *over and done with* mean? That her husband had died? That they'd gotten divorced? Surely not—nobody but movie actresses ever got divorced. No, she must be a widow. Maybe that was why she didn't want anybody to know; she didn't want to be reminded of her grief. I watched her dance past with a skinny fellow whose ears stuck out like flags, telling him a joke, laughing so hard she could barely talk. That's what the customers liked about Peggy, how peppy and upbeat she was.

Not like any widow I'd ever met.

By closing, at two o'clock, neither of us had snagged a fish. I finished scrubbing my face at the sink—when I didn't have an after-hours date, I liked the warm water at the Starlight a lot better than the freezing tap at home—and padded in my stocking feet back to the lockers.

"Want to split a cab?" Peggy asked.

"Sure," I said.

As soon as we got in the cab, I scootched around to face her. She groaned and laid her head in her hand. "You're not going to leave it alone, are you?" she said.

"I didn't say a word all night. Not one syllable."

"I don't suppose you can keep it that way."

I leaned toward her, my chin cupped in my hands.

She sighed. Glanced up at the ceiling of the cab, as if it might have an escape hatch. Then she said to the cabbie, "We've changed our minds. Drop us at Bennie's on Jackson."

Bennie's was an all-night diner. I ordered a hot dog and a cola, Peggy a piece of apple pie and a coffee. "One bun pup, one Eve with a lid on!" the waitress bawled to the cook.

Peggy had met her husband a year ago, at another

taxi-dance hall near the Loop. They'd dated for six weeks, then got married.

"Talk about head over heels," she said. "From the first time I saw him, I was a goner. He could've asked me to live in sin in an igloo in Alaska, and I'd have done it."

Her husband, Vidal, had come to America for college. "That's why most of them are here," she said. "But then the law changed, so if they leave the States, they can't get back in. The problem is, there's no Filipinas here to marry. So a lot of them marry American girls, instead."

Four months after their wedding, Vidal found out his mother was dying. She wanted him to come home, and he went. End of story, Peggy said. She sliced the edge of her fork through her apple pie.

"But you . . . how come you didn't go with him?" I asked. "If a man I loved . . . I mean, it wouldn't matter where he went, so long as we could be together!"

Peggy took a sip of coffee, wiped her mouth. "He never told his family about me." Her voice light and dry, as if she were talking about a pair of shoes. "His mother warned him, see. About us American girls." She arched her fingers like claws, bared her crooked tooth in a Dracula grimace. Then shrugged and picked up her fork.

"But he can come back now, can't he? I mean, he's married to you; they can't keep him out, can they? Or, or you can go there. Now that his mother's . . ."

"He won't come back," Peggy said. "He got married. Again. To a nice Filipina girl his mother approved of. For all I know, Vidal Jr. might be on the way right now." She folded her napkin and tossed it down by her empty plate. "Like I said. End of story. So what's yours?"

"My what?"

"Your story. Every taxi dancer has a story. I spilled mine, now it's your turn."

My hot dog was cold in my hands. I put it down. "Are you still in love with him?"

"Does it matter? Look, if he'd stayed, I'd have divorced him. He wanted me to become a Catholic and he wouldn't pick up his socks."

How could she sit there and talk like it was nothing more than a story in one of Angie's magazines? At least those had happy endings. I tore off a piece of bun, rolled it between my fingers. "What about your family?" I asked. "What did your mother say when she found out?"

She sat back in her chair, her coffee cup in both hands. Looked at the blackness of the window. Outside, or at her reflection, I couldn't tell.

"The last thing my mother said to me was, 'Don't come home. It'll kill your father.'" Peggy glanced at me. Shrugged again, a quick lift of one shoulder. "I told you," she said. "Every taxi dancer has a story."

•   •   •

Manny became one of my fish. So did Tom. Between them, and a few others here and there, I started picking up three, sometimes four dates a week. Pretty soon, I got to know every chop suey joint and after-hours club for ten blocks around the Starlight, and most of the black and tans, too. Maybe Peggy thought I didn't fool Del, claiming to be eighteen, but I fooled every nightclub I ever walked into. Or maybe they didn't care. After my first week at the clubs, I never thought about it.

If my date was a white fellow looking for a little adventure, then I'd steer him to Lily's. White fellows always seemed to think the black and tans were dangerous, and they especially liked Lily's because it was so cramped, the bandstand practically on top of the customers. Authentic, they said, whatever that meant. I just liked it because nobody played fast, hot, finger-popping-foot-stomping swing the way Ozzie and the band did.

Lucky for me, Manny was as wild for Lily's as I was. I liked Manny. He was fun, and he could tear up a dance floor like nobody's business. Plus, he was the only college boy I'd ever met. Had his degree, too. But nobody would hire a Pinoy architect, he told me, so he'd gone to work for Pullman as a railroad porter. Dressed up in a white jacket, showing passengers their compartments, fetching toothbrushes. He liked me because I laughed at his jokes and, in the cab on the way home, I didn't mind a kiss or two. The first time he kissed me, I was shocked. Not by how strange it was, but how ordinary. It got so where, except for the fact that we couldn't go to the regular clubs, I almost forgot he was a Pinoy.

Was that how it'd been for Peggy? If, once you got to know a fellow, you didn't think of him as foreign anymore? He was just Vidal, who left his socks on the floor. Head over heels for him, she'd said. Sometimes I wondered if Alonso reminded her of him. They seemed to be getting awfully close, and I'd noticed her studying him, almost, with an odd look on her face, like she was trying to remember something she was afraid of forgetting.

Sometimes I felt guilty, for Tom's sake. I'd promised him I'd stay white. And when he talked about it, or Nora or the other girls did, it seemed pure and noble, and sometimes I thought I ought to. But I couldn't give up Lily's, not in a million years. And I had so much fun with

Manny, and he brought me gifts, too. An adorable Scottie dog brooch, in black Bakelite with a sparkly glass eye. A silver charm bracelet with a tiny cross. Best of all, a new wool coat, hunter green with a plaid lining, warmer than any coat I'd ever had. I gave it to Ma, along with a pair of thick wool gloves. When she saw it, she put her hands to her face and cried. I had an elaborate story all ready to trot out, to explain where the money had come from. But Ma only asked, "You didn't get another advance, did you?" I told her no, and after that she didn't ask any more questions.

I'd grown up listening to our Polish neighbors make nasty remarks about the Lithuanians, the Croats, the Irish . . . shanty Irish, they called them, turkey birds. No offense to your mother, they always added hastily. But in a black and tan, nobody cared my mother was Irish. Nobody cared I was from the Yards. What difference did it make to them? I was a white girl, that was all. I could be anybody, and the black and tans let anybody in. No one seemed to care who danced with who or sat with who or talked with who—so long as you weren't dumb enough to poach another girl's fellow, but that was true anywhere.

At the Starlight, though, it was different. We had to be careful. Most of the white customers didn't mind a girl dancing with Orientals once in a while; we told them it was our job, Del made us, what could we do? If a girl took too many tickets from Orientals, though, then the whites figured she must like it. They called her cheap or worse, and they kept their distance. As if she might make them dirty, somehow.

And then, of course, when Tom was at the Starlight I

didn't dare look at a Pinoy at all. Thank God Manny was savvy about it; if I snubbed him, he knew why. Still, I was afraid some night Tom would come in while I was dancing with him or one of the other Pinoy boys I'd met. Not that it mattered, I told myself. After all, it's not as if he owns you. Still, on the nights Tom was most likely to show up—mainly Fridays—I was extra careful.

I always knew when he was there. I'd get a tickle up the back of my neck, like a tiny spider climbing into my hair. I'd turn around, and there he'd be. After three or four dances he'd go sit in the stag line, with the men who only watched. Tom would watch only me. Sometimes, if he thought I was dancing too much with a particular fellow, he'd come to the sidelines and stare. If I sat down to coffee with someone, Tom would hover at the next table or over by the wall. His long face getting longer, as if everything below his eyes was rubber and someone was doing pull-ups from his chin. The bouncer, O'Malley, caught him at it once and told him to knock it off or get out. That made things better for a night. Then he was back at it.

"He gives me the creeps," Peggy said. "Now that you've paid him back, why don't you tell him to shove off?"

"I feel bad for him," I said. Which was mostly true. When we went out, he'd go on and on about how hard it was to meet nice girls. How they only went out with him because he made a good wage, how none of them seemed to really care for him.

"But you care, don't you, Ruby?" he'd ask.

"Sure I do," I told him. I didn't, but what could I say? I didn't want to be rude. Besides, he was still giving me money. I always said no, but he always insisted.

"Put it on your tab," he said. "Buy yourself something nice. I like for you to look pretty."

I knew I shouldn't take it. But the problem was, as much as I danced, I never made the fifty a week Paulie had promised. Thirty was more like it. Which a month ago would have been a fortune, but now, somehow, it never seemed to be enough.

Every night, when I got home, I stashed my earnings in an old pillowcase I kept hidden in the far corner of the closet, behind shoes we'd outgrown. Ma couldn't bend that low anymore, and Betty would never look there; she'd been terrified of dark narrow places like that ever since a spider had crawled on her under the porch of our old house. The first few times I lifted the pillowcase out, I froze at every clink and rattle. But Betty's snoring never hitched. She could sleep through Mr. Schenker; compared to that, a few coins must be nothing.

On Saturdays, I squirreled the pillowcase under my housecoat and carried it to the hall toilet. There I counted out a week's wages, eighteen dollars. If I'd been out after hours, I put in extra for "overtime." Tucked the cash into an envelope and left it on the kitchen table. Ma complained that the telephone company was working me to death, that I wasn't getting enough rest. But every Sunday morning, when I got up, the envelope was gone and she was sitting with pencil and paper, figuring how much back rent we still owed and how soon it could be paid.

We ate meat every day now. Pork chops and sausage and meatloaf and even a roast. Not a bean in sight. We made cakes. We got the coal bin filled, a full ton, to last the entire winter.

And then there were all the things I needed for work.

Nylon stockings, a dozen pairs, and a cunning quilted box with a dozen compartments to keep them in. Two new bras. A new girdle. Half a dozen satin step-ins. Hair ornaments to match my gowns, and earrings to match the hair ornaments. I bought two more gowns from Reinhard's, which meant two more pairs of shoes. I would've bought more after-hours outfits, too, except I would have to wear them home, and I couldn't explain to Ma where I'd gotten the money for them. The wool coat from Manny had been dicey enough. Everything else, I kept in my locker at the Starlight. I never wore the lime green dress anymore, and I kicked my old, creased saddle shoes under the bed.

Thanksgiving came. For the first time in years, we could afford a turkey to roast. Ma made stuffing with walnuts and celery; Betty made an apple pie. At work, that night, I could barely zip myself into my gown. But I really regretted how much I'd eaten when Del insisted that the band play "The Turkey Trot" three times every hour.

"Give us a break, Del, wouldja?" Nora begged him. She'd had three kinds of pie at her brother and sister-in-law's house, and by ten o'clock she was panting, her broad face tomato red. "If I have to jump up and down and flap my arms one more time to that old-timey crap, I'm gonna puke."

"Thanksgiving, customers expect the Turkey Trot," Del said. "Next year don't eat before you come to work."

I caught Ozzie's eye. He cocked his finger and thumb like a gun, held it to his temple, and fired. I laughed out loud. But there was no getting out of the Turkey Trot, not for Ozzie or for us. Like Del always said: in this business, if you don't have illusion, you don't have anything. To-night, the illusion was of a happy holiday.

"Well, I think he's right," Alice said in the Ladies'. The rest of us groaned, and someone threw a roll of toilet tissue at her. "No, really!" she insisted, untangling the tissue from her curls. "Look at them out there. Most of them tonight are old. They don't have anyone to spend Thanksgiving with except us."

She was right, and for a while I was sorry. I'd do better, I'd be sweet to the customers. Then the band swung into the Trot for the umpteenth time, and I wished they would all go home.

The weather got colder. We got a dusting of snow. In the Yards, it lasted just long enough to turn into blackish-gray lumps before it melted. We never had white snow for long, not with the soot from the trains and packinghouse incinerators. Betty took to rolling herself inside one of the blankets, like a cocoon, so that when I got into bed my chilly skin wouldn't touch hers.

The night after Thanksgiving, Tom came to the Starlight. He didn't dance with me at all. Just sat, smoking one cigarette after another. Which was strange all by itself; I'd never seen him smoke more than one cigarette, and usually not even that.

After hours, he was outside waiting for me just as usual. He seemed different, though. I could feel it, like static on a phone line. A hum of tension. At the steakhouse he hardly touched his food. And then there was the way he looked at me. I didn't mind him staring, at least not much. He always stared. But tonight, he stared everywhere but at me. His gaze darting at me from time to time, like a snake's tongue flicking. Every time I looked away, I felt it.

Well, whatever mood he was in, I hoped it wouldn't stop him from loaning me a little more money. I had a dry cleaning bill to pay. I should've had enough, but somehow it had all gotten spent. I decided to wait to ask until we were in the cab, going back to the Starlight. Tom got sentimental then. He'd talk about how much it hurt him, seeing a kid like me trying to make it all alone in the world. How he hated to leave me at the end of the night. He'd beg me to let him see me home. I always refused. Peggy had taught me that. Don't ever let a fish know where you live, she said. You never know when one will take it into his head to pay you a visit. I guessed that if a fish paid your rent—like Yvonne's did—it might be a different story. Peggy had laughed. "That," she'd said, "is a whole different book."

I still had half a steak on my plate when Tom reached over and took my hand.

"Let's get out of here," he said.

His fingers were rough and tight on mine. I smiled at him and tried to loose my arm. He wouldn't let go. "I need to go powder my nose," I said.

"You're fine. Come on." He got up, still holding my hand.

In the cab, Tom gave the driver an address I didn't recognize. "Where's that?" I asked.

"No place," Tom said. "A club."

I frowned. The cabbies knew every night spot in Chicago, so unless a club was new, like Lily's, a man just told the cabbie its name. Tom slipped his arm around me. "Don't worry," he said. "You'll like it."

Outside, the tires whooshed over the wet streets. Here, inside, it was warm and dark. Tom bent his head and kissed me.

He didn't kiss as well as Manny, not a tenth as well as Paulie. But I never kissed anyone I didn't like, and I supposed I liked Tom well enough. He was even handsome, in a deep-eyed, long-jawed sort of way.

The kiss ended. I sighed and laid my head on his shoulder.

"How's your mother?" he asked.

Surprised, I twisted my neck to look at him. He'd never asked about Ma before. But this would make it even easier than usual. "She's okay, I guess," I said. "Really, it's nothing." That slick weasel Artie had taught me, and I never forgot. Nobody likes a sob story. I'd never told Tom anything more than the fact that I had to work to support my family. He didn't even know what Ma was sick with.

"Ruby," he said. "Tell the truth now."

I sighed again. "It's the landlord," I said. I kept my tone low and flat, as if I was sick of having to think about such a horrible person. "He's raised the rent." I'd thought of it during dinner. December first was Monday, the timing was perfect. Plus I might be able to play this out. Rent day came every month, after all.

Tom's mouth pushed out as if he was thinking. "How much?" he said.

"Five dollars," I said.

"All right," Tom said. But he didn't reach for his wallet.

"Tom, really, I couldn't . . ."

"You can." Now his voice was the flat one. The cab pulled over; Tom got out, paid the cabbie, and came around to my door. "Come on," he said. I took his hand and stepped out onto the curb. Ahead of us, on the corner, was a rundown brick building. I looked up; a neon sign running down its side said, in vertical letters, HOTEL. No name. Just HOTEL.

"The club's in there?" I asked. Some hotels had them, sure. But the only ones I'd ever heard of were the ritzy places, where the swells went. Not a broken-down fly-trap like this. And where were the people? At the clubs I'd been to, folks were constantly coming and going, the streets outside bustling with cabs. Here, just a few people drifted up the sidewalk. All men, every one by himself.

"Come on," Tom said again. He took my arm and steered me into the hotel lobby. It was tiny and smelled sour, like laundry that hadn't been washed. On one side was a booth, almost exactly like the ticket booth at the dance hall. Directly ahead was a flight of stairs. Tom tapped the bell sitting on the booth's counter. A sallow, tired-looking boy about my age appeared.

"For how long?" the boy asked in a bored tone.

Behind us, the door opened, and another couple crowded inside. I pressed against the wall to make room. As they pushed past, the woman bumped into me. " 'Scuse me," she said. For an instant, our eyes met. The light was bad, but I could still see the heavy rouge on her cheeks. Like a painted doll's. The man shoved ahead of Tom and slapped a dollar bill onto the counter. The boy scooped it up. "Half an hour," the man told him. The woman nudged her fellow and jerked her head at me. I edged closer behind Tom.

"Someone's cherry's gonna get popped," the woman

said. The two of them whooped with laughter and staggered up the stairs, the man goosing her from behind.

"Wait outside a second, Ruby, will you?" Tom said.

I was already going. If he'd hoped to keep me from figuring out what kind of place this was, he was thirty seconds too late. I was already halfway across the street when I heard him panting behind me. "Ruby! Ruby, wait!" he called. I started to run, but he caught up to me and clapped one of his big mitts on my shoulder, spinning me half around. I slipped on the slick pavement and grabbed his coat sleeve to keep from falling.

"What the hell's the matter with you? Where are you going?" he said.

"Where do you think?" I tried to shove him, but he wrapped an arm around me, squeezing me close to his side. I squirmed, and he squeezed tighter.

"Listen to me," he said. "Listen! It's nicer upstairs. I promise."

Nicer upstairs? Did he think it was the goddamned *drapes* I was mad about? I kicked at him and missed. Tom started back toward the hotel, dragging me with him.

"Can the act, Ruby," he said. "Time to pay the piper. Now come on."

"What act? What piper? What the hell are you talking about?" HOTEL flickered in front of me, in bright red neon. Had he gone crazy? Was this how crazy people behaved? Frantic, I swiveled my head, searching up and down the street. No cops. The few men in sight had turned to stare, but none of them came our way.

Tom hauled me up the sidewalk and pushed me back against the building. The roughness of the brick scraped my coat like sandpaper. I could feel his breath riffling my hair.

"Fool me once, shame on you," he said. "You ever hear that saying, Ruby?"

At the coldness in his voice, my anger leaked away. Leaving me hollow and shaking. I didn't know what he meant, except that he meant to make me go upstairs with him. But why? He'd always called me a sweet kid. Sweet Ruby. Not like those other girls. "I don't understand," I said. Sobs crowded my chest like bubbles, aching tight. I fought them down. Don't you dare cry, don't you dare let him see you're scared . . .

"Fool me twice, shame on me." He leaned his arm against the wall, bending down so that his face was only an inch from mine. So close, my skin felt the warmth of his. "Your rent got raised. You needed another dress. How much, Ruby?"

The money. He wasn't crazy, he was upset about the money. I almost gasped with relief. *He'll make sure you pay, one way or another.* Peggy, in the shadows of a cab, weeks ago. But I'd tried! I fumbled for my pocketbook, crumpled under my arm. "Here, Tom, look . . . I have six dollars from tonight, take it. I'll get the rest as soon as you say, I'll—"

"I work hard. Twelve hours a day. Five days a week. My wife and my kids, they deserve that money."

I blinked. The back of my throat ached from cold, and I realized my mouth had fallen open. Wife and kids? Tom was *married*?

"I met you," Tom was saying, "and I thought, Here's a poor dumb kid who needs some help. So I helped you.

Didn't I? And all this time, I didn't ask nothing from you."

All these weeks, boo-hooing how he couldn't get a girl to care for him. Making me feel sorry for him, while all the time he had a *wife* . . .

"Tell the truth, Ruby." Leaning closer. His lips brushing my cheek. "How much of my money—my *family's* money, my *children's* money—did you spend on your nigger boyfriends?"

The cold went all through me then. All the way down in my belly, a block of ice. I started to babble. "We have to, Del makes us, we'll lose our jobs—"

Tom grabbed my shoulder. He jerked me forward, then shoved me against the brick, banging my head hard. I gasped. Tears stung my eyes.

"Liar," Tom said. "I saw you. Two days ago. I saw you leave with those two flips, you and that brunette friend of yours." His eyes, just a few inches from mine, as narrow and cold as his voice. "Jack warned me. He told me you were nothing but a little tease. But I said, No, not Ruby. Ruby's just a kid." He laughed, short and bitter. "You sure pulled the wool over my eyes."

"You don't understand. Those men, they're not . . . We dance, that's *all*. I've never . . ."

He yanked me away from the wall. "Can it, Ruby. You've played that hand out. I'm not asking for nothing you haven't already done. Nothing I haven't paid for already, a dozen times over. I'm through talking. Let's go."

The woman in the hotel. The blonde on the sidewalk in front of Lily's. Tom thought I was like them. He'd make me go upstairs with him, and after that—I would be like them. Ma . . .

"No, I *won't*!" I shouted. I twisted away, but he grabbed both my hands. I spit in his face. I'd never spit at anything before, and a lot ended up on my chin, but I must have got him because he jerked back with a disgusted "*Aargh!*" I wrenched my arms loose and ran.

"Ruby!" he yelled. "Ruby, come back here!"

Fat chance. I glanced behind and saw him stumbling after me, scrubbing at one eye with his sleeve. Good. I hoped I'd blinded him. As I turned back around, I ran into one of the men drifting on the street. He grinned at me, slimy as the man in the hotel, and grabbed at my arm. I yelped and dodged away. Behind me, Tom hollered, "Hey! Leave her alone!"

I skittered out into the street. A cab was coming, its light off. I waved anyway, both arms over my head. It stopped and I scrambled inside, slamming the door just as Tom caught up. He pounded on the window.

"Ruby! We're coming back here, we're finishing this thing!"

"Go to hell!" I yelled through the glass. What was wrong with the cabbie, why weren't we moving? I leaned forward and drummed my fingers on the cabbie's shoulder. "Go, please!"

"Where to?" he said.

"Just *go*!" I shouted, at the same time Tom yelled, "You bitch, I'm gonna get what I paid for!" The cab started rolling. More pounding on the window. "Fifty-three dollars, Ruby! You hear me? Fifty-three dollars' worth, flat on your back!"

That louse, that no-good rotten jerk . . . I grabbed the first thing in my pocketbook I could find and rolled the window down, fast jerks. Tom was already a few feet behind, standing in the middle of the street. "You better see this thing through," he shouted, "or I'll tell that boss of yours what a whore you are, and he'll kick your ass out on the street! What'll happen to your poor sick mother then, huh?"

I leaned out the window and threw the thing in my hand. It flew a yard wide of his head but he ducked anyway, hands in front of his face. The last thing I saw was the compact shattering on the pavement, powder exploding in a pale cloud. Then the cabbie hit the gas and I fell back inside. Freezing wind roared over me. The sobs I'd stuffed down broke free, wracking me in two.

TEN

The next morning I slipped out of the flat without Ma or Betty seeing me. I couldn't face them. Not with Tom's words still careening through my head. *Liar. Tease. Whore.* Just remembering made me feel fouler than the packing-house ever had.

My heels rang on the frozen sidewalks. Up and down Honore Street, lights glowed behind window curtains. Neighbors clumping down their front stoops waved or tipped their hats to me. I hurried past. Ashamed to look at them, as if Tom's words were branded on my skin.

Fifty-three dollars! Was he lying? He must be lying. I'd lain awake the rest of the night, trying to tally how much money he'd given me, where it had gone. Every time I thought I'd accounted for it all, I remembered something else. Like the dress I'd bought this week: a moss green wool crepe de chine with a matching leather belt. Not from Reinhard's, either—I'd bought it full price, from Goldblatt's, the neighborhood department store, because I'd seen it in the window and it looked cute. And the shoes I was wearing this minute, brown leather oxfords, with darling wide Cuban heels. I'd taken the money to pay for them out of my new change purse. My old one had been fine, but this was embroidered all over in white and blue beads, with a blue silk lining, and when I saw it, I couldn't resist. Hair ornaments and nylons and earrings . . . I pictured my locker at the Starlight, stuffed with things I couldn't bring home because I'd never be able to explain where I got the money, and guilt wrung my stomach like poison.

I'd meant to get us out of the Yards. Fifty-three dollars could have been a month's rent in a nice flat, in a nice neighborhood with trees and clean air. Fifty-three dollars could have been doctors' visits and medicines for Ma, or half a year's tuition at a good parish school for Betty. Fifty-three dollars should be filling the pillowcase under the bed. Instead, I had barely enough to fill the pay envelope tomorrow.

We're coming back here, Tom had said. *We're finishing this thing.*

"Well, look what the cat dragged in," Angie said when her mother called her to the door. Angie was still in her flowered housecoat, her hair wrapped up in pin curls and tied under a net. It made her cheeks look wider, her face more kittenish. Commotion poured out of the kitchen behind her, kids' voices swooping and diving.

"We're eating breakfast, Ruby, would you like some?" Mrs. Wachowski asked. She was short, like Angie, but where Angie was delicate, Mrs. Wachowski was solid as a kielbasa, her face almost as red.

Angie swept toward me and pushed me back out the door. "Go finish eating, Ma. This'll only take a minute." She closed the door behind us. We stood on the stair landing that led down to the street, Angie facing me, her arms wrapped tight against the cold.

"What'd you come here for?" she said. "To say you're sorry again?"

"No," I said.

Angie's face tightened. She spun around and put her hand on the doorknob.

"Wait!" I said. "Angie, I'm in trouble. I need to talk to you."

She hesitated. Turned her head just a sliver. "What kind of trouble?"

I didn't answer. She glanced at me over her shoulder, biting the inside of her cheek, the way she always did when she wasn't sure.

"Please," I said. "You're the only one I can tell."

For another breath, she didn't say anything. Then she nodded.

Angie shared a room with three younger sisters. Her little brothers slept on the sofa in the parlor. Seven kids in all, including Clara. Angie envied me having only one sister, but I loved the Wachowskis' hullabaloo. Always something going on, jokes or fights or secrets. Never boring, never quiet. All my life I wished I was one of four, six, eight kids, like every other family I knew.

Angie's sister Reena was in their room. Angie kicked her out, slammed the door on her complaining and hollering, then snapped on the radio so Reena couldn't hear us talking. "Woodchopper's Ball" jumped into the air, good and loud. Angie swiped a pile of clothes off the nearest bed. Sitting down, she eyed my brown oxfords. "Those are kind of cute," she said.

"Thanks. I like your necklace."

That made her smile. She lifted the silver cross from her chest, tucking her chin to look down at it. "Isn't it pretty? Stan Dudek gave it to me yesterday. We're going together. Almost two weeks now." She looked up at me. "I didn't think you'd care. You never seemed to be interested in him one bit, and he's been so sweet to me . . ."

"No, I think it's wonderful," I said. "Really." Angie and Stan Dudek! When just three weeks ago she'd been crazy for Steve Bajovinas, from Holy Cross parish. What else had changed I didn't know about?

"I know it's awfully fast, but we're thinking about getting married." Angie let the cross fall, stroked it against her skin. "Stan's pop can get him a good place on the beef kill. Skinner would be best, but they'd probably make him start lower, you know, a shackler or a driver . . ."

Tossing around the words like she knew what they meant. Angie'd never been in a packinghouse in her life. I dropped my coat and pocketbook on the pile of clothes and wandered to the window.

"So what happened?" Angie asked. "Your ma find out about the dance hall?"

I brushed aside the window curtain, although I knew the view outside as well as my own: the narrow alley, the gray two-flat next door. Now that I was here, I didn't know how to start. We'd shared all our secrets in this room. But never anything like this.

"I've got this customer . . . ," I began.

"'Customer'?" Angie interrupted. "That doesn't sound very romantic."

You have no idea. "Sometimes the cus— . . . the men, you know, they take us out. After the hall closes."

"Really?" Sharp with sudden interest. "Where? Have you been to the Aragon?"

The Aragon wasn't even open at two in the morning, didn't she know that? "No, just clubs. And restaurants. So I was out with this man, and he . . . well, he propositioned me."

"Are you in love with him?"

"No!"

"Is he in love with you?"

I hesitated. Tom, in love with me? The way he watched me all the time, the way he got jealous . . . I didn't know what to call it, but I didn't think it was love. If it was, it sure wasn't any kind I wanted.

Angie had flopped onto her stomach and was digging through a stack of magazines by the side of her bed. She sat up with a copy of *Love Fiction Monthly* in her hand.

"Where is that . . . oh. Here." She sat up straight, one leg tucked under her, and began to read. *"In these modern days, any girl who spends time with a fellow is sure to be asked a certain question—but not the one she hopes for! The answer to this particular question, of course, is No . . ."*

"Angie, that's not . . ."

"No, wait, listen: *Pretending not to understand what he means often does the trick . . ."*

Not understand what he meant? After a prostitute laughed at me in the hotel, after Tom yelled those horrible words at me? "Angie—"

". . . especially when accompanied by a show of innocent confusion."

Not to mention a compact hurled out the window of a taxicab. I remembered the way he'd ducked—like I'd fired a gun at him, for Pete's sake!—and my mouth twitched up at the corners. I felt a twinge of satisfaction, like a tiny flame licking across dank coal.

"*Just because a girl gets a proposition now doesn't mean she won't get a proposal later—maybe from the very same fellow, if she plays her cards right!*"

Angie dropped the magazine to her lap, her expression triumphant.

"Oh, for goodness' sake, Angie. He's married!"

"*Married?*"

The song on the radio ended, and in the fade of music the word *married* rang out like a church bell. Angie leaped up and switched stations. A commercial for Lux soap boomed.

"You didn't say he was *married,*" she hissed at me.

"Yeah, well, you didn't let me finish. But listen, it's not just that." I sank down next to her and covered my face with my hands. Then dropped them to my lap. Hiding wouldn't help. "He says . . . he says I have to. He says I owe him. Because I borrowed money from him and spent it and now I can't pay him back." It sounded even worse, out loud.

Angie didn't say anything. I was afraid to look at her. Then: "How much money?"

"Fifty-three dollars." At her gasp, I shut my eyes. I remembered sweet-and-sour pork soaking through Clara's gown, sticky against my skin. How stunned I'd been, holding a ten-dollar bill for the first time in my life. How fast I'd gotten used to it.

"Fifty-three . . . Mother Mary on a shingle, Ruby, how could you?"

"I had to! You don't understand, you don't have to worry about . . . about coal. Or food." I pushed away the thought of my locker at the Starlight. "Anyway, compared to some of these other girls . . ." I told her about Yvonne's fish paying her rent. About Nora's bump and tickle. Angie listened, not saying a word, her eyes wide. When I described the scams Yvonne and some of the other girls pulled, promising to do things for money, then scramming with the dough before the chumps wised up, she raised her hands like a wall.

"Stop," she said. "Don't tell me any more." She stood up and crossed to the mirror and began undoing her pin curls.

"But see, borrowing money from a fi—a customer— that's practically nothing." I hadn't mentioned Manny, or the black and tans. She didn't need to hear about that. "I mean, I know I shouldn't have. But I did, and he's being awful about it, and now what am I supposed to do?"

"Don't you think you should've thought of that?" She yanked a pin out of her hair and turned around. Loosened curls corkscrewed over her cheek. "You knew those other girls were bad. A married man goes to a place like that and you borrow fifty-three dollars from him, why wouldn't he expect what he expects?"

"You don't understand! I tried to pay him back before, but he—"

She threw her hands in the air. " 'You don't understand, you don't understand!' If I don't understand, then how come you're telling me all this?"

I didn't know anymore. The radio blared "One O'Clock Jump." Funny how even Benny Goodman seemed tame after Lily's. But if I told Angie that, she wouldn't know what I was talking about. Even if I explained about the black and tans, how could she understand swing so new it didn't even have a name, if she'd never heard it? *Love Fiction Monthly* and *True Confessions* and Stan and the Yards—that was all Angie understood.

"Well, it's obvious what you have to do," Angie said. "You have to quit." Her fingers dancing quick and light, one pin after the next. She rolled every scrap of her hair up, and it always took her forever to get out all the pins. "You could go back to your old job. Or anywhere, so long as it's respectable."

Respectable. No more Lily's. Back to jitterbugging with neighborhood boys at Pulaski's drugstore. Back to twelve and a quarter a week, and our gloomy narrow flat, and any chance ever getting us out of the Yards gone straight down the toilet.

"I can't quit," I said.

"You'd rather cheat men out of money? Let them . . ." She jiggled her hands tits-high.

"I told you, I don't do things like that!"

"Lie down with dogs," she said, "get up with fleas."

I made Ma's aggravated noise, her exasperated, growling sigh.

"That place has changed you," Angie said. "Listen to me. You have to quit. Find some nice boy. Stan was just saying the other day you and Hank Majewski—no, listen! He's always been crazy about you, and he's an apprentice mason now. His mother's a dragon, but you could do worse, and—Say, whatever happened with you and Paulie Suelze?"

Paulie. He'd gotten me into this mess, the creep. I didn't even want to hear his name.

"Nothing," I said. "I have to go. Don't tell anyone about this, okay? Pinkie secret, right?"

"Sure, but—Ruby, wait! What are you going to do?"

I picked up my pocketbook and coat from where I'd dropped them on the pile of clothes.

"I don't know," I said.

. . .

It wasn't until I was almost home—dragging my feet, I still didn't see how I was going to face Ma—when it hit me.

Paulie'd gotten me into this mess. Paulie could damn well get me out of it. I wasn't sure how, but I didn't care. Paulie would know what to do about Tom, never mind the details.

But how to find him? I hadn't seen him since my first week at the Starlight, six weeks ago. All I'd heard since then were the rumors Betty passed along. Something about a poolroom—or was it a tavern?—on Fiftieth. Or Forty-ninth. I played it safe and searched both streets, every poolroom between Damen and Racine, a mile in either direction. He wasn't in any of them. Or in the taverns or the saloons or the barbershops. I dodged around women sweeping their sidewalks, little kids playing tag in the streets. Everywhere I went, I asked about him. Most people shrugged. One woman crossed herself. The young men in the poolrooms grinned at each other. "Popular guy, that Paulie," one of them said. The old men glanced at me and muttered things in Polish and went back to drinking their beer.

"If you see him," I said, over and over, "tell him Ruby Jacinski's looking for him."

Almost an entire day wasted, and I was no closer to figuring out what to do about Tom than I had been last night. I went home just long enough to eat dinner. Fought with Ma over sneaking out without telling her, then fought with Betty because she'd had to scrub the kitchen floor by herself, which made her miss the matinee of *Shadow of the Thin Man*. And then Ma jumped on Betty because, after all, where did the eleven cents for the movie come from? From her big sister, that was who, who was working herself half to death keeping this family afloat, and Betty better not forget it even for a second.

I thought the guilt might reach right up my throat and choke me. I grabbed my coat and fled for the Starlight.

It wasn't any easier there. It was Saturday, the hall packed with hundreds of men. I quickstepped and waltzed and Peabody'd like a windup doll. The band could've played "Tiptoe Through the Tulips" a dozen times in a row and Ozzie could've done a back somersault off the bandstand and I wouldn't have noticed. Every half minute, I felt a spidery tickle up the back of my neck. But every time I drummed up the nerve to look around, Tom wasn't there. "I'm the one you're dancing with, over here," one customer complained, the third time I glanced over my shoulder. He didn't tip me. I laughed at something another man said— the tone of his voice sounded like the punch line of a joke— only to realize he'd been telling me about his mother's funeral. No tip there, either.

If only I could be at Lily's! Dancing to wild, stomping music, dancing so hard I couldn't think, so hard all I could feel was my feet flying and my heart banging and my partner's hand pulling on mine—swing in close, whirl out wide, shim sham shimmy, until I was so tired I didn't care anymore about anything.

By the end of the night, Tom hadn't shown his face and I was exhausted. In the Ladies', while everyone else hurried into their street clothes, I dawdled, leaving only after everyone else had gone. Under the glare of lights, the hall seemed like nothing more than a stale-smelling box with a low ceiling and a scuffed, dusty floor. No swirling colored dots, no dark romantic corners. No illusions.

I cashed in my tickets, ignoring the grumbling of the ticket man about dames who had no respect for folks who wanted to call it a night and go home. On the stairs, I found Peggy waiting.

"Will a cab ride do the trick?" she asked. "Or are we gonna need Bennie's?"

"I'm fine," I said, edging past her. I didn't want to talk to Peggy. As far as she knew, I'd paid Tom back two weeks ago. Telling Angie had been painful enough. Peggy would make sarcastic remarks and call me a ninny, and I'd end up feeling a hundred times worse than I already did. "I just have a headache, that's all."

"A headache, huh?" Dogging my steps all the way down. "What's his name, and what's he done?"

I pushed through the door onto the sidewalk. We both clapped our hands to our hats to keep them from being blown off. "Come on," Peggy said. "You spent all night looking like the Headless Horseman was after you. The grapevine says two customers complained to Del about you. Seems like a milkshake and apple pie might do you some good."

The wind stung my eyes, making them tear up. Angie hadn't been any help. Paulie was nowhere to be found. Tomorrow, or the night after or the one after that, Tom would be back.

"Do you promise not to call me a nincompoop?" I said.

"Do you promise to take my advice?" She cocked her head at me. Then looped her arm through mine. "I'll take my chances if you will. Come on, let's get that milkshake."

At Bennie's, as soon as we ordered, Peggy sat back and lit a cigarette. "Spill it," she said.

As it turned out, telling her was easier than telling Angie. First of all, nothing surprised her. "I *knew* it," she said when I told her Tom was married. Second, I didn't have to leave anything out. When I described how I'd spit in his face, she laughed so loud a couple of high school boys across the diner turned to look. "Hey, sister, what's the joke?" one of them called.

"Your hat size," Peggy called back. "Well, go on," she said to me. "Then what?"

I told her the rest. Tom saying we were coming back to finish things. Threatening to get me fired if I didn't go with him at the hotel. I expected her to laugh at my throwing the compact. But she'd gone suddenly broody, her hazel eyes squinty at the corners.

"So this creep said he'd go to Del?" Peggy said. "And tell him what, exactly?"

"That he saw you and me leaving with Manny and Alonso and . . . you know. He'll probably tell Del I do it with all the customers." I pushed my milkshake away, my stomach suddenly sour. "It's what he thinks," I said bitterly.

Peggy tapped her cigarette into the ashtray. "No he doesn't. He wants to think it, because then he can tell himself he's right." Delicately, she pinched a speck of tobacco off the tip of her tongue. "I suppose you can't pay him back."

"Not a chance." Then, with sudden hope, "Not unless . . ."

She laughed one of her short, dry laughs. "Believe me, kid, if I had the cash I'd donate. But I've never been able to keep that much in one place in my life. I hate to say it"—she shook her head—"but you got yourself good and caught."

I'd had another spoonful of milkshake; at that, I put down the spoon, not caring it was sticky. "What do you mean, 'caught'?"

"I mean either you get canned, or you go through with it."

"Go through with *what*?"

"Didn't we just have this conversation? Or did your elevator skip a floor on the way up?" She leaned forward, tapping her temple with a forefinger. "Tom, remember? The hotel?"

I stared at her. "Are you crazy? You're supposed to tell me how to get out of this!"

"I did tell you how to get out of it. Or have you forgotten that already, too?"

"I *tried* to pay him back, he wouldn't—"

"All right, all right, keep your voice down. It doesn't matter now anyway. That skunk could make up any kind of story to Del, and you'd be out like that." She snapped her fingers. "And not just the Starlight, either. Don't you know if a girl gets fired for being loose with the customers, she's done? Not a dance hall in this city will hire her." She tamped out her cigarette, the brooding look heavy again around her eyes. "And I'll tell you what else. If that weasel gets real creative, he'll make up stories about me, too. I don't know about you, but I'm not going back to the goddamn box factory for a goddamn eleven bucks a week."

"I could quit," I said.

"Yeah. You could." Blunt as a baseball bat.

Quit or get fired. I knew what lay down those paths, and I didn't like it. But to go through with it . . . looking down that road was like peering into gray fog. Six weeks ago I'd been a girl in pink dotted swiss. Now I was a different one, in silk and sequins. After the hotel with Tom, who would I be?

I didn't know who. I knew what, though. The skinny blonde on the sidewalk in front of Lily's. The woman bumping into me at the hotel. Their faces hard and painted as wood.

"My mother—," I began. And then I stopped because I'd begun to cry. *How many times have I told you, you have to be careful!*

"Hey." Peggy reached across the table and took my hand. "Hey, it's not so bad. Really."

I yanked my hand away. "Yvonne has all those fish buying everything for her and paying her rent and nobody's running to Del about her! Nora, either, or Gabby or you or any of them! How come I'm the one who gets caught, huh? How come?"

"I'll thank you not to lump me in with those piranhas. And if you want to know why not, it's because their fish get something for their money and what they get is plenty more than a fox-trot. Your problem is, you tried having it both ways. It won't wash."

"But you—"

"I pay my own rent. I pick my fish careful, and I'm careful what I take. This business is a slippery sidewalk, kid. Too easy to slide right into the gutter, and too many people happy to give you the first shove."

She searched through her pocketbook, came out with a handkerchief. I wiped my eyes, my cheeks. A ghost of rouge came away on the white linen. I'd have to wash my face again at home. Illusion, Del said. Lies.

"This isn't how I expected it to be," I whispered.

Peggy sighed. "Look, I know it's not the white dress and veil. But I'll let you in on a secret." She leaned forward, matched my whisper with her own. "It's never how anyone thinks it'll be. Not even the girls who save it for the ring and the little house in Archer Heights. Maybe especially not them." She patted my hand and sat back. "Finish drying your eyes and let's go, huh? Like the lady said, tomorrow's another day."

In the cab, before she got out, she said, "You know, some girls are kind of glad to get it over with. Saves them having to worry about it. If you decide . . . well, anyway, I'll take you out for a drink, after. If you want."

Thank you hardly seemed like the right thing to say. So I kept my mouth shut.

I lay awake a second night. I knew the score, but . . . maybe Paulie would come tap on the window. Say, *Hey, Ruby. I heard you were looking for me.* I waited for him, listening, thinking, maybe Peggy's right. Maybe it's not so bad. Then I'd remember that fleabag of a hotel, and Tom touching me, and I felt sick to my bones, and I knew she was as wrong as she could be.

If only it had been Paulie, not Tom . . . Of course I'd still say no. Wouldn't I? But I wouldn't feel like his hands were spiders crawling on me. I wouldn't feel like jumping out the window to get away from him.

Every five minutes, I made up my mind to quit the Starlight. Every five minutes and thirty seconds, I changed my mind back.

It shouldn't have been so hard. St. Lucia had let her eyes be gouged out rather than be forced into sin. St. Agatha had let her breasts be sliced off. Both of them walking around afterward with their cut parts on golden plates. What was bean soup, compared to that?

I prayed to Lucia and Agatha for strength. It didn't help. Maybe I was too bad of a girl already.

Paulie never came.

ELEVEN

As soon as Ma and Betty and I came out of Mass, I saw him. Across the street from Sacred Heart Church, leaning against a telephone pole. The wind bitter cold, but he wasn't wearing a hat. Dark blond hair, jug ears. Just standing there, one knee raised with the foot flat against the pole, reading a paper.

Betty saw him, too. I could tell from the sudden stiffness in her walk, the way she pushed her shoulders back.

After we'd walked another half block, I said, "Ma, I need to run to the candy store."

"I'll go with you!" Betty said.

"No, you won't. Take Ma's arm. I'll be right home!"

Paulie was gone. I stood on the corner, peering up and down the street.

"I heard you were looking for me," he said behind me. I spun around, my heart leaping like a dog for a biscuit.

He wore a heavy red plaid wool coat, a blue muffler. His paper tucked under one elbow. In the daylight his eyebrows seemed even paler, like ghosts of eyebrows. He had a way of looking out from under them, without raising his head. I smiled at him. He didn't smile back.

Last night, when I'd hoped he'd appear under my window, I'd pictured him grinning up at me. I'd rehearsed a dozen things to say. But his gray eyes glanced past my shoulder, like he was already thinking ahead to whatever came after me, and my breath skimmed high in my throat from nerves. I couldn't remember anything.

"So, what'd you want?" he said.

"Just . . . to see you," I answered.

"Yeah, well, you're seeing me," he said. "You and everyone in your parish. Come on, let's get out of here." He led me into an alley that ran between two rows of flats. "Scram," he told a nest of boys playing craps. They did, disappearing behind the fences and sheds of the back lots. One kid lingered by a fence post, watching us. Paulie feinted at him, and the kid vanished.

"Thank you for the dress," I blurted out.

The boys had grabbed up their money before they ran, but a penny glinted on the pavement. Paulie picked it up, flipped it high, and caught it. "That why you decided to make me a laughingstock in every poolroom in the Yards? To say thanks?" He shot a look at me sideways. "That's all I been hearing since yesterday. Some little girl running around yelling my name. You know how dumb that makes me look?"

Little girl? Was that a little girl's gown he'd given me? I opened my mouth to ask, but before I got a word out, he said, "Don't come running after me like that. That's all I got to say." He slipped the penny into his trouser pocket and walked away.

He was leaving. While I stood here like an idiot.

"You didn't come here just to tell me that!" I yelled after him. Part of me—*squirt, baby*—expected him to keep walking. But he *had* given me that gown, not just any gown but one that made the men at the Starlight head for me like bees to a flower, and a bigger part of me knew he'd seen the dark, smoky blue and imagined me in it, and that's why he'd come here when he heard I was looking for him.

He kept walking, two more steps. Another and he'd be on the street.

He turned around.

I felt a blaze of triumph, as scorching and quick as a blush. But I didn't grin. I didn't smirk. He was coming back now, his head turned a little so that he was looking at me from the narrow corners of his eyes, and I tipped my chin up and watched him and I didn't say anything.

He stopped a few feet from me. "All right, since you know so much," he said, "why *did* I come here?"

"Because you like me," I said, as if it was the most obvious thing in the world.

His pale eyebrows lifted. "Oh, that's so, huh? And what makes you think that?"

I didn't say anything. He took two more steps. One more and we'd practically be touching.

"The dress is beautiful," I said.

His gaze fell down the length of me. He nodded. "Yeah," he said, "I thought it would look good on you."

I let myself smile then. He did, too, slowly, like a fanned ember warming to life. His eyes roaming over my face. The flecks of color, deep in the gray, just the same as I remembered.

He took the last step.

Both arms around me. I let him pull me close. His gaze flicked from my mouth to the top of my head and back again. He pushed a curl of my hair behind my shoulder, and then he kissed me. Longer and deeper than the first time, the night we'd met. His hands moved slow, hard, across my back. I wound my arms behind his neck, ran my fingers up through his hair. Against the dark of my closed eyes, yellow lights danced.

A sudden hooting made my eyes fly open. A few feet away, on the sidewalk, the boys he'd chased away leaped around, scratching their sides like monkeys. Paulie bent down and grabbed a stone and the boys took off running. He winged the stone at them. One of them yelped.

"Punks," Paulie muttered. He turned me so my back was against a rough wood fence. I felt a moment's panic; it felt too much like Tom, the other night. Trapped. But Paulie bent down and kissed me again and when I tasted him, cigarettes and earth, I forgot Tom. Paulie unbuttoned the top buttons of my coat.

"I do like you," he murmured. "You like me?"

I smiled again. "When you're nice I do." I felt dizzy with how beautiful he was. His hand slipped inside my coat, drifted over my left breast, cupped underneath. I should be mad. I should tell him to stop. Only I didn't want him to.

His voice murmured on, buzzing in my ear. "You let all the nice fellows do this?"

I shoved him hard, making him stagger back half a step. Then I stormed past him, wrapping my coat tight.

Jerk, what'd he have to go and ruin it for? In that second all of it had come pouring back, Tom, the hotel, the whole stupid mess. "Hey!" he yelled. He dodged in front of me, blocked my way. "What are you getting mad for? I ain't some dumb joe, I know what racket you're in."

"At least I'm not a low-down thief!"

"Didn't stop you from wearing that dress, did it?"

"I take it back. I don't like you. I hate you. If I'm in a racket, it's your fault, and it's your fault the trouble I'm in!" I tried ducking past him, but Paulie caught me around the waist.

"Wait a minute. Hold on. What trouble?"

"Forget it. Let me go!" I hauled my fist back, but he grabbed it.

"You hit me again," he said, "you'll wish you hadn't. I didn't think you'd chased me all around the Yards just to say thanks for some lousy dress. What is it?"

I told him. When I was done, he reached into his back pocket and pulled out his wallet. Three twenties, counted, folded, and on top of them a matchbook he dug out of his coat. He held the money and the matchbook out to me. I didn't take them.

"I ain't one of your fish," he said. "You think I have to pay girls to like me?"

I stared at the money. Shook my head.

"Look, it's a gift. Like the dress. You took that, right?"

He had a point. But still . . . "Why?" I asked.

"You just told me, didn't you? I guess I like you." He smiled his rumpled smile. "No strings," he said. "I swear."

I took the money. His fingers were warm, just like they had been the first time we'd met. *Ed's Garage,* the matchbook said on the cover, in plain black letters, and underneath, a phone number. "You need me again," he said, "don't go shouting my name all over. Call there and leave a message. They'll make sure I get it."

. . .

Tom didn't come to the Starlight that night, either. Having Sunday dinner with his wife and kiddies, no doubt. Monday was my night off. When he didn't show up Tuesday, I thought maybe I was home free. But I figured I'd give it another week. If he hadn't come by then, I'd return Paulie's sixty dollars. I was through spending money that didn't belong to me, on things it wasn't intended to buy. Peggy told me I was being commendable.

When we stepped out of the Starlight Tuesday night, though, there Tom was, waiting for me at the bottom of the stairs.

"I've got a cab waiting." He looked at Peggy, half a step behind me. "Tell your friend to get lost."

"Why, hello, Tom," I said. "I'm doing swell, how nice of you to ask."

That shamed him a little. He shifted his feet and licked his lips. "Yeah, well," he said. He jerked his head toward the street. "Let's go."

When you offer to give something to someone, they don't think fast enough to refuse. I held out my hand and Tom, frowning, reached out his. I slapped Paulie's money into his open palm. He blinked, his mouth hanging open, like I'd just forked over a horse turd.

"What the hell is this?" he said.

"What does it look like?"

He fanned the bills in his fingers. "This doesn't get you off the hook. What about all those dinners I bought you? What about all that cab fare? You gonna pay all that back, too?"

"She doesn't owe you for that and you know it," Peggy said. She'd stuck behind me like a barnacle on a boat; that was our plan. "You loaned her cash and she paid you back. So scram."

"I don't take marching orders from whores," Tom said.

"Good thing we're not, then," I said.

"You'll take them from O'Malley," Peggy chimed in. Shoulder to shoulder with me, cool as butter out of the icebox. "O'Malley doesn't like customers who bother the girls."

Tom licked his lips again. "I'll go to your boss," he said. Less sure, but not ready to give up yet. "I'll tell him you're both whores. I'll tell him the hotel was your idea. I'll tell him I've seen you there with dirty flips."

"You go to my boss," I said, "I'll go to your wife."

That surprised him. Then he smirked. "As if you—"

"Mrs. Thomas Eames," I said. "STEwart-3358."

It was hard to tell, under the streetlight, but I thought he went pale. "You bitch," he said. His tone a mix of mad and uncertain. He settled on mad. "You stinking *bitch*." He took a step toward us, and Peggy and I scuttled backward to the door. I opened it, hollered, "O'Malley!" Tom stopped.

"You keep quiet, we keep quiet," I said. "You make up a bunch of lies about us . . ." I paused—let him stew, just for a second. ". . . then we tell the truth about you."

I sounded tough. Inside, I was shaking. We were

bluffing about O'Malley; it was his night off. We'd had Underwood, a string bean of a retired cop who'd skedaddled as soon as the band stopped playing. If Tom decided to get rough . . .

He shoved the money in his pocket. That was when I knew it was over.

"Goddamn whores," he said. He spit on the sidewalk in front of our feet. When he stalked away, I yelled after him, "STEwart-3358! Hear that, Tom? Don't ever come back!" When he got in his cab and slammed the door, I felt like I could Lindy Hop across Lake Michigan. I felt like I could grab the moon right down out of the sky. Paulie may have given me the money, but I'd put in the fix, and I'd won.

"Now that we got you out of this jam," Peggy said, "try to keep your nose clean, huh?"

I whooped and gave her a lip-smack on the cheek so loud she jumped and rubbed the spot, laughing. "You got it, sister," I said.

With Tom went all my worries. We had coal, we had meat, and now that the back rent was paid off—our last debt—we were even getting milk delivered again, for Betty to pour over her Rice Krispies and all of us to stir into our coffee. The lines in Ma's face didn't go away, but they eased some. I was spending a lot more time with Ma now than Betty. Between her school and my work, practically the only time I saw my little sister was when she was asleep. I missed her, and worse, I felt guilty. I paraded in satin and silk every night, going to clubs, while she was stuck in worn wool skirts and cotton blouses, working math problems in the circle of light on the kitchen table.

I couldn't buy her a new wardrobe—but I did buy her first pair of nylons. When she saw them, she squealed so loud Ma almost came in our room, afraid one of us had hurt ourselves. I had to run out and tell her Betty had only seen a spider. "I better go kill it," I said, then went back to show Betty how to unroll the seams nice and straight up the backs of her legs.

Best of all, though: the trouble with Tom threw me straight into Paulie's arms.

He called for me at Hirsch's candy store. Didn't leave his name, just said to call Ed's Garage. When I got him on the phone, he said, "Hey, squirt. Want to go to the movies?"

The next day, and every day for the rest of that week, we met at Peoples Theater. Peoples was the fanciest movie house in the neighborhood, as fancy as any uptown in the Loop. Me and my friends never went there much—the Olympia was smaller and closer—but as a place to meet Paulie it was perfect: so enormous and so crowded, even during the day, I doubted anyone I knew would spot me. Three afternoons in a row, I waited for him under the huge scalloped awning. Inside, Paulie bought us Hershey's bars or Old Nicks and sodas. Then, our hands full, we fumbled past people's knees to empty seats in the last few rows, far from the housewives and the little kids. We always arrived in the middle of *Tarzan's Secret Treasure*. It didn't matter. We didn't watch. All through the movie we kissed like fiends, Paulie's hands sliding under my blouse, Johnny Weissmuller and Maureen O'Sullivan ten feet high on the screen, the screeching of Cheetah the chimp a beautiful nonsense noise in my ears. After the credits rolled, we sat back and ate and watched the cartoon and the newsreel. We left before the second feature started, so that I could get home and help Ma make dinner before I left for work.

I loved Paulie. I knew because when I kissed him, the world disappeared. All that was left was him. His warm hard hands and his lips and his tongue. I wanted to climb inside him. Every time he left and I watched him go I felt raw, as if part of me had been cut away and the rest of me left open. I'd never felt that with anyone before, not Tom or Manny, not any of the boys I'd kissed in school. The way he looked at me sometimes, I thought I made him feel the same way: staring like he was trying to memorize every bit of me, the light from the movie flickering over his face, staring like he would devour me if he could.

Surely only love could do that.

Before Paulie, I'd liked spending time with Ma every day, just the two of us, talking while we worked, gossiping about the neighbors, sipping coffee at the kitchen table when the chores were done. She told stories I'd never heard before, about when we were little, before Pop died. Or from even further before, how they met and fell in love. The scandal of a boy with a Polish name marrying a girl with an Irish name. The uproar in the families, the tears and threats from all my grandparents.

Now the mornings at home dragged, because they were time away from Paulie. In order to get away, I made up stories to tell Ma, most of them about Peggy deGroot. Not the real Peggy. This Peggy was a telephone operator. She lived in Canaryville, the Irish neighborhood next to us, and we rode the el back and forth to work together. I went to the movies with Peggy or met her for lunch at a hamburger joint. Other times, we went shopping. Ma liked her. "I'm so glad you've made a nice friend," she said. "I know you were fond of Angela Wachowski, but really, Ruby, she always was a little wild for my comfort."

"I know," I said, and I told Ma how Peggy deGroot had helped wallpaper the bathroom in her grandma's flat.

I was scared Paulie wouldn't like me going out after hours, or going with Filipinos. But he didn't care. It's a racket, he said, and if you were going to make it in a racket, you had to go in the whole way. "A girl with your looks and pep, I bet you take the chumps to the cleaners," he said. I didn't like when he said that; it reminded me too much of Yvonne and Gabby and their scams. But it was just the way he put things, he didn't mean anything by it.

In fact, I was getting antsy to get back to Lily's. I hadn't been there in over a week, not since before the mess with Tom. Manny's schedule had changed; Pullman had put him on some long runs, and I wasn't sure when he'd be back.

"You'd love it," I told Paulie. "You've never seen Lindy Hopping like they do it there. Why don't you pick me up at the Starlight some night and take me?"

"Go with your fish, I don't care," he said. "But me, sit in the same room with a bunch of dumb shines? Not on your life."

It was like I'd given him a flower and he'd stepped on it. Lily, a dumb shine? The way she'd built her place up— still a hole in the wall, sure, but so popular now she'd had to get twice as many tables and three more waiters. And Ozzie and the band, they were cooking so hot that white musicians from the white clubs had started coming to hear them play. The doorman razzed them, asking if they'd come for more lessons.

I tried explaining all this, but Paulie only said, "Pipe down, the newsreel's on." As if I wanted to look at stupid Hitler. He had nothing to do with us, and it was all the way across the world, so who cared? I ate my Old Nick and breathed the delicious scents of chocolate and Paulie. I'd get him to Lily's somehow. It'd just take some work. He'd love it, once he was there. Once I decided that, everything felt all right again.

That night, my head was so full of Paulie I couldn't bear to think about anything else. The noise and chatter of the hall wore on my nerves so that by the break, I ached for quiet.

Silence this time from the little dark room, except for the scratching of a pen on paper. I stuck my head around the door. Ozzie leaned on the windowsill, in the rectangle of streetlight, scribbling notes.

"Can I come in?" I asked.

Ozzie jumped so hard his fountain pen left an ink blotch on the paper. He muttered under his breath and waved the paper to dry it. "You know, you can go anywhere you want in this place," he said, his voice tight with irritation. "Why you gotta come here?"

"I thought maybe I could listen. Like before."

"You can hear it at Lily's. We've been rehearsing; we'll play it tonight. You gonna be there?"

I felt suddenly shy. I wondered if he thought I was a good dancer. The Negro girls didn't think much of me, I knew. They always tried to steal Manny away: *Say, daddy-o, aren't you ready yet for a real rug-cutter?* Like I wasn't standing right there.

Girls—colored and white—asked Ozzie to dance, too, whenever he wasn't playing. He always smiled and shook his head no, quiet, his gaze slipping to wherever Ophelia, the slim, freckle-chested singer, was. The other musicians razzed Ophelia as if she was their little sister. Called her "Coatrack" and "Broomstick," that sort of thing. But not Ozzie. When they started in on her, he'd frown and fidget, looking half-embarrassed and half-exasperated, like he was thinking, *Come on, girl, zing 'em back already.* Which she should have. But she sang her heart out and ignored them all, so, of course, the other fellows never let up on her for a minute.

Ozzie pointed his fountain pen at the doorway. "Please. Miss."

"My name's Ruby," I said.

Ozzie acted like I hadn't spoken. The pen pointing like an arrow. I sighed and flounced back around the door. "All I wanted to do was listen," I said, stomping into the hall. "If this is how you treat girls, no wonder Ophelia won't give you the time of day."

Through the open doorway, I heard him say, "What?"

"Ophelia," I repeated, a little louder. "The singer, the one you're always making sheep's eyes at?"

I heard his chair scrape back, heard the scuff of shoes on the bare floor. Walking a tight circle, I guessed. Stopped with one hand on his hip, the other holding his trumpet. I'd seen him do that on the bandstand, once, when he'd gotten good and fed up with Hamp's direction. I was pretty sure Ozzie'd gotten in trouble for it.

"What would you know about colored girls?" His voice suspicious—but underneath, a tiny, little hope.

I tipped my head back, laughed silently in the dark.

Then said, "I know one particular colored girl doesn't think much of musicians."

For half a minute, he didn't say anything. Didn't move, as far as I could tell. Then, slow, the door swung open wider. When I went inside, he was sitting by the windowsill again, jotting more notes, the trumpet an upright glimmer on the floor by his chair. He didn't look up. But he pulled a cigarette pack and a matchbook out of his shirt pocket and tossed them onto a broken chair between us. I lit one of the matches, found another chair, and set it by the wall behind the door, so that if anyone came in, they wouldn't see me. Then I shook a cigarette out of the pack, tore a second match out of the book, and sat down.

· · ·

Later that night, Manny and Alonso showed up. They clocked me and Peggy out early. Gonna do the rounds, they said.

We hit the Hoot Owl Café first. The Hoot Owl was a black and tan, but unlike Lily's, the customers were mostly white, and it seated a few hundred people, not just a few dozen. It wasn't on any dark side street, either, but on South Garfield in Bronzeville, where the neon signs of the after-hours clubs lit the air, and even at three in the morning, people of all colors jammed the sidewalks. We ate chop suey and hamburgers, listened to the swing band cook, and sipped our drinks: rum and Cokes for me, gin fizzes for Peggy, shots and bumps—whiskeys, with beer chasers—for the fellows.

From the Hoot Owl we went to the Jelly Roll, and from there to the Palm, before finally we ended up at

Lily's. By then, all I knew was I was having a damn good time. Paulie still on my mind, of course, but farther back, tucked somewhere behind the rum and jazz and laughing crowds. Lily's was jammed; a waiter had to squeeze another table next to the bandstand for us. Ozzie was there, his shirt already soaked down the back, trumpet growling. I hoped they hadn't played his new song yet. He'd told me the name—"Candy Apple"—but he didn't have to say who he'd written it for. Ophelia wore a few different dresses onstage, and all of them were red.

We'd barely sat down when an excited sway ran through the crowd. I craned my neck, but I couldn't see anything. "What is it?" I shouted over the music. "What's happening?"

"Horace Washington just came in!" a fellow at the next table shouted back, just as I glimpsed a colored couple strolling behind Lily and a waiter hoisting another table overhead. The man was big, not tall, but wide across. His coat was thrown over his shoulders; underneath, he wore the sharpest pinstripe suit I'd ever seen on anyone, black, Oriental, or white. People shuffled and scooted aside, making room. Calling out hellos. The man nodded, slapped shoulders, tipped his hat. The woman with him wore a full-length mink coat, and she nodded around, too, smiling.

Alonso leaned to the middle of the table; we all leaned in with him to hear what he was saying. "That's him, all right. I've seen him a couple of times before, at the Rhumboogie."

"All I see is a colored man in a nice suit," Peggy said.

"All the black and tans you've been to, you've never

heard of Horace Washington?" Manny said. "He's the biggest policy king in Chicago. You know policy, don't you?"

Sure we did. Policy was Negro gambling. Pick three numbers. If they came up lucky, the player might win a few dollars. Or a few hundred. One night at Lily's, a fellow had come in wearing a brand-new zoot suit with a diamond tie pin. Bought rounds for everyone in the place, tipped every member of the band ten bucks each and fifty for Lily. Word around the club was, his numbers had hit for almost a thousand.

"The policy kings own the games," Alonso explained. "A nickel a bet, hell, everybody in Bronzeville plays. The kings pay off the winners. Pay off the cops. Keep the rest. Thousands and thousands of dollars, every day. The kings are worth millions."

"Millions!" I popped up in my chair, trying to get another glimpse. But the couple had sat down; with the dancers in the way, and the cigarette haze, I couldn't see. Manny flipped a coin onto the table. A buffalo nickel.

"A million bucks built on that," he said. "Hard to imagine, huh?"

Not for me. Everything I ate these days, everything I wore, came from nickels. Nickels added up just fine. I imagined stacks of them, shining soft gray, reaching up to the sky.

"If he's such a big shot, then what's he doing *here*?" Peggy wanted to know.

Before Alonso could answer, the band swung into "Candy Apple." When Ozzie's solo came, he stood up—he always stood for his solos—bobbing and swaying as though the notes rose from deep inside, rattling him as they came through. Eyes closed, his face tense as a fist and then suddenly lifting, as if the music asked some question he was half-afraid to hear the answer to. I snapped and shimmied with Manny, my feet flying, feeling strangely jealous. To have someone make something so beautiful, out of his head, just for you . . . Ophelia better appreciate it.

"But don't make a big deal out of telling her," I'd advised. Thinking of Paulie, and the blue silk dress. "Drop it casual, then scram. Let her stew a little. Oh, and," I said, heating up, "the next time those boneheads in the band start calling her Broomstick, tell 'em to knock it off. Make sure she hears you, too."

"They only pick on her because she's a kid," Ozzie said. "That's just musicians, it doesn't mean anything. Hell, I've gotten crap every place I've ever played."

"You're a boy. She's the only girl up there and she's got eight fellows calling her Mop Handle—"

"*I* don't!"

"—and you wonder why she doesn't give two hoots for the whole pack of you. You tell 'em to knock it off. You've at least told her she's pretty, haven't you?"

Ozzie picked up his trumpet, fingered the keys. Bent back over his papers.

"You haven't said one word to her," I accused. Sudden commotion at the far end of the hall, girls' voices swooping and diving. Break almost over. I stood up and stubbed out my cigarette in the ashtray. "Well," I'd told him, "I'd start with hello."

I didn't know what time it was when we finally left

Lily's. Or how many rum and Cokes I'd had. Peggy and I staggered up the stairs to the sidewalk, screeching laughter and hanging on to each other, Manny and Alonso on either side of us to keep us from falling.

I had the cab let me off at the usual spot. Two blocks away from our flat, so nobody on our street would see me get out of a taxi when I was supposed to be coming home by the el. Walking, I could barely feel my feet. I seemed to be floating, almost, held to Earth only by the pocketbook over my shoulder. Once home, I noticed the walls were swaying. Careful not to hit them, don't wake anybody—careful past Ma's room—the floor rising in waves under my feet, don't look—my room, the door open, like always, to get the last bit of warmth from the coal stove. Just as I stepped inside, the floor tipped. I pitched sideways. I put my hand out, to catch myself, but the wall seemed to jump backward. I heard a crash, and then someone gasping.

"Ruby?" Betty whispered. "Is that you, what happened?"

"Shh. Don't wake Ma. Go to sleep." All I had to do was find the bed and get in. I moved my feet, but I didn't seem to be going anywhere.

"You're *drunk*!" Thrilled or outraged, I couldn't tell. I started laughing. As if I could be drunk. I'd just been jitterbugging with the best hoofer in Chicago. I'd showed them a thing or two, those colored girls who laughed at me behind their hands. I almost said that. Then I remembered: "I was at work," I said.

"You smell like a tavern." Betty's voice bounding somewhere above me. I wished she would hold still; I couldn't see her, and trying to figure out where she was

was making me dizzy. "You were out with Paulie, weren't you? Did Paulie get you drunk?"

"Stop saying that word, I—" A sudden glare blinded me. It was as if someone had taken the sun and hung it directly over my face. I moaned and raised my arm over my eyes. Still too bright. I turned my head. Not two inches from my nose were Ma's slippers.

"Ruby! What on earth are you doing on the floor like that? Get up!"

"She's drunk," Betty said.

I raised my head. It seemed like I had to raise it a long time. Not sun, I realized. Lightbulb. Hanging overhead. I was on my back. The light dimmed and Ma's face hovered over me.

Sweet Ma. I smiled at her. "Hi, Ma," I said. She must be kneeling over me. Ma didn't kneel well. Even in church, she mostly sort of sat forward on the edge of the seat. Hands clasped on the back of the pew in front of her. "Bad Ma," I said. "Don't kneel."

She grabbed my arm and shook me. She couldn't shake hard but my hand flopped as if all the bones had gone out of it. "Where have you been?" She leaned close, peering. "What is all that makeup doing on your face?"

No. No makeup. I'd washed my face. Hadn't I? Better wash it now . . . I tried to push myself up, but the floor bucked again.

"Put her in bed," Ma said.

"With *me*?"

"You can go in my bed. It's almost five, I might as well stay up."

Bed. Like the floor but softer. I scootched to the warm spot where Betty had been. Ma was upset. Ma thought . . . I didn't know what Ma thought. Ma mustn't think anything. I was a telephone operator.

"Ma?" I said. No answer. I called louder. "Mama?"

"What is it?"

I couldn't see her. She'd turned out the light. "I went to a party," I said to the dark. "At work. They had a party . . ." Were there different kinds of parties? It seemed like there ought to be, but I couldn't think of any. ". . . they had a party, and . . ."

"We'll discuss it in the morning." Her tone cold and hard as iron. I hadn't heard her iron voice in a long time. Not since the money I brought home started paying all the bills.

There'd been a party . . . I'd tell her in the morning. Then I'd go see Paulie at the matinee, Paulie who I loved . . .

"RUBY!"

I jerked awake. Light shot like knives into my skull. Daylight. I groaned and pressed my hand to my forehead. Rum. Lily's. Ma had seen me come home . . .

"RUBY!"

I winced. I was going to beat Betty black with the nearest hard thing I could find. As soon as I could find my feet. As soon as the daylight stopped driving spikes into my head.

"Close the curtains," I said. I thought I said. Maybe I didn't say it out loud, because Betty's voice kept hammering, hammering.

"Get up! Right now, come on, get up!" Panicking. Betty was panicking. I sat up. Pressing the heel of one hand into an eye socket.

"Is it Ma?" It must be. I'd upset her, and now she was

sick. I pushed myself to my feet and teetered forward and grabbed Betty by the shoulders. More to keep from falling than to make her talk, but from her wild-eyed look, she didn't know that. *"Is something the matter with Ma?"*

She shook her head. "The Japs," she said. "It's the Japs. They're bombing someplace called Pearl Harbor."

TWELVE

We crowded into Mr. Maczarek's parlor. We had our own radio, but we could hear his through the open door of his flat, and for some reason it felt better for us all to be in one room. When we came in, he was leaning out his front window in his undershirt, the wattles under his chin flapping, not caring about the cold, talking to someone in the street. "The Japanese, that's who! The radio says it's still going on. Yes, as we speak!" He saw us and pushed a chair close to the radio for Ma, then went back to the window. It was sunny outside, and I had to duck my head away from the light; after a second, the stabbing in my head lessened to a throb, and then I could stand it.

I never listened to news programs. Why be bored by men yapping about President Roosevelt and Hitler, when *The Romance of Helen Trent* or *The Guiding Light* were on? Now, though, words jumped out and I grabbed at them. *Attack. Counterattack. Oahu. Nomura. Cast the die.* Excitement rippling through the voices like electricity. After a while, the words became harder to follow: *diplomatic ties, naval blockade, president's authority, meetings of the secretaries.* Ma sat unmoving, as pale as marble, the lace she wore to Mass pinned to her smooth hair. Betty perched on the arm of her chair. Both in their good dresses and shoes. It must be close to time for church . . . no, surely not, Ma would never have let me sleep so late. I looked around Mr. Maczarek's parlor for a clock but didn't see one. I shifted my feet. They ached almost as badly as my head. My mouth tasted rotting sour, like the milk Betty had left out of the icebox last summer. From the sidewalk, Mr. Schenker's voice boomed into the flat; Mr. Maczarek shouted back. Hitler and Japs and Hawaii. I tucked my chin and pressed my hands over my ears.

"Hush! Hush!" Ma said. Mr. Maczarek popped his head inside to listen, then waved out the window: *pipe down.* Silence. I let my hands fall to my sides.

From the radio, a faint male voice. . . . *hello NBC . . . KGU in Honolulu . . .* Mr. Maczarek twisted the volume knob higher. . . . *battle has been going on nearly three hours . . . it is no joke . . . it is a real war.* Then a woman's voice, clear and loud. *This is the telephone company . . . emergency call . . .* More static. The regular announcer: *One moment please.* Mr. Maczarek frowned at me, as if I were the telephone operator who'd cut off the broadcast.

From the street, Mr. Schenker bellowed, "He'll have to declare war now, he's got no choice!"

"Who does?" Betty said. "Who's he talking about?"

"Roosevelt, of course," Mr. Maczarek answered. He went back to the window.

But the war was in England. Poland. Far from here. Wasn't it? I looked at Ma to see what she thought. But she was staring at me like she was seeing me for the first time, and her lips were set in a thin line.

"Get out of that housecoat and wash your face," she said. "Make yourself look decent."

I fled back to our place. How could I possibly explain last night to Ma? I had to come up with something . . . Crossing through the parlor, I glanced at the clock on the table. It couldn't be. I ran into Ma's room, dug her watch out of her dresser. Three fifteen. I forgot about Ma, and last night, and the Japs.

I was supposed to meet Paulie at Peoples Theater at three o'clock.

No time to heat water on the stove. I scrubbed off last night's makeup with cold out of the tap, gooseflesh all over, clenching my teeth so they wouldn't chatter. Realizing that Ma and Betty weren't ready for Mass, they'd already been and gone. Why hadn't Ma woken me up? Maybe she'd tried, I thought, remembering Betty's yelling, how she'd practically had to drag me out of bed. My face burned with shame. All that rum last night . . . Lying on the floor, looking up into Ma's face. Babbling something about a party. Stupid, *stupid* . . . I hustled into the one new dress I kept at home, at the same time chewing two of Ma's aspirin, the way she did when she needed them to work fast. Almost gagging at the bitterness.

"I'm going to work!" I called into Mr. Maczarek's parlor from the hallway.

"You wait right there!" Ma yelled back. "I want to talk to . . ."

But I was already at the front door. "The switchboard's probably going crazy. Emergency calls . . . you heard that operator just now!" I shouted, and then I was running down the front stoop. I wasn't the only one hurrying; everybody was hustling home or crowding into the nearest tavern. At Hirsch's candy store, the line of people waiting to use the phone stretched out into the street. "What are they saying now?" they asked each other. "Our boys . . . dirty Japs . . ." On Marshfield Street, I almost ran into Stan Dudek and Charlie Baczewski coming out of a poolroom. "Ruby, have you heard?" Stan said. His knobby face alight in a way I'd never seen.

"I can't stop to talk . . . ," I began, but they ran past me.

"First thing tomorrow, we're going to enlist!" Stan shouted, and Charlie hollered, "We're gonna beat them Japs!"

"Enlist!" I said. "In the army?"

"Better than waiting to get drafted!" Stan yelled. Charlie whooped and clapped him on the shoulder, and they disappeared around the corner.

Drafted.

"Paulie," I said. And then I broke into a run.

It's no joke . . . it's a real war, the man on the radio had shouted. And Mr. Maczarek, once when he'd been going on about Hitler, and Poland: *old men start wars. Young men fight them.*

Young men like Paulie. But they couldn't take him away from me now. Not when everything was finally perfect.

Only a few people under the theater awning. No Paulie. I paid for a ticket and went inside. Sunday afternoon, the place should've been packed. It was less than half full. I wondered if the people watching Veronica Lake up on the screen even knew what had happened, what was still happening. I wandered up and down the aisles, whispering Paulie's name, ignoring the scoldings to shut up.

No luck. From the pay phone in the lobby, I called Ed's Garage. No answer.

I wasn't worried anymore about being late. All I could think of was Paulie being sent to war. Killed, maybe. All those newsreels about the battles in Europe . . . soldiers slogging through mud, filling row after row of hospital beds. I'd paid hardly a scrap of attention.

Don't come running after me, he'd said. But we hadn't been at war then. I crisscrossed the streets, looking in every poolroom, every tavern and saloon, all the same ones as before. This time, nobody was playing pool. The tavern owners had turned up their radios and men and women clustered three-deep, four-deep around the bars. This time, when I asked for Paulie, nobody made jokes and patted stools for me to join them. All the stools were taken and nobody paid attention to me.

I couldn't find him. It started to snow. I got to the Starlight with just enough time to get ready.

Turned out I wasn't the only one worried about a fellow. "But what about the boys who've already been drafted?" said a petite, pretty brunette named Joan. Her husband had gotten called up for the peacetime draft, back in April. "He's only supposed to be there a year. The army'll stick to that, won't they? They can't go back on their word, can they?"

"Of course not, honey," Nora said. The rest of us busied ourselves with our gowns and our nylons and our makeup. None of us looked at Joan.

By nine o'clock, when only thirty men had wandered in, Del sent half the girls home. At eleven, the rest of us got the boot. Nobody wanted illusion tonight. Before I left, I called the garage twice more. Still no answer.

Monday morning, on the little table radio in the parlor, Ma and I listened to President Roosevelt. Mr. Maczarek came over and sat on our sofa with a cup of Ma's coffee. The president's voice crackled: *". . . date which will live in infamy . . . last night Japanese forces attacked the Philippine Islands"*—Manny's family was there, and Alonso's, all the Pinoys—*"the American people in their righteous might . . . state of war."*

That afternoon, I waited for Paulie at Peoples Theater. He didn't show up. I stood under the awning, fretting at a tiny rip in the hem of my handkerchief, and watched the people hurrying past. Yesterday they'd looked stunned. A few angry. Today, their faces were grim. They walked past, heads down, not glancing at the theater or the shops. Stopping only to buy newspapers from the newsboy crying the headlines at the corner. All anybody wanted to know was what was going to happen now. But nobody knew.

Three hours later, my handkerchief was gone. Shredded and blown away, tiny pieces of cotton snow. I let go the last of them, watched them whirl and dance into the street. The daylight faded, the streetlights had come on. I wiped my eyes with my fingers, my nose on my sleeve. Then, my legs aching from standing on the sidewalk, I walked home.

Tuesday night, when the Starlight closed—at the usual hour, business had picked up a little—I walked out of the dance hall to find Paulie waiting for me, just like Tom had, exactly a week before. I yipped and ran toward him, but he backed away from me, his eyes dark as thunderclouds.

"What'd I tell you about not running all over town after me?" he said.

I stopped, stricken. The other girls drifted around us; I could feel them pretending not to watch, and not missing a word. I blushed hot. "I was late getting to the theater," I said, "and everything had just happened and I thought . . . I was afraid . . ." He shook his head, started to turn away. "Wait, Paulie, don't be mad!" I ran forward and reached for him, but before I could touch him, he'd swung back around, and he was grinning. The relief felt like being drenched in a sudden rain. Exhilarating, a little shaky. "You jerk," I said, but I was laughing, too. He put his arm around me then, and I snuggled close, relieved, too, at his solidness. Every time we were apart more than a day, I couldn't let go the feeling that I'd imagined him.

Peggy sauntered up. "So this is the dreamboat you're always going on about," she said.

They shook hands. Peggy was impressed, I could tell. So were the other girls; they tossed their hair, walked away slow. Peeked at him over their shoulders. I slid my arms around his waist. The look on Yvonne's face—like she'd swallowed a knife, blade first—*that* was the cherry on top.

In the cab, when I told Paulie my fear he'd get drafted, he started laughing. "*That* was why you were after me like a bloodhound?" he asked. I nodded. I'd already figured out that Paulie didn't like sappy girls, and he didn't like clingy girls, and I was one teardrop away from begging him not to go if the army called.

"The army locked me up and then they kicked me out." He looked out his window. "Believe me, after what I did, they ain't about to invite me back."

Paulie was safe. Safe from the draft. Safe from the war. I reached out and touched his knee. He was solid, he was real. He wouldn't be taken away. The fear and fretting of the past two days vanished, and I laughed, and then the relief overwhelmed me and I burst into tears.

"What's the matter?" Paulie said. "Don't tell me you had your heart set on the Japs using me for target practice."

"I'm so glad," I said between sobs. I heard him laughing low, under his breath. Then his arms were around me and it was all right. When I stopped crying, my head lay on his chest. For a minute, I watched the shops rolling by on Ashland Avenue. Then I asked, "What was it that made them lock you up, Paulie?"

"A private moved on my girl. I busted him up." He ran his hand up and down my arm. "Nothing I wouldn't do again."

So the rumors were true. I wondered how bad Paulie'd hurt him. "What happened to the girl?" I asked. Playing with a button on his coat.

"Don't know. Don't care."

I smiled against the rough plaid wool.

The cab let us off a block from home. Paulie pulled me into a gangway between two flats and kissed me.

"What if I did get drafted?" His voice thick and rough, almost a whisper. "What if I had to go fight? You'd be sweet to me then. Wouldn't you?"

"I'm sweet to you now," I whispered back.

"No. *Sweet.*" He pressed his hips against mine, kissed my neck.

Those terrible days worrying about Tom, thinking, *Why couldn't it be Paulie? If only it was Paulie . . .* Then, I'd told myself I'd still say no. Then, I hadn't had a shred of hope that he could be mine. Now here he was, his dark gold hair and good earthy smell and strong, warm hands under my coat.

"Would you?" he said again.

I looked him in the eyes, his beautiful rain-colored eyes, with the little flecks of color deep inside. Too dark to see them, but I knew they were there.

"Get drafted," I said, "and we'll see."

Whatever answer he'd expected, it wasn't that. His mouth hardened. He did a quick odd twist and then shoved his hand up under my skirt. I gasped in surprise and dodged away from his grabbing fingers, then slapped him. My palm cracked hard across his cheek. He caught my arm. Squeezed. I felt my bones bend. My stomach flipped with nausea and a sudden stabbing fear.

I busted him up. But this was me, I hadn't done anythi—

As suddenly as he'd seized me, he let go. Laughed, and flicked his fingers against my cheek. "I'll see you tomorrow," he said. "One o'clock at Peoples. Don't stand me up this time." He tilted my chin up and kissed me. Then he walked away, leaving me shaking in the alley.

Stupid to have gotten scared like that, I thought the next day. So he'd grabbed me a little too rough. How many times had I practically done the same to Betty, when we were little?

I made sure to keep my arms covered, so nobody would see the bruises.

•   •   •

This is what I told Ma about coming home drunk: one of the girls I worked with had gotten engaged, and she'd invited a few of us to her flat to celebrate after work. Her parents were there. Well, to tell the whole truth, they'd been in bed. The girl had served brandy Alexanders. She'd made them awfully strong, but they tasted so good, with the chocolate and the cream . . . And then someone said it was about time I learned how to put on makeup, and they'd started smearing things on my face. Yes, it felt awful to be drunk. I knew better now. I was sorry.

I put it over okay. Better than okay, actually. The telephone company, I told Ma, wanted us to look nice. It was a rule. And I was the only girl whose mother wouldn't let her wear makeup.

In the end, she agreed to powder and lipstick. Pink or coral, nothing dark. Yes, Ma, I said.

As far as the war, everything was unsure. Depending on who was talking, it would be over in a few weeks or would go on forever. Flags flew up and down the streets. Boys from all over Chicago lined up at recruiting offices to volunteer. Stan Dudek and Charlie Baczewski had both dropped out of school to sign up; others from our neighborhood, too. I knew I should be ashamed that Paulie wouldn't be going to fight. I wasn't. I was glad.

In the dance hall, the Chinese customers had a hard time. Some of the girls who usually danced with them wouldn't anymore, and the other customers gave them the stink-eye. The week after Pearl Harbor, a Lithuanian who'd been nipping from a hip flask all night knocked a cup of coffee onto a Chinese man's lap, saying, "Dirty skunk, go back to Japan!"

"I not from Japan, I spit on Japan!" the Chinese hollered. "You so stupid, you go back to Poland!" Well, of course that got the Poles and the Lithuanians mad, because they hate each other, and before you could blink, six or eight Slavs were swinging away at three Chinese, who swung right back. We girls jumped up on chairs or scrambled onto the counter to get a good view. There were a couple of good sluggers in the mix, but for my money, Del took the prize. He threw off his coat, rolled up his sleeves, and waded right into the thick of it. Between him and O'Malley, it took only a few minutes until the last of the contenders got a boot down the stairs. The band played right through it. Ozzie told me later that Hamp, the band leader, figured it was his job to play the music. If customers wanted to fight instead of dance, that was between them and Del.

After that, the Chinese stayed away. It wasn't just us; we heard it was the same at taxi-dance halls all over the city.

"If only the flips would scram, too," Nora said, "I'd be happy as a clam."

"That just shows how ignorant you are," I said. "Don't you know the Pinoys hate the Japanese as much as we do?" Last night at Lily's, Manny had been in such a blue funk, worried about his family, that he wouldn't dance. He sat at the table and drank whiskeys, one after another, getting more and more broody until finally he wouldn't talk even to Alonso.

"Hey, Cinderella, that boyfriend of yours know you date flips on the side?" Yvonne said.

I smiled at her. "He knows what the racket is." Chew on that, I thought, and I hope you bust a tooth. Actually it was getting kind of thorny, juggling Ma and Betty and the Starlight and my fish and Paulie—more and more, I felt like I was being pulled in a dozen different directions at once. I remembered how none of Yvonne's four fish knew about any of the others. Not for the first time, I wondered how she managed that.

"Any of you who don't want to dance with Orientals don't have to," Peggy said. "But did you stop to think that if they stay away, that's less dough for all of us?"

"The only thing I stopped to think is that any Jap can come in here and call himself a Chinaman and none of us would know the difference." Yvonne slipped a heel on one foot, balancing on the other.

"What on earth would they do that for?" Alice asked.

"So they could spy what Yvonne stuffs into her bra," I called. The whole Ladies' erupted in laughter, a few scandalized *oooohs*. For a second, Yvonne got the swallowed-knife look again, and her neck flushed red. So I was right. I didn't think she'd been working just what God gave her. I walked past her in my bra and girdle, then leaned down to a mirror and pretended to check my makeup. Let her see what a set of real tits looked like.

Aside from the Chinese, the war made other changes at the Starlight. The first was that every granddad suddenly remembered all his doings in the Great War. You'd see a girl trapped in the lounge, looking desperate, some geezer waving his hands in her face: "And then what do you think we did? We marched right back *up* that hill . . ."

"If another grayhair tells me one more story about his dysentery, I'm going straight home to blow my brains out," I told Ozzie.

"You should hear Hamp," he said. "Every word out of his mouth is either *foot rot* or *trenches*. Or both."

I'd started spending some of my breaks in the little back room. Not all the time, not even regular. A week or two might go by. Then a night would come when I wanted nothing more than to close my eyes and listen to Ozzie work out a new solo. Since he'd taken my advice and landed Ophelia—by New Year's she was kissing him behind the bandstand at Lily's—Ozzie was about the only person who didn't want something from me. Him, and maybe Peggy.

I never stayed the whole break. One cigarette, that was all. I didn't want him to think I was a nuisance. At first I only listened. Then, after a while, we started talking. He told me he'd started playing trumpet when he was nine. Moved to Chicago last year, when he was sixteen. The Starlight was his first gig.

"But if you hate it here so much," I said, "why don't you just work at Lily's?"

"This here is rent money," he said. "Lily's don't pay. That's where I'm developing my sound."

I'd never known anyone who'd developed anything. Ozzie talked about someday playing the Savoy in New York, the Century Room in Kansas City.

"Kansas City!" I said, and laughed. "What's in Kansas City?"

"See, this is what I mean. Chicks don't know nothing about music. Some cats who are hot in Harlem can't keep up in Kansas City. You hold your own in K.C., you can go anywhere."

I told him I'd settle for a flat that didn't build up ice on the inside of its windows. Stubbed out my cigarette, then went back to the floor. Night after night, I waltzed and single-footed, and listened to war stories smiling, and collected my nickels one at a time. Once I got a hundred dollars saved, I figured I'd have enough to get us out of the Yards.

Then came the boys in uniform, and the dance hall turned upside down.

Not just Chicago boys, either. These fellows came from all over, and they came in every stripe. Army privates in their khakis, navy sailors in their blues. Every one of them pressed and starched, fresh out of basic training and turned loose for two days, sometimes three, sometimes a week, before shipping out. If they weren't all handsome, at least they were all eager to have a good time. Happy as I was that Paulie was safe, still it thrilled me to see those boys.

The regular customers weren't thrilled a bit. The young bucks were horning in on their turf. They especially didn't like how the boys tipped. Spoiling us girls, they complained to Del. They claimed we sulked unless we got at least a dime tip, where before we were happy with a nickel. Well, that was true. So what? The boys treated us good and we liked it. Go figure.

Del kept an eye out, made sure we weren't turning our backs on the regulars, that we still treated them okay. Other than that, he didn't do much. The recruits rolled into Chicago by the trainload. Del put the steer to some of the cabbies, then sat back and raked it in.

Sure, a few of the recruits were obnoxious. Tried to feel us up, that sort of thing. Nothing worse than the worst regulars. The big difference was, these boys didn't know we were supposed to be sports. So if they got out of hand, I found a good hard crunch on their toes with my heel usually did the trick. I have to say I got some satisfaction out of that.

But that hardly ever happened. Most of the boys just wanted to share a laugh and a dance and after hours, step out to a nightclub. After a couple of beers, they got senti-mental. They told us about their families and girlfriends back in Iowa or Nebraska or Minnesota, they scribbled their names on napkins and matchbook covers and asked us to write. "Don't know when I'll see a girl pretty as you again," they said, and then they kissed us.

Business at the Starlight was booming, and any girl with a bit of pep—like me—was making money hand over fist. By February, I had six gowns, and four regular outfits to go out to clubs. The gowns I kept at the Starlight, of course, but I ran out of room in my locker, so I'd started bringing the regular dresses home, one every few weeks. Ma didn't ask where I'd gotten the money. She'd started giving me an allowance out of my wages; maybe she thought I was saving it up to buy clothes. By this time she had all new housedresses, herself, and two pairs of new shoes, from all the "overtime" I worked. I stayed out late almost every night now.

Betty was the one who was giving me headaches.

Ever since she'd seen Paulie waiting for me outside church, she wouldn't let it alone. Wanting to know if I was seeing him. If he'd kissed me again. Doing her dog-with-a-damn-bone act. Truth was, part of why I'd bought her those nylons was to distract her. Maybe even bribe her a little. It had worked, sort of. But after I'd come home drunk, she was convinced.

"He wears cologne," she whispered, one Saturday after-noon when we were scrubbing the kitchen floor. "I know, I smelled it on you."

"You didn't smell anything, you idiot." It must have been Manny's aftershave. "Someone spritzed me with per-fume at the engagement party."

"Well, which is it, then? Nothing, or perfume?" I flicked soapy water out of the bucket at her, and she shut up, but in no time at all she was back at it.

The minute I began bringing home clothes, she began stealing them to wear to school. Since I was never awake at six thirty, when she got dressed, she always got away with it. I'd pull out a dress to wear to work and find a stain on the bodice or a mustard spot on the skirt. When we fought about it, Ma took my side, telling Betty that those were my work clothes, to leave them alone. Betty said "Yes, Ma," and kept right on doing it.

"She's a pest," I complained to Paulie.

"Is that right," he said, looking out the window of the diner.

I sighed. Sometimes it was hard to find things to talk about with Paulie. We weren't seeing each other every day anymore—no one could keep that up forever—but we got together two or three afternoons a week, usually at Peoples Theater. Sometimes, a diner or chop suey joint in Canaryville, where nobody knew me, although Paulie didn't like that as well because we couldn't make out. Afternoons suited him just fine, though. Like me, he worked at night. Angling for the big score.

That was the one thing he loved to talk about. The big score. And the old-time gangsters. Al Capone and Frank Nitti, Bugs Moran and Jack McGurn. What they'd done and how they'd done it. He talked about how easy Capone had had it, with Prohibition and bootlegging—millions of bucks just waiting to be scooped up. He'd shake his head and say, "It ain't that easy anymore. And then Capone let the feds get him. Stupid." He sneered at what he called the small-time operators and their penny-ante schemes.

They didn't understand it was all about the big score. Once you had that, you had it made. You'd be on top, and then anybody who gave you crap, you could make eat it.

He was on his way up already. You could see it, the way the neighborhood toughs pissed themselves like puppies when he walked by. Paulie would make it big, I knew it. Thinking it, I'd get that cold-shivery thrill again. But when I asked him what the big score might be, all he ever said was, "I got my fingers in some pies."

The one time I got Paulie's entire attention—aside from kissing—was when I told him about the policy king. He knew what policy was, of course. But he'd never heard of Horace Washington. When I got to the part about millions of dollars, he stopped me. Up on the movie screen, Clarabelle Cow was baking a cake for Mickey Mouse's birthday. Everyone around us was laughing, but Paulie had gone dead serious.

"Tell me that again," he said. So I did. "And they call him what? The king?"

"The policy king. Maybe he'll be at Lily's again. You could come with me and see for yourself."

But Paulie had slouched back in his seat. "I told you once already. I don't go to places like that."

Where I fit into his plans for the big score, I couldn't tell. Capone had had his Mae. Why shouldn't Paulie have me? But by the end of February, our dates had slid from three times a week to twice to once. Even making out in the theater seemed to bore him. "This is kid stuff," he'd say, and then, "If you'd just be a little sweet to me . . ."

"I am sweet to you," I'd tell him, and he'd give an irritated shrug.

He started staying away. A week would go by and I

wouldn't see him. I called the garage until the man who answered finally told me not to call anymore. Then Paulie would show up, waiting outside the Starlight, or on the corner near my house. Those first times, everything would be wonderful. Then we'd fight, and he'd disappear again. I cried so hard one night, I woke up Betty. When she asked what was wrong, I told her to go jump in the lake.

And then, suddenly, Paulie wasn't my only problem.

THIRTEEN

One night in early April, I was doing a kind of shuffle-step waltz with an army private when across the dance floor someone yelled, "Ruby? Hey, Ruby!"

I didn't pay attention. If you were popular, like I was, some customer or another was always calling your name. But then the man said, "Ruby Jacinski!" and I was so startled, I stumbled over my partner's feet.

None of the customers knew my real last name. Not even Tom, not even Manny. I'd picked that tip up from the other girls: don't give the customers a handle to find you outside the hall. If a man insisted, I said my name was deVere. I'd seen it in an ad somewhere, and I thought it was elegant. *Ruby deVere.*

"I think that fellow wants you," the private said, just as Stan Dudek came up and tapped his shoulder to cut in. He was dressed in navy blues. Under his hat his face looked even more angular, his cheekbones and chin sticking out like the corners of furniture.

He smiled at me. "It *is* you. I thought it couldn't be, because everyone said you'd gone to be a telephone operator. And the light's so bad in here. But then I got a little closer and I thought, Nobody but Ruby Jacinski is that tiny, with such pretty hair." The song ended. "Sorry to interrupt your dance." Stan took two tickets out of his pocket, tore them apart, gave one to the private. "Here's another to make up for it. Ruby?"

I nodded. My brain felt frozen. He put the ticket in my hand, and then we were swinging onto the floor just like we were back at Pulaski's drugstore, jitterbugging to the jukebox, with all the kids from school.

I'd been at the Starlight six months. In all that time, I'd never thought I might run into someone I knew. Why should I? There were dozens of taxi-dance halls in Chicago, and the Starlight wasn't anywhere near the closest one to the Yards. All through the dance, I smiled at Stan, but inside I was terrified. Mrs. Dudek lived two doors up the street. It wasn't possible that Stan would know I was here and my mother not find out.

After the dance, Stan kept hold of my hand. "I've never been to one of these joints before. Can you . . . I mean, is it okay if we sit and talk, instead of dance?"

Tell him no. Tell him you can't.

But this was Stan. I'd always liked Stan. He was one of the few boys in the neighborhood who looked me in the face when he talked to me, instead of eight inches lower. He'd been sweet to me since the first day my family arrived on Honore Street, when I was five and he was seven. Now he was going to war, and I couldn't be any less sweet to him.

"Buy us two sodas," I said, "and I'll grab a table."

When he came back with the drinks, before he could ask a question—before he even sat down—I said, "So, I hear you and Angie Wachowski are getting married."

I hadn't heard any such thing, except from Angie herself, and that had been almost five months ago, when I'd told her about Tom. I hadn't seen her since then, except passing on the street, and then we pretended not to notice each other.

But the question distracted Stan better than I'd hoped. He turned red and cleared his throat, and took some good long sips of his soda.

"Yeah, we weren't . . . we're not . . ." He grinned and rubbed his forehead, not meeting my eyes. "Oh, hell, Ruby. The truth is, I jilted her."

"Jilted her!" Angie Wachowski had never been jilted in her life.

"When I signed up, see, she wanted to get married right away. I guess to square things away, you know, before I left. But the thing of it is . . ." Stan gazed at the far end of the hall, squinting a little, as if he was seeing a horizon instead of a ten-piece band. "I don't want to spend my life on the killing floor, Ruby. You worked there, you understand."

I nodded. I understood perfectly.

"When I heard you'd quit the packinghouse to go be a telephone operator, I said to myself, That's just like Ruby Jacinski. Not gonna settle for anything." He picked up his napkin, creased it in half, then half again. "Angie and me, we were going along pretty good, and I thought it'd be all right. But then, when the Japs bombed Pearl Harbor . . . I felt like I ought to do something. A lot of us did. I signed up so I could pick the navy, and I busted my hump and I made good. I don't want to brag or anything, Rubes, but . . . I got accepted to navy pilot school."

"Pilot school! You mean flying planes?"

Stan laughed, and I clapped my hand over my mouth. *Of course a pilot flies planes, you dope!*

But what he said was, "Yeah, I know. A Back of the Yards punk who thinks he can fly. Some nerve, huh?" He leaned forward, his eyes shining on mine. "But that's the thing, Ruby. The navy don't know the Yards from the North Shore. They don't care my pop's been a beef skinner all his life. All they care is, can I do it or not?"

His face reminded me of Paulie's, when Paulie talked about the big score. Or Ozzie's, blowing a solo at Lily's. Not hope. Not wishing. But a wanting so deep, it was like he would grab the world and shake it until it did what he told it.

Where would you go, if you could go anywhere you wanted?

I felt something stir, a little excitement, a thrill. But it was Stan leaving, not me.

"So?" I asked. "Can you do it?"

"Yeah," he said. No bragging, no fancy talk. Just *yeah*. He knocked back his cola. Then, setting his glass down, he said, "So what about you? What happened to the telephone job?"

It had to come around to this sooner or later. "I didn't . . . it didn't work out." I bit my lip. The burning had gone out of Stan's face. He looked at me from across the table, patient as a dog. "Stan, listen. My mother still thinks I work there. All right? If she knew about this . . ." I waved my hand at the couples swaying across the floor. "We don't do anything but dance, I swear. And the money's good, and we need it. But if Ma found out, she'd think I was . . ." Heat flamed up my neck, my face. "You know what she'd think. And she'd hate me. She'd call me a tramp and kick me out. She'd . . ."

"Hey," Stan said. "Hey, it's okay. Don't cry, Ruby." He reached over and brushed his thumb across my cheek. "I can see it's not . . ." He glanced at the far corner of the lounge—I didn't dare turn around, but I heard Nora giggle and I guessed she was rubbing up against some guy. ". . . you know, not such a bad place. We do what we have to, right? I thought my ma would bean me with the iron when I told her I'd volunteered." He grinned for a second, then got serious again. "Look, don't worry. I won't rat you out."

But he wasn't looking at me anymore. His gaze wandered around, and when it finally came back, it rested a good long moment on my tits. I was wearing a red gown, high cut but with a keyhole opening that showed nice cleavage. For the first time since I'd started working at the Starlight, I felt like covering up. I did the next best, and rested my elbows on the table, hands clasped under my chin. "Thanks, Stan. You're a real brick."

He lowered his voice. "Say, you want to blow this joint? Go to a club, get some real drinks?"

"Gosh, I wish I could." I put on my best know-nothing face. "I know some of the girls do . . . but I can't keep Ma waiting. She expects me home at a certain time, you see."

"Oh, sure. Of course."

Stan fished a piece of ice out of his glass, popped it into his mouth, and crunched it. The noise frayed my nerves. Stan might be sweet, but he was no dummy. He wasn't fooled, not about this place. As far as me . . . all I needed was for one of my fish to show up and say, *Ready to hit the town, Ruby?* and Stan would tattle to his mother sure as God made the grass green. After that, the news would be all over the parish in two seconds flat. *That's right . . . a taxi-dance hall . . . I always said that girl was flighty . . . the shame must be killing her poor mother.* And then no story in the world could ever make it right with Ma.

"Well," I said, "this has been really nice . . ."

"Stan-O!" a fellow hollered. I looked up to see two other navy recruits headed our way, each of them with his arm around a girl. My mouth went dry. As they got near, Stan stood up.

"Stanley Dudek," one of the recruits said, "meet Gabby and Yvonne. Gabby and Yvonne, this strapping handsome fellow is Stanley Dudek."

"Ruby Jacinski," Stan said. "George Roberts, Bill Costa."

"Stan's a good friend of mine," I blurted. "From the old neighborhood."

"Could've knocked me over with a feather when I saw her," Stan said.

Yvonne glanced between the two of us. She smiled, her slow wolf smile. "Is that so?"

The other recruit spoke up. "We're clocking these angels out and going on the town. Why don't you wrap up your friend, Stan, and bring her along? Yvonne here says she knows a great little place just off the Loop."

"Best vodka tonics in Chicago," Yvonne said. "Ruby just loves a good vodka tonic, don't you, Ruby?"

I tried to laugh. It came out shrill. "Don't be silly, you know my mother expects me home."

"Old lady can't expect you back before, what, two thirty?" the first recruit said. "It's only eleven now. Plenty of time. Come on, get your coat."

"Come on, Ruby," Stan said. "One little drink won't hurt."

"I'm sorry, I can't. I don't drink," I said.

Yvonne's smile widened. "Really? Just the other night, I thought—"

I jumped to my feet. "Yvonne, before you go, I need to get that . . . that lipstick for you." I grabbed her wrist. "This won't take a second," I called over my shoulder, and I pulled her to the Ladies'. Once there, she shook me off and stalked to her locker.

"This better be good," she said, lighting a cigarette.

"Look," I said. "Promise me you won't tell him things. Please. My mother . . ."

Yvonne lifted her eyebrows. "Things?"

"About the Pinoys. About the clubs. Please, it's the only thing I'll ever ask you."

Yvonne walked slowly back toward me. Head tilted to one side, like she was thinking. She leaned against one of the dressing tables. Crossed one long leg over the other. "You know," she said, "I always thought *promise* is an expensive word."

She couldn't just say, *Sure, Ruby.* She couldn't make it easy. I strode to my locker and yanked it open. "What do you want?"

She reached over to an ashtray, tapped her cig. "Nothing you've got," she said. "Unless . . . say, everything you earn for the next two weeks."

Two weeks? Either she was nuts, or she thought I was. "One week," I said, adding, "I don't have fish paying *my* rent."

She flicked a bored gaze across me. "That's not surprising. Two weeks, or nothing."

I added quickly in my head. I had the money I'd been saving in the pillowcase at home, but it wasn't enough to cover two weeks' rent and groceries. Could I ask Paulie? Just yesterday we'd had another fight . . .

"Time's wasting," Yvonne said. "Put up or shut up."

No way around it. I'd have to figure out something later. I nodded. Yvonne tamped out her cigarette—Del didn't let us smoke on the dance floor—and sauntered out of the Ladies'.

The thought of giving my money to Yvonne hurt. Hurt me in my body, an actual ache, as though a hand grabbed low in my belly and squeezed.

"Lipstick," Stan said, when we rejoined them. He chuckled. "The stuff dames get worked up over. So, Ruby, you coming or not?"

"Ruby's such a baby, I bet she's never even seen the inside of a club," Yvonne said. "We'll get you a real gal to step out with." She waved her hand. "Stella!"

"Then I guess I'll see you around, Rubes," Stan said. "Kiss for old time's sake?"

I stood on tiptoes, let him peck me on the lips. "Look, Stan," I whispered. "If they lay a line on you about going to a hotel after, don't fall for it. They'll get you to give them the money up front for . . . well, you know. Then they'll run out the back with the dough and leave you standing out front like fools."

"How do you . . ."

"Because they laugh about it later, that's how. The recruits are shipping out, they can't come back to settle the score. Easy money."

"Come on, Stan, time to leave the little girls in the playground," Yvonne called.

Stan nodded to me. "Thanks, Ruby. I owe you one."

Right after they left, the band took a break. A soldier

asked if he could buy me a soda, but I turned him down. I went back toward the Ladies', then, when nobody was watching, slipped down the hallway. I stood outside Ozzie's room and laid my head back against the wall and listened to him singing notes in the dark. Wild music. A wanting so deep, you would break the world open, just to get your chance.

Ozzie and Stan, they knew what they wanted.

What did I want?

Paulie. You want Paulie.

Yes. And no. At least, not only him. Something more, I didn't know what. A nameless want that reached down, grabbed me by the roots. Felt like it was about to shake me apart.

FOURTEEN

The next night, after the Starlight closed, Yvonne glided over to my locker. She'd changed out of her gown into a midnight blue cocktail dress, and had a cashmere coat— once the weather got warmer, she'd stopped wearing the fox—slung carelessly over one arm. She leaned the other against Peggy's locker, and said, "Hand over your haul, chickie, and be quick about it. I got fish to fry."

I made her wait until I finished unrolling my stocking. "Did any of you say anything to Stan?"

She shook her head, smiling her slow wolf smile. "No sirree. We didn't say a thing." Three lockers away, Gabby made a noise like she was choking back a laugh.

I'd expected Yvonne to gloat, but this was more than gloating. She had a stuffed-to-the-gills look, as if she was bursting with something. Gabby, too. But the rest of their pack—Stella, Valerie, a few others—shifted curious glances back and forth, and Stella shrugged. Stella had gone out with them last night; if there was a trick, she'd be in on it.

I shuffled my tickets into a neat pile. "If you said one word . . ."

"Not one syllable, chickie."

I scooped up the tickets and shoved them at her. Then I grabbed my pocketbook and shut my locker.

"Not so fast!" Yvonne flipped her hand toward me, palm up. "Your tips."

Tips made up half our income, sometimes more. Between them and my savings, I'd be able to scrape by without bothering Paulie. "Go lay an egg," I told her.

It was a gamble. Stan might come back—navy pilots trained right here in Chicago, after all—and if he did, Yvonne could still spill the beans about me and clubs and the fish. But I didn't think he would.

"Listen, sister, you're safe as houses," Peggy had told me earlier. "You know why? Because now he's an officer. Who do you see in here?" She'd waved to take in the entire dance hall. "Servicemen, that's who. The officers go to their Officers' Clubs, or to the Aragon and the other fancy places with the other swells in this town. Face it, kid." Peggy had raised her orangeade and winked at me. "We're the low-rent girls."

Low-rent girls. Of course—when had I ever seen a swell at the Starlight? Even Artie, that slick huckster, for all his good suits, he'd been only a traveling salesman.

Yvonne studied me a moment from behind her hat veil. Then shrugged one silk crepe shoulder. "All right, Little Miss Cow"—behind her, Gabby sputtered into giggles—"if that's how you want to play it, fine by me." She took my tickets, every night for the next two weeks, and she and Gabby snickered behind my back. Whatever they were up to—and they were up to something—I didn't care. Compared to my other worries, they were small fry.

I couldn't relax. Ever. I'd never paid attention before to the hundred or so men who came to the Starlight just to watch us girls. But now I peered at their faces in the hall's half-light. Any of them could be someone I knew. They could come and go whenever they wanted, while I was trapped here, on display, for everyone to see.

At home, the cozy routine I shared with Ma began to splinter. She'd bragged about me until I couldn't go outside without neighbors repeating back to me the stories I'd told her. Stories I'd made up about being a telephone operator, all those long mornings together in our flat. It had been a kind of game. Now when I saw Mrs. Dudek, I ducked down an alley. Thanks to the tickets I'd promised Yvonne, Stan might not know about the fish, and the black and tans, and the Pinoys. But he knew enough that one slip could make my world collapse. Every lie I'd told in the past six months, crashing down on our heads.

I started sleeping later and later. When I did finally get up, I came out to the kitchen already dressed. Instead of sitting down for coffee and a chat with Ma, I ate breakfast over the sink. Then I did the daily shopping. As soon as I got home with the groceries, I left again.

"Where are you going?" Ma would say. "You just got back."

"I'm meeting friends."

"Every day? Who's going to do the ironing? Who's going to help me make supper?"

I'd throw my coat on the floor. Or my pocketbook, or my keys. "I pay for our suppers, don't I? I pay for everything! Now you want me to spend all day slaving, too?"

Ma tried to reason with me. I refused to be reasoned with. I slammed doors and hollered until finally she said, "Go. *Go!* God in heaven, just leave us in peace, will you?"

The dark circles came back under her eyes. She hurt all the time. Her hands, her knees, her ankles. I knew it, and I wore her down. And then I could do what I wanted.

I went to the theater—whether I had a date with Paulie or not—and I watched movie after movie, newsreel after newsreel, until it was time to go home for supper. I always washed the supper dishes. That was fair. Ma couldn't say I wasn't fair.

After two weeks of losing my tickets to Yvonne, my savings in the pillowcase were spent. The minute I was earning for myself again, I sashayed peppier, snapped my fingers faster, smiled at the men more. As much as I wanted to hide in the meatpen, I couldn't. I needed dances. I needed that money back, and more. I had to get us out of the Yards, for all the reasons I'd had before, plus this: I needed to go where nobody knew me. Where I wouldn't worry that every time a neighbor slid a look across me, he might be recognizing me from the Starlight.

Once we were someplace new, I could breathe. Then things would go back to how they used to be.

In May—the freezing weather long gone, the swampy heat of summer still ahead—we were given our first ration books. One for each of us, issued on a sunny Saturday morning by a tired-looking teacher at Sacred Heart School. He tore a stamp out of Ma's, to account for the sugar we already had at home, then went through the rules in a speeded-up mumble none of us could understand.

When we got home, Ma stopped in at Mr. Maczarek's to see if he could explain how the ration points worked. I went to the bedroom and started putting on my makeup. After staying away almost two weeks, Paulie had shown up at the Starlight last night. I smiled to myself, remembering how he'd kissed me on the sidewalk in front of everyone, then in the cab on the way to a Chinese supper. Every time he came back I hoped that this time, he'd stay. That this time, he'd tell me he loved me.

He hadn't, last night. But we'd closed the Chinese joint down, Paulie talking about rackets in Detroit and Philly and I don't know where all, and then we'd made out in the back of the cab until the cabbie said he'd turn a hose on us if we didn't knock it off. My skin thrilled, remembering. The last thing Paulie'd said was to meet at Peoples Theater at one o'clock today. I wasn't taking any chances being late. Paulie never waited.

Betty came in the room and shut the door. "Have you noticed anything strange about Ma lately?"

"Like what?" I opened my Carnelian Red lipstick, examined its tip. "Did you use this?"

"No." A little too quick.

"How many times do I have to tell you, keep your hands off my stuff? I already gave you the Peach Blossom, what more do you want?" I rolled on the lipstick quick, blotted my mouth on a tissue.

"You know how she said she joined the altar society at church?"

"Yeah? So?"

"So I don't think that's where she's going." The bed creaked as Betty sat down. In a sulkier tone, she said, "I look better in that red than you do."

I glanced at her in the mirror. Then took a good second

look. When had she started wearing her hair like that? Parted low on one side and waved to her shoulders. No ribbons, no bows. She'd plucked her eyebrows, too. A little archy, but not bad. With that rich chocolate hair of hers, she was right about the lipstick; in fact, put her in the Carnelian Red and a gown and she could be at home in the Starlight.

I slung the lipstick back into the dresser drawer. "Forget it. You're not old enough for a red this dark." I rummaged for my mascara. "What do you mean, that's not where Ma's going? Are you saying she's lying?" Just the thought made me laugh. In the mirror, Betty flushed.

"How would I know? All I know is, last Saturday my friend Evelyn saw her on the streetcar going east on Forty-seventh Street. That's *away* from the church," she added, as if I didn't know which way east was. She stepped over to the dresser, picked up the mascara. "Does Ma know you have this?"

"Ma doesn't say anything anymore about what I wear. So you can just keep your nose out of it." I picked up my watch. 12:35. Better hustle. "Do me a favor, will you? Ma wants a pork loin for tonight, but I don't have time. There's money on the kitchen table. Try Stawarz's first. If he doesn't have it, he might know who does." Certain cuts of meat had gotten hard to find. The war, everyone said. Last week I'd had to go to three shops to find beef brisket.

"I already do everything else around here. I'm not doing your shopping, too. Who are you meeting anyway? Your friend Peggy?"

I didn't like the sneer she used with Peggy's name. As if she didn't believe me. "That's right," I said. "Look, don't be a pill. Just do me this one favor. I'll make it up to you."

"What about Ma?"

I slammed the dresser drawer shut. "What about her? Evelyn Terasek is so dizzy, she probably didn't even know which way the streetcar was going. Have you asked Ma?"

"No, but—"

"Then what are you bothering me for? Now are you going to get that pork loin, or not?"

She'd dropped the mascara and was glaring at me, arms crossed. I fought down the urge to smack her. What did she know about anything? About what I did to buy the saddle shoes on her feet and the pretty sweater on her back? Nothing. So she could just keep her snotty looks to herself.

Still—Paulie wouldn't wait.

I plucked the Carnelian Red out of the drawer. Held it out. Betty made like she was considering. I started taking it back.

"Okay, okay," she said, and she snatched the tube out of my hand. I grabbed my pocketbook.

"Tell Ma I might not be home for supper," I told her.

At Peoples Theater I stood under the awning, searching the faces in the crowd. Suddenly warm hands covered my eyes, warm breath tickled my ear. "Paulie!" I said.

"No, the Easter bunny," Paulie said. I turned in his arms and put up my face and he kissed me, and something that was cranked tight in me relaxed.

The Saturday matinee was a double feature—*Son of Fury* and *Ghost Town Law*—and the place was jammed. We got in line for sodas and candy. A couple of little boys careened between the pillars in the red-carpeted lobby, waving toy guns in the air, hollering *Bang, bang!* From somewhere ahead of us, over the babble of voices, I heard a girl talking loud.

". . . so they pair me up with an absolute battle-ax, a Mrs. Hotty-totty from Lincoln Park, and for the first hour nothing I swear but one ugly serviceman after another, nobody higher than a corporal, so I let her wait on all of them . . ."

"You didn't!" another girl exclaimed. I started. That was Angie's voice. I peeked between the people behind me, and sure enough there she was, coming through the lobby with Lois Terasek and Viola Bauer. I edged behind Paulie's shoulder. Angie was still wearing Stan's cross. I wondered if she'd really loved him. If he'd broken her heart when he jilted her.

"Good thing I did," Lois was saying, "because the battle-ax was showing some private how to get to the Greyhound station, when up comes a *dreamboat* of a marine, and he's asking directions to the Auditorium. So I told him I'd tell him, but only if he took me bowling there . . ."

"You *didn't!*" Angie and Viola cried together, and suddenly I wanted to run and join them, talk at the top of my voice about boys and double over laughing, the way I always used to. It hadn't been so long ago.

"I'm telling you," Angie said, "Traveler's Aid is *the* ticket. Much better than serving coffee at the USO . . ."

"Ruby!" Fingers snapped in front of my face. I jumped and blinked at Paulie. "I asked you twice already. You want a Snickers, or what?"

"I'm sorry. It's just, I know those girls." I turned and nodded toward them. Paulie stepped out of line to get a better look. "Don't *stare,*" I whispered. "They'll see us!"

Paulie grinned. Then he tilted up my face and kissed me, good and deep. Showing off. *Tsk*'s all around, mutterings like bees. Angie's voice stopped, sudden as turning off a radio.

I came up from the kiss like I was drowning. Flailing, gasping for air. "What's wrong with you?" Paulie said. I put the back of my hand up to my mouth and looked over at the girls—afraid to, and unable to stop myself. Lois and Viola were giggling and whispering, their faces twisted with scandal. But Angie looked like she was seeing me through the window of an el train, moving. Like she'd caught the last glimpse of me she'd ever see.

I'd never laugh with her again about boys or anything else. I'd have to not know too much. I'd have to go backward, and I didn't know how.

I walked past them across the lobby, not seeing who I bumped into and not caring. Someone crashed into me from behind, knocking the breath half out of me. Coins fell in a sparkling shower at my feet, bouncing on the thick red carpet. I dodged around a fat fellow coming through the door, and then I was outside. A storm had come up. The sun was gone; rain spattered the asphalt.

Paulie hit the sidewalk right after me. "Goddammit, what the hell's the matter with you?"

I hugged myself. I was shaking. "I can't go back in there."

"Damn right you're not going back in there. I ain't paying admission twice. I've had as much as I can take of this kid stuff, Ruby. You ain't dangling me on your string anymore. I told you at the beginning, I ain't one of your damn fish."

Me and Angie, Lindy Hopping to a jukebox with Stan

Dudek and Hank Majewski at the corner drugstore. Dreaming about the Aragon Ballroom, swapping pinkie secrets. I put my head in my hands, squeezing my eyes shut tight, as if I could push myself back into the shape I used to be. People eddied all around me, shaking out their umbrellas as they stepped under the awning.

"You're right," I said suddenly. I lifted my face to his. "This is kid stuff."

Paulie pulled out a cigarette pack, tapped one out into his palm. His eyes under their pale brows not leaving mine.

"Tomorrow night," he said. "After you get off work."

"No. My night off. Monday."

I thought he might say forget it. I thought he might walk away. He didn't. He didn't smile, either, or say all right. But his eyes changed. Cold to warm, like March to May, as if all this time I'd been struggling in the cold and the rain, and all I'd had to do was open a door and on the other side was summer.

I couldn't go back. I could only keep going the way I'd begun.

"Eight o'clock," Paulie said. "I'll pick you up here."

FIFTEEN

At five minutes to eight on Monday night, I was in front of Peoples Theater. Evenings at the movies were even more crowded than the matinees, and the sea of faces under the awning were all starting to look alike. At the curb, a car honked. Then honked again, and again.

"Stuff a sock in it, buddy!" someone yelled. I turned to look—and saw Paulie leaning against a car. Kelly green, with a white convertible top. As I pushed through the crowd, he came around the front and opened the passenger door. I scrambled inside.

"Is it yours?" I said, once he was behind the wheel.

"No. Borrowed it from a friend. Not bad though, huh?"

I'd never been in someone's own car before. This one had stains on the seats, a crack in the dashboard. It smelled a little like an old shoe.

"It's beautiful," I said. Paulie draped his arm across the back of the seat. I scootched close, laid my head against his shoulder and watched the lights spool past on Ashland Avenue.

Sunday morning, when I told Ma I was going to

Peggy's on my night off, I was ready for an argument. But all she said was, "We'll both be out, then. I have an altar society meeting."

Betty looked up from the ironing board. "You just had a meeting last night. And one on Thursday."

Thursday? Nobody told me about that.

"We're getting ready for the Confirmation ceremony next week," Ma said. "Father O'Donnell wants the church to look extra nice."

O'Donnell? Sacred Heart's pastor was Father Redisz, not O'Donnell. "Oh, didn't I mention it?" Ma said, when I asked. "These are ladies I met a few weeks ago. From Rose of Lima."

The Irish parish. So that explained the streetcar going east. I passed behind Betty and flicked her on the neck, making her jump. I didn't stop to wonder how Ma had met women from a whole different parish, or why she'd joined their altar society instead of Sacred Heart's. Rose of Lima wasn't far, in distance. But in Back of the Yards, it might as well have been on the other side of the world.

Whoever these Irish ladies were, Ma was out to impress. The next morning, when I came into the kitchen, she said, "Oh, good, you're up already. I want to go shopping today. Just you and me, to buy a new dress. Won't that be fun?"

I blinked at her, not sure I'd heard right. *A new dress? What for?* I almost asked. Ma was standing at the sink, so I couldn't see her face; but I saw her back go stiff, as if she was waiting for me to say it. As if she didn't deserve something pretty, instead of the simply useful, like her wool coat, like gloves.

So we went to Goldblatt's, and right off that was

strange. Ma never went to department stores. She always bought clothes on Maxwell Street: shops and pushcarts selling almost anything you could imagine, for cheap.

But Ma wasn't looking for just any dress. As soon as we stepped into Goldblatt's, Ma collared the nearest salesgirl, a little timid-looking redhead, and the hunt was on. I forgot about Angie, and Stan and his mother and the Starlight. Even Paulie I hardly thought about at all. The world shrank down to me, Ma, and a store full of possibilities.

We about ran the feet off the little redhead. In the fitting room, I did and undid buttons and zippers and hooks until the tips of my fingers were sore. Ma was steaming past cranky, right into cantankerous ("Is there a *single* dress in this store that doesn't make me look either six or sixty?"), when, finally, we found it. A divine pale yellow, dotted with navy blue, a navy leather belt to match.

After the salesgirl rang up the dress, Ma dropped her nine cents' change into her change purse. "Well, that's that," she said.

"No, it's not," I said. I snatched the ugly, out-of-style cloche off her head ("Ruby! What are you doing? Ruby, stop that!"), and I ran with it to the hat department. By the time she caught up to me—limping, poor Ma, she was tired—I'd picked out a felt side-brim hat, navy blue with a black eyeline veil. "Oh, Ruby," she said, "I can't afford that."

"I can," I said, and I bought it for her.

Somehow in Goldblatt's fitting room, with rayons and cottons and linens heaped all around us, we'd found a truce. Fragile as a soap bubble, but it held.

Maybe she'd just needed time to adjust. After all, I

was the oldest, the first of Ma's girls to grow up. No wonder she had trouble realizing I wasn't a baby anymore. Betty ought to give me a medal. She'd have it easier, when her turn came.

Before I left to meet Paulie, I helped Ma into the new dress. Then I sat her down at the kitchen table and took the rollers and pins out of her hair and brushed it into soft, shining waves, swept back from her face. She reached for the hand mirror. I stopped her.

"Wait," I told her. "Close your eyes. Don't move." I darted into my bedroom and came back with a compact and rouge and lipstick. I kept a light hand. Ma had delicate coloring; too much would drown her.

"There," I said. "Now you're beautiful."

The Ma of the past year—faded and drab, strained thin—was gone. Here, in our ugly, cramped kitchen, was the Ma I remembered. The pale yellow of her dress made her skin seem rich as cream; her face, free of tight clinging curls and the cloche hat, wide-open as sky.

She stared at herself in the mirror. Touched the sleek upsweep over her ear, the soft bright waves at the back of her neck. Her carmine lips. "Oh, Ruby," she whispered.

"You should be going out dancing," I said. "You should be going to a *ball*!"

A red flush spotted her cheeks. "Do you really think so?" In that moment, she seemed as young as Betty. As young as me. Not even her knotted hands could ruin how beautiful she was.

"I know so," I said. I laid my head on her shoulder; Ma raised the mirror high, and we studied ourselves together. My dark blond hair against her shining gold. Our eyes both blue, hers pale, mine dark. Ma kissed my temple.

"You're a good daughter, Ruby," she said. "I know it's been hard for you . . ."

She didn't know. She had no idea . . . and if I watched my step, she never would. Then again, had I ever known how hard it had been for her? Pop gone, me and Betty to raise. Under the shoulder pad of her dress, I could feel the sharp bone. Ma, dance? Some days, she could hardly walk. In the mirror, I watched the tears rise and spill over my cheeks. A glass too full.

"No time for that." Ma put down the mirror. "Go get ready. You're going to be late."

• • •

The green convertible flew down streets I didn't recognize. At every stoplight, Paulie leaned down and kissed me. "Where are we going?" I asked.

"Uptown," he said.

I sat upright. "The Aragon Ballroom!"

"That richie-rich joint? I'd rather chew glass. Just keep your shirt on, you'll find out."

The instant I saw the Ferris wheel, lit up bright as Christmas, I knew. "Riverview!" I cried.

We had a long hike from the parking lot—for some reason, Paulie drove what seemed a hundred miles past the other cars, to the far end. "What are we all the way out here for?" I asked, getting out of the convertible. The air was warm and damp and smelled like steel. It had rained earlier.

"Don't want anyone dinging the paint job." Paulie took my hand. "Come on, you can hoof it."

I'd only been to Riverview Amusement Park a handful of times in my life. Never at night. The lights dazzled me, the smell of hot dogs and popcorn, the music pouring out of the banjo speakers. Just inside the enormous arched entrance, the Silver Flash roared by on its tracks. Screams floated like ghosts in the air behind it.

"Where first?" Paulie said.

I didn't hesitate. "The Bobs." The last time I'd been at Riverview, when I was ten, Ma refused to let me ride the Bobs. Too dangerous, she said. Someday, someone's going to get killed.

"Atta girl," Paulie said.

As the Bobs train clicked up the first hill, Paulie put his arm around me. I never could get enough of his scent. Car leather and earth and something faintly metallic, which reminded me of automobiles. His mouth tasted like the Lucky Strikes he smoked. Dark and strong.

The clicking slowed.

"I'd hang on, if I were you," Paulie said. And then the train fell away under me.

I felt myself flying off the seat. I grabbed the thin metal bar in front of me with both hands, and I shrieked living daylights. I could hear Paulie laughing, and behind me someone screaming, "Jesus, Jesus! Mother of *God*!" At the bottom, a hairpin turn; Paulie slid sideways and smashed me against the side of the car. I bounced off him, bounced off the seat, bounced in the air. My sharpest memory, afterward, was his arms, hands gripping the bar and never budging, the shadows of his muscles sharp as if drawn on his skin with ink.

After the Bobs, we wandered up the Bowery between rows of booths and games. "Win me a doll," I told Paulie, but he shook his head. "All rigged," he said. "Waste of money."

"Hey, you! In the sissy yellow shirt!" someone yelled. I turned to see. A few other people had stopped, too; one of the men wore yellow. "Yeah, you!" The voice came from what looked like a row of tall cages. "I saw you over there at the duck shoot. What's wrong with you, you blind?"

Laughter scattered through the crowd. The man in the yellow shirt glanced right and left, as if unsure what to do. The woman with him pushed his arm. Urging him.

"I ain't never seen nobody miss so many duckies in my *life* as that boy there!" The voice was deep, with a harsh rattle to it. Louder than the music, louder than the roar and clack of the roller coasters nearby.

The man in the yellow shirt seemed to make up his mind. "You want to see aim?" he called. "I'll show you aim." He turned and headed toward the cages, the woman trotting to keep up. Paulie started walking away. I tugged at his sleeve.

"Wait, I want to see."

"Nothing to see except that guy waste a dime," he said. But he came with me.

A row of chain-link cages, set maybe six feet off the ground, stretched down a length of the Bowery. In each cage, a Negro man in a white shirt and white pants sat on a platform over a tub of water. They were the only Negroes I'd seen in the park all night. The sign overhead read AFRICAN DIP.

The Negro who'd hollered at the man in the yellow shirt cupped his hands to his mouth. "Hey, sissy! That ain't the same girl you brought here last night!" That got more laughter, some rude hoots. The crowd was getting bigger. The man paid the attendant, got three baseballs in return. He rolled up his right sleeve.

"Uh-oh, here he comes," the Negro shouted. "Looks like I better shut my mouth."

"Don't worry. I'll shut your mouth for you," the man called. He drew his arm back.

"Winding up for the pitch," the Negro said. "Watch out, now, there's a breeze from the east . . . gotta figure that in, too . . ."

The man leaned forward. Just before he let fly, the Negro yelled, "Pansy!" at the top of his voice. The ball hit the back of the platform, barely two inches from the button that would have dropped the Negro into the water. Groans and laughter from the spectators. The man shook his head—one quick, angry jerk—and picked up a second ball.

He took longer to aim this time. The Negro kept up a steady patter. "Anybody got spectacles he can borrow? Maybe your eyes ain't the problem, though . . . that arm of yours looks no bigger'n a chicken wing . . . looks like you're gonna hurt yourself—"

The man hurled the baseball. It missed the target by a good foot.

"Now that's a darn shame."

Fewer groans, more laughter. By now at least fifty people had gathered around. Most had wide grins. A group of sailors started chanting: *Dunk the nigger, dunk the nigger, dunk the*— The man picked up the last ball. Someone whistled.

I tried to imagine Ozzie up there. Ozzie with his long hands and wide, serious eyes, in a baggy white uniform and cap. Ozzie taunting white boys to earn money. I couldn't picture it. I didn't want to.

"Maybe you ought to get someone to throw the ball *for*

you," the Negro was saying. The Negro in the next cage yelled, "How about him?" and pointed to a little boy wearing enormous glasses. The crowd roared.

"How about you shut the hell up?" the man shouted.

"Why don't you ask your girl there to throw for you? I bet she can—"

The baseball smashed into the cage with a ringing *clang*. I jumped, my hand to my mouth. More whistles and laughs. Some people clapped. If the cage hadn't been there, the ball would've hit the Negro square in the face.

"Three strikes," the Negro hollered, "he's out! Better luck next time, pansy!" The man dug into his pocket for another coin, muttering.

"The way that shine's got him worked up, he'll pitch balls until he either dunks the nigger or runs out of dimes," Paulie said. "Come on, let's do the Flying Turns."

We walked up the Bowery. Waltz music floated from the banjo speakers. People strolled past, laughing and talking. With Paulie's muscled arms tight around me, I felt like nothing on earth could hurt me. Still I couldn't get the thought of Ozzie out of my head. Ozzie with his talent, the way his trumpet made all of Lily's swing and sweat. Put him in a cage over a tub of water, and men would hurl baseballs at his face. I hadn't understood the cage, at first. I did now. I thought of Ozzie's face, bleeding, and pushed the image away.

Once we got to the picnic area, instead of heading to the roller coaster, Paulie led me into the picnic grove. "Nice and quiet in here," he said.

And dark. The only lights were from the Flying Turns, glimmering on the picnic tables. Barely enough to see Paulie's eyes, black here in the dark, not a trace of color left. He closed them and kissed me, harder than before, rougher. His hands skimmed down the front of my dress, undoing the buttons . . . one, two . . . I shivered as the night air hit my skin. I'd never let a boy undo my dress before, not even the fish at the dance hall. Paulie's hands were warm and I shivered again. He moaned. I felt the vibration of it in his jaw, his tongue, felt it pass from his mouth to mine. He pushed me back against a tree, slipped one hand inside my dress, ran the other one under my skirt. No grabbing this time; his fingers caressed the garter along my thigh. My skin felt electric where he touched me. The whole world was Paulie, and my skin.

"Be sweet to me," he whispered. "Are you gonna be sweet to me?"

"I love you, Paulie. I love you more than anything . . ."

"Show me. Show me you love me." He kneaded the girdle at my hip, then slid a finger underneath, pulling at it. He groaned, a long, deep rumble of frustration. "Come on," he said. He pushed himself away from me. "Button up, quick," he said. I did.

"Where are we going?"

"The car. Come on." He pulled me along, stumbling over the grass tufts, and then we were on the path again, lights and screams and laughter all around us, the smell of hot dogs, waltz music lilting over everything. The car, parked all the way at the end of the lot. More alone than we'd ever been anywhere.

My steps slowed. My weight dragged against Paulie's arm like an anchor. "Paulie, wait. Can't we just . . ."

"Just what?" He stopped and turned to face me. "Just what, Ruby? Make out at the movies? Feel you up through your damn clothes?" Startled glances from the people around us. I ducked my head so they couldn't see my face.

No more kid stuff. This was what I wanted. Wasn't it?

Paulie leaned close. His breath was soft in my ear. "Look, don't worry. You won't get caught," and at first I thought he meant Ma, but then he said, "I have protection. You'll be all right."

Ma's face and mine, side by side in the mirror. *You're a good daughter.* But I wasn't, because every time I saw her, every time I talked to her, I lied. I wasn't who she thought I was.

Paulie slid his arm around my shoulder. "Ruby. Come on. It'll be all right, I promise."

I shook my head. His face tightened, the pale brows drawn down. I opened my mouth to explain, but no words came. I wanted him. And I wanted one thing that my mother believed about me still to be true. How was I supposed to explain that?

"I've waited, Ruby. A long time. Haven't I?"

"I know, Paulie, it's just . . ."

His voice rose. "Why do you think I keep leaving, huh? You think this is fun for me, your little games?" He stepped back, hands jammed in his pockets. Guilt twisted inside me. He was making me choose. How was I supposed to choose?

"I'm not playing games," I whispered.

"Not anymore, you're not," he said. "I'm done waiting. You say you love me, you better prove it."

You've played that hand out. . . . I'm through talking. Tom's voice, mocking. A sliver of anger cut through the guilt. I lifted my chin. "Do you love *me*?"

He stared like I'd asked him to climb into the dip

cages with the Negroes. "Look around! Am I here with another girl, or with you?" He held out his hand, palm up. "You want to be with me, then come on. You want to play with babies, go back to the sandbox."

He waited. One heartbeat. Then he walked away.

I should have run after him. But I thought he'd come back. An hour later, when I went to the parking lot to look for him, the kelly green convertible was gone.

. . .

I got home a little after eleven. I hadn't thought to bring money for a cab—why would I?—so I'd had to take the el and the streetcar. Almost an hour to get home, the whole time thinking, *He left you. He left you.*

How could I have been so stupid? *You should have gone with him. You love him, don't you? You should have proved it.*

This time, I knew, I wouldn't get another chance.

As I walked up Honore Street to our flat, I saw the kitchen light was on. Ma must still be up. Of all nights . . . Please, God, let her not ask any questions. It'd been all I could do not to bust up sobbing on the el. If I had to start making up stories, I'd lose it for sure, and then God only knew what I'd say.

At least I could walk in and look her in the face. An hour ago, that had seemed like everything. Now Paulie was gone and I didn't know anything anymore.

I expected Ma to be in the kitchen, in her housecoat. But as I stepped inside she was coming into the parlor and she was still dressed to the nines. A curl had come undone over her ear. Her bare lips were as pale as her cheeks; the lipstick I'd put on her earlier was gone. Betty was following behind her, yawning in her nightgown, as if she'd just woken up.

"Ruby, it is you!" Ma said. She laughed a strange, gusting laugh. Like wind blowing through her throat, not reaching deep. "I thought I heard someone in the hall. Don't worry about your coat, sit down. Betty, come sit next to your sister."

She was radiant. "You must have had a good time," I said.

She laughed again. "I . . . well, I did. Shall I tell you?"

From the sofa, Betty and I stared up at her like a couple of lambs. Ma pulled off her gloves. First the right, then the left. She held out her left hand, draped downward at the wrist, fingers pointing toward the floor.

My first thought was, She's cured. There was a miracle at the church, and she's cured.

Ma wiggled her fingers. That was when I saw the scrapes over her knuckle. And the ring. Not her wedding ring. A different one, with a flashing diamond.

"Girls," Ma said, "I'm getting married."

Three days later, she did.

SIXTEEN

It wasn't a church ceremony. Father Redisz told Ma she'd have to wait three months, to allow for the banns—but the Catholic Church wasn't in a hurry, and Ma was. So that Thursday, without telling me or Betty, she and a bus driver named Chester Nolan nipped over to City Hall.

We'd met our new stepfather once by then, on Tuesday, when he took us out for dinner at a steakhouse in the Loop. Before he arrived at the flat, Ma made Betty wash off her Peach Blossom lipstick and me my new Victory Red, and she insisted I change my Cuban heels for saddle shoes. I didn't even own saddle shoes anymore. So I wore the brown oxfords with the chunky heels instead. Ma frowned, but she didn't say anything.

"He looks like an icebox," Betty whispered to me as Ma ushered Chester Nolan into our parlor. I felt too numb to laugh, even though it was true. Square shoulders dropping straight down to short legs. A flat, square face. Not ugly, not handsome. He could've been a customer at the Starlight. For a panicked second, I wondered if he was. Then he doffed his hat, showing gingery hair, combed straight back, a white streak over his right eye. I let out my breath, relieved. I'd remember that hair.

He kissed Ma on the cheek—he didn't have to bend far to do it, he was only half a head taller than she was—then stood with his hands folded in front of him while Ma introduced us. His hands were broad, spangled with fine gold hairs. His palm moist when he gripped mine.

"Shall we go?" he said. He offered Ma his arm. She smiled and slipped her hand over his bent elbow, as though she'd been walking with him for years.

At the restaurant, Chester told us bus driver stories. No different from the Starlight. I knew how to pretend to listen without hearing a word. I watched him pick up his fork and knife and, with hardly a hitch in his story, begin cutting Ma's steak. He sprinkled salt and pepper for her; he broke her roll in half and buttered it. Through everything, Ma beamed at him.

"Thank you, Chester." Again and again. "Thank you so much."

"You bet, sweetheart," he answered her. "Sure I cut those small enough?"

Like they'd done it a hundred times before. Ma smiling and frail and brave, Chester hovering and protecting.

Ma touched the glinting gold hairs on the back of his hand. "Tell the girls about the blind woman. Remember that radio story about the Seeing Eye, girls? Chester had one of those wonderful dogs on his bus last week!"

She was trying too hard. I tried to catch Betty's eye, to see if she'd noticed, but her gaze kept flicking between her menu and the other diners and the waiters carrying plates back and forth. I realized with a start that this dumpy steakhouse must be her first real restaurant. I wondered if my eyes had been as big in that little Chinese dive with Tom and Jack and Peggy. It embarrassed me to think they must have been.

I interrupted Chester in the middle of his Seeing Eye dog story. "So how did you meet, anyway?" I asked Ma. Beside me, I felt Betty snap to attention.

They fidgeted and threw little glances at each other. Ma laughed her new gusty laugh. Two months ago, she said, she'd been on her way to see a new doctor in Avondale. (Ma had been to a doctor? How come she hadn't told me?) She'd stumbled getting on the bus, and Chester had jumped up and taken her arm. He settled her in the seat closest to the front, and they chatted all the way up Western Avenue. Her next appointment, the next week, was at the same time, and Chester was the driver again. Over the next few bus rides, she'd told him everything there was to know about her, and us, and the Yards. Chester turned to Ma and, as though cradling the finest, most delicate porcelain, took her hand in both of his. "I guess that's why I fell for your mother, here. All she's been through, brave little thing, and still she can smile like that!"

She was beaming at him, all right. But her eyes were nervous, and suddenly I knew why she was talking too loud and laughing too much, why she'd insisted on little-girl saddle shoes and made us wash off our lipstick. She was afraid. And I realized something else: all those hours in the fitting room at Goldblatt's, running the salesgirl off her feet, Ma had been thinking of Chester Nolan. I'd helped her pick out the pale yellow dress. I'd done her hair, her makeup. And it'd worked. She'd hooked her fish. No wonder he knew chapter and verse about her arthritis. *Brave little thing!* But she was scared to death he'd drop the bait.

I felt something breaking apart the numbness inside. Pressure around my heart, pushing its way out.

I scraped my chair back. "I have to go."

"But you haven't touched your steak," Chester said.

Ma must have seen something in my face, because she laid a hand on his arm and said, "It's all right. We'll wrap it up and take it home." Then, to me, "You should get moving. You don't want to be late." I understood. Better for me to leave than queer the deal.

Half a block from the restaurant was a pay phone. I took the garage matchbook out of my pocketbook and called the number. No answer. It was six thirty. I had to be at the Starlight ready to dance by eight. I took the el to the Yards and headed down Fiftieth Street to the poolroom where, months and months ago, Betty's classmate had seen Paulie.

Third time was the charm. Halfway there, I spotted him, sitting on a stoop with two other guys.

"Paulie!" I started to walk toward him but he threw out his hand—*Stay there*—and said something to his friends that made them laugh. He grinned at them, but as soon as he turned toward me, his face went cold. He sauntered across the street, glancing this way and that, as if his coming this way had nothing to do with me.

He stopped a good six feet away. Beautiful as a statue. He reared his head a little when I went up to him, but he didn't back away. I knew he wouldn't. Not with his friends watching. I stepped close enough to feel his warmth on my bare skin—my neck, my face. I didn't touch him with my hands. Instead I leaned up, and I kissed him on the mouth.

Behind us, his friends hooted and whistled. I didn't care. Last night, I'd watched Paulie walk away. I'd lost him, just so that one thing Ma believed about me would still be true.

She didn't know anything about me. And, it turned out, I didn't know anything about her.

I swayed on my tiptoes. A touch on my elbow— Paulie's touch—steadied me. I looked into his eyes, rain-gray and wary.

"I want to be sweet to you," I whispered.

That night, when I left the Starlight, he was waiting in the kelly green convertible.

Three days later, Chester piled us and our few trunks into his old-fashioned black Ford, and we left the Back of the Yards and its slaughterhouse stench behind forever.

SEVENTEEN

In our neighborhood, the houses and flats were mostly wood, mostly gray, mostly narrow. A saloon or a tavern or a poolroom on almost every block. Hardly any grass at all, except in vacant lots. Just a few miles away, where Chester lived, lay street after street of brick houses. Tan or red, or with the bricks laid light then dark, like checkerboards. Lawns like welcome mats, rosebushes and daisies and irises and flowers I didn't recognize. Cheerful-looking corner stores, not a tavern in sight.

"Now, don't you girls get your hopes up about the inside," Chester said, pulling up in front of a checker-board brick house. "It's just a little bungalow, as plain-Jane as they come." He said that after having seen our flat, after he'd carried our few things out past all our staring neighbors. He said it knowing we would be dazzled.

No more mopping up floods when we forgot to drain the icebox pan; Chester's house had an electric refrigera-tor. No more scrubbing painted pine boards on our hands and knees; Chester's waxed oak floors shone a smooth red-dish gold. No more running to Mrs. Hirsch's in rain and snow to use the phone; a telephone hung in the hallway. Chester's house had a sleek gas stove, not a speck of coal soot anywhere. A real bathroom, all white tile, and a porcelain tub. No more washing our hair bent over the kitchen sink, or shivering crouched in the galvanized washtub. And thank you, God, no more hall toilet, with its smell, and buzzing flies in the summer, and icy drafts in the winter.

Chester had grown up poor in Canaryville. But he'd worked and saved his money, and ten years ago he'd bought this bungalow for himself and his mother. Last year his mother had passed away, and he'd lived here alone. Until—at this part of the story he took Ma's hand—we came along.

"Look at this!" Betty cried. "Look at this!" I followed her through the arched doorway to the stained-glass windows in the living room. The brick fireplace. Betty begged Chester to build a fire for her. He laughed. His voice rattled like a truck on gravel, and when he laughed, the truck revved speed. No fires until winter, he told her, when she'd appreciate it more.

He took Betty on a tour of the house. I stayed in old lady Nolan's room, which Betty and I were going to share. Wondering if Ma had helped Chester pick out the brand-new furniture. Two white dressers with gold trim, two matching bedstands and headboards. A pink and green tufted floral rug. It smelled of paint and clean wood.

Ma came in behind me. I knew it was her from the unevenness of her steps. I crossed to the window and looked outside, pretending I didn't know she was there.

"Do you like it?" she asked.

I didn't know if she meant the house or this room or the neighborhood or the fact that she was married to a man she hadn't told us existed until a few days ago. Even as I'd watched Chester carry our trunks inside, I couldn't believe this was where we lived now. I still had my hat on, and my gloves, as if the cab that would take me back to the Yards would arrive any minute.

But that wasn't why I didn't answer her. After what Paulie and I had done in the the kelly green convertible, I felt entirely changed, as if the old me was our dark, dingy flat, and the new me this airy, light-filled house. Before, I thought I'd loved Paulie. I'd had no idea, then, how love could seize you so absolutely. In the shock and flurry of the past few days, I'd closed my eyes again and again, imagining his arms around me, crushing me close, feeling every time a jolt of joy zag through me, holding it tight as if that feeling in my body could conjure his actual, solid self. I missed him so much, at moments I thought my heart might stop. Surely Ma could see it. She'd read what had happened in my face, my eyes, in the way I stood, or walked, or breathed. And then she would never look at me the same way again.

You're not my daughter anymore.

Ma came close, stood just behind my shoulder. "I know what's going on," she said. My heart lurched, my fingers tightened on the windowsill. Of course she knew. What could I tell her, what could I possibly . . .

"You miss your father," she went on. "It's not as hard for Betty, she doesn't remember him. But you . . ." She laid her hand on mine. Her voice anxious. "This is a good thing, Ruby. You can see that, can't you? Chester is a good man. He'll be able to give you everything you deserve. You and Betty both."

She was so wrong, she might as well have been talking to someone else. I swallowed, closed my eyes. I should've been relieved. I supposed I was.

Mostly what I felt was that my mother was a complete stranger.

She was waiting for me to say something. I didn't know what to say. I nodded my head.

"Good." She patted my hand. She was almost at the door when she added, "Now you can quit your job." Not a question.

"What?" I said, surprised. But the room was empty.

I found out what she meant at dinner.

"Shame you've lost this year," Chester said to me, as he divvied up the roast chicken. "But the nuns at St. Casimir's will get you up to speed quick enough, come September."

Nuns? St. Casimir's? Betty gawped at me from across the table. "You mean she's set back a year? But that means we'll be in the same class! I don't want her in my class!"

"Well, we tried to get your sister into school now, like you. But they said Ruby would have to wait until fall." Chester passed me a plate.

"I can't go to school. I have a job." I handed the plate to Betty. I wasn't hungry.

Chester shook his head. "School's the proper place for a sixteen-year-old girl, not cooped up behind a switchboard. I tell you, what I wouldn't give sometimes to have some-body tell me I could skip on back to classes! Nothing to worry about the livelong day, huh?" He winked at Betty. To my disgust, she winked back. I stared at her, but she just stared back, cool as you please, and took a big bite of chicken.

"I have a job," I repeated. "I'm not going back to school." Chester stopped carving and blinked at me, his flat, square face perplexed, as if I'd said I'd seen pigs fly.

"That's enough, Ruby," Ma said. "We'll talk about it later. Pass the gravy, please, dear."

She didn't say anything that night when I left for work, so I forgot about it. A couple of servicemen clocked me and Peggy out and took us to a supper club. I had two rum and Cokes and taught my guy to dance the boogie-woogie, and on the way home in the cab, I let him kiss me. Dreaming the whole time of Paulie. Tomorrow, after work, he'd be waiting for me again outside the Starlight . . . Letting myself into Chester's house, I realized I'd forgotten the mouthwash back in the hall toilet at our old flat. I tiptoed to the white tile bathroom, searched through the medicine cabinet. Bingo. I topped the bottle up with water, after, so no one could tell I'd used it.

The smells in Chester's house were different. No hot metal of coal stove, no naptha soap. No smoke plumes rising in the air outside, and instead of a dead animal and incinerator reek from the packinghouses, when the wind was right we could smell Oreos baking at the Nabisco factory nearby. No packinghouse whistles, no trains rumbling past at all hours. We couldn't even hear the streetcar. The strangeness made me feel unsettled. And every day Ma got after me about quitting, until I was ready to scream.

"Then what am I supposed to do?" I asked her. "Mop Chester's floors? Iron his shirts?"

"What's wrong with that? After all he's done to make you feel welcome, you can't show the slightest gratitude? Any other girl would be jumping for joy!"

In no time we were fighting. Worse than we ever had in the Yards, because now Ma wouldn't back down, not one inch. She searched my dresser and my pocketbook and took away my lipsticks and mascara and rouge. When I yelled that she had no right, she said, "I'm your mother. I may have let things go before, but from now on, this family's going to be the way it ought to be."

Meaning me.

Betty slipped into Chester's house and her new school like they were a dress made just for her. Not two days had gone by before she was helping organize a scrap drive for the war and going with her new friends down to Sixty-third and Central Park to wave at soldiers on the troop trains. If she wore makeup, she was smart enough to get rid of the evidence before she came home.

As for Ma, since we'd moved her nerves had disappeared like smoke. Still frail, still hurting, but more like her old self than she'd been in almost two years, before the rheumatoid. She'd made up her mind I should quit, and that was that. She had Chester, and Chester's house, and Chester's money. Betty was toeing the line, so all Ma had left to get straight was me.

The funny thing was, I half wanted to quit the Starlight. Del always said without illusion, we didn't have anything. Ever since I'd fallen in love, *real* love, with Paulie, I couldn't see the illusion anymore. All I saw was a bunch of men who couldn't get a girl to dance unless they paid her, and a bunch of girls out for every nickel they could charm, fish, or scam. I was sick of acting peppy, sashaying around for dances, laughing at the same joke I'd heard a million times before. Bruises on my toes from clumsy galoots stepping on them, those same galoots pinching my keister whenever they thought they could get away with it.

What good had any of it been, anyway? All my grand plans—moving us out of the Yards into a nice neighborhood, where Ma didn't have to pinch every penny, where Betty could go to a good school—were for nothing. Chester had swooped in and taken care of everything. All those months I'd spent hoarding one damn nickel at a time, and Chester just snapped his fingers.

But if I quit, then what? St. Casimir's and the nuns? I tried to imagine wearing a drab plaid uniform, like Betty, not a sequin or bow anywhere. Making Welsh rarebit in home-ec class, watching other girls swap issues of *Romance Weekly* and swoon over their friends' older brothers. Girls who'd never heard of black-and-tan clubs or policy kings or Reinhard's. Girls who thought a wonderful evening was a dance at the high school gym.

No more wild swing at Lily's. No more silk and satin, or dishing with Peggy over milkshakes at the all-night diner, or cabs whooshing through the streets in the black hours of the morning. No more listening to Ozzie dream about New York and Kansas City; I'd never again hear his music first, before anybody else in the world.

No more money of my own, to spend how I liked. I would get an allowance from Chester, same as Betty. Fifty cents a week. She thought it was a fortune.

"Ma's done good for us," Betty told me, "and you're

ruining it." Whispered fights back and forth in old lady Nolan's room. "Chester's an okay guy. You don't have to work anymore, so why don't you just quit?" The makeup I'd given her, the clothes I'd bought her, the coal, the Rice Krispies: all of it forgotten.

I couldn't quit. Because even if I could live without everything else, I couldn't live without Paulie. And if I didn't have the Starlight, I'd never see him at all. Ma wouldn't let me skip out to movie houses in the afternoon anymore, so he and I had worked out a system: he called Chester's house, let it ring twice, then hung up. Then I knew he'd be at the Starlight when it closed, waiting.

That whole first week, me and Ma, nothing but fights. Never in front of Chester, though. Ma insisted on that. He's never lived with a family before, she said. He's not used to this sort of thing.

But the tension in the evenings, before I left for work, was thick enough to choke a horse. Chester skulked like a hangdog and shot me baffled looks over the top of his newspaper. One evening, just before dinner, he came across me crying in the hallway. Took one look and rushed away. Big baby, scared of a few tears, I thought, and snuffled my way into the bedroom. Less than a minute later, two hesitating taps at the door. I opened it. There he stood with a glass of milk and two Oreos on a plate, the red turkeyish skin around his eyes crinkled in worry, the white streak in his hair like an exclamation point.

If he'd started lecturing me or yelling about my ingratitude, I would've given as good as I got. But I didn't know how to fight Oreos.

I took the plate and the glass. He looked down at the floor.

"It's not my place to step between you and your mother," he said, "but . . . this job, it's pretty important to you, huh?" He darted a look up at me, as if he was unsure whether I'd burst into tears or throw the milk at him or kiss him on the cheek. He was wearing his jacket with the Civil Defense arm patch Betty had sewed on for him. Chester was air raid warden for the block; this must be one of the nights he was scheduled to walk house to house, looking for chinks of light through the neighbors' blackout curtains.

I stared at that arm patch. "It is important," I said slowly. "It's . . . we're vital to the war effort. I mean, if you think about it, without operators to put the calls through . . ."

"Sure, sure," Chester said. Enthusiasm growing in his voice. Just tonight, we'd listened to a radio story about women building warplanes in a factory in San Diego. Ma remarked that sort of thing turned girls' heads, but Chester said anything that freed up more men for the fighting might be a darned good idea. Chester believed in the war effort. He'd dug a victory garden in the backyard; he even had Ma saving cooking grease to take back to the butcher. The government was supposed to collect it, make it into explosives.

Hope rose like a butterfly inside me. "So you can explain to Ma. Tell her I can't quit."

He raised his hands. "Like I said. I'm not going to get between you and your mother. But what I'm thinking is . . ."

It was only right, Chester told Ma, that I give fair notice. Especially since the telephone company was short-handed and I was still working all that overtime. Ma was suspicious, but Chester had peace in his sights, and she had to give in.

I got a two-week reprieve. And then I had other problems to worry about.

Manny and Alonso joined the U.S. Navy. Although, Manny told me, before they could fight the Japanese, it looked like they might have to fight the navy first. Lots of Pinoys were assigned work as stewards, but Manny wasn't enlisting to peel potatoes and swab decks.

"America gave me an education," he said. "Then they told me I was only good enough for servant's work. I've done enough of their cleaning and fetching. I want the chance to fight for my home."

I cried when he left. But Peggy was a wreck. She and Alonso had gotten engaged, the night before he shipped out.

"I'm just a sucker for flips, I guess," she said, wiping her eyes in the booth at Bennie's.

I squeezed her hand, and she gave me a soggy smile. Pinoy or not, it didn't matter; Alonso and Peggy were a good match. Him quiet and her cracking wise, but both of them street-savvy and smart. She'd fallen for him hard, and now she didn't know if she'd ever see him again.

Some other girls whose boyfriends volunteered, or got drafted, acted hysterical. But that wasn't Peggy's way. She danced like a windup toy, barely said two words to anyone. I tried to cheer her up, but she didn't want to go out after hours anymore, or shopping at Reinhard's. With Alonso gone, I could hardly ask her advice on what I should do about Ma, and Paulie, and quitting. I was just glad she didn't look at Paulie like he was dog poop on her shoe, like the other girls had started doing.

Makes me sick to see an able-bodied fellow not lifting a finger for his country, they told each other in loud voices, *while other men are putting their lives on the line.* Those girls had always been friendly to me, but now when I walked by, they turned their backs. Between them and Peggy's moping, it was no wonder I spent nearly all my breaks in the storage room.

It was only a matter of time before somebody noticed.

"Hey, Bo Peep, what are you always creeping down that hall for, anyway?" Stella called across the Ladies' one night.

"Got a hip flask hidden somewhere," Gabby said. Just the week before, Del had fired a girl for keeping a flask of gin stashed in her locker. Someone had snitched on her. Nobody knew who, but since one of Gabby's fish had been giving the girl tickets, we had a pretty good idea.

Yvonne swayed into the middle of the room, adjusting the taffeta bow at her hip. "*I* know what she's doing," she said. Grins broke out all around the Ladies', waiting for what was coming. I bent forward at the dressing table with my mascara and pretended I wasn't listening.

"The band takes their break back there," Yvonne went on. "What do you want to bet Bo Peep here is knocking back a few with the boys?"

My hand slipped, smearing black across my eyelid, as the Ladies' erupted in whoops of scandalized laughter. Yvonne raised her voice over the uproar. "She doesn't have to bring her own booze, she's tipping a flask with the coloreds! Aren't you, Bo Peep?"

Panicked, I shot a look at her. Could she possibly know about Ozzie? I should say something cutting. Put her in her place. But rattled as I was, it was all I could do to fix my mascara and escape to the dance floor.

At the break, I made double sure nobody was watching, then headed down the hall. I hadn't taken two steps, though, before I saw a man coming toward me in the dark.

"Looking for something?" Del asked. He stopped in front of me.

"No," I said. I hadn't done anything wrong, I reminded myself. So why did I feel like a thief caught with money in my hand? "It's just, that's the only window you can see out of in this whole place." I pointed toward the end of the hall.

"And what? You like to look out the window?"

I shrugged. Acting like I didn't care, but my heart tripping hard. "Sometimes."

Del drew a deep breath, let it out slow. "No," he said, as if he'd thought it over. "You don't need to be doing that."

Maybe Yvonne didn't know about Ozzie and the storeroom. But she'd said something to Del, and Del knew. *That pipsqueak sees ashes on the floor,* Ozzie had said, *he'll run me out of here.* At the end of the hall, shadows of leaves flickered over the glass. I listened, but I couldn't hear anything. Del took my arm, turned me back to the dance floor.

"Stay out," he said.

Later, I couldn't catch Ozzie's eye. Even during "Tiptoe Through the Tulips," he never looked up. So Del had said something to him, too. Had he threatened to fire him? Or just kick him out of the storeroom, make him take his breaks with the rest of the band?

So that was that. My only refuge at the Starlight, gone. Maybe Ozzie's, too. At home, thanks to Chester, Ma had called a truce—but a whole day could go by without her saying a word to me except *Bring in the laundry* and *Turn on the radio,* Our Gal Sunday *is on.* More and more, I felt her watching every little thing I did. I got the uneasy feeling again that she knew, she could tell, and no matter how often I decided I was being silly, this time I couldn't shake it.

The next night, Paulie picked me up at the Starlight. Now he came only when he could borrow the convertible. We used to take a cab to a diner, or to the Yards. Not anymore. We hardly talked. We always went to a place Paulie liked, a dead-end side street by a park, with trees all around and no lights.

Paulie drove us to our spot. He switched off the car and the headlights vanished, the radio cut out. The only sound was his breathing, and the squeaking of the leather seat as he turned toward me.

"I told you already," Paulie said when I asked him, for maybe the dozenth time, what I ought to do. "Move out. Take a room in a hotel, like your pal at the dance hall. That'd be sweet, huh?" His hand brushed my thigh. A long way away—too far to touch us—a single streetlight shone on a park bench.

It would be sweet. But to leave home . . . "I just don't know," I said.

"Then shut up about it already." The streetlight disappeared in blackness and warm breath as Paulie kissed me, pushing me back on the seat.

Afterward, I cried. Paulie groaned. "Waterworks again?" he said, starting up the car. "What is it with you?"

I couldn't answer him. He was the man I loved. I didn't understand why, after what we'd just done, I felt lonelier than I ever had in my life.

€IGHT€€N

The next night I picked up a fish, a skinny black-haired buck private from Nebraska, and browbeat him into taking me to Lily's. I hadn't been in almost two weeks, since Manny and Alonso's last night at the Starlight. My reprieve was almost up, but I still didn't know what to do. Ma pushing me to quit. Paulie pushing me to move out. Either way, one of them would be mad at me. Already Paulie was getting impatient with our system; just the other day, Betty had snatched the phone from me and demanded to know who kept calling and hanging up. He told her only the Shadow knew, and she'd busted up laughing.

"You shouldn't have said anything," I complained. "Betty's no fool. She'll figure it out."

"She won't have anything to figure out if you don't live there," Paulie had answered. I'd dropped it, irritated.

I led the buck private down the concrete steps to Lily's. He kept looking back over his shoulder at the folks milling around the sidewalk above. "There's a lot of Negroes around," he said. "You sure this is safe?"

"What are you, scared? Big strong fellow like you?" I

hooked my arm through his and pulled him along. "I told you, you'll love it."

He'd clocked me out a little before the Starlight closed, so Ozzie wasn't here yet. Ophelia was up on stage, though, belting her lungs out, and the place was hopping. Lily put us at a table near the front; good, but not so good as she would've given Manny.

I tried to get the private to dance, but he wouldn't, so I sipped my rum and Coke and listened to Ophelia. The past few months, she'd come into her own. Every bit of awkward polished off her. Her songs seemed to bubble up from some deep well inside, and when she leaned back and closed her eyes, watch out, because she'd let it rip and get the whole joint on its feet. Every night, she wore the cloisonné earrings Ozzie'd bought for her. Red, to match her dresses. I knew they were from him, because he'd asked me what I thought a girl might like for her birthday. If Paulie'd given me those, I'd have been over the moon.

She finished up her set, took her bow. All of Lily's clapping and whistling. She stepped off the stage, half a dozen men waiting to get her a drink, a seat, a handkerchief, anything they could think of. Good thing Ozzie'd made his move when he did. He might not have a chance now, I thought, just as Ophelia stepped down into another man's arms and kissed him on the lips.

I blinked, thinking I hadn't seen right. But then she kissed the fellow again. The musicians slipping looks at each other sideways, then back at the curtain behind the stage. I stood up, but I couldn't see if Ozzie had come in. "What are you doing?" the private asked.

"Dancing," I said, and grabbed his hand.

At the Starlight, the private had danced okay. Here, though, he was too busy staring at everyone else. Maybe he'd never seen a Mexican dancing with a colored. Or a white girl and a Filipino boy holding hands, or colored and white sitting at tables together. Another night I might have joshed him, smiling and laughing so he knew he was having a good time. But while he stared, I watched Ophelia cozy up at a table to the fellow she'd kissed. Did Ozzie know?

He came in just as we finished dancing. I tried to keep the private on the floor, but he aimed for the table like it was a foxhole. He lifted my wrap off my chair. "How about we find someplace more . . . regular," he said.

I snatched the wrap from him, tossed it back on the chair. "Go ahead," I told him. I sat down. He shifted and glanced around and made noises and I ignored him. Finally he slouched down in his seat and nursed his beer. I ordered another rum and Coke. Another one after that.

"Trumpeter's blowing some clinkers tonight," I heard a fellow behind us say. It was true; Ozzie was playing like a fire half-lit. I'd heard him put more pizzazz into "Cheerful Little Earful." After only five numbers, he left the stage. The other musicians shaking their heads. A few looked like they felt sorry for him. A couple grinned.

I leaped to my feet, snaked my way past the tables, past Ophelia and her new boyfriend. I couldn't see Ozzie. Had he left already?

"Excuse me," I heard him say, and as Ozzie brushed past me, I put my hand on his arm. He jumped, startled. Startled again when he saw me. The miserable in his face disappearing under *What the hell does she want?* I realized I didn't know. What did I think I'd do? Tell him she wasn't worth it? Tell him it would be all right?

"Dance with me," I blurted. Stupid. Ozzie never danced.

He glanced over his shoulder at Ophelia. Then lifted his head and looked down at me, his jaw pushed out a little.

"Yeah," he said. "All right."

I couldn't tell if Ozzie was good or if he was just good and mad. He flung me out and hauled me in, strong as hell and twice as fast. My skirt whipped around my legs and my hair over my face and he flipped me upside down and I couldn't see but I threw my hand out and he grabbed it and there was the floor and then it was gone again, and I forgot everything except the screaming horns and the drums pushing my feet faster and the grip of Ozzie's fingers in mine. He stepped the wrong way coming out of a turn and we collided hard, knocking the breath half out of me, then he yanked my other hand and I was flying again. The number ended, too soon, but the next was starting and I was ready to go, grinning like a fool. I looked up at Ozzie, but he was staring past me and his face was closed up like a door. I turned around. Ophelia sat next to her fellow, but she wasn't cozy anymore. Eyes like thunder cracking, her freckled chest heaving.

I took Ozzie's hand. "Forget her," I said. "What's she got to be mad about, anyway?"

He looked at me then. His expression so unhappy and so mad, I dropped his hand quick as if it burned. He opened his mouth like he was going to say something. Then shut it again, shaking his head. Like there were no words. He stepped back, hands raised, palms out, then he was walking away, away from me, from Ophelia, from everyone. Shoved past the curtain behind the bandstand and disappeared.

Couples jostled me off the floor. At our table, the black-haired private was gone. I grabbed my wrap and pocketbook and made my way out to the street. I gulped the muggy air, trying to clear my head of rum and confusion.

I'd only wanted to help. I didn't understand how I'd made everything worse.

. . .

The next day I didn't get up until almost noon. I slipped on a blue shirtwaist dress and slippers and padded out to the kitchen. The moment I stepped onto the smooth green linoleum, Ma said, "I had a lovely chat this morning with Mrs. Burns, next door. She was nice enough to copy out her war cake recipe for me." No *Good morning*, no *Did you sleep well?* Mad about something. My insides ratcheted tight a notch; I tried to think what I'd done but came up blank. Through the window, I saw Chester and Betty in the backyard, him with a spade and her with a hoe, working in the victory garden. The sky a hard, bright blue, the kitchen already steamy and Ma hadn't even turned on the oven yet.

I poured myself a cup of coffee. "What's war cake?" I asked. Sometimes, if I acted like everything was fine, Ma would come around.

"Like Depression cake." Ma stood at the counter, measuring flour into the sifter. She was wearing a new apron, I noticed, a pretty blue gingham with ruffles that matched her eyes. "But that calls for sugar and this takes corn syrup and molasses. Now that you're up, you can help."

I remembered Depression cake, all right. No eggs, no milk, no butter. It had tasted like a sweet brick. One of the first things Ma had made, once I brought home enough money, was a real cake with every ingredient God meant a cake to have. The three of us had eaten the entire thing in one day. Now, half a year later, the war was taking everything away again. Meat, sugar, coffee, all rationed. Butter impossible to find. Nylons, too. The government needed them to make parachutes.

"Mrs. Burns saw you trip coming up the steps at three o'clock this morning," Ma said. "She wanted to know if you were all right. Very kind of her." She didn't sound pleased with Mrs. Burns's kindness. Our neighbor had a sweet round face and battle-ax eyes that didn't miss a thing. Worse than Mr. Maczarek because as far as I could tell, she never slept.

"I didn't trip," I lied. I actually had, had caught my toe right on the edge of the step. I'd cussed a blue streak, too. Mrs. Burns must have heard every word, the nosy old bat. No wonder Ma was on her high horse.

"I see," Ma said, her tone saying, *You're lying.* "Still, you can imagine how relieved she was to find out tonight will be your last night at work. Get the molasses. It's in that cupboard." Ma pointed. I didn't move.

"But it's not been two weeks yet," I said.

"You'll tell them you're needed at home. Your supervisor will understand."

From the street, a car horn honked. I barely heard it. "But Chester—"

"That's *enough*!" From the corner of my eye, I saw Chester glance up at the window, then away. Ma saw it, too; she lowered her voice. "What you do reflects on me. On Chester, on all of us. We're a real family now, and we're going to act like one. For God's sake, Ruby, can't you see that's why . . ." She made her aggravated noise and turned away. Like Ozzie, last night. As if there were no words to explain how much worse I made everything. "I'm through arguing," she said. "Tonight is your last night."

"No," I said.

More honking. Three short blasts this time. Someone was losing his patience. And then, floating clear as day into the kitchen, a different voice. Paulie's voice.

"RUBY!"

I darted through the living room, threw open the front door. There, in front of the house, purred the kelly green convertible, Paulie leaning across the front seat, grinning at me from the open passenger window. I ran, barelegged and in slippers, down the front stoop, across the neat rectangle of lawn, Ma yelling behind me, "Ruby, come back here! Where are you going? Ruby!"

I yanked open the door and threw myself onto the seat just as Paulie popped the clutch. "Go," I said. "Go!"

Paulie never messed around when something needed doing. The tires squealed, the car leaped forward. I glimpsed Mrs. Burns's startled face peering out her front window. I flipped her the bird. As the car took the corner, I leaned halfway out the window, laughing as a warm muggy wind lifted my hair, sent it flying all around my head. I'd practically just gotten out of bed anyway, I didn't even have lipstick on. What did I care if my hair was a mess? Paulie tugged on the back of my dress and I plopped down onto the seat, still laughing with the miracle of it.

We rolled up California Avenue, the sun striking stars off the green hood. The fight with Ma faded more with every block. I'd get around her somehow. Maybe another good cry in front of Chester . . .

Paulie put his arm around me. "Where you want to go, baby? Anywhere you want, name it."

"The beach."

"You got it."

I laughed. "I was joking, silly. Does it look like I have a bathing suit?"

"That all you need?" He swung onto Sixty-third Street; two minutes later, the car rolled to a stop in front of Sears. Paulie handed me a twenty. "Get whatever you want," he said. "And don't take all day!" he hollered as I ran into the store.

Less than ten minutes later, I was shoving myself and two Sears bags into the front seat of the convertible. "Got it," I said. "Let's go."

But he didn't start the car. Instead, he sat back against his door and stretched out his legs.

"Show me," he said.

First, the pair of sandals on my feet. Then the beach towels. Finally, I held up the green and purple striped bathing suit. "What do you think?"

He looked so doubtful I burst out laughing. "I know, it's hideous." I pushed it back into the bag. "But if you don't like it, it's your own fault. You're the one who told me to hurry."

"Guess that's why you forgot the most important thing." He reached past me and popped open the glove compartment. "Lucky for you, I remembered."

I peeked inside the glove compartment and gasped.

Paulie slammed it shut, so fast I wondered if I'd imagined the gun, inky black and smooth, lying like a rock in a clutter of papers and gadgets. Then I saw the velvet box in his hand and snatched it from him, and in the tiny dart of disappointment—*too big for a ring*—I forgot about the glove compartment. I snapped the box open. Later, Paulie said I launched myself like a torpedo straight for him. All I remembered was smacking my knuckles on the window glass when I threw my arms around his neck.

"Put it on me, put it on!" I said.

The necklace was even prettier in his hands than in the box: a chain of white gold daisies, each with a dark blue rhinestone center. Paulie frowned, trying to undo the clasp. "Turn around," he said. I held up my hair, and the gold slipped heavy and cool against my skin. I propped myself up on the seat so I could look in the rearview mirror.

"I saw those blue bits," Paulie said, "and I said to myself, That's exactly the color of Ruby's eyes." His fingers slid up the back of my neck, under my hair.

"It's beautiful," I whispered. He'd stolen it, I knew. The cold-shivery thrill tingled through me to my fingertips, to the tips of my toes. He pulled me to him, and we kissed, and the thrill warmed and tingled, like my insides waking up after a long sleep.

A cracking rap on the window. We jumped apart. A beat cop bent down, peering inside, a nightstick in his hand. "Take it somewhere else!" he bawled at us.

"Yeah, yeah," Paulie muttered. "Goddamned flatfoot."

I smiled at the cop. *If you only knew what I knew.* He stared back at me, stone eyed. Behind him, four girls stood in a little knot, laughing behind their hands at us.

High school girls in saddle shoes, their hair pulled back with ribbons.

A year ago, that would have been me. I smiled and laid my head on Paulie's shoulder. He turned the ignition and gunned the motor.

It seemed like all of south Chicago was at the lakeshore. We picked our way over blazing sand through what seemed like thousands of shrieking children and their clammy-looking mothers; picnic baskets and girls already tanned the color of roasted peanuts; white lifeguard towers and the lifeguards themselves in their brilliant red swim trunks, like spots of blood spattered down the beach. I let Paulie get a little ways ahead of me. I'd been with him in the convertible's backseat, but I still didn't know what he looked like with his shirt off, and I didn't want him to see me staring.

Muscles shimmied across his back as he dodged around a toddler. The toddler's mother—thirty if she was a day, with another kid hanging on to her legs and a baby in her flabby arms—craned her neck to watch Paulie go by. "That one can rub coconut oil on me any day of the week," she said to her friend.

As if Paulie would give the time of day to an old broad like that! I trotted to catch up to him and slipped my hand in his. He shook free and pointed.

"There's a spot," he said.

Instead of sunning on the towel, though, Paulie coaxed me out into the lake. "It's just wading," he said, when I told him I couldn't swim. "Even that grandma over there can do it."

In the water, the air seemed less muggy, the smells of suntan lotion and sweat and hot skin less. Pretty soon, I was in up to my waist. When he tried to get me in deeper, though, I planted my feet.

"Gee, Ruby, I'm sorry. I didn't mean to scare you," he said, and reached out his hand. I took it and he yanked me hard off my feet. The water rushed cold up my body and I shrieked, but then he had me in his arms, one around my shoulders and the other under my knees, and I was safe against him, his belly sliding smooth and warm against my hip. The shrieking and splashing of kids faded; it might have been only the two of us in the entire lake. All around, the sun glittered like fireworks.

"See?" he said. "I wouldn't let you fall."

Holy Mary, I prayed, let me live in this moment forever.

By dinnertime, the crowd had thinned out. I felt lazy down to my bones: sleepy from sun and the water and hot dogs and root beer. The necklace lay warm as a cat over my collarbones. Paulie sat up.

"We gotta go," he said. "I got someplace to be tonight."

We bundled up the towels and walked to the beach house. Ahead, the downtown skyline rose like sharp-cornered mountains, the sun low behind, gleaming orange around the edges. Changing into my dress, I realized I should've grabbed my pocketbook and shoes before dashing out the door; then I could've gone straight to the Starlight. There was going to be hell to pay at home. Chester wouldn't help me now, not even if I bawled like a baby.

I had to decide. Quit the Starlight, or move out on my own. My family, or Paulie.

Whichever I chose, it felt as though I'd be leaving half of me behind.

The answer came to me in the car, so suddenly I must have been blind not to see it before. Paulie's hand was on the gearshift; I grabbed his arm with both hands. Something in the engine ground and snarled and the car lurched. Paulie stomped the clutch hard.

"What the hell are you doing?" he snapped.

"Let's get married," I said.

For a long, horrible moment, Paulie just stared. Then he started laughing.

It was like he'd squashed me flat under his foot. I yanked open the door and started to scramble out of the car, but he grabbed me and pulled me back inside, still laughing.

"You're just a kid," he said. "Married? You're joking, right?"

I hit out at him. Missed, because of the tears blinding me. "You didn't think I was such a kid before!" I shouted. "I'm sixteen. Plenty of girls get married at sixteen. My own mother did!" I snatched up one of the beach towels and wiped my eyes. Sand gritted across my cheek. "We'll be getting married sometime anyway. Don't you see? If we do it now, it'll solve everything." His face skewed, as if it'd slipped on ice. A sudden panic fluttered like bird wings around my heart. "Paulie! We're getting marr—"

"Yeah, yeah, just shut up a second, all right?" I could feel the impatience rising off him, like steam. He ran his hand through his hair, rubbed his face.

"This is the thing," he said. "I got something going. I can't say what, but this . . ." He gestured at the inside of the car, at me. "It's not a good time, Ruby."

I closed my eyes. Wrung the corner of the towel in my lap. All this time, I'd been so sure . . . His fingertips brushed my temple. Pushing a curl behind my ear. Still irritated, I could tell by his touch, but trying to be gentle. He was trying. I grabbed at that like a lifeline.

"Don't you think if we could get married now I'd have asked you?" he said. "I thought you understood, Ruby. I'm trying to get a foothold in this town, you know? And I'm close. *Real* close." His thumb wiped tears across my cheek. "Gimme a little while. Just until things settle down. Then yeah. Sure." His gray eyes gazing steady into mine. Flecks of gold and green and blue. My heart slowed down. *A little while.*

"This thing with your mother's got you all riled up," he said. "It's driving you nuts. And it's driving me nuts. I'm tired of sneaking around, Ruby. I want to be able to see you when I want. You get your own place, we can do that. You want that, don't you?"

As he talked, I looked at our hands twined together on my knee. Peggy had been right; nothing had happened the way I'd imagined it would. But those were little-girl dreams, babyish as the stories in Angie's romance magazines. Runaway heiresses and dukes in disguise. If you were savvy, you knew real life wasn't like that.

I was savvy.

"Yes," I whispered. "Yes, that's what I want."

"That's my girl," Paulie said.

NINETEEN

I was right: there was hell to pay. Thank God, Ma hadn't gotten a look at Paulie. I told her Hank Majewski from the old neighborhood had just bought a car and had come to show it off with a bunch of the old gang, Angie and Lois and some of the others. If Mrs. Burns had looked closer, she would have seen them in the backseat.

We were in old lady Nolan's room, Ma sitting at Betty's desk, me on the bed. Ma said Chester was so humiliated by what I'd done to Mrs. Burns, he couldn't bring himself to make his air warden rounds. He hadn't even looked at me when I came in. I wished he'd never brought me those Oreos, that he'd never been nice to me at all. Then I wouldn't feel so bad about it.

"Tell your supervisor tonight's your last night," Ma said. "Or tomorrow I'll call him myself. Understand?"

I'd made my choice. No question of quitting now. But I said, "Yes, Ma," and as soon as the door closed behind her, I started unbuttoning my dress. It was already after seven; I had just enough time to change clothes and get to the Starlight.

Betty came into the room. "Get out," I said. Instead,

she flopped down on her bed, the cat-watching-a-mouse look on her face that meant she knew something. Well, whatever game she had in mind, I wasn't going to play. I went to the closet and sorted through the hangers.

"Where's my russet dress?" I asked.

"Which russet dress?"

"I only have one and you know it. Did you wear it?"

"Maybe." I turned and glared at her. Her cheeks flushed pink. "I couldn't help it. It's cuter than anything I have."

I snatched my red skirt with its matching peplum jacket off the rod. "If you don't keep your hands off my clothes, I swear I'm going to scalp you," I said, stepping into the skirt. Realizing, with a jolt, that Betty wouldn't be able to borrow anything anymore. Tomorrow night, Ma would expect me to stay home. Which meant that I had to leave before then.

My hand lay on the jacket lapel, ready to flick it free of the hanger. What could I possibly say to Ma, how would I explain? At the thought, my fingers dug into the smooth gabardine.

Later. I couldn't think about it now. I shrugged on the jacket.

Behind me, Betty said, "Was it Paulie who told you to flip Mrs. Burns the bird?"

My fingers jerked, slipping across a button. I managed a little breathless laugh. "Paulie? *Suelze?* What on earth would he be doing here? No, it was Hank Majews—"

"I saw him, Ruby." Lying on her stomach, cheek propped against one hand. Smug as if she'd not only eaten the canary, but dipped it in chocolate sauce first. "I heard the honking and went up the side yard and

I saw him. Besides, Hank Majewski joined the army, remember? You better hope Ma doesn't."

The breath went out of me, sure as if she'd punched me in the stomach. "Did you say anything to Ma?"

"I *knew* it," she said. "You've been seeing him all along, haven't you? When the phone rings twice, that's him, isn't it?"

"I'm asking you, did you tell Ma!"

She rolled over and sat up. "Of course I didn't. What do you take me for?"

I drew a deep, shaking breath. Ma didn't know. In a little while Paulie and I would be married, and after that none of this would matter.

Betty leaned back against the wall, stretched out her legs. "So have you done it with him?"

"Have I . . . ? That's . . . I don't know what you're talking about!" I snatched up my black pumps, sat down at the desk to put them on.

"Oh, come on. How stupid do you think I am? I know all about it. Some of the victory girls have done it. Or they say they have."

"Victory girls?" I frowned at her. "Who are they?"

Instead of answering, Betty glanced away, an odd half smile on her face. For a moment, I saw her the way I had that afternoon in the Yards: not the sister I'd grown up with, but a girl with a high-bridged nose and chocolate-dark hair and a figure better than most girls out of high school. She'd just turned fifteen. A little practice, and she could pass for eighteen. Like me.

"Betty! What have you done?"

She looked up, startled, and then she was my baby

sister again. "Nothing." She shrugged. "Gone to the USO a couple of times. That's all."

"You're volunteering at the USO?"

She laughed. "Volunteer?" she said, as if I was talking about cleaning a pigpen. "Pour coffee and wash dishes? As if the boys want to sit with those drippy do-gooders, anyway. We hang around outside and they're happy to see us." She scootched off the bed and stood up. "And you can save your looks, it's not like you're any angel. Besides, me and my friends, we don't do anything bad. They take us to the movies. Or out for burgers. They're nice."

Organizing scrap drives for the war effort, she'd told us. Going to wave at the troop trains with the neighborhood kids. Instead she'd been running around with soldiers. The movies! Oh, I knew about the movies.

"So have you?" Betty picked a file up off her dresser, drew it across her thumbnail. "Done it, I mean. With Paulie."

"Don't be ridiculous." Stuffing things from my brown pocketbook into the black one. Handkerchief, change purse . . . I glanced at the clock. If I didn't leave right now, I'd be late.

"The girls who have talk about it," Betty said. "They say it's not such a big deal." She looked almost wistful. *It's not so bad,* Peggy had told me, that night at Bennie's. *It's never how anyone thinks it'll be.*

I snatched the nail file out of her hand and pointed it at her. "If you go near those girls again, I'll tell Ma. She'll make sure you never see another USO as long as you live. Got that?" I smacked the file down on her dresser. She picked it up again, leisurely, ran it over another nail.

"You tell Ma about me," she said, "and I'll tell her about Paulie. Got *that*?"

We stared at each other, not speaking. Then I stormed past her out of the room.

• • •

". . . so the army doctors stamped my papers 4-F," the young blond fellow was saying. "Unfit for service, all because I broke my ankle back in '39! Is that fair?"

I was stuck on my third dance with this chatterbox. What with all his yammering, I could hardly hear myself think. And I had to think. If I'd known, two months ago, that I'd have to worry about my own sister, under my own roof, I wouldn't have lost one minute's sleep over Stan Dudek.

The band closed the number with a trumpet flourish. That was another thing: Ozzie wasn't on the bandstand. Oh, they had a trumpeter—couldn't have a dance band without one—but he was some tubby fellow, without half the pizzazz Ozzie had in his littlest finger. Ozzie couldn't be at Lily's, it was too early. What if he'd gotten into a fight with Ophelia's new boyfriend? He'd looked mad enough last night to do anything.

"Looks like they're taking a break," the blond fellow said. He seized my hand. "And here I was just going to tell you what the second army doctor said. Buy you a soda?"

"Gosh, thanks, I can't." I jimmied loose and didn't wait for my tip.

The Ladies' was packed, as usual. Three deep at the long mirror. I couldn't see myself even when I stood on tiptoes. All the dressing tables taken, too. Except Yvonne's, of course.

"If you're looking for a fight, keep doing what you're doing," Gabby said, when I walked to Yvonne's table. "Otherwise, scram."

I didn't answer her. As usual, Yvonne's red fox fur hung draped over the back of her chair. She wouldn't wear the coat again until October, but she left it here. Not even in her locker, but out where everyone could see. It had made Peggy mad, back when anything besides Alonso mattered to her. A nice fur like that ought to be stored for the summer, she said. Not shown off like a trophy. I brushed my palm across the collar, the hairs prickling the inside of my wrist. The tabletop was cluttered with makeup and combs and hairspray. No one else left their things lying around, not unless they wanted every girl in the place to help herself. But no one dared touch Yvonne's stuff. Peggy was wrong, I thought. Yvonne didn't leave her coat here to show off. She left it as a sign: *Queen Bee. Keep Out.*

I sat down and picked up Yvonne's compact case. It was a gorgeous thing, beaded in red and gold, with a matching cigarette lighter. Whatever fish gave this to her, he didn't buy it at any five-and-dime. I dusted the powder over my nose, my chin. It smelled creamy, slightly sweet. Expensive.

"Just lemme know where to send the flowers, after," Gabby said. Two tables down, Nora laughed and repeated the remark to somebody else. Behind me, the everlasting chatter and yapping quieted down a moment. Then picked up again.

I know all about it, Betty had said.

She didn't. And she wouldn't, if I could help it. I didn't want her knowing the things I knew. Like the backseat of a kelly green convertible. Although you could call that by name, at least. Confess it to a priest. But what about all the other things I couldn't possibly explain? Like, knowing whether I'd get a bigger tip by flirting with a fellow or acting like it was my first time in high heels. Whether I could hook a fish for a date by suggesting cocktails and wild jazz, so he'd think I was the life of the party and a sure thing . . . or by mentioning a sweet little chop suey joint, quiet, away from all this noise, so he'd think I was fascinated only with him . . . and a sure thing. How far to let the hands go before putting on the kibosh, whether to joke or act offended, to keep the fish coming back, keep them believing, surely next time . . . How best to drop the hints, the sighs, the wants, so the fish would think the meals and dresses and makeup he bought me were all his own idea, and not me fishing him for everything I could get. If you went into the confessional and knelt in front of the musty-smelling screen and said, *Bless me, Father, for I have sinned,* how exactly would you describe what you'd done?

Illusion, that's what Del would say. You're helping them believe what they want to believe. Was illusion a sin? Did it make you hard, put a shell over you, paint you like an Easter egg?

My eyes looked back at me in Yvonne's mirror. Mascara and eyeshadow were supposed to make them bigger. All the magazines said so. But mine struck me now like two glints of blue at the bottom of the cellar stairs. Was this what people saw when they looked at me?

Something hot brushed across my bare arm. I jumped and dropped the compact case. A red bead skittered free across the table. Cigarette ashes drifted from my skin to the floor.

"Oopsie," Yvonne said. She stood next to me—sneaky, she knew not to come from behind, not when there was a mirror—one hand on her hip. Behind her stood Valerie and Stella, grinning. Gabby at the next table, an *I-told-you-so* expression on her thin face.

"Get out of my chair," Yvonne said.

"It's not your chair." I rubbed the sore spot on my arm. "And I'm not your damn ashtray."

Yvonne took a long, deep drag. The cigarette paper glowed, turned black, shriveled. Yvonne held the trembling gray ash over my hair. *Tap.* I ducked, twisting, but the ash caught my cheek. I jumped out of the chair, batting at my face, and the ash broke apart, fluttering to the floor like a hundred fly's wings.

"Good doggie," Yvonne said. Behind her, Stella laughed.

I snatched the cigarette from her fingers. She wasn't expecting that. I clamped my lips to the blurry scarlet marks of her lipstick, drew in hard. When the ash was good and hot, I plunged it into the collar of her red fox coat.

"Woof," I said. Smoke curling from my mouth. Curling from the fur. It smelled stronger than the cigarette and worse. Gasps around the room. I didn't look up. I buried the cigarette, my fingers disappearing up to the knuckles in bright, shimmery red.

"You *bitch*!" Yvonne shoved me away, but I'd already let go. Yvonne snatched up the coat and ran with it to the sinks. The cigarette dropped to the floor. I ground it out with my toe, smiling. I felt better than I had in days.

Walking out of the Ladies' was like swimming upstream. Everyone crowding toward the sinks. I had to turn sideways to get through the door, past the girls pushing their way in, jabbering, mouths open like babies waiting for spoonfuls of cereal. They stopped their yapping and stared at me as I went by.

The Starlight wasn't air-conditioned, and the hall had been jammed hotter than blazes all night. I could use a nice cold cola. I plunked my nickel on the counter, picked up my glass. Turned around and ran smack into Stella. Her elbow jerked upward, and in an instant I was freezing wet all down my front, ice cubes scattered around my feet. My breath disappeared somewhere deep inside.

"Oh my *goodness*, I'm so *clumsy*!" Stella wrung her plump hands. Snickers all through the lounge. My dress clung to my girdle and the girdle clung to me. When I moved, the fabric smacked against my belly like lips. I arched my back, held my arms wide. "I'm so *sorry*! You *do* have a clean dress, don't you?" A good little actress, Stella.

"Get out of my way." I stalked past her, back to the Ladies', trying to hold the dress away from my skin. I had one clean gown, thank God. All the others were at the cleaner's.

When I pushed open the door to the Ladies', I grit my teeth, ready for the chorus of cackles. But Yvonne wasn't there, or any of her gang, either. The only girls in the room were the usual stragglers, the two or three who never could time a break right, who Del was always yelling at to hurry up and get on the floor before he canned their asses. As I shuffled to my locker they looked up from the dressing tables, but none of them said anything. Not a single "What happened?" or "Jesus on a pogo stick, Ruby, what did you *do*?"

No doubt they'd heard Yvonne plan the whole thing. Of course Yvonne had put Stella up to it—that dizzy redhead could never come up with a stunt like that on her own. I peeled my sopping gown off just as the saxophone started wailing. Hustling now, I wet a handkerchief and blotted cola off my skin. The girdle would be sticky the rest of the night. But girdles could be cleaned, and the dress, too. Unless Yvonne found a way to hex a dead fox to grow new fur, though, she better get to work fishing a new one. That gave me a little satisfaction.

"Ruby?"

I glanced up. Alice, the girl who wore her hair in ringlets like Shirley Temple, who spent half of every night dozing in the meatpen, stood at the end of the row of lockers.

"The band's starting, Alice," I said.

"I know, Ruby, it's just . . . it's just that . . ." Her hands were clasped in front of her; she nudged them in the air at me. Why was she blushing? What on earth was wrong with her?

Whatever it was, I didn't have time for it. "Del's going to be pounding that door down any second," I said, "and I don't plan on being here when he does." I grabbed the clean dress—the one Paulie had given me, the smoky blue silk—and stepped into it.

"But Ruby . . ."

"For God's sake, Alice, leave me *alone*!"

I half expected she would cry. She did, sometimes,

when Yvonne teased her. I felt bad, but some people just didn't have the sense God gave a rat, and how was that my fault? But Alice only said, "Suit yourself, then." Which was an un-Alice-like thing to say. No time to ponder. I zipped up my dress and still made it out of the Ladies' before she did.

The band was in full swing. Del wasn't anywhere in sight, thank goodness. I straightened my shoulders and lifted my head and sashayed down the dance floor. A fellow bobbed over to me with a ticket. I took it from him and slipped it under the top of my stocking. The little colored lights floated across the floor, the walls, the faces. My partner was a good dancer, for once, and better yet, not a talker. Three couples to my left, Yvonne single-footed with a dark, Italian-looking soldier. She glanced my way and smiled, and at that moment, the lights came up.

Not the swirling colored dots, but the big overhead lights. The ones that signaled the show was over. Time to go home. Everyone looked up, looked around. My partner blinked, frowning. Even the band stopped playing.

Behind me, a girl shrieked with laughter. I turned to look. Off to my right, someone else—I couldn't see who—called, "Hey, Ruby! Over here!"

"What is it? Where?" I pivoted and craned my neck to see. More shouts of laughter, still behind me. Scattered guffaws from the men, while the girls' laughter rose into whoops. My partner backed away, a look on his face like I'd suddenly sprouted whiskers. "What's wrong?" I asked him, but he glanced left and right and shrank backward into the crowd. That was when I realized that the crowd was outside me. Fingers pointing. Girls nudging each other. I saw the direction of their stares, and my hand flew around to my rear. I'd changed dresses so fast . . . was my skirt hem caught in my girdle, was my underwear showing? But all I felt was the smooth fall of silk. And something sticky.

I looked at my fingertip. Bright orange red, heavy. I'd seen the color somewhere before. I touched it to my thumb, smeared it.

Lipstick.

Over the laughter, I heard Del roaring, "What the hell! What the hell!" And then I saw Yvonne.

She was hanging on to the arm of her soldier. Both of them laughing fit to die. Yvonne lifted her nose. Sniffed. "What is that stench? My God, it smells like . . . like a *slaughterhouse* in here." Screams of laughter from Gabby, from Valerie, from Stella. From everyone.

Red bloomed like roses at the edges of my sight. I didn't know I was moving forward until something jerked me back almost off my feet, Peggy's voice in my ear: "Don't, Ruby! Del's coming—if he catches you fighting, he'll fire you!"

"I don't care. Let me go!" I wrenched hard, left and right, put my head down to charge, but they hauled me off the floor, Peggy on one arm, Nora on the other, someone else's hands on my shoulders. They banged my head against the doorjamb, shoving me into the Ladies'. Once inside, they let go. I staggered, the heel of my hand pressed to my eye where I'd hit it.

"Hold still," Peggy said. I felt her unzip my gown, a loosening. I shoved it off, stumbling forward, one foot and then the other until the silk fell in a heap on the linoleum.

A fist hammered on the door. "Everybody out of there!" Del shouted. "Back to work!"

"Ruby's sick!" Peggy hollered back.

"So what! For that you gotta turn on all the lights? Half of you gotta be in there with her? Get your asses out here right this goddamned second, or all of you— canned!"

They left, all except Peggy. She bent toward the dress, but I bent quicker and scooped it up. Still she hesitated. "You sure you're all right?"

"Don't worry. I don't have a knife, I won't stab her."

"She deserves to get stabbed. I bet Nora's white gown will fit you. I'll ask her, if you want."

The notion of going back out there made my stomach shrivel. Tomorrow. I could do it tomorrow. Not tonight. I shook my head. I thought Peggy would argue, but she only said, "I'll tell Del you got sick to your stomach."

When the door shut behind her, I carried a chair over and wedged it under the knob so no one could come in. Then I held the gown at arm's length.

Written across the rump, in Gabby's brilliant orange red lipstick: STOCKYARD COW.

We didn't say a thing, Yvonne had told me.

But Stan must have said plenty to her. About the packinghouse. About the Back of the Yards. I could see her, resting her chin in one hand, smiling her lazy wolfish smile, asking Stan question after question. All that snickering she and Gabby had done, after.

Stockyard cow.

I plucked the tickets out of the top of my stocking and tucked them into my garter purse along with my tips. I stripped off my stockings—careful not to snag them with my nails—then the girdle. The ruined gown, the gown Paulie had given me, I stuffed into the trash. It didn't matter if cleaners could get the lipstick out. I'd never wear it again.

Yvonne had slung her fox coat back across her chair. The burn hole in the collar looked like a crater in grass, like a den a tiny monster had dug. In my bra and panties, barefoot and barelegged, I carried it to the sink and held the left sleeve under the tap. When it was soaked through, I washed the sticky sheen of cola from my breasts and belly. I used the right sleeve to dry off with. The fur pushed the water around, it didn't absorb a lick, but I didn't care. The soft coolness felt good. It was the only thing that felt good. I left the coat in the sink, went back to my locker, and put on the red suit.

Del's fist hammered again on the door. "You, Ruby! Get out here!"

I cracked the door open, just enough to see his angry face. "I'm sick," I said.

"I don't care if you got the Spanish flu. Get your Polish fanny in a gown and get out onto that floor."

"I'm sick," I repeated. "I'm going home."

"Then you better clean out your locker right now, because you ain't coming back."

I opened the door wider. "I'm going home now," I said, "and I'll be back tomorrow night. You know why? Because I'm your best earner."

It was a shot in the dark. I figured he was going to can me. I figured he'd say, *You, the best? You're nothing, compared to Yvonne. Don't let the door hit you in the ass.*

"What do I care about that?" he yelled. Stabbing a finger at me. "This time tomorrow, I could have a dozen girls lined up to take your place."

"And none of them as good as me." A little spark of victory catching inside, burning. *Queen Bee.* "Eight months, Del. I haven't missed a night. You can give me three hours." I coughed. Rubbed my throat and winced. *Give him what he wants to believe.*

Del looked like he'd stepped in manure. I supposed in a way, he had. "Something went on tonight. I don't know what. But if it happens again . . ." He jerked his thumb over his shoulder. "You savvy me?"

I nodded.

"You're one minute late tomorrow, I'll can your ass. See if I don't."

I ducked back into the Ladies' to get my pocketbook. On the way out, I stuffed the fox jacket into one of the toilets and pressed the lever.

The lights were down on the dance floor, the colored spots swirling. The band playing "If I Didn't Care." Everything back to normal. Nothing the same. Even walking felt strange, without a girdle. As though my body might spill in any direction. Bigger, but lighter somehow. Girls turned their heads away, pretended not to see me. I didn't look for Yvonne, but I knew she was watching.

Good doggie. Her eyes dark and brittle in the mirror. The beginnings of wrinkles at their corners.

I passed fifty men on the way out. None of them recognized me; none of them spared me more than a glance. They never noticed our faces much. A green gown instead of blue, pin my hair up, and I'd bet tomorrow ninety-nine out of a hundred couldn't pick me out of a lineup.

Let Yvonne think she'd won. Let her think she'd run me out for good. She was old; her time was over. Tomorrow I'd take her best fish away from her, that plug-ugly man with the big ears, and by the end of the week, I'd be wearing a new gown he'd bought me, and come the end of summer, I'd have my own fur coat, and I'd dangle it in front of her and watch her choke. Starting tomorrow I'd have my own place, and every night I didn't see Paulie, I'd go out on the town and have myself a ball.

I was the Queen Bee now.

TWENTY

Eleven o'clock and outside it still sweltered. The day's heat rose onto my bare legs as though coals burned under the sidewalk. No taxis in sight.

Just as well. I wasn't in any hurry to go back to Chester's house. I'd walk up Madison Avenue, take in a late show at the movie theater. I could think better in the air-conditioning. Maybe I could figure out how to tell Ma I was leaving.

In winter, people walked fast, their heads down. A hot night like this, they ambled. No hurry. Nobody wanted to be cooped up inside their houses. I kept near the curb, where there was a little more room. I was almost to the theater when an enormous, gleaming black coupe slowed up next to me, honking. The driver leaned across the seat. Even before the passenger door popped open, I started running toward it.

"What on earth are you doing here?" I said as I got in. Instead of answering, Paulie slung his arm behind my neck and hauled me close for a kiss, deep and wet and steamy. Someone on the sidewalk whistled. When he let go, I was breathless. He grinned his messy, crumpled grin.

"You up for a celebration?" he asked. He didn't wait for an answer. He shifted gears, and the coupe leaped away from the curb. I ran my hands over the smooth burgundy leather of the seat, feeling like I'd wandered into a dream, a dream where Yvonne was nothing more than a pesky fly, and Ma . . . Ma I would worry about when I woke up. If ever I woke up. For the second time in a day, Paulie had swooped down, snatched me out of my blues, swept me away. It's fate, I thought. We're meant to be together.

"Where'd this car come from?" I asked. Chrome glimmered on the dash; not a stain or a crack in sight. If the convertible had smelled like a shoe, this smelled like money.

"It's mine," Paulie said. "Nineteen forty-one Lincoln Zephyr Club Coupe. You like it?"

"Yours! Since when?"

"Since an hour ago. I swung by the Starlight to pick you up, but Del said you'd gone home sick. Glad I found you." He kissed the top of my head. "Wouldn't be a celebration without my girl."

I'd never seen Paulie in this good a mood. "What are we celebrating?" I asked. But he wouldn't tell me. Not until we got to the restaurant, an all-night diner off the Loop.

"Sinkers and suds," he told the waitress. "Blond and sweet, no cow."

"You got it," she said. And still he wouldn't tell me. Just sat there with the same stuffed-to-the-gills look Yvonne had after she'd found out I'd bottled hog's feet for the packinghouse. I pushed the thought of her out of my head. Yvonne would get what was coming to her later. Tonight, all that mattered was Paulie.

When the doughnuts and coffee arrived—cream and sugar for me, black for him—he leaned close across the table.

"I shouldn't even tell you this, but . . ." He took my hand. "I can trust you, can't I? You can zip it?"

"Zipped," I breathed, and drew my finger and thumb across my lips. His fingers tightened on mine, warm and strong. Then he let go. He picked a doughnut off the plate, broke it in half.

"You remember a couple months ago, you told me about that jumped-up colored in the pinstripe suit? The policy king?"

"Sure I do."

"That got me thinking. So I did a little sniffing around. In New York and Detroit, the mob's got policy all buttoned up. But here, the mob ain't got a hand in. The colored run it themselves." He dunked the doughnut half, shoved it in his mouth, chewed. "Millions of dollars, built on nickels. That's what you said, and I never forgot it. Millions, in the hands of some dumb shines. Seemed to me like a couple smart white boys ought to be able to figure something out."

A bad feeling began to stir in my chest. Like coffee in a percolator, when the heat's on, bubbling. "Paulie, what did you do?"

"Me and my buddy Steve, we took our time. Studied the operation. The guys who take the bets, the runners, they're small fry. Maybe they got fifty bucks on 'em at a time. The runners drop the dough at a policy station, but that ain't no good, either. Stations are crowded. Folks going in and out all hours placing bets. On top of that, they got maybe ten, twenty coloreds working the joint and the cash squirreled away like Fort Knox. Safes and everything. But the money can't stay there, can it?"

He didn't wait for an answer. "See, they got to move it. Pay off the winners. Pay off the cops. Kick the rest upstairs. These fellows who run the policy games, you know why they call 'em kings? Because they live in *palaces*, Ruby. Right over there in Bronzeville. They got Rolls-Royces and chauffeurs to drive 'em, and they don't so much as lift their little fingers for it. While I have to borrow a lousy dinged-up Chevy to take my girl out."

The bad feeling boiled right up into my throat. "Paulie, *what did you do?*"

"A few fellows take the moolah out of the stations. Same fellows, every day. They got routes. Same routes, every day." He chuckled. "Nice cars they use on those routes."

I leaned forward, whispered, "You *robbed*—"

"Shh!" He glanced around. Then back at me. "We were just going to case one of 'em tonight, we weren't planning to do it. But everything came together and we made our move. Easy as kicking a kitten. Shine never knew what hit him."

The gun, lying like a rock in the convertible's glove compartment. "Paulie, you didn't—did you shoot him?"

"What do you care? We got the loot, that's what matters." He swept up my hand and kissed it. "A cool thousand and a sweet car, and all thanks to you."

"Me!"

"It was you told me about it, wasn't it?"

My coffee cup slipped from my fingers. I grabbed for it, but not before coffee splashed across my peplum jacket. I snatched up my napkin and blotted the stains.

Paulie shot someone for money.

All those grilled cheese sandwiches I ate with him in diners just like this. Snickers and Old Nicks in Peoples Theater. Listening to him talk about the big score, while movies flickered light and shadow across his cool gray eyes. Me soaking up every word, thinking, *He'll be big as Capone someday.* Feeling that old, cold-shivery thrill.

How'd you think Capone got big, Ruby? By stealing dresses off delivery trucks? What'd you think he might do?

Not shoot someone. I never thought that. And the policy kings . . . mansions, Rolls-Royces . . . millions of dollars, built on nickels.

"They'll get you," I said suddenly. "Paulie, they'll come after you!"

He laughed. "That's the beauty of it, Ruby. They can't. They'd have to go through Canaryville to get to the Yards, and no colored in his right mind is gonna step foot in either one. If the Irish don't beat the tar out of 'em, the Poles will. As far as the law, fat chance. Policy's illegal. The coloreds pay off the cops so they don't get raided. It ain't protection money." He swallowed the last of his second doughnut, started on a third. "Best of all, Frank Nitti and all the big boys in the mob, they won't care. Whatever happens to policy ain't no skin off their nose." The doughnut piece fell into his coffee; he fished it out with his fingers. "See? Home free."

He made it sound easy. Maybe it was. But then, how come nobody thought of it before?

Either Paulie was the first one ever to hit the policy kings. Or . . . or somebody *had* done it before, and everybody knew better than to try again.

Paulie shot someone for money.

No. He couldn't have. He couldn't have done that, then sit across the table from me, eating a doughnut. He wouldn't be the same Paulie, with his hair gold on top from sun, his ears that stuck out just a little too much, his rain-cloud eyes.

"You know," he said, "a friend of mine is moving out of some sweet digs over on Van Buren."

Paulie shot someone for money. I shivered. Goose walked over your grave, Ma would say. I took a swallow of coffee. Not hot enough to chase away the sudden chill. I signaled to the waitress.

"I've seen it. Upstairs of a swell two-flat. Soon as I heard, I thought, that's the place for Ruby."

It took me a second to realize what he'd said. "But I can't afford a flat. I was going to see about the hotel where my friend Peggy lives. Like we talked about before. It's nice enough and I don't need much room."

"You can do better than a fleabag hotel. As far as the rent"—Paulie pushed the crumbs on his plate into a little pile—"I could take care of that for you."

I frowned. Take care of the rent? Like Yvonne and her fish? "No. I couldn't do that," I said.

"What's the matter, you think God's gonna send a lightning bolt?" He grinned up at me. "Seems to me he'd have done it already, if he was going to. Look, I'd pay the rent if we were married, wouldn't I?"

"But we're not." I flushed, remembering our fight in the car earlier.

"So?" The waitress came over, topped up our cups. Paulie waited until she was gone. Then he slipped his fingers under mine, stroking my knuckles with his thumb. "We do other things married people do, don't we?"

A shiver zigged down my back. I nodded.

"This'll make us more like being married. Isn't that what you want?"

"Sure it is, but . . ."

"But what?"

Maybe it wasn't the same as Yvonne at all. She did it for money. When you loved the man, though, like I loved Paulie . . . and we were going to be married soon, anyway . . .

"So that's settled." Paulie leaned forward and took my other hand, folding them together in both of his. "You know, Ruby, I been thinking. Taxi-dance halls—that's old stuff. In your racket, where's the real dough? Hooking the fish, right? But you gotta dance your feet off all night first. The smart dames, they don't wait for fish to come to them."

"Oh, yeah? What do they do, put an advertisement in the paper?"

Paulie didn't smile, but he had the same light in his eyes as when he talked about the big score. His fingers tightened on mine.

"See, this is how it works. I find the fish. You show 'em a good time. I'm telling you, the way this town is booming with GIs, we'll clean up. How does that sound, huh? Dress up in your pretty dresses and go out on the town, and not have to hop around a dance floor for nickels?"

The uneasy feeling stirred again; the coffee felt like acid in my stomach. *Their fish get something for their money,* Peggy had said. *And what they get is plenty more than a fox-trot.*

I pulled my hands free of his. "I don't get it. How are

we supposed to clean up, just from fellows taking me out to clubs?"

Now it was Paulie's turn to frown. "Well, that's not all they . . . Look, it's not anything more than you're doing already. My way, you'll get to spend more time off your feet than on 'em." He shrugged. Acting casual. But his shoulders had gone tense, and his face. Watching me.

I'm not asking for nothing you haven't already done. My back shoved up against bricks, Tom's breath in my hair. I looked at Paulie's rain-cloud eyes and I couldn't see past the flecks of color. I couldn't see inside. I wondered if I ever had. Or if that had been an illusion too.

Earlier, when I'd charged Yvonne, I'd been so angry I'd literally seen red. Now my vision was sharp as glass. My hands were in my lap, the tablecloth brushing across their backs. I wadded fabric between my fingers, crumpled it small into my palms. Then I stood up and yanked. The tablecloth upended into Paulie's lap.

I should've ordered the egg plate, with toast on its own dish and orange juice. As it was, there were only the coffee cups and saucers and the doughnut plate and the water glasses and water pitcher and silverware and napkin holder. Although, the water pitcher was full. That was something. I dropped the tablecloth while the pitcher was still tumbling, but from Paulie's yell I was pretty sure it got him.

There's your big score, I thought.

I walked to the door while glass still crashed behind me and knives clattered (maybe it was spoons, I didn't turn around), Paulie hollering, "Goddamn bitch, what the hell's the matter with you!" Then I was outside, heat slapping across my face like wet laundry fresh out of Ma's new washing machine.

I hadn't gone two steps up the sidewalk when a hand grabbed my hair and yanked backward. Pain shot across my scalp and I fell. I screamed and beat at Paulie's arm—it was his arm, of course, the muscles hard edged and taut— but he didn't let go. He yanked again and my leg and hip scraped across the sidewalk. I dug my nails into his wrist, trying to make him let go, trying to pull myself up, to make the agony on my scalp go away. From the corner of my eye I saw his knee draw back. I swung one fist high. Hit something. Couldn't tell what. The next instant, pain exploded down my side.

He let go then. When I could breathe again, I pressed a hand to the back of my head. My scalp tingled and stung. My side felt numb. I knew that would change soon. I heard Paulie panting above me. He'd panted above me in the backseat of the kelly green convertible. I'd thought it meant he loved me.

I heard an anxious voice asking something. "It's all right," Paulie said. "She's my wife." Footsteps walked away. To me, Paulie said, "You bitch, I'll teach you to make a fool out of me. Goddamn whore."

"I'm not a whore." I didn't know if he heard me. I pushed myself up along the wall. My fingertips scrabbled against the brick. My breath came in short gasps, every one like the stab of an ice pick into my right side.

"All those fish you bragged about, what'd they give you all those gifts for, huh?" Paulie said. "To look at that piggy-eyed face of yours? I know your racket, Ruby. You don't get something for nothing."

Illusion. That's what they got. They got to believe a girl thought they were handsome. Funny. Interesting. They'd pay for that. Every time. But that was one of those things you couldn't explain.

Illusion was what I'd paid for, with Paulie. I got to believe he loved me.

Now his face hovered above mine, the corner of his lip raised, a glimpse of white teeth showing. His eyebrows pale smudges in the shadows. Big man. He'd shot someone for money.

"Problem here?" a man's voice said. Paulie spun around. The cop—I could see it was a cop now—peered past him at me. Paulie edged in front of me, blocking my view.

"No, officer, no problem," he said. "My wife just fell down. Had a little too much, you know. She'll be fine in a minute."

"Wife, huh?" A big red hand appeared on Paulie's shoulder and shoved him aside. The cop looked me up and down. "You all right, miss?"

I didn't snitch. Maybe I should have. But what difference would it have made?

"I'm fine," I said.

He frowned. Glanced at Paulie, then back at me. "You make sure she gets home safe."

"I will," Paulie said. When the cop was gone, he turned around on me.

"Touch me and I'll scream bloody murder," I said. "That flatfoot will be back here in two seconds, and I'll spill everything I know. I swear to God, Paulie. I will."

He put his face up close to mine. "You breathe one word about me to anyone," he whispered, "and I'll hurt you. I'll hurt you so bad, you won't ever get better. You got me?"

I worked my lips like I was going to spit on him. He drew back fast. Raised his fist. I opened my mouth, drew a double lungful of air.

He turned and walked away.

TWENTY-ONE

The priest raised his arms high overhead, holding the white circle of the Host high before the altar. The jangling of bells scraped my nerves. I shifted on the kneeler, my arms on the back of the pew in front of me, trying to find a comfortable position. There wasn't one.

When I got up this morning, my entire right side throbbed. Just taking a step made me catch my breath. I'd hobbled to the bathroom, peeled off my nightgown, and stared at myself a long time in the mirror. At what Paulie had done. A bruise the size of my palm bloomed across my ribs, the color of raspberries in the center, spreading to grape and lime at the edges. Oddly enough, the girdle helped a little, once I'd managed to get it on. Betty had tried coming in our room while I was getting dressed, but I'd yelled at her to stay out. I didn't want anyone seeing.

"What happened to you?" Ma cried when I limped into the living room.

"It was the dumbest thing," I said. "Last night I tripped and fell down the platform stairs at the el station."

Chester hustled off for aspirin and a glass of water. "Let me look," Ma said, pulling off her gloves. "Do you want to stay home from Mass?" Behind her, Betty tried to catch my eye. I ignored her.

"It's okay, Ma, there's nothing to see. And I'd rather go." The phone had rung three times already this morning. If Paulie came, I didn't want to be alone.

Getting in the car, Chester insisted I lean on him, as if I might break in half. It certainly felt like a possibility.

At the altar, the jangling stopped. The priest lowered his hands. I bowed my head, but I wasn't praying.

I'd been in fights before. But I'd never been kicked and beaten. If it'd been some rough kid, some stranger, maybe I wouldn't feel so undone. Like even the ground under my feet might buckle and collapse, no warning, nowhere to run.

I never should've made Paulie so mad. I knew he had a temper; I could still feel his grip on my arm, that night months ago in the Yards, the stomach-flipping sensation of my bones bending. Last night, he as good as admitted he shot a man. So what did I do? I dumped a tablecloth in his lap. I remembered his yell, when the water pitcher landed, and shame washed over me.

At the same time, a little part of me said, He deserved it.

". . . *nos inducas in tentationem,*" the priest intoned.

"*Sed libera nos a malo,*" the congregation replied. Betty's clear voice to my left, Ma's slightly huskier tone to my right, Chester proclaiming loud on the other side of her. I moved my lips along with them, not making a sound. The ends of the lace covering my head fell like white fences at the edges of my vision. Keeping everyone out. I wished I could make them walls and hide forever.

We stood for Communion. As soon as Ma and Chester turned toward the end of the pew, their backs to us, something nudged my elbow. I glanced down, saw a folded note in Betty's hand. I took it.

> Paulie called this morning. He said to tell you he was stupid and he's sorry and he wants to see you. 8 p.m. at Maddie's Diner in the Loop. He said please. Five times.

I turned to Betty, as far as the stabbing in my side would allow. "You *talked* to him?" I whispered. "Why didn't you tell me?"

"I *tried* but you—"

"Psst!" From the aisle, Ma frowned at us. We hushed and followed her.

The minute we got home, Betty and I made a beeline for our room. I unpinned the lace from my hair, tossed it on my dresser. "Tell me exactly what he said. *Exactly*."

Betty nodded at my pocket. "Just what I wrote. I figured it was him calling. Two rings, nobody there. Then he called a third time and I grabbed it and said his name, and at first he didn't say anything but then he asked for you. I tried to tell you. You wouldn't let me in the room, and I couldn't say it was him because Ma was right there."

"Did she hear anything?"

"I told her it was a girl, Polly, from your work. I told her you forgot something there and this girl would bring it for you if you met her tonight." Betty stepped out of her good dress, pulled on the skirt she used for gardening. "Pretty good thinking, huh?"

It was. "Where'd you learn to make up a story like that?" I asked. "Your friends the victory girls?"

"Are you kidding? I'm teaching *them* a thing or two." Betty pulled her hair back into a ponytail. "All those whoppers you told Ma about going out with your friend Peggy. When all the time it was Paulie, wasn't it?"

Guilt settled on my shoulders like a crow. A fat, black, sharp-clawed crow.

"And Ma," Betty went on, "rooking us with all that la-di-da about the altar society. I bet there never was any altar society."

No. There wasn't. I'd figured that out about half a second after Ma announced her engagement. I hadn't said anything to Betty, I thought it'd hurt her. But here she was, half smiling at me, that kind of smile that says you know what's what. Nobody's pulling the wool over your eyes.

Betty gave a final tug to her ponytail. "You should've heard him, Ruby. He sounded awful. What happened, did you catch him with another girl?"

"Just forget it, will you? It doesn't matter." I kicked off my shoes and unbuttoned my dress. My girdle covered the bruise, Betty wouldn't see it.

"Whatever it was, my friend Susan says you should never forgive a fellow right off. She says make them beg first. Otherwise they think they can take you for granted."

I took Betty's note out of my pocket and reread it. *He sounded awful . . .* Did Paulie feel as bad about what happened as me? Maybe he wanted to take it all back, the way I wished I could. Maybe last night was just a mistake. A misunderstanding. Those terrible things he'd said, out on the sidewalk; he'd been upset.

The little part of me spoke up. *My way, you'll get to spend more time off your feet than on 'em.* He'd said that, too, and he hadn't been mad then. Pushing me to move out. Paying my rent, just like Yvonne's fish did for her. Only not a fish. Something else.

The way this town is booming with GIs, we'll clean up. It's not anything more than you're doing already.

Tears pricked my eyes, blurring Betty's handwriting. Paulie believed the worst about me. And even worse than that: he didn't mind. All the times I'd told him about the taxi-dance racket, he'd never cared how many fish I had. All he cared about was how much I'd soaked them for.

I crumpled the note into a ball and dropped it on the floor. Betty stared at me like I'd lost my mind. "Aren't you going to go see him? Aren't you going to talk to him?"

"No," I said.

Because to Paulie, I was just another Yvonne. And I couldn't forgive that. Not ever.

. . .

I took two more aspirins, then joined everyone in the kitchen. Ma and Chester sat at the kitchen table, eating sandwiches. At the counter, Betty chopped rhubarb stalks from her garden. Ma had said she'd make a tart for dessert.

"Betty said something about you meeting your friend Polly tonight," Ma said to me. "Now, is it Polly or Peggy? Or are they two different girls?"

At the sound of the name, I flinched. "No, she's . . . they're different. But it's just a . . . a magazine I loaned her. I don't want it back."

Betty shot me a look, her lips tight. She'd yammered at me about how awful I was being to poor Paulie until finally I threatened to stuff a shoe down her throat. That had shut her up.

Chester put down his sandwich. "Shame if you lose all your friends, just 'cause you're not working anymore. Say, tomorrow when I make my air defense rounds, why don't you come with me? There's some girls up the street I bet would love to meet you." He turned to Ma. "The Gorman sisters. You remember?"

"What a wonderful idea! Why don't you, Ruby? I believe you and Betty will be in Amy Gorman's class this fall. It'll be good to make some friends before then, don't you think?"

I'd seen the Gorman sisters walking to school in their St. Casimir's uniforms. Their faces looked as sweet and blank to me as whipped cream. I opened the refrigerator, looking for the lemonade; suddenly I felt as if I were inside it, the walls pressing down hard. I shut the door.

Betty and Chester went to work in the victory garden. Chester invited me, too, but I wasn't up for hoeing, or for more of Betty's sour looks. The day whiled itself away, one radio program after the next, a different one every fifteen minutes. The news came on. I listened to war news now, with so many boys I knew gone overseas. The navy had just won the Battle of Midway; I wondered if Manny or Alonso had been there. A merchant marine vessel had gotten torpedoed by the Japanese. The news finished. When *Scattergood Baines* started, Ma switched the station to music. A minute later, she was humming along to the radio. More cheerful than I'd seen her anytime since we'd moved here. Well, why not? Now that I'd fallen in line, we were a real family. Acting the way a real family should.

Yesterday, Paulie shot a man for money. Yesterday, I was the top earner at a taxi-dance hall, and yesterday, I'd burned a hole in a woman's fox coat.

Yesterday, I'd thought that today I'd be leaving home for good.

Now today was here, and I was rolling out tart crusts for Ma. I didn't have Paulie. I didn't have a job, or my own place. In a little while, I wouldn't have any money left out of the stash in my pillowcase. Fifty cents a week allowance, and come fall I'd be walking to school with Betty and the cream-faced Gorman sisters. Four of us, in matching plaid uniforms.

I was back where I started, nine months ago, before I pulled Ma's wedding ring off her finger and went to work stuffing hog's feet into bottles. A school kid. No worries except whether or not a boy liked me, and if I'd get called on to read poetry in class. But I wasn't that girl anymore. Chester came in, red faced and sweating. I poured him a glass of lemonade. He smiled at me and I smiled back. He and Ma nattered on about the war going on six months already. I put the tarts in the oven. The days marched ahead of me, I could see them, every single one exactly the same, and I wondered how I was supposed to unlearn all the things that I knew.

"I'm going to lie down," I told Ma.

"Are you feeling all right?" she asked. She felt my forehead. "Do you need more aspirin?" Chester shifted in his chair, ready to dash off for the bottle. I shook my head.

"I'm just stiff, that's all. A headache. Maybe I overdid it."

In old lady Nolan's room, the sun threw deep gold rectangles across the bed. I drew the curtains. Six o'clock. I could change into Paulie's favorite dress, the sweet little pink and black number, catch the el, be waiting for him when he walked into Maddie's Diner.

No—he should have to wait for me. I imagined strolling in, in my own sweet time. Paulie taking my hand, swearing over and over he'd never do it again. I imagined the tears rolling from his beautiful eyes. In the dark, sticky heat of the room, I built a shining picture of the two of us, just married, sitting down to dinner in a little flat of our own. Pretty curtains in the window, a quilt on the bed. Paulie carving the roast. Peggy and Alonso coming over, the men talking baseball in the parlor while Peggy and I sat over coffee in the kitchen and talked about them.

Knuckles rapped on the door and I jumped. Pain stabbed my side. I eased down onto the bed as Ma poked her head in.

"Chester's running some things to St. Rita's for the jumble sale next week," she said. "I know you're tired, but I thought you might like to go. Here it is two weeks since we've been here, and you two have hardly had a chance to say more than good morning and good night to each other."

I've decided to meet my friend after all. I could say it, and she'd let me go.

The stabbing in my side faded to a throb. I tried to call back the picture of me and Paulie and the pretty little flat. I couldn't.

Even if you made Paulie lose his temper, the little

voice said, you didn't make him kick you like you're a low-down cur. He did that himself. And as good as he did it, what do you want to bet it wasn't his first time?

Maybe not. But it would be the last time for me.

The words came like they were being dragged in chains, but I spoke them. "Sounds like fun," I said.

Ma crossed the room, leaned down, and kissed the top of my head. "Thank you, sweetheart," she whispered. From the doorway, she threw me one of her old smiles, blue eyes flashing. "I'll call you when Chester's ready to go," she said.

As soon as the door closed, I laid my head in my hands and cried. For Paulie. For the Starlight. And for whoever I was now.

TWENTY-TWO

Betty begged off coming with us. Said she didn't want to miss *Truth or Consequences*. So Chester and I drove to St. Rita's in his old black Ford. I thought he could tell I'd been crying; he didn't say much, but as he drove he seemed to be listening extra hard, as if anything I might say or do could give him a clue how to help. It was the kind of thing that ought to rub me exactly wrong. But somehow, the way Chester did it made me feel safe. I couldn't remember the last time I'd felt safe.

I could get used to it.

An hour later, though, after drinking three cups of coffee and listening to the St. Rita Jumble Sale Committee argue over how to arrange the sale tables, I was ready to run screaming around the parish hall. Right at this moment, the Ladies' would be hopping. Yvonne crowing at the top of her lungs about how she'd run me out, I bet, Gabby and Stella and all the others congratulating themselves. I wondered if Peggy missed me, if she was watching the door, rooting for me to come in. I glanced at the clock on the wall. Quarter to eight. Fifteen more minutes, and I'd officially be canned.

Fifteen more minutes, and Paulie would be waiting at Maddie's Diner.

I got up from my chair and poured myself another cup of coffee. By the time I finished it, the meeting was breaking up and it was three minutes after eight o'clock.

"Sorry we got stuck there so long," Chester said, on the way to the car. "I hadn't meant to get caught up in all that. Hope it wasn't too boring for you."

"No, it was fine."

"Your mother and sister'll have dinner waiting for us, I expect. I'm starved, how about you?"

"Starved," I said. He opened the car door for me, and I smiled at him. It felt strange, like putting on a favorite dress that you've outgrown. A little tight. The good-girl dress.

On the way home, the shadows stretching long across Sixty-third Street, I decided. I couldn't unlearn what I knew. But I could make Ma happy, I could get along with her husband. And I could damn sure watch out for Betty. Betty and those friends of hers. Victory girls? Know-nothing idiots was what they sounded like. Trouble.

Keep Betty on the right road—that much, I could do. It would have to be enough.

I'd make it be enough.

The house smelled good, pork roast and potatoes and the rhubarb tarts. I'd eat, then plead another headache and go to bed. I was tired and I hurt. My heart, more than my body now. But that was worse.

I followed Chester into the dining room. "How come the table's only set for three?" he asked. "Where's the munchkin?"

"On an errand," Ma called from the kitchen. "She'll be back soon."

"Errand?" Chester said. "At this time on a Sunday night?"

Ma appeared in the doorway, a bowl of mashed potatoes carefully cradled in one arm. I went and took it from her. "It's Ruby's fault, really," Ma said. Winking at me, so I'd know she was joshing. "Apparently, when Betty spoke with your friend Polly this morning, she promised you'd meet her tonight."

My fingers froze around the bowl.

"Then you said you weren't going to go," Ma went on, "and Betty felt badly. So she went instead."

"She *what*? And you let her? You let her go?"

Ma frowned. "Well, we couldn't have your poor friend sit there for hours waiting. Betty said she'd explain what happened, then come right back. I would have sent her with Chester but—for goodness' sake, Ruby, what's wrong?"

I didn't answer. I dropped the bowl and ran for the door.

• • •

Maddie's Diner lay around the corner from the USO. Servicemen of all stripes—literally—crowded the place, along with their dates. The radio was blaring, but you could barely hear the music over the riot of laughter and joking. I picked my way around a soldier's outstretched legs ("Go ahead, step over 'em, honey, they don't bite") and squeezed past a bunch of sailors blocking the path between tables. ("Say, darlin', what's your address? I'm lost without you.") A waitress would need hazard pay to work this joint. I searched for a dark blond head, but the few there were all in uniform. Had he taken her somewhere else? How would I possibly find her? Stand in the streets, scream her name? Call the police?

Maybe I was panicking for nothing. After all, what would he do when Betty showed up instead of me? A kid like her, probably he'd tell her to scram. She might this minute be on an el train headed back to Chester's house, boo-hooing because Paulie had called her a squirt and a baby. And when I got home, by the time I got through with her, she wouldn't know which way was up. I was almost comforted, imagining how I'd lay into her.

But what if he hadn't laughed at her? *I'll hurt you,* he'd told me last night. *I'll hurt you so bad you won't ever get better.* I'd thought he meant he'd break my arm, or my leg, or cut a cross into my cheek like Eduardo Ciannelli did to Bette Davis in *Marked Woman.* What if he looked at Betty and saw a way to get back at me? She could be anywhere in this bedlam of a city with him, a man with the backseat of a car, a man who'd shot someone just last night.

I pushed my way past two marines. And caught my breath in relief. There, in the very last booth. Dark blond, facing me. All I could see of Betty, the sleek chocolate crown of her head.

It's easy to sneak up on people when you're short. It's also easy when the people you're sneaking up on are sitting with their heads practically touching, holding hands between glasses of cola and vanilla milkshake. When I was almost to their table, Paulie raised his eyes. "Hey, waitress, gimme—" Then he saw me. His face went through an odd kind of struggle. He ended up smiling, but I'd seen the anger in his eyes before he pasted on that grin. He didn't let go of Betty's hand. No struggle on Betty's face; she wasn't happy to see me, and she didn't care if I knew it.

"What are you doing here?" she snapped.

"I thought I'd ask you that." I turned to Paulie. "Let go of my sister."

He shook his head slowly at Betty, as if she was a naughty child. "Looks like your big sis thinks you're horning in on her turf." He glanced up at me. "You want to send her on home? Slip into her spot?"

"Paulie!" Betty cried, at the same time I said, "Gee, thanks. But we're both going home." I jerked my head toward the door. "Come on, Betty."

"You go wherever you want. I'm staying."

"The hell you are." I took her by the arm. She yanked free and glared up at me, mad as an alley cat and ready to bite.

"Go on back to your dance hall, why don't you! You and your clubs and your booze, who are you to tell me what to do?"

I felt myself go cold. I felt my mouth flapping. No sound coming out. Paulie raised a pale, cool eyebrow at me and shrugged. Then he lifted Betty's hand to his mouth. Kissed it, all the while watching me, one corner of his mouth curling up.

I grabbed Betty's hand out of his and wrenched her half out of the booth. *"No!"* she yelled. Give her credit, she was a quick thinker; instead of pulling back, she stuck her foot out to trip me. I'd have been proud of her, except that it was me she was doing it to. I kicked her in the ankle and hauled again and got her to her feet.

"NO!" she yelled. "You hypocrite, you *liar*! Leave me

alone!" Kicking and flailing so hard, I couldn't keep hold of her wrists. So I got behind her and crooked one arm around her neck and the other under her tits and dragged her backward to the door. The servicemen about choked, they laughed so hard. Shouting bets to each other, shouting to Betty: *Sock her, sis! Land her a good one!* She did, too. Knuckles right in my eye, which got her a whooping round of applause. Finally, though, we got to the door. A grinning sailor pulled it open for me. I dragged Betty onto the sidewalk. I let her go to catch my breath and that was a mistake; she put her head down like a bull and aimed straight for the diner. This time I threw both arms around her waist and lifted her clear off her feet, spinning us both around.

My side was killing me and I was gasping for breath, but Betty had plenty of fight left. I realized I had no idea what to do now. I couldn't possibly wrestle her on the el the whole way home; I'd expire before we got to Western Avenue.

"Ruby? Ruby!" A man's voice, familiar. Tall, a natty blue uniform. A navy officer. I had to stare at his face a second before I recognized him.

"Stan!" I said, just as Betty twisted her neck and tried to bite me. I pinched her ear as hard as I could and she yelped.

"Need a hand with anything?" Stan said. He was grinning too. What was it men found so damn funny about girls fighting?

"God, yes," I said. "Whistle us a cab, will you?"

"Let me GO!" Betty bellowed. "I'm old enough to do what I want, and you can't stop me, you liar, you phony, you—"

Christ on a shingle, it was like trying to hold a giant cat in a dress. Where the hell was that cab? "Betty, so help me God, if you don't quit, I'm going to rip your ear *right off* your head!" I gave it a good wrench. Show her I meant business. That calmed her down some.

A cab pulled up to the curb. "Here we go," Stan said, and opened the door.

That set Betty off again. "If you send me home, I'll tell Ma everything! I'll tell everyone, I'll—"

I hauled her around and slapped her across the face as hard as I could. Her hand flew to her cheek; red blotches spread from under her fingers. I shoved her toward Stan, making sure to keep her sideways so she couldn't kick him. "Take her home, please, Stan. I have to—I have to clear up something here. Will you? Please!"

He glanced at the window full of laughing sailors. Then at Betty. "Tell me which one it was. I'll take care of it."

"No, you're an officer, you'll get in trouble. I can handle it. Just please, take her home!"

"No," Betty whimpered. "No, I won't . . ."

"You will. Or I'll belt you so hard you'll think God himself smote you." To Stan, I said, "You better get in first. Or she'll jump out the other side."

"You always were the sharp one, Ruby." He bent forward swiftly, kissed me on the cheek. Then he grinned and folded himself into the taxi. I pushed Betty in after him. The slap had taken the wind out of her sails; as soon as her fanny hit the seat, she collapsed on Stan's shoulder, sobbing. I leaned in the cab window and babbled the address to the driver.

"Make sure she gets in the house," I told Stan. "Hand her to her stepfather. He'll take care of her from there."

"Will do," Stan said. "You sure you don't need a hand? I could call a few fellows . . ."

"No. But thanks."

Betty raised her head. Her face was ugly, contorted with tears. "I'll tell Ma!" she shouted. "I'll tell her everything!"

Yeah? Tell me something I didn't know.

I walked back into the diner to a chorus of whistles and applause. "Watch out, here comes the wildcat," someone called. I shouldered past them but didn't look left or right. My eyes were fixed on Paulie. He was leaning against the diner counter, his hands in his pockets. Then he straightened up and crossed his arms. Tough guy. Paulie was a tough guy, all right. Won all his fights, in the ring and out. Half killed a fellow with his hands. Beat up a girl on a sidewalk.

The trick to punching somebody, he'd told me once, *is aim six inches behind where you want to hit. Then follow through. Where most chumps make their mistake is, they don't follow through.*

I drew my fist back, still walking. The soldiers hooted. Paulie tilted his chin up, out of my reach. Gray eyes hard as walls slanting down at me.

Last step, dip of my knee, fist swinging underhand. Paulie knew where I was headed then. Tried to scuttle backward but I'd figured on that and I kept coming. Eight months of dancing, my legs strong as hell. Fist coming up. Knuckles scraped cotton trousers, kept going. Followed through so hard I felt his heels lift off the ground.

I staggered a little, recovering. Almost tripped over Paulie jackknifed on the floor. I put a hand on the counter and steadied myself, and I said, "You come within a mile of my sister again, I'll kill you."

Paulie didn't answer. He was puking.

I walked a clear path to the door. God parted the Red Sea, I parted a khaki one. Nobody crowding. No catcalls. The only sound, Paulie retching.

I stepped outside and I didn't look back.

TWENTY-THREE

Out on the sidewalk, the streetlights had come on. I stood panting. My side throbbed deep. My arm hurt from my knuckles clear up to my elbow. Behind me, I heard the diner door squeak open. I brought my fists up, but it was only a GI holding out my pocketbook. I took it from him. He glanced back into the diner and said, in an easy Southern drawl, "You might oughta lay low a bit, miss. The stuff he's starting to say, it ain't too pretty."

"Thank you," I said. The GI touched his cap and went back inside.

I didn't even think where I was going. I took the el and then the streetcar and twenty minutes later I was smelling a smell as familiar to me as Ma's lavender water. Summer strong, as if the heat boiled the stench down thick as gravy. I stumbled off the streetcar at Forty-seventh and Damen. Ahead, in the fading light, rose the smokestacks of the Yards. I'd come home.

Boys played line ball in the street. Crack of the bat, sprinting, a flying catch. All up and down the block, folks sat on their front stoops or leaned out their windows. So many windows with stars. Mostly blue, but every once in a while, gold. The Majewskis' flat had one of each. Hank and his big brother, Les. Which one wasn't coming home?

Union Hall. Paulie and I met there. That night, the only time we ever danced. He'd kissed me, then left me staring after him like a fool. But he'd always come back. Never when I was looking for him. But I'd turn around and there he'd be. Crooking his eyebrow at me, grinning.

He wouldn't stop now. I knew it, even before that GI said what he'd said. I'd humiliated him, I'd laid him out like a ninepin in front of an entire diner. He'd be coming back, all right. But . . . I remembered the shift of his eyes to mine as he kissed Betty's hand. I'd seen the look on her face when his lips touched her fingers. She was a smart girl. But when it came to Paulie, smart wasn't nearly enough.

Just look at me.

Nothing could stop Paulie from crooking his eyebrow at my sister. Nothing could stop her from running to him when he did. And he would. He'd do it just to get even.

Whistles blared from the packinghouses. Shifts changing. I rubbed my knuckles, feeling the ghosts of scabs, the sting of brine in cuts and scratches. I could go back. Tell Chester. And Chester would do what? Call the police? What good would that do?

I could go to the police myself. Say that Paulie attacked me. I had the marks to prove it.

But it would be my word against his. The word of a taxi dancer. A girl who went with men for money. No one would believe that all I'd done was let the customers kiss me. Paulie would say he'd given me sixty dollars, and they'd say I deserved whatever I got.

No. I needed something better than police.

Honore Street. Our old flat, five doors up. Folks walked

past me like I was a rock in a stream. Any second, some-body would recognize me, and the next thing you knew, I'd be answering a dozen people's questions about Ma, and Betty, and Ma's new husband and our new house . . .

I turned back the way I'd come. Across the street was the Wachowskis' tavern, the same Hamm's beer signs in the windows that had been there as long as I could remember. I missed Angie, her kitten's face and her bluntness, with a sudden ache in my throat, sharp as thirst. Where was she tonight? At the movies with Lois Terasek. Or dancing to the jukebox at Pulaski's drugstore. Who did the girls dance with, now that the boys were gone?

She might be home. She was sometimes, Sunday nights when her mother helped out in the tavern and Angie had to watch the kids. I could climb upstairs, knock on the door. And say what? I saw Stan Dudek an hour ago, he helped me out of a jam. He looked great, Angie. Like he was going places.

Or I could say, last night, Paulie Suelze beat me in the street. Right after he shot somebody. Stole the man's car and a lot of money. You've heard of policy, haven't you, Angie? Millions of dollars, made out of nickels.

The Hamm's signs faded. In my mind I saw Paulie's face, the corner of his lip raised like a dog snarling. *You breathe one word about me to anyone,* he'd said, *and I'll hurt you.*

You breathe one word about me to anyone.

I started walking back to the streetcar. After half a block, I started to run.

. . .

Four hours later, I stepped inside the Club Tremonti. Before this, the closest I'd been to the Club Tremonti was when the newspapers ran pictures of movie stars and millionaires beaming for the flashbulbs, drinks scattered in front of them like dice. The Club Tremonti was the best nightclub on the South Side. Maybe the best in Chicago. On my own, a low-rent girl like me would never have gotten past the doorman in his yellow-braided coat. As it was, the man who brought me had to do some fast talking.

Inside, the first thing I saw was ten Negro girls dancing on the raised stage. They wore tiny two-piece outfits and enormous ruffled sleeves, and their heels *ratta-tatt*ed, whooshed into a sideways shuffle-slide. So smooth, they looked like ten pieces of one girl. A trumpet growled, and my heart shivered. By the dim red lights around the walls, I could barely make out the dozens and dozens of tiny round tables, the sequins and beads of the women's dresses, the silhouettes of officers' hats. Men's voices rumbled below the music, women's laughter slid high. The air solid with smoke, reddish from the lights, soaked in a hundred perfumes.

The man who'd brought me tapped my shoulder and pointed at the white-jacketed maître d'. *Follow him.* Then he left, winding his way through the tables to the ones nearest the stage. I spotted the one he was aiming for. A dark island in a sea of white faces. I couldn't tell anything more than that. I didn't have to. Only a policy king could get one of the best tables in a club that seated only whites. Only a policy king could break those kinds of rules.

It had taken me four hours to find Horace Washington. Four hours, and half of Bronzeville turned upside down. But I'd done it.

The easy part was over.

"Miss," the maître d' said. "This way." He had to lean close to be heard over the booming of the bongo drums. I nodded and followed him to a curved carpeted staircase, leading down. At the bottom was another room, almost as big as the lounge upstairs, but more brightly lit. Through a forest of suit jackets and officers' uniforms and shimmering dresses, I glimpsed green-felted tables. The maître d' was hurrying now, weaving past the swells, and I hustled after him. I bumped into a woman holding a highball glass, and she gave me a look like I was an iceman's mangy horse. An excited call rose above the din of voices—*Hundred on the black six!*—and then the maître d' opened a door ahead of me and waved me inside.

"Wait here," he said, and closed the door.

An office. Big. Plain brown wallpaper with an odd pebbly sheen. I looked close and rubbed it with my finger. I made double sure nobody was in the room, and then I sniffed it. Leather. I'd never heard of such a thing. Leather chairs, too; a leather sofa in one corner. Pipe tobacco smell in the air, instead of cigarettes.

Bongo drums pounded through the ceiling. I couldn't hear them, so much as feel them. Not loud enough to drown out my nerves. How long would they make me wait in here alone? If I could be upstairs, with the music and the crowd, that would be better. Then maybe my heart wouldn't be skipping like a little girl's hopscotch foot.

I sat down in one of the chairs. Then sprang up again and roamed around the room. Dark green carpet, a shiny dark wood desk. Next to this, Del's office was plain as a flour sack.

Del. The Starlight, and Ozzie. I wondered where he

was. I thought of Ophelia and her new fellow, and I wondered if Ozzie had been fighting his own battles, the same time I'd been fighting mine.

It was Ozzie I'd gone looking for first. From the Yards, I'd gone straight to the Starlight. O'Malley, the bouncer, met me at the head of the stairs.

"Del said to tell you you don't work here no more." Not a bit of interest on his broad cop's face, as if he didn't know who I was, as if he hadn't seen me practically every night for the past eight months.

"I need to talk to Ozzie," I told him. O'Malley looked blank. "Look, just ask Del, will you? Ozzie, in the band! He'll know."

A minute later, O'Malley was back. He shook his head. "Quit," he said.

Quit? The Starlight was his rent money, he'd said. Where could he have gone?

"Please, can you find Peggy? Tell her I'm here. Tell her I need to talk to her." Alonso knew all about the policy king. Maybe he'd said something to Peggy, maybe she'd know where to find him.

O'Malley didn't budge this time. "She's working."

"Just for two seconds! Please, O'Malley!"

"Scram." Pointing one of his big mitts down the stairs. Through the closed doors behind him, I heard the strains of "Sweet Sue, Just You." How many times had I hoofed it to that groaner! I wished I was in there now, laughing with Peggy, not worried about a thing except whether or not I could hook a fish to take me to Lily's.

"You must make your mother proud, O'Malley," I said, and then I beat it out of there.

It was early, barely nine o'clock. Lily's wasn't open yet.

I pounded on the door until a boy in a white apron answered.

"I need to find Ozzie," I told him.

"Ain't here," the boy said. He started to close the door. I stuck my foot in the opening and pulled a bill out of my change purse. I didn't look to see what it was. A ten at least, I guessed, from how quick the boy snatched it. He tucked the bill into his shirt. "He plays a dance hall up on Madison somewhere."

The Starlight. I could've punched him. "Then where's Lily?"

He eyed my change purse. I swore under my breath and pulled out another bill. He considered it. Probably considered Lily, too, and if he'd still have a hide when she got done with him. The bill won. He plucked it out of my hand and pointed down the street.

"The apartment house with the geraniums," he said. "Second story, in the front."

"Who the hell are you?" Lily said, when she opened her apartment door. She was wearing a housedress, her hair tucked under a flowered scarf. The light in the hallway was dim, but still brighter than I was used to seeing her by. Her jaw looked heavier than in the club, her lips dull without their carmine shine. But I'd have known her by her eyes in any light. Not a bit cowish, like so many big-eyed girls, but sharp as two tacks, and with those luscious curling lashes. They flicked down to my shoes, narrowed when they arrived back at my face.

"Okay, yeah," she said. "You're one of the taxi dancers. You used to bring those Pinoys." She didn't seem happy about it. In fact, she edged close to the jamb, pulling the door along with her, so that she filled the open space. As if she thought I might push past her into her apartment. "What do you want?"

"I need to find the policy king."

Whatever she'd been expecting, it wasn't that. Her eyebrows arched higher than the busboy's had. "What do you mean, *the* policy king? Which one? And why in hell are you bothering me about it?"

"There's more than one?"

From inside the apartment came a man's voice. I couldn't hear—some kind of question, I thought. Lily waved her hand—*hush*—without taking her eyes off my face. "Yeah, there's more than one," she said. She sounded more amused now than hostile. "Don't matter, though, 'cause ain't none of them going to talk to a little white girl like you. Now go on. Get out of here."

This time I didn't stick my foot in the door. Boys are nicer about that kind of thing. A girl like Lily, she'd bang the hell out of it without a second thought. I would, if I was her.

"The policy man who got shot last night," I said. "I know who did it."

Except that the door stopped closing, I might have said the sky was blue. Not a sign showed on Lily's face. If she shut me out, what would I do? In all of Bronzeville, she was the only person I knew by name. Except for Ozzie, and I didn't know where Ozzie was.

Lily stepped back. "You'd better come in," she said.

． ． ．

From the other side of the office door, I heard men's laughter, getting closer. I looked right and left—should I sit? Stand by the bookcase? By the desk? Before I could decide, the door opened, and Horace Washington—the king of Chicago policy kings—walked in. He was still chuckling. Behind him drifted a haze of cigar smoke and two other men. The men arranged themselves by the wall, hands in their pockets. Horace Washington strolled past me to the desk. He didn't look at me. I'd barely gotten a peep at him that night at Lily's, but this was him all right. The slow, rolling stride, like he had all the time in the world.

I licked my lips. They were dry. Bare. I wished I had a gown on, instead of a sweat-damp, polka-dotted house-dress. Or even just some lipstick. Something to make me feel savvy. I needed to be savvy.

I lifted my chin, brushed tangled curls behind my shoulders.

Mr. Washington pushed aside a stack of papers on the desk and sat on the edge. He was mostly bald, and his top eyelids drooped, which made him seem sleepy. His suit—double-breasted, navy pinstripe—looked like it cost more than everything in my closet and my locker at the Starlight combined.

"Gracious of Mr. Tremonti to let us use his office," Mr. Washington said. "I understand you went to a bit of trouble to find me."

"Yes, sir."

He took a short puff on his cigar. "They tell me you're a taxi dancer."

"I was. At the Starlight. I saw you once, at Lily's."

"Mmph." Cigar in his mouth. Rolling it a little between his fingers. "They tell me," he said, "you know who hit my man."

"Yes, sir."

"Mmm-hmm." He shifted his weight. "You going to tell me this person's name?"

I'd thought about this hard, the past four hours. "Not if you're going to kill him," I said.

The drooping eyelids flickered. He lowered the cigar. "Don't believe it was your man got put in the hospital. Or your money stolen. Was it?"

"He's not dead?"

Mr. Washington chuckled. "Whoever this sumbitch is—excuse my language—he can't aim worth beans. Jerry'll be okay. One arm a little shorter than the other, maybe."

I let my breath out. Whatever else Paulie was, he wasn't a murderer. Not yet. "If he wasn't killed, then . . ." Trying to keep my voice from trembling. If Mr. Washington didn't agree . . . "He wasn't killed. So you can't kill this . . . this person. Please. I can't have that on my hands."

The two men stirred near the wall. One coughed. Mr. Washington reached behind him and tapped his cigar into an ashtray. "I'm sure you don't know," he said, "being as you seem like a nice young lady. But this isn't the first time the mob has tried muscling in. You see, they're tempted by the money. For some reason," he went on, in a dry voice, "they think some of it ought to be theirs."

They got Rolls-Royces. . . . While I have to borrow a lousy dinged-up Chevy.

"He's not in the mob," I said.

Mr. Washington nodded. "Thinks he's going to be the next Capone, then. Get enough dough, take over the city. Us, the mob, everyone. We've seen those, too. I call 'em mad dogs. You know about mad dogs? Generally they need to be shot. Before they spread the infection."

At the word *shot*, I flinched. "If he leaves Chicago . . . if he promises never again . . ."

"Oh, he'll do it again. See, that's the problem with mad dogs. Smack 'em with a newspaper, they just get madder." Mr. Washington took another puff on his cigar. Studied me with his sleepy eyes. I met him look for look, but inside, my head was in an uproar. If he didn't agree, would I still give him Paulie's name? Would I let Paulie die, to keep Betty safe?

"If he leaves Chicago," Mr. Washington said, as if to himself. Then, "Morris."

"Yes, sir," one of the men by the wall answered.

"You remember Eddie Johnson?"

"Yes, sir. Could work."

"Mmm." Mr. Washington looked back at me. "This mad dog of yours. He 4-F?"

4-F. Unfit for service. "He's been in army prison," I said.

"We can take care of that." Mr. Washington stood up. "This is what I'm going to offer. Your mad dog joins the merchant marine. Or we take care of him ourselves. One or the other."

The merchant marine! On the newsreels and the radio, almost every week, there were reports of merchant marine ships hunted by the German U-boats. Torpedoed and sunk, one after another, dozens of ships in just the last six months. Hundreds of men killed. Died in explosions, drowned in the Atlantic. Another ship just today, in the Pacific, blown up by the Japanese.

"It's a fair deal," Mr. Washington said. "We both of us want him gone. Isn't that right?"

I stared at him, but I hardly saw him. Paulie's dark

gold hair, matted with blood. Paulie tossed in the ocean, screaming, his hand outstretched for help that wouldn't come, like the mariner in that horrible poster you saw hanging everywhere. *Loose Lips Sink Ships!*

"Merchant marine, he stands a chance." Mr. Washington turned, ground out the stub of his cigar. "He won't, with me."

Paulie's rain-cloud eyes, the same color as seawater, slipping beneath the surface of the waves. I closed my eyes. Saw Betty instead, in a St. Casimir's uniform, walking to school with the Gorman sisters.

"All right," I said. And then I told.

It took only a few minutes. When I was done, Mr. Washington offered his hand. For a big man, he had a gentle grip. Or maybe he just saw that if he squeezed too hard, I might break apart.

"Tell you what, Miss Jacinski," he said. "I'd hate to have you mad at me." He pulled a gold cigar case from his pocket, flipped it open. "You know, this Paulie makes it, he'll come back home. Might not be too happy with you. I'd think about that, between now and then."

I nodded. If he makes it . . .

Please God, keep him safe. And keep him far, far from here. Forever.

TWENTY-FOUR

I walked through the door that night to find Ma in her armchair, a rosary twisted through the hands in her lap. Under the little table lamp, her face was gray and grim as old snow. She didn't say anything. She didn't look up. Her knotted fingers working the rosary beads into her palm, one by one. The last time I'd seen Ma with a rosary, Pop had been in the hospital.

I dropped my pocketbook on the sofa and went to her. "Ma, you shouldn't have sat up. Are you all right? Do you need some aspirin?"

She didn't answer right away. Then she said, "I've been praying to the Blessed Mother. Asking her for understanding. Because I don't understand, Ruby."

I sank to the floor in front of her. "It's okay, Ma. What happened tonight . . . it won't happen again. I made sure. That's why I was gone so long, I—"

"Tonight?" She looked at me then. The lines around her eyes, her mouth, harsh in the small light. "And the past eight months? What about that?"

Betty had told.

"Why, Ruby?" Her voice bewildered. Not a trace of iron in it. Somehow, that was worse.

I would be anywhere, rather than here. Back in front of Horace Washington. Back with Paulie, or Tom. I could fight them. Because I was right, and they were wrong. But now I was the one who was wrong.

I'd had reasons, though. All along, I'd had reasons. I tried to remember what they were, back in the beginning. I couldn't. Not with Ma looking at me, disappointment drowning her eyes and every line in her face. All the times I'd imagined her finding out, terrified she'd find out, I'd imagined her furious. *You're not my daughter anymore.* I'd never imagined her disappointed. Seeing it felt worse than Paulie beating me. It felt like standing by while Paulie beat *her.* I couldn't meet her eyes.

"It wasn't enough money," I said. "The packinghouse. It wasn't enough, and . . ." The smell of relief beans, I remembered that. But there were other things, important things, what were they? My eyes grew hot, my throat closed with tears. If only she'd stop *looking* at me . . . "I dropped out of school, didn't I? I got a job, I paid for everything. The coal. And your gloves, and Betty's shoes and the groceries and the rent. I got your ring back . . ."

"Did you buy the coat?"

I wiped my eyes on the back of my hand. Ma reached into her pocket, held out her handkerchief. I took it. "What coat?"

"My winter coat. Did you buy that?"

The hunter green wool. Manny had given it to me, and I'd given it to her. Ma had cried when she opened the box.

"It was a gift," I whispered. Her face changed. She

hadn't wanted to believe. But now she did, and she believed the worst. Like Paulie. "Ma, it's not what you think. The Starlight"—I saw her flinch, but I kept going—"it's not a bad place, it—"

She shook her head, looked away. "Don't tell me. Please, Ruby. I don't want to know."

"I'm a good girl, Ma. I never—" I bit my lip. "I did everything you asked. I worked so hard, I was saving money. I was going to get us out of the Yards."

Her fingers tightened on the beads, her swollen knuckles paled to white. "I never asked you for that! For you and your sister to be decent girls, that's all I ever asked!"

"Mary?" Chester's voice, anxious, from the hallway. I heard Ma's breath catch.

"It's all right," she called. "I'll be right there."

If I'd gone along with what Paulie wanted, she'd still think I was a decent girl. I'd be turning tricks for him every night, and she would have no idea.

"You never asked me about the coat before," I said.

"What are you talking about?" Tucking the rosary into her pocket.

"The coat." I raised my eyes to hers. "How come you never asked me about it before?"

Ma braced her hands on the arms of her chair and stood up. The hem of the cherry-print dress fluttered in front of me. She took two steps and stopped.

"We won't talk about this anymore." Then her voice sunk to almost nothing. "You've broken my heart, Ruby."

Chester came and took her arm. Delicate, the way he always was with her, as if she was made of something rare and precious. He didn't say anything. Ma's steps were stiff.

Painful. She shouldn't have sat up so long. She'd hurt tomorrow.

After a long while I got up. My side ached now only when I moved. In old lady Nolan's room—our room, Betty's and my room—Betty lay still and quiet. Pretending to be asleep. I didn't bother undressing. I curled on my bed in my clothes and lay awake until morning.

. . .

I never found out what story Betty told Ma and Chester about that night. I didn't ask her, and she wasn't speaking to me. But from the way they treated her—making her favorite dishes, buying her a phonograph—I guessed she'd told them that finding Paulie, instead of Polly, had come as a complete shock. It seemed easier to let them believe her.

Ma wouldn't look at me. She talked at me: *Good morning, dear. Clear the table, please. Mercy, it's so humid today, I'm afraid the laundry won't dry. Would you like milk or coffee with your dinner?* But her glances skimmed across my hair. My elbows. The top of my head. Betty pretended I didn't exist. If it wasn't for Chester, I might have disappeared altogether.

I didn't leave the house for two days. Trying to be the good girl. It got hard to breathe, for all the unsaid words in the air. The evenings were the worst. I tried sitting in the living room with the rest of them, listening to radio shows and sewing. When *Amos and Andy* came on, I knew men would be streaming into the dance hall. Staking out their territory along the stag line, giving us the once-over. I'd have danced five or six numbers already, slipping the tips into my garter purse, giving the boys an eyeful.

On the third day, in the middle of the afternoon when none of the girls would be there, I went to the Starlight. I climbed the stairs and pounded the door until Mack, the janitor, let me in.

"Thought Del fired you," he said.

"He did. I came to clear out my locker."

Mack pushed his dry mop away over the floor. "Help yourself," he said.

It wasn't until the fourth time I tried undoing the lock on my locker that I noticed the new piece of tape on the door. *Doreen,* it read. I went to go find Del.

"Chucked it," he said when I asked him about my stuff. He leaned back in his office chair and spread his hands, palms up. "Does this look like a warehouse? Most girls skip, I never see them again. It's not my job to save their lipsticks and hairbrushes."

"Hairbrushes! What about my outfits? And my garter purse? I had half a night's tickets in there!"

"Shoulda cashed 'em when you had 'em," Del said.

After fifteen minutes of squabbling, he finally pulled out his wallet. Peeled off two bucks like he was peeling the skin off his own arm. That garter purse had had three dollars' worth of tickets, at least, but I didn't have the juice to keep arguing. I took the money and left.

Two bucks. Forty nickels. Forty waltzes, two-steps, fox-trots, jitterbugs. Smiling and snapping my fingers and acting perky as all get-out. Acting half in love. Acting all in love. Pretending whatever fellow in front of me was the shiniest thing in shoe leather, just so I could get a lousy ticket and a tip after. And he might have been terrific, too. He might have been swell. But I was savvy. Figuring I'd already found my perfect guy.

The hall was stifling hot. Sun leaked through the smeary windows, showing up every smudge on the walls, every ding and scratch on the dance floor.

I walked out without a backward glance.

· · ·

Del might have chucked everything else, but I still had four gowns at the cleaner's. I picked them up and took them to Peggy's, thinking maybe she'd let me keep them in her armoire until I could figure out what to do with them. But when I got there, the armoire was empty, and a flowered cloth suitcase lay open on the bed. I stood gaping in the doorway, the four gowns draped over my arm.

"You're leaving?" I said.

"Looks that way." Peggy nodded at the gowns. "I hope those aren't a going-away gift. I don't think I've got room for another handkerchief, let alone all that."

I dumped the gowns onto a chair. "But I don't understand. What happened?"

Peggy went back to the bed and started sorting through a pile of undergarments. "I should've married Alonso when I had the chance. He wanted to, before he left. But I figured the last time I rushed into wedded bliss, it sank like the *Titanic.* This time, I thought"—she tapped the side of her head—"I'll play it smart." She held up a white satin slip, looked it over.

"Yesterday," she said, "I saw a notice in the paper. About a fellow from Englewood who was in the Philippines. At Bataan." Her hands closed into fists on the satin. "The War Department told his folks he's been killed. Or captured. They don't know which." She tossed the slip on the floor and turned to me. Her hazel eyes were glassy with tears. "If we'd married, I'd get a telegram a from the War Department. Like that boy's parents. And then at least I'd know. But no, I had to be *smart*." She laughed, one of her short, dry laughs, but it slid into a sob. I put a hand on her shoulder. She shook it off.

"You shouldn't worry," I said. "Alonso could be halfway across the world from the Philippines. Anyway, he's written you, hasn't he?"

Peggy picked up an envelope from her bedstand. Thick, the white paper smudged with grime. "Just once." She brushed her thumb across her name. "I've called the newspapers, I've called everyone I can think of. All those boys at Bataan, nobody knows what happened. Nobody knows where they are."

"But Alonso's in the navy, not the army. Besides, the mail takes forever to get out. Remember the other night Linda said . . ."

She set the envelope back down. "You're sweet, Ruby. And probably you're right and tomorrow I'll get a letter and he'll tell me he's fat and happy and dumping me for some island princess." She smiled a trace of a smile. "But in the meantime, I'm no good."

I sank onto the chair. I couldn't think of anything else comforting to say. *Killed. Or captured.* I'd meant to pray for Manny and Alonso every day. For all the boys. I'd meant to light candles . . .

Peggy threw a girdle at me. "Buck up," she said. "If you get blue, I'll start bawling. And then I'll never get this packing done and I'll miss my bus and it'll be your fault."

"Where are you going?" I folded the girdle and handed it to her.

"Back to Wisconsin." She smiled at me again, stronger this time, and shrugged. "At first I thought about going to Seneca. Fellow at the *Daily News* gave me the poop about a new shipyard there. Said there'll be plenty of good jobs for girls who don't mind getting their hands dirty. But then I decided I'd better mend some fences. God knows that'll keep me busy awhile." Peggy nodded at the gowns behind me on the chair. "So. What's your story?"

I'd planned to tell her about Paulie and Horace Washington. Everything. But seeing the weariness and worry in her face, I changed my mind. "I guess I just had enough, that's all."

"Keeping it to yourself, huh?" I looked up at her in surprise, and she grinned at me, her rare Peggy grin, not as bright as before but enough so the crooked tooth showed in front. "I told you," she said. "*Every* taxi dancer has a story."

. . .

I took the gowns back to the cleaner's. It took some haggling, but the owner finally agreed to keep them for me for a week. I figured I'd have made up my mind by then.

Three nights before, at the Club Tremonti, Horace Washington had offered me a job.

"Friend of mine's opening a class joint," he said. "Looking for gals to work as hostesses. You got the kind of moxie that would make a real splash. Interested?"

"I'll think about it," I told him.

He jotted the club's address on a piece of paper. "Don't think too long."

I knew the jobs would go fast. Half the girls at the Starlight would give their eyeteeth to be hostesses. You did most of your work sitting down, and instead of cola and coffee, the fellows kept you knee-deep in champagne and cocktails. The more they drank and gambled, the more commissions you earned.

The club address was only three blocks from Peggy's hotel. "Owner's out of town," the guy who answered the door said. "But he'll be here tomorrow. You want to leave your name?"

I couldn't have said if I was more disappointed or relieved. "No," I told him. "No, I'll come back."

. . .

That night, just like the last three nights, I lay in bed and listened to Betty snore. For eight months I'd stayed up until the wee hours, then slept until noon. Now I couldn't seem to switch back. Just like the last three nights, I watched the moonlight drift across the ceiling, and just like the last three nights, I stewed about Paulie.

Before I'd spilled his name to Horace Washington— and the fact that he was driving the stolen Lincoln Zephyr—I said, "You have to promise me to tell me when he's . . . when it's done."

"Promise you, huh?" Mr. Washington said. "Okay, I'll send you a telegram." I hadn't known he was joking until one of the guys by the wall snorted laughter.

"I don't have to tell you anything," I said. The guy who'd snorted ambled behind me. I could feel where he stopped by the prickling in the small of my back. Mr. Washington frowned at him. The guy drifted again to the wall.

"You were right," I said. "I want him gone. He's after my sister. I have to know. Please."

Mr. Washington took the cigar out of his mouth and inspected the end, as if he'd gotten a taste he didn't care for. "Five days," he'd said. "Then you check with Lily. I'll leave word."

In bed, I counted on my fingers. Five days would be Friday. Today was Wednesday. Thursday, really. Two thirty in the morning. Lily's would be hopping. I wondered if Ozzie would be there. I'd asked Lily if he'd gotten another gig, if that was why he quit the Starlight.

"He keeps his business to himself," she'd told me, "and if I were you, with the kind of trouble you got going on, I'd do the same."

I could get to Lily's and back before anyone was up. Better than lying here, wondering if Horace Washington had kept his word. Wondering if they'd killed Paulie anyway, or if he'd escaped, if he'd found out I'd ratted on him. If he was waiting for me, or Betty, gun in hand.

I eased out of bed and felt around for my shoes. My side twinged, but it wasn't slowing me down much anymore. The bruise had turned plum colored and black. It was spreading in rings, like motor oil in a rain puddle.

If that was the worst any of us got, I'd count us lucky.

· · ·

I heard the music all the way out on the sidewalk. As I paid admission, a trumpet wailed high and loud. Hearing it, my feet itched to fly. I pushed my way through the curtain, into the club. Ozzie wasn't on the stage. Neither was Ophelia.

A waiter nodded at me. *This way.* I shook my head. "I need to see Lily!" I shouted in his ear.

The waiter jerked a thumb at a closed door behind the bar. "She's busy!"

I signaled I'd wait by the entrance. The waiter shrugged and gestured to the people who'd come in behind me. I waited until his back was turned, then I made for the closed door. Lily might be busy, but I didn't have all night.

I knocked on the door. No one answered. "Lily!" I bawled. "Lily, it's Ruby! Open up!"

The door swung open. I was about to say *Lily* again, but instead of her face I saw a man's checked shirt, open at the collar. Strong curving cheeks, a sharp-edged mouth. Eyelashes curling, just like his cousin's.

"What do you want?" Ozzie said.

• • •

By the time I left Lily's, the eastern sky was pink, the streetlights pale. Already the air was warm and damp. Even on the wildest of the nightclub nights, I'd never been so late getting home. I trudged from the streetcar stop to Chester's house, dog tired and hungry, hoping Ma hadn't noticed I was gone. But even that thought couldn't shake the relief soaking down to my bones.

Paulie was gone.

Horace Washington had turned up the heat so high, he hadn't needed five days. Papers had been rushed through, signatures gotten, and yesterday, Paulie had been put on a train bound for St. Petersburg, Florida. His ship had come in, all right. Shanghaied into the merchant marine.

Chester had already left for work. Ma sat in the dining room, looking out the window. I picked up her empty coffee cup and carried it into the kitchen. Got a second one and filled them both from the electric percolator.

When I sat down, she said, "I thought you were still in bed." She cradled both hands around her cup, as if we were back in the old flat, in winter. "I used to think I knew where my daughters were, every second of the day. And night."

"I'm sorry," I said.

She didn't answer. We watched the sun rising between the houses across the street. It lit Ma's cheekbones a pinky gold, struck sparks of yellow and blue from the diamond on her finger.

"I'm going to leave," I said.

Her mouth wobbled, just for a moment. I got up and crossed behind her chair. Bent down and wrapped my arms around her. Her cheek soft. Scents of cold cream and raisins, and setting lotion, and a trace of the Coty perfume Chester had bought her as a wedding present.

"I tried, Ma," I said.

She laid a hand on my arm; it felt dry and light as a leaf. "I know," she said.

After a moment, I knelt by the side of her chair. "Ma, listen. I have to tell you something."

Betty would be furious. But even if I put on the St. Casimir's uniform every day and walked to school with the Gorman sisters—even if I played the good girl to a T—Betty would know it was just another lie. She'd do what she wanted, and she would never listen to me.

But she still might listen to Ma. And she liked Chester. Maybe she still had a chance.

"Some of Betty's friends," I began, "call themselves victory girls."

TWENTY-FIVE

August 17, 1942

Dear Ma,
I just got home from my first day at work, and I'm
dead-dog tired.

I rubbed the sore spot at the base of my right thumb, where the bucking bar had pressed. My writing paper lay in a pool of blue light. I'd thrown a scarf over the little table lamp so that my roommate, Lu, could sleep.

A breeze came through the open window. Before I went to bed, I would shut the curtains tight so the sun wouldn't wake us up too early. I liked sitting up late, the only one awake. I guessed I'd gotten used to night habits.

I finished the four weeks of training which I told
you about in my last letter. The instructor said I learned
as fast as any girl he ever taught and made the fewest
mistakes, so you see I finally did good in school.

I added an exclamation point. Then scribbled it out. I should have written in pencil. Too late now, I was too tired to start over.

The plant we work in isn't like the packinghouse, men in some places and the women in others. We're all of us on the floor together. I don't know yet if I like it.

I put down my pen.

This morning we'd followed a supervisor through the largest building I'd ever set foot in. We walked between a double line of B-24 bombers stretching as far as I could see—not seeming like much except scattered hunks of metal where we started, then the farther we went in the building, they began looking more and more like planes. Ships, the supervisor called them. If I'd ever thought the Ladies' at the Starlight was loud, it was nothing compared to this: the pounding of rivet guns and screaming drills, hundreds of them, and hundreds of men shouting to make themselves heard. As we walked, the supervisor parceled us out, two and three at at time. "You and you, what's your names?" he'd call, then "Flight deck" or "Fuselage" or "Wing. Go on, get to work! You in the red scarf, what's your name!"

"Ruby Jacinski," I said.

He pointed to another girl. "Irene Petrovsky," she said. Her voice pitching up at the end, like she was asking a question.

"Nose turret," he said, and pointed to a bomber.

Some fellows were laying wiring in the wing. One of them looked us up and down. Sneer on his face. You could tell he thought he was a tough guy.

Paulie could clean this guy's clock. You wanted to know tough—Paulie was tough.

But I'd turned out tougher.

"I'll buck," I told Irene. "You rivet." I'd picked up the bucking bar and climbed into the half-built plane.

I bent again to my letter.

> *They put me in the nose because I'm small, I can get where men can't, or even the bigger girls. We have to wear Sanforized coveralls and keep our hair tied up in scarves, and we can't wear any jewelry.*

We could wear makeup, though. A few of the girls said what was the point, wearing makeup in a factory? But after all those months at the Starlight, I didn't feel dressed without it. Besides, I had to stay in practice. The USO held dances every weekend. The bands were all right. Nothing like what I was used to in Chicago, though.

Another breeze through the window. I closed my eyes. Remembering Ozzie, the last time I'd seen him. Shirt open at the neck, no tie. Sleeves rolled up to just below his elbows. Frowning down at me from the doorway of Lily's office.

"I, I have to ask Lily something," I said.

"Not here. She'll be back pretty quick though. You want to wait, you can sit at the bar."

Nothing seemed swollen or broken on him. Maybe he hadn't been in a fight over Ophelia after all. But his face was stern, the usual quickness gone. Like he'd never thought it was funny I'd almost walloped a dirty old man on a dance floor. Like I'd never given him advice on how to romance his girl; like we'd never sat in a little room across from each other, shadows and music and talk between us.

I looked past him into the room. "Can I wait in here?"

He shrugged and stepped back. I walked past him. An office, small and bare. Nothing like the Club Tremonti. A beat-up desk and two hard-backed chairs. I sat down.

"I heard you quit," I said.

"That's right." Ozzie's hand on the door, about to leave.

"I'm glad." As soon as I said it, I realized how it must sound. But he took his hand off the doorknob.

"Thanks." He hesitated, then said, "I got the gig in Kansas City. Went down there to play and I got it."

"No more Turkey Trot," I said.

"Goddamn, I forgot about the Turkey Trot." His face eased, and he laughed his low, rolling laugh. "You know, I almost quit that night, I was so sick of that tune?"

"You and me both." He looked at me, and I looked at him, and we both grinned.

High heels clacked in the doorway. Lily came in, saw me. Her mouth screwed down like she'd sucked a lemon.

"Oh, *you*," she said.

When she found out what I'd come for, she got right on it. She wasn't doing it to be nice. In fifteen minutes, word came from one of Horace Washington's men.

"That's that," Lily said. "You can go on home."

Ozzie was onstage, taking over for the other trumpet player. The rest of the band razzing him fierce. Calling him the "K.C. Kid." Saying, "They better watch themselves down there, now you're coming."

"I'm staying awhile," I told Lily.

He played all of it, the stomping, yowling down-dirty and the wake-up-and-kick-it. One high, sweet, sad melody made me want to cry and scratch Ophelia's eyes out at the same time. Nobody played music like that whose heart hadn't gotten sledgehammered like a steer on the killing floor. I knew about that, all right.

Ophelia never showed. Gone to sing at a fancier black and tan on Garfield, I heard people say. A heavy-set girl with a reedy voice took the stage, not nearly the power-house Ophelia was. Ozzie didn't look at her once.

When I got up to go to the ladies' room, Lily followed me in.

"You come here with one of your taxi-dance customers, that's one thing." Starting right in, not an *Excuse me* or *Can I have a minute of your time.* "But a girl by herself, that's not good for business. Makes the place look seedy."

The mirror was crowded, no place to shove in. "I'm not bothering anybody," I said.

Lily was shorter than even me, but the way she set her weight back on one foot, chin tipped high, she might have been tall as Ozzie. "You white girls. Coming in here looking for who knows what. You got plenty of your own men, why don't you go sniff around them?"

"Amen, sister," said someone from inside the stall.

Lily rapped the stall door. "Mind your own business!" To me, she said, "The luckiest day Ozzie ever had was when that puffed-up piece of work Ophelia dumped him over the side, though it took him long enough to see it. Girl hanging on his coattails is just going to slow him down. Especially a little white one like you."

Behind me, the girls at the mirror said, *mmm-hmm*, nudged each other. "Now," Lily said, "do I have to throw you out?"

"I guess so," I said, and marched back to my table. Somone else had taken it. I snagged a chair. Lily told the waiters not to serve me. I didn't care. I didn't want anything anyway, except to hear Ozzie play.

Five thirty in the morning, the band wrapped up. Ozzie set his trumpet back in its case. Hardly anybody in the club except musicians: Lily's bunch, and six or eight from other joints, come to play with Ozzie a last time. Ties and jackets off, cigarettes in everyone's hands. The men still razzing Ozzie, slapping him on the back. He grinned, said something that made them shout with laughter. A numbers runner wandered in, pulled up a chair, fell into the conversation. From behind the bar, Lily gave me the stink-eye. She was the only one who seemed to know I was still there.

I'd found out about Paulie. Ozzie'd finished playing. Nothing left to stay for.

Bright outside; I squinted, shaded my eyes. A scrap of breeze blew in from the lake. By midmorning, it'd be snuffed out by the heat. People already out and around. Man carrying newspaper bundles. Milkman carrying bottles. No cabs. I started walking to the streetcar stop.

"Ruby."

I turned around. Ozzie was climbing the steps to the sidewalk. His shoes scuffed the concrete, loud in the early-morning air. He held something in his hand.

"I saw this under a table," he said. "Thought it might be yours."

It was a compact case. Silver, with a fancy monogram.

C.S. I shook my head and handed it back to him. He turned it over, looked at the lid. "Oh, yeah. Guess not." He glanced up the street. Started to turn back down the stairs to the club.

"I'm sorry about the other night," I said. He stopped. Shot me a quick, doubtful look. "When I asked you to dance. I didn't know it would make Ophelia so mad. Not that I care about her, but if . . ."

Ozzie ran a hand over the back of his head. He kept his hair short. Not straightened, like some colored men's. "You might know girls," he said, "but you don't know *colored* girls."

I thought back to what Lily had said in the ladies' room. "Oh. *Oh.*" Baby sees the light.

"She was playing games. You know, trying to make me jealous. So I thought, Let's see how she likes it."

"I guess she didn't."

Ozzie stuck his hands into his pockets, blew air through his lips. "You could say."

We stood a moment, not talking. Then he said, "Just as well." I thought he meant, Just as well since I'm going to Kansas City. But he went on, "Turn eighteen in November. After that . . . bunch of musicians gone already. Not just the sidemen. Bandleaders, too." Gazing up the street, not looking at anything. "I figured I ought to get in as much playing as I can get. Before they send all of us to fight the Jerries."

Paulie shanghaied. Manny and Alonso and half the boys in the Yards signed up or drafted. A gold star in the Majewskis' window. A few more months, Ozzie might be slogging through mud in Europe, or on an aircraft carrier in the Pacific. Or dead. I swallowed hard.

· 345 ·

"So when Hamp starts up that Turkey Trot," Ozzie said, "you think about me. Okay?"

"I can't." His face knotted like I'd jabbed him with a fist. "I mean, I would, but . . . I quit, too. Well—I was fired. Both, sort of."

"Got tired of Del, huh?" He smiled, his eyes still somewhere else. "So, where to now, another dance hall? Plenty of 'em around."

Where would you go, if you could go anywhere you wanted?

"I don't know," I said. I remembered Peggy. The tip from that fellow she'd talked to, at the *Daily News*. Slowly, as if to hear how it sounded, I said, "I think maybe I'll go build ships."

His eyebrows arched. His smile grew into a grin. "Little different from what you been doing."

"A little bit." Different felt good. I was ready for different. I tried to imagine what it might be like, but I couldn't. Find out when I got there, I supposed.

A jitney cab came up the street. I waved, and the driver cut over and swept up to the curb. I reached for the door, but Ozzie's hand was on the latch before mine.

But he didn't open the door. We stood so close that if either of us turned, we'd bump the other. The hollow of his throat a few inches away. I saw a tiny fluttering under his skin. He smelled like the club, like cigarettes and booze and Lindy Hopping.

"You happen to drop by Kansas City the next six months or so," he said, "I'll be playing the Century Room. Jay McShann's band."

I raised my eyes to his face. My own, without a stitch of makeup on. Eyes too deep. Lips too pale. I didn't care.

"Take care of yourself." He dropped his gaze. Held out

his hand. I took it. His palm wide and warm. Fingers strong from the trumpet. I popped up on tiptoe, quick. Kissed his cheek. Tickly with stubble. Him up all night. Me, too.

"I'll listen for you on the radio," I said.

. . .

Why San Diego? Ma had wanted to know. It was one of the few times we'd talked before I left. Once I'd made up my mind, I hadn't seen what there was to wait for.

"If you want to do war work, you could stay right here in Chicago," she said.

"They said San Diego on the radio," I explained. "That story about women taking men's jobs. Remember?"

She didn't. "I just don't see why you have to go so far away."

"Because it *is* far away, that's why."

All I'd meant was, if I was going to go someplace and start over new, across the country seemed like a good place to do it. I tried to explain, but I'd hurt her feelings. After that, we hardly spoke. When Chester drove me to the bus station, she stayed home.

I wrote my first letter to her before the bus was out of Chicago. The next, as soon as I had an address for her to write back. I wasn't sure she would. But a week later, she did. Her letter short, a little stiff. Not saying anything important. Mine didn't, either. It didn't matter.

Once I was here, I'd thought of how to explain better. It was like how Ozzie's music made me feel. Not just like dancing, although at the beginning that had been most of it. But then his music changed, or I did, and the scream and soar of his trumpet made me feel bigger than the

Starlight. Bigger than all Chicago. No one to say, *You can't.* Like what I'd imagined it might be like to go somewhere new, nobody knowing what you'd done or who you'd been. To see who you could become next.

Ma was right. I hadn't wanted us out of the Yards for her sake. I'd wanted it for mine.

Where would you go, if you could go anywhere you wanted?

Listening to Ozzie play, that last night, I knew it wasn't to a club. No matter how swanky, no matter how many sequined gowns I could wear. Pretending to be in love for a commission, while the love of my life might be standing a few feet away and I'd never know it.

I frowned and chewed my pen cap. Even if I could write all this on paper, Ma had never heard Ozzie's music. She thought even Benny Goodman was too wild. The Lindy Hopping at Lily's would've sent her into a conniption. I grinned, imagining what she'd say.

The breeze gusted, riffling the curtains. I lifted my face to it, closed my eyes. I loved listening to the rustle of the palms. Smelling the ocean. If the beginning of the world had a scent, it would be ocean. Sharp and strong and new. It had surprised me, how different it smelled from Lake Michigan, back home.

I bent to the paper again. Humming a scrap of something I remembered Ozzie playing. I'd been there when he wrote it. Developing his sound, he'd said.

Like me, here, bucking rivets.

Love to Chester and Betty. Tell Betty I haven't seen any tomatoes out here yet that could beat the ones in her garden. Don't worry about me. I like it and I'm doing good and I have a place to stay, which is more than some,

so many people are pouring into town and not enough
room for everyone. I'll write more in a few days. I'll tell
you about the leadman on our ship, he thinks he's pretty
tough but he's not met a Yards girl yet. He'll learn.
I miss you.

Your loving daughter,
Ruby

A NOTE FROM THE AUTHOR

If I'd never found out about Aunt Sofia, I never would have written *Ten Cents a Dance*.

Sofia was my mother's aunt, my grandmother's baby sister. For most of my life, that was all I knew. When I asked my grandmother about her, she'd act as though I hadn't spoken. She wasn't pretending to be deaf; it was as though I'd ceased to exist. Which, let me tell you, is a pretty effective way to convince a kid to leave a topic alone. It wasn't until years later, after my grandmother passed away, that my mother finally told me the story.

Sofia was the youngest of five children growing up in a small town in Sicily. When she was about fifteen, the family emigrated to New York. We don't know what happened, but we know that within a year of arriving, Sofia's father had kicked her out and declared her dead to the family. Any contact with her was forbidden. To my mother's knowledge, her grandfather—Sofia's father—never spoke Sofia's name again, to the day he died.

Fast-forward to 1939. My mother was eleven. One afternoon, a beautiful, tiny, elegantly dressed woman walked into the candy store my grandparents owned in the Bronx. She and my grandmother threw their arms around each other, sobbing. To my mother's astonishment, she was introduced to an aunt she never knew she had. Sofia had returned.

After her father disowned her, Sofia had supported herself as a taxi dancer. Many taxi dancers married and went on to lead perfectly respectable lives. Others slid into prostitution. Sofia was one of the lucky ones: she married a Jewish cabdriver and lived in a lovely apartment in the north Bronx. Over the next several years, she and my mother became very close. My mother's family was poor, but somehow Sofia never had to worry about money. She took Mom to the horse races and out shopping; she bought Mom her first high heels, her first fur coat. My mother and grandmother visited Sofia at her apartment. Once, they even went to her mother-in-law's apartment for coffee. All this time, however, the rest of the family not only refused to meet with Sofia, they refused even to acknowledge her existence.

One day, when my mother was seventeen, Sofia's husband came to see them with devastating news: Sofia was dead. She was only thirty-six years old.

My mother and grandmother—alone, again, out of the entire family—went to the funeral. There, they discovered that nothing Sofia had told them about herself was true. Sofia wasn't married, and she didn't live in that lovely apartment. In reality, Sofia was the longtime mistress of a prominent Jewish gangster. She lived in the Hotel Taft, in Manhattan. Her cabdriver "husband" was one of the men who worked for her lover.

A taxi dancer and mob mistress, a woman who for years led a double life—in *our* family?

"How come we never heard any of this before?" I asked my mother. Surely, a cousin . . .

But none of the cousins knew about her. My great-grandfather's word was law, and none of his children—Sofia's brother and sisters—ever mentioned her name. And my grandmother? She never stopped grieving for her baby sister, my mother said, and she never could bear to talk about it. When my grandmother passed away, the only person in our family who knew Sofia had ever existed was my mother. And then, me.

Why had Sofia gone to such extremes of deceit? My mother's theory—which I believe—was that she was most likely driven by loneliness. With the apparent backing of her gangster lover, she arranged the trappings of a respectable married life—including, bizarrely enough, even a mother-in-law—in order to reconnect with her family.

After hearing Sofia's story, I had to research her life. Along the way, I became fascinated with the world of taxi dancing. I'd been vaguely aware of "dime-a-dance" girls, but I really didn't know who they were or what they did. I was surprised to find out that taxi-dance halls were enormously popular in the United States from the 1920s until after World War II. Sometime in the 1950s they began to decline, although they've never entirely gone away; to this day, taxi-dance halls can be found in most major cities.

Taxi dancers inhabited a kind of gray area: they weren't prostitutes, but the profession certainly wasn't respectable, either. Men paid, not for sex, but to be able to hold a pretty girl close for the length of a dance, a girl who would listen to them and pay attention to them. Girls (and they often were girls) chose it because it seemed fun, and because they could earn easily twice as much money as they might in a factory or other socially acceptable job.

It must have been difficult enough for Sofia, with all her resources, to maintain a double life as long as she did. How, I wondered, might a teenager manage—and why might she have to? As I started imagining the kind of girl who could pull it off, Ruby Jacinski, from Chicago's Back of the Yards, was born. Her story is not my aunt Sofia's; it's not as dire, and it certainly has a happier ending. Writing it, though, I got the chance to explore what fascinated me most about my aunt. Here she'd climbed up from the street, to a life with furs and money and everything she could possibly want—yet none of it was enough to fill the hole where her family used to be. I study her photographs and wonder: what choices might Sofia have made differently if she'd had the chance?

A(KNOWL(DGM(NTS

My sincere thanks to all who helped throughout the writing
of this book: Dr. Mary Meckel, for her knowledge of the
taxi-dance industry and her warm encouragement; Kathleen
Headley, for patiently answering all my questions about
Chicago neighborhoods in the 1940s; Karen Karbo, Dan
Berne, Charlotte Dixon, Debbie Guyol, Connie McDowell,
and Laura Wood, for their thoughtful critique and unflag-
ging support; Choi Marquardt, whose astute insights
inspired me to dig deeper, think harder, and write better;
Ketzel Levine, for her enthusiastic reading of multiple
drafts; Margot Monti, for vetting my music references;
Andrea Carlisle, for never failing to ask how the writing
was going and allowing me to vent; and the members of
the Fedora Lounge (www.fedoralounge.com), who helped
me get period details right. My thanks also to Don and
Melinda McCoy and the staff of North Portland Veterinary
Hospital, for being the best at what they do, and for making my day job more fun than should be strictly legal.

My deepest gratitude to my family, and to Barbara
Newman, who started me laughing on a ninth-grade field
trip to see King Tut and who has kept me laughing ever

since; her sharp wit and steadfast friendship have stood me through many a rough patch.

Many affectionate thanks to my agent, Dorian Karchmar, for her help and wise counsel, and to my editor, Melanie Cecka, who gives the lie to the common plaint that editors no longer edit. She does, and brilliantly. Thanks also to Deb Shapiro, Stacy Cantor, and everyone at Bloomsbury Children's Books, for their enthusiasm and dedication.

A full bibliography would take pages, but I want to mention the following outstanding resources: Paul G. Cressey, *The Taxi-Dance Hall: A Sociological Study in Commercialized Recreation and City Life* (1932); Mary V. Meckel, PhD., *A Sociological Analysis of the California Taxi-Dancer: The Hidden Halls* (1995); Robert A. Slayton, *Back of the Yards: The Making of a Local Democracy* (1986); Thomas J. Jablonsky, *Pride in the Jungle: Community and Everyday Life in Back of the Yards Chicago* (1992); Edith Abbot, *The Tenements of Chicago 1908–1935* (1936); Dominic A. Pacyga and Charles Shanabruch, *The Chicago Bungalow* (2003); St. Clair Drake and Horace R. Cayton, *Black Metropolis: A Study of Negro Life in a Northern City* (1945); Dempsey J. Travis, *An Autobiography of Black Jazz* (1983); Nathan Thompson, *Kings: The True Story of Chicago's Policy Kings and Numbers Racketeers (An Informal History)* (2003); Emily Yellin, *Our Mothers' War: American Women at Home and at the Front During World War II* (2004); and Constance Bowman Reid and Clara Marie Allen, *Slacks and Calluses: Our Summer in a Bomber Factory* (1944). I have strived to portray the era and its events accurately, and any errors are mine alone. For more information on the topics explored in this book, please visit www.christinefletcherbooks.com.